The ambush didn't come from the horizon. It came from inside the camp.

Almost faster than Hollister could see, two of the bodies he hadn't inspected yet rose from the ground and launched themselves at his troops. The bodies moved impossibly fast for a human being—not the least dead guys—and each one snapped the neck of the trooper closest to him with a wicked cracking sound.

Hollister couldn't speak. Couldn't shout out a warning in time. For some reason his brain kept telling him that these people were dead bodies. They grabbed the next troopers and snapped their necks as well, but this time, instead of letting them slump to the ground, each one took a dead trooper by the shoulders and bit into his neck. Hollister watched in horror as these dead things ripped the flesh from the throats of his men with their teeth.

MICHAEL P. SPRADLIN

Blood Riders

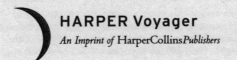

HARPER Voyager
An Imprint of HarperCollins Publishers

This book is a work of fiction. The characters, incidents, and dialogue are drawn from the author's imagination and are not to be construed as real. Any resemblance to actual events or persons, living or dead, is entirely coincidental.

HARPER Voyager
An Imprint of HarperCollins*Publishers*
10 East 53rd Street
New York, New York 10022-5299

Copyright © 2012 by Michael P. Spradlin
Cover art by Don Sipley
ISBN 978-0-06-202309-4
www.harpervoyagerbooks.com

First Harper Voyager mass market printing: October 2012

Harper Voyager and) is a trademark of HCP LLC.

Printed in the U.S.A.

10 9 8 7 6 5 4 3 2 1

To Kelly.
For thirty more years.

Acknowledgments

I've often said before it takes a village to raise a book. Sometimes it's an entire city. *Blood Riders* wouldn't be possible without the efforts of so many friends and colleagues. I thank my editor, Emily Krump, for suggesting, listening, and collaborating, and helping me bring a world to life in ways I couldn't have imagined. And the book is so much better for her efforts. Thanks to my agent, Steven Chudney. Having me as a client is an endless game of whack-a-mole, yet he always manages to keep me on task.

I thank my friends and colleagues at HarperCollins, especially Mike Brennan, Carla Parker, Mark Hillesheim, Rachel Brenner, Jeff Rogart, Dale Smith, Liate Stehlik, Adrienne DiPietro, Kristine Macrides, Pam Spengler-Jaffee, Donna Waitkus, Michael Morris, and my sales reps buddies in the field. Space prevents me from listing all of you, but know that I'll never forget your efforts on my behalf. You are the best in the business.

A special shout out to Tom Egner for giving me a cover far better than anything I could have dreamed of. You've been a friend for more than twenty years, and your talent has never ceased to amaze me.

And, of course, my family, without whom none of this is possible. For my daughter, Rachel, my son, Mick, and my daughter-in-law, Jessica, who find new ways to inspire me every single day. For my mom and sisters, who keep me on my toes. And my eternal love and thanks to my wife of thirty years, Kelly. Every time I have stood before the abyss, you have been there to pull me back. My heart is big enough for all of you. Come on in.

Blood Riders

Chapter One

Eastern Wyoming Territory
August 1876

It wasn't right, that's all Captain Jonas Hollister could tell. Three hundred yards away, two wagons were overturned and smoldering with arrow-riddled bodies strewn about. Not far away from a still smoking campfire, a horse lay dead in the dust. He couldn't tell if the dead people had been shot or scalped from this distance, but something was wrong.

The dead horse.

Lakota raiders would go to any lengths to avoid killing a horse. An animal they could use.

And there were no birds.

Buzzards should be everywhere, but there wasn't a one in sight.

It was just before dawn and in the low light the camp looked like it had been attacked a while ago. Jonas Hollister returned the small spyglass to his saddlebag and raised himself up in his stirrups to stretch.

He and his eleven troopers had been riding patrol for nearly forty-eight hours with little rest.

Three days ago a young girl had wandered into Camp Sturgis, not far from Deadwood in the western South Dakota Territory. She was delirious and nearly dead.

She had cried and screamed and wailed nonsense, until she finally fell into a deep, fitful sleep in which, the regimental surgeon told the colonel, she had fretted over "blood devils."

The colonel had sent Hollister into Deadwood to look into it. He'd learned a party of settlers had left Deadwood heading west toward Devil's Tower, over in Wyoming Territory, a few days before the girl had stumbled into the fort. Some of the town folks remembered a young girl, about nine or ten years old, who had been with them. Maybe it was this girl, maybe it wasn't. No one could say for sure. No one remembered their exact destination. Deadwood was booming after all; wagons and people were moving in and out all the time. So the colonel told Hollister to pick a sergeant and take a platoon and check it out. And it seemed they'd found what they were looking for.

"Cap'n?" Hollister heard Sergeant Lemaire ask him. Lemaire had silently ridden his horse right up next to him without his noticing. The man moved like a ghost, one of the reasons Hollister had wanted him in his company.

"Sergeant?" Hollister replied.

"Shouldn't we see to them, sir?" Lemaire asked.

"Yes, Sergeant, I suppose we should."

"Is there something wrong, Cap'n?" Lemaire swiveled in the saddle to look at Hollister.

"Can't say for sure, Sergeant. But yes, something feels wrong," Hollister replied. He drew his Colt from his holster, snapped open the cylinder and checked the load.

"Sir?" the sergeant asked, his voice indicating concern over Captain Hollister's mood. "Your orders, sir?"

Hollister let out a long, slow breath and stared down at

the ruined camp. His heart was pounding. In truth, every instinct was telling him to turn his horse and ride like hell for Camp Sturgis without looking back.

"Tell the men to advance carbines. You ride with me toward the center of the camp. Tell Corporal Rogg to take the left with four men and, have Private . . . what's the new kid's name . . . Hawkins?"

"Harker, sir. Private Harker," Lemaire answered.

"Harker. He's green, but seems steady. Have him take the other four and approach the camp from the right."

"Begging the Cap'n's pardon, sir. But . . ."

"I know, Sergeant, something isn't right down there. Tell the men to stay sharp. Order them to wait until you and I start forward before moving out."

"Yes, sir." Sergeant Lemaire deftly turned his horse and gave the command quickly, efficiently, and with zero wasted effort. Just like always.

It was getting lighter. Yellow and red had started to fill the dark eastern sky as the wind picked up. Hollister didn't usually believe in what his mother had always referred to as "blasphemous nonsense," but for just an instant he thought the wind carried whispers: a quiet moaning, like a lost soul crying out for mercy. Hollister shuddered, worried that he was losing his mind.

He heard the squeak of leather as the platoon spurred their horses, moving along the ridge and into position. He checked his load again, rolling the cylinder along the blue sleeve of his cavalry blouse, and snapped it shut.

"Ready, sir," the sergeant reported. He didn't wait for the captain, but spurred his horse and trotted gently down the slope toward the camp. Lemaire knew Hollister was no shave-tail. If he said be careful, then careful Lemaire would be.

The prairie grass was burned off to knee height in the late, dry summer. If it had been spring, when the rains came, the grass would have been ten to twelve feet tall and an entire company of soldiers could have ridden past this camp a dozen times and never even noticed it, if not for the smoke.

No one made a sound as the men approached the camp. Hollister hadn't spotted any movement, but he knew the Lakota wouldn't leave anyone alive. How the girl had managed to escape was a mystery. Perhaps she'd been able to hide somehow. But whatever happened here, it was clear the girl had witnessed it. And what she'd seen had been two counties past horrible.

Lemaire and Hollister reined up at the edge of the camp, not far from one of the overturned wagons, when Hollister spotted another thing that bothered him. The two wagons had been tipped over, and a few articles of clothing scattered about, but most of the supplies and tools were still lashed to the sides of them. A Lakota raiding party would have torn through everything, looking for food, whiskey, ammunition, and anything of value. Something must have spooked them. But what? And one of the two was burned but not completely—it was just smoldering. It was almost like someone wanted them to be spotted. And the one wagon remaining upright? Jonas couldn't get a handle on it. Nothing added up.

He looked closely at the two arrows protruding from the nearest body, a woman who lay sprawled facedown in the dirt about ten yards away. Even in the dim light of predawn he recognized the markings on the shaft: definitely Lakota arrows. The woman had been shot in the lower back and in the leg. From where he stood, he still couldn't tell if she'd been scalped, but the arrows hadn't killed her, unless she had bled to death from the wounds.

Every instinct in Hollister's mind and body was telling him to pull back. To run. The wind howled louder and in his imagination he thought it called out a warning to him. He stepped slowly and gently toward the woman, kneeling when he reached her side. She wasn't breathing and there was a dark red stain where her face lay buried in the grass and dirt.

"She's dead," he said to Lemaire.

"Yasser," the sergeant replied. "Looks like all of them are, sir."

"If this is Lakota work, it could be Fool's Elk and his bunch. Instruct the men to surround the camp, and tell them to keep a sharp eye out. Wouldn't be the first time he's tried to ambush a rescue party. You and I will check the victims."

"Yasser!" Lemaire shouted out orders. Hollister studied the bodies. It would be sunrise in a few minutes, and the thought of sunlight made Hollister feel safer for a reason he couldn't identify. He stood, making his way toward the center of the camp. Another body lay near the fire. This one was a young man, maybe in his late teens or early twenties. He wore wool pants and a white poplin shirt with black suspenders. Like the woman, he was facedown. A single arrow protruded from his back. Again, most of the shaft remained sticking out of his body. It had not gone in deep enough to kill him, and there were no signs of gunshot wounds. But he had the same dark red stain, seeping into the grass and dirt near his face. And he still had his hair.

Hollister started thinking maybe it *wasn't* Lakota at all who had done this. It might have been somebody else trying to make it look like a Lakota raiding party. Ever since gold had been found in the Black Hills, hordes of men had rushed in and there weren't enough legitimate claims to go around. Some just packed up and went home. Some turned to thieving. A few did worse.

Hollister looked to the east. The sky was getting lighter by the minute. He counted six on the ground, plus the girl who had staggered into the fort. And who knew how many captives had been hauled off if it was Lakota? Why not burn the other wagon? Who ever did this took the horses or cut them loose, but why leave a perfectly good wagon for someone to scavenge?

Hollister couldn't really blame the Lakota for being angry.

They'd been promised this land forever and had been lied to every day for the past forty years. You push a man far enough, he either breaks or he starts pushing back. The Lakota were far from broken. So why leave a perfectly good wagon for some other white person to come along and use, to tear up more of their land with cattle and plows? Why, indeed?

"Sergeant? Anything?" Hollister asked.

"No, sir. All dead, sir," Lemaire replied. Hollister waited, hoping and praying for Lemaire to speak, to confirm his suspicions and recommend leaving immediately. But if the sergeant noticed anything, he didn't say it.

Hollister was about to order the sergeant to begin a burial detail when he noticed movement out of the corner of his right eye. His four troopers were spread out, dismounted and grasping the reins of their horses. Each man held his carbine at port arms and stood with their backs to him, following his orders to keep an eye on the horizon.

But the ambush didn't come from the horizon. It came from inside the camp.

Almost faster than Hollister could see, two of the bodies he hadn't inspected yet rose from the ground and launched themselves at his troops. The bodies moved impossibly fast for a human being—not the least dead guys—and each one snapped the neck of the trooper closest to him with a wicked cracking sound.

Hollister couldn't speak. Couldn't shout out a warning in time. For some reason his brain kept telling him that these people were dead bodies. They grabbed the next troopers and snapped their necks as well, but this time, instead of letting them slump to the ground, each one took a dead trooper by the shoulders and bit into his neck. Hollister watched in horror as these dead things ripped the flesh from the throats of his men with their teeth.

"Sergeant, open fi . . ." Hollister raised his Colt, pointing at the corpse attacking one of his men. But there came a sharp blow to his arm as someone grabbed him and attempted to twist his gun from his grasp. It was the woman who had lain dead on the ground only moments before.

"Sergeant! Retreat! Get out of here!" he cried, struggling to free his arm from the grip of this shockingly strong woman. Off to his left he could see Sergeant Lemaire, locked in a struggle with the young man in suspenders who, also, had definitely been dead.

A shot went off somewhere, and Hollister heard a scream. He struggled with the woman, not understanding her incredible power. How was it possible? She held his arm with one hand and he thought she might break it if he wasn't careful. He then looked—really looked at her—and knew why he had been right to feel afraid.

Her throat was a mass of twisted, bleeding flesh that appeared to be healing itself. Something was wrong with her face and eyes, which had turned bright red, and her mouth grew to an alarming size as she opened it and fangs descended from her gums.

He couldn't move his gun arm. He heard more shouts and the sounds of muffled struggles. For some reason it struck him as odd. Hollister had seen his share of hand-to-hand combat in the war years earlier. He'd killed men up close and he knew he should be hearing the screams and wails of fighting and dying men. Grunts and groans at least. But it was eerily silent.

A quick glance to his left showed Sergeant Lemaire had been pummeled to the ground. Hollister tried to shake the woman loose but couldn't, he was going to lose his grip on the Colt and die if he didn't do something fast. With desperation he reached down, feeling for the arrow stuck in the flesh of her thigh. With all of his strength he pulled hard on the shaft and jerked it free.

Momentarily confused, his attacker loosened her grip on

his gun arm and tried to stop his other arm; but before she could prevent it, Hollister had hit her straight in the chest. He pushed with every ounce of his strength and finally felt it pass her ribs and enter her heart. The woman—body, creature or whatever she was—shrieked in agony and let go of him immediately. She staggered backward, her hands suddenly like talons, clawing at the wooden shaft piercing her flesh. Hollister watched in disbelief as she threw back her head, howling a death scream like none he'd ever heard. Then she disappeared.

It took him a moment to realize the woman's body was gone. On the ground where she had stood an instant before was a pile of ashes, the clothes she had been wearing, and two Lakota arrows.

Hollister looked at the four troopers to his right. They were dead; he knew it already. The creatures continued feeding, ripping flesh and lapping up the blood as it still flowed from the veins of his men.

He raised the Colt and took aim. His bullet took one of the creatures square in the back, knocking it and the trooper in its grasp to the ground. He fired again, missing the second creature as it dropped the body it held and dived behind the closest wagon for protection.

"Cap'n." He heard a mournful groan from behind. He turned to see Lemaire, on his knees in the clutches of the boy wearing suspenders, the boy's arm around the sergeant's neck and throat.

"You killed Caroline," it said to him. But it wasn't a human voice; it was a strange whispering sound, from deep in its throat. Hollister didn't answer, he raised his Colt and fired a bullet into the center of the boy's forehead, and he flew backward, his grip on Lemaire relinquished.

As Hollister staggered toward Lemaire, he saw the same thing had happened to his troopers stationed on the other side of the camp. Two of them were dead on the ground and the others were being attacked by whatever these things were. Hollister nearly tripped as he bent to pull Lemaire to his feet.

"Cap'n!" Lemaire shouted, pointing behind Hollister.

Hollister whirled about to see another one of the creatures nearly upon him. He lifted his gun and pulled the trigger. The bullet took the thing square in the chest, knocking it off its feet.

"Open fire! Open fire!" Hollister commanded. But only he and Lemaire remained alive. "Sergeant, shoot!" There was no response and Hollister turned in horror to see another creature, taller and bigger than the rest, suddenly tearing at the flesh of Lemaire's neck. He had no idea where this one had come from. The sergeant's eyes were open and empty. His arms and legs still moved and flailed against the being holding him, but he was already dead.

Hollister shot the attacker, his first bullet taking him high in the shoulder. The creature stood up straight and faced Hollister, blood and flesh covering its mouth and chin. Hollister shot again and again. Both bullets entered the creature's chest, but it didn't even flinch. He was a giant. Hollister was six feet four inches tall and the thing towered over him, at seven feet tall, at least. It had shoulder-length white hair and the wind seemed to pull it behind him like a cape. His eyes blazed red and his mouth was elongated; fangs descended where teeth should be, just like the woman Hollister killed moments before. It was all wrong.

Don't let it touch you, Hollister thought. He was out of bullets. It kept coming forward and Hollister threw his pistol at the beast, but the heavy Colt bounced off its head with no effect.

Keeping the thing in sight, he backed slowly away in the direction of the horses. A quick glance over his shoulder showed his own mount still standing there, pacing nervously at the edge of the camp—disturbed by what was happening, but too well trained to leave its master. Lemaire had just broken a mare two weeks ago and the not-quite-tame horse had skittered away. Jonas thought of turning and running, but instinctively knew the creature would be upon him the moment his back was turned.

Reaching into his boot, Hollister pulled out his Bowie knife with one hand and drew his saber with the other. Most times he didn't carry the sword as it only got in the way. But the colonel was a stickler for it, always insisting officers carry one on patrol. And for some reason, the saber seemingly gave the creature pursuing him more pause than the other weapons, for it slowed its advance. Its gaze locked on his and it made him feel like a frightened buffalo calf staring into the eyes of a wolf.

"You have taken one of ours," the creature said to him in a voice tinged with anger and hatred. It made Hollister cringe to hear it. He found himself losing his breath and he tried to calm himself, but he was too afraid.

"You killed my men!" Hollister shouted at him.

"Yes. We feed," it replied. "My followers feed. And you have taken one of mine. Caroline. You will die for this."

"Murdering bastards! I'll kill you all!" Somewhere Hollister found the courage to step forward and take a mighty swing at the man with his saber, but the creature dodged it easily.

Hollister had overswung, and with his next step backward, tripped over something and fell to the ground on his back. Without warning the creature was straddling him, pinning his arms to his sides. The creature struck him with a fist the size of an anvil. Hollister felt his nose crunch, and the warm taste of blood filled his mouth as it hit him again. He screamed in agony at the fangs descending toward him. He knew he was going to die and wished to close his eyes against it but found he could not.

Suddenly and without warning the creature straightened up, looking off to the east. Hollister was still pinned beneath him, struggling to free his arms. But day was breaking as the sun topped the horizon and light spilled across the prairie. The creature shouted out something in a language Hollister had never heard and stood up. For a moment, Hollister thought he saw smoke coming from the fiend's skin and clothing, but was sure his own loss of blood must be playing tricks on him.

"Some other time," the creature hissed at him, "for Caroline." He moved backward toward the camp, into the shadows and away from the advancing sunlight. The smoke coming from his clothes and body disappeared. Hollister sat up and watched in horrid fascination as these living monsters moved among the camp, dragging the bodies of his dead men behind them. Each body, in turn, was tossed into the back of the upright wagon effortlessly, as if it were a sack of flour from a general store. Six creatures remained, including the one with the white hair. He counted his blessings they hadn't all attacked him at once. All of them moved with speed and precision, as if it was important for them to make some unknown deadline.

They had taken four of the dead trooper's horses and cut loose the saddles, hitching them to the wagon. The white-haired giant looked back at Hollister as he donned a long robe he had pulled from the back of the wagon. The robe covered him completely and before raising the hood, he studied Hollister again. He took a few tentative steps in his direction.

"Another time. For Caroline," it reminded him. It stood there staring at Hollister for a long moment. Hollister felt as if the giant man were toying with the idea of finishing him now instead of waiting. It looked down at its robe and then off to the east and the rising sun. For a reason he didn't understand, it left him there in the dirt.

In two steps it vaulted into the seat of the wagon. The other creatures had disappeared into the back, and Hollister could hear awful sounds coming from behind the canvas covering.

He stayed on the ground, too terrified to move, watching

until the wagon disappeared from sight. Hollister tried to stand, to reach his horse and give pursuit, but had taken a frightful beating. His head was bleeding and the pounding was so loud in his ears, he thought his skull might cleave in two.

"Bastards!" he shouted. "I'll find you! I'll kill yo . . ." the world spun and he collapsed in the dirt, flat on his back. As he drifted into unconsciousness, the morning sunlight washed over him like a blanket and the last thing he remembered was its warmth on his face.

From a small hillock to the west, Shaniah watched and waited. She knew the troopers were doomed the moment they approached Malachi's camp, but there was nothing she could have done to stop it. Not yet. Malachi and his group were feeding, drinking what the Old Ones called *Huma Sangra*—the name for human blood in the ancient language of her people—and growing more powerful every day. Though she was strong and nearly an immortal herself, she did not feed on human blood, and because of it, could not match their speed and strength. It frustrated her to stand idly by with Malachi so close. But she would not be able to end it now.

The human who'd survived intrigued her. Though it was the sun that had saved him, he had fought bravely, and she'd watched in fascination as Malachi hesitated briefly, cautious of the human and his saber. One of the few ways to kill an Archaic was to cut off its head, but there was no way for the man to have known that.

She rode into the camp. The man was still alive, but she would be gone before he regained consciousness. Standing over him a moment, she pulled her hood wide in order to study him more closely. He was a handsome man, for a human. For a brief instant she thought his eyes opened and he looked at her, but he had been beaten so severely that she was sure he was only semi-conscious at best. His eyes closed again. She could not stay much longer. The leather gloves and cloak she wore were too warm in the morning sun, but she could die without them, for she was a creature of the night, an Archaic herself.

Malachi had captured and turned a band of settlers. Humans were turned when they were bitten and then drank the blood of an Archaic. The change happened in a few hours. Some could not survive the process and those who proved unable were merely drained of their blood and their bodies discarded. She had watched for three days, unable to stop Malachi or help any of the humans they had fed upon.

Malachi had then used his new recruits to stage a scene looking like a Lakota attack. They waited for a rescue party to show up, with the intent to feed upon or turn more humans. Malachi was becoming more and more daring, gathering more and more followers.

Shaniah inspected the camp, peering inside the wagon, looking for any clue of where Malachi might be headed.

She remounted her horse, turning the great stallion west. The animal, named Demeter, was one of many that had been specially trained since birth not to fear her kind. He would not spook or shy away from her as most creatures would, and as a result the horse had saved her life on more than one occasion.

She could not ride for long in the sun and heat, even with the cloak, and would need to find a place to hide until the night came. Then she would think about Malachi again. Where he might be going next and what his plans were.

And more important: how to stop him.

Chapter Two

Ft. Leavenworth, Kansas
June 1880

"Where you goin', Chee?" Sergeant McAfee asked as he poked a sausage-sized finger into the young man's chest. Chee, thin and rangy, with dark eyes, said nothing, but Hollister saw his fists clench. There were seven of them on prison work detail, digging another well, and it was unseasonably hot for June, with the afternoon sun high in the sky moving the temperature just past hell. Hollister kept digging, not caring about their conflict, but watching from the corner of his eye just the same.

McAfee was a huge Irishman, nearly three hundred pounds and solid, his skin pale and ruddy from drink. The lines on his face were a map of booze, fights, and hard living. He was hot-tempered and foulmouthed; he smelled like a stable and was quite likely insane.

The officers who'd served on McAfee's court-martial board had deliberated for less than three minutes at his trial.

He had shot his commanding officer, a lieutenant, in the head. The lieutenant had taken issue with McAfee's handling of a half dozen Sioux prisoners. According to rumors, he'd pulled his sidearm and put a round between the man's eyes and left him on the ground. Then he'd shot his prisoners for good measure.

He had been a master sergeant, and had been incarcerated at Leavenworth since it opened. When Chee arrived two months ago, McAfee had chosen the kid as his personal punching bag. Hollister had a feeling someone was going to break, soon, one way or the other.

Whenever there was no other meaningless labor for them to perform, the warden decided the prison needed a new well. Hollister hated digging, but he had at least another six years of it. He didn't know the length of Chee's sentence; the kid never talked much. McAfee was in for life.

"I said, where you going, boy?" McAfee was in front of Chee, blocking the path to wherever.

"Let me pass, please, Sergeant," the boy said quietly. Hollister guessed Chee was in his early twenties, just a boy compared to everyone else behind these walls.

McAfee laughed and his crew laughed with him. McAfee had a group of vultures following him around Leavenworth, watching and sometimes participating in his terrorization of the prison's population. There was a moment of quiet. Hollister knew the sound of this silence. With every altercation— any fight, every battle he'd ever witnessed since he'd left West Point in 1864—there was always a calm before the storm. A brief moment of silence before the screams and grunts and dying began.

"Huh. Let you pass. I'm sorry. Why of course, you mongrel-breed, dog-shit-eatin' son of a whore. I don't know what I done with my manners. By all means, you little sack a' shit, pass by." McAfee made a show of stepping back, bowing at the waist and slowly throwing out his hand like a matador. *Don't do it kid*, Hollister thought to himself. There were two guards, both armed with Springfields and black-jacks, talking in low tones to each other more than forty yards away, up by the barracks. Hollister knew the guards wouldn't do much of anything. They were probably as terrified of McAfee as everyone else.

Chee stood still a moment. He closed his eyes and stepped past McAfee. The kid was a hard worker, and he'd dug up more ground this morning than anyone in the detail, Hollister included.

As he moved past the ex-sergeant, Hollister wanted to shout out a warning, but he knew better. Chee needed to deal with this, and if Hollister got involved he'd have to handle McAfee himself somehow, and so far the giant ape had left him alone.

As McAfee remained bowed, pretending to give Chee a pass, he flexed his arm, fist clenched behind his back. Hollister saw the big man's arm swing forward and winced. He'd watched McAfee fight before and knew he was deceptively fast. This blow might just separate Chee from his head.

But it never landed. McAfee swung hard, but Chee was no longer standing where he should have been. The ex-sergeant's momentum twisted him around and off-balance so fast that Hollister didn't see how Chee got behind him. His foot shot out and connected with the back of McAfee's knee, and the giant man crumpled. Chee's left hand shot out like a sidewinder, grabbing a handful of McAfee's hair and pulling his head back. With his other arm he drove his elbow into the bully's nose. The crunch and crack of bone and tissue made McAfee bellow in pain. One of the other men moved on Chee, swinging his shovel like an axe. Chee released McAfee, who fell to his hands and knees, blood darkening the ground beneath him.

Chee easily ducked beneath the shovel and kicked the man solidly in the groin. He dropped the shovel, clutching his crotch with both hands. Chee took the man's head in both hands and drove his knee into his face. He slumped to the ground, finished.

McAfee was standing, his mouth and nose a mass of twisted gore and blood, his eyes watering.

Three of McAfee's men down in the hole with Hollister grabbed their shovels, thinking about climbing up to join the fray. Hollister moved in front of them and with a commanding look at the first one, an illiterate trooper named Smith, said quietly, "Don't."

The man looked at Hollister with hooded eyes. He tried to shrug past, and Jonas put his hand on the man's chest. "I said, *don't.*" The three of them saw something in Hollister they didn't like and backed off.

Up above them, McAfee charged at Chee, trying to get his hands on the younger, faster man. His primitive brain told him if he could do that, he could rid himself of the pain he felt by pounding away at Chee until it was gone. What he didn't realize was that the fight was already over. Hollister, with one eye on the three dregs in the hole with him, watched in quiet fascination as Chee leapt in the air, his foot flicking out and taking McAfee square on the chin. McAfee went down and didn't move.

"The hell you doing, Chee?" said one of the screws, a blue-coated corporal named Larson. He and the other guard had finally arrived, waiting as usual until the two men had settled things before taking action. Chee said nothing and the corporal drove the butt of his Springfield into the young man's gut. He groaned and doubled over, dropping to his knees.

What the corporal hadn't noticed was the rifle butt had hardly hit Chee at all. He'd managed to bend his body away with it and take most of the force in his hands. He was acting. With Chee on the ground and Hollister in the hole, they were at eye level, and when the dark-skinned man winked mischievously at him, Hollister couldn't help but smile.

"You're going in the box, half-breed," the corporal sneered as he and the other guard lifted Chee to his feet. "You men, drag this fat tub o' lard to the surgeon." McAfee's followers scrambled out of the hole, pulling the sergeant and the other man to their feet, leading them away toward the administration buildings.

Hollister watched them for a while and returned to his digging.

Hollister dug on through the afternoon, then climbed out of the well, taking a break for water and hardtack with a piece of wormy bacon for lunch. The meat was inedible so he threw it over the wall of the fort. McAfee's three varmints had never returned after hauling him to the infirmary. It was all the same to him; he preferred solitude.

As always, his mind returned to the ridge in the Wyoming Territory where he'd watched his men die four years ago. He remembered passing out as the wagon pulled away, and he'd woken up with the sun beating down on his face and his mount snorting at him from a few yards away. He was grateful he'd taken the time to train his mount, who he called Little Phil. The horse hadn't spooked like most horses would. Besides mourning the loss of his men, the destruction of his life and career, and being locked up in Leavenworth for ten years, Jonas really missed that horse. Little Phil had been the best ride he'd ever had.

All that was left there on that ridge were the smoldering wagon and his horse. He mounted up and tried to follow the wagon trail, but quickly lost it. He was no tracker. He'd counted on Lemaire for that. As he rode back toward Deadwood, the face of the woman leaning over him kept returning to his memory. Had she been real or imaginary? He was convinced she was there, but why? Was she one of them? Or was she one of the party who had been able to escape somehow?

It was nearly a two-day ride back to Camp Sturgis, where he arrived sunburned, his horse nearly dead and wild with thirst. He staggered into the colonel's office and reported what had happened. The next day the colonel got him a fresh mount and sent two companies back with him to the site.

There was nothing to see. The wagon was still there, but there were no bodies, no other evidence. There was another thing that bothered Hollister: the wagon was still full of goods. No one, not even the Sioux, had salvaged anything. In his heart he knew it was because there was a veil of something evil over the place where his troopers had died. His eleven murdered troopers had disappeared without a trace.

After returning to Camp Sturgis, Hollister slowly came to the realization that his colonel didn't believe him. The old man had sat Hollister down and gone over the story with him again and again. *What had he seen? How had his men died? It must have been the Sioux, wasn't that how it happened? Not some strange and unbelievable story about blood-drinking creatures.*

Hollister never wavered, and after nearly six hours of nonstop interrogation, a private walked in with a telegram for the colonel. Hollister remembered him running his hand through his white hair as he read it. He barked an order and a detail of troopers entered the room, ordered Hollister to attention, and arrested him.

He was held in the brig, and court-martialed two weeks later for dereliction of duty, conduct unbecoming an officer, and several other made-up charges. The next thing he knew, he was in Leavenworth.

Hollister rarely thought of anything else but that day. He remembered the look on the face of the man-creature as the sun had risen. How the smoke had rolled off his clothes and skin as the light peeked over the horizon. He heard the serpentlike hiss of his voice. "We shall meet again. For Caroline," he'd said.

Well, he'd have a hard time finding Hollister now. Hollister thrust his shovel into the ground and climbed back into the hole. He was wearing his striped cavalry pants and a red undershirt, soaked through with sweat and grime. The sun was almost gone behind the western wall of the prison fort. It would be chow time soon. Hollister laughed at the thought.

He had lost about thirty pounds since being incarcerated, and he'd never tended toward heavy anyway. The food in Leavenworth was awful beyond description, as long as the description commenced at disgusting. Hardtack was about all a man was able to choke down here.

"Hollister," a voice called behind him.

He turned to find the duty officer; a first lieutenant named Garrick was headed his way. He figured now he'd have to make some kind of report about the fight. Whether he liked it or not, it looked like he was involved. Hollister scrambled up the ladder and came to attention, feet together and shoulders back. He made sure not to look the lieutenant in the eye when Garrick reached him. In his time in Leavenworth, Hollister had learned eye contact was a tool to be used in very specific ways: avoided with the guards and officers, used as a means of intimidation with the other prisoners.

"Sir," he said.

"Colonel wants to see you. On the double, inmate."

"Yes, sir." He saluted and started for the administration building. Strangely, the lieutenant followed along. Word of Hollister's story had made its way through the population and command structure at the prison. It had only served to isolate him because he was considered crazy. Luckily, in a place like Leavenworth, craziness was one way to stay alive: even thugs like McAfee gave him a wide berth. Yet he felt something changing. Jonas suddenly realized this shitty day had the potential to grow much worse.

"What'd you do, Hollister?" Garrick asked him. With the sun gone behind the western wall, the heat had subsided a bit and twilight shadows were racing across the grounds.

"I don't understand, sir," he replied.

"Like hell you don't. You been writing letters again? You might've stepped in the cow shit, Hollister."

"Yes, sir. I'm sure I did, sir," Hollister said.

When he'd first been sentenced to prison, Hollister had used whatever meager privileges he could muster to write letters to his former comrades, commanders, and even the congressman who'd appointed him to West Point. Asking for a new trial, he had pleaded his case and begged his friends and former classmates to investigate the disappearance of his men and find the creatures that'd killed them and destroyed his life.

All for naught. He was shunned by everyone he'd once called a friend; standing up for him was a sure way out of the army. He had given up after a year.

"Colonel Whitman ain't going to be happy, if you been stirring up the shit, inmate. You been stirring up shit again, *Captain*?" The lieutenant sneered. It was a grave insult to a prisoner, especially a former officer, to be referred to by his old rank. He took a deep breath, determined not to let the lieutenant draw him in to his little game.

"No, sir," he replied quietly.

The two men crossed the main yard, reaching the wood-plank walkway leading to the main gate. Passing through, they entered the administration building with the lieutenant in the lead, climbed the stairs to the second floor, and proceeded to the colonel's office. The lieutenant knocked on the door and they heard the gruff man answer from inside.

Lieutenant Colonel Whitman was a pompous little rooster. He was about five feet five inches tall, gray haired and clean shaven. He was approaching thirty years in the army without ever seeing combat, and as a result had never risen above his present rank, even during the war, when promotions were handed out like wooden nickels.

"That will be all, Lieutenant," the colonel said. He was standing at the window of his office, which overlooked the yard of the main prison. Running the nation's military prison was no plum assignment no matter how you tried to frame it. Whitman would be here until he retired or died.

"Inmate Hollister, your appearance is, as usual, appalling. You are out of uniform. I can smell you from here." The tone in his voice was measured. These were facts, not to be disputed, and Hollister knew he would be punished for his transgressions. More digging lay ahead.

"No excuse, sir," he said, hoping it would save him from the lecture on the importance of an inmate's personal hygiene. The colonel remained at the window, looking out on the prison grounds. This was unusual as he normally was all business, sitting at his desk and dispensing whatever orders he needed to in a clipped and efficient manner.

The colonel's body language made him look bound up and angry, as if he had been forced to swallow something and could not bear the taste. Hollister then noticed the other man, sitting in the corner. Medium height, thick chin whiskers and a hard, granitelike face, which implied he knew a thing or two about trouble. He sat with his legs crossed and his hands folded in his lap. Hollister noticed the rough, scarred skin on his hands, especially on a few broken fingers that had never healed right. Whoever he was, he'd been in few scraps. Hollister remained at attention and turned his eyes to the practiced middle-distance stare of a prisoner, and waited.

"You have a visitor, Inmate Hollister," the colonel said, his back still turned to Jonas. Jonas saw Whitman's stance go straighter as he spoke, and he clasped his hands behind him. Neither man said anything, as if waiting for Hollister to speak.

"Yes, sir," he finally replied.

The stranger stood up, striding confidently across the creaking office floor to Hollister and stuck out his gnarled right hand.

"Captain Hollister," he said. "My name is Allan Pinkerton.

Chapter Three

Hollister knew the name. He reluctantly shook Pinkerton's proffered hand, but returned quickly to attention. Whitman turned around to look at him, and he was determined not to do anything that would bring the colonel's wrath down on him. At least not yet.

"It's a pleasure to meet you, Captain Hollister," Pinkerton said, with a trace of a Scottish brogue.

"*Private* Hollister," the colonel corrected.

Pinkerton glared at him. "For now, Colonel. For now," he said. He stomped back to his chair, picked up a leather satchel, and placed it on Whitman's desk.

Out of the corner of his eye, Hollister saw Whitman blanch and press his mouth into a straight line at Pinkerton's growing list of violations of proper procedure.

"Please, Captain Hollister, at ease, at ease," Pinkerton said as he rifled through the satchel. Jonas glanced at the colonel for approval before allowing himself to go to parade rest, his posture relaxed but on the alert. He was concerned. This wasn't about McAfee and the fight. This was something unfamiliar. One of the most famous men in America was here to talk to him. But not knowing why made Hollister edgy.

"Yes . . . yes here it is," Pinkerton said, pulling a small ledger out of his case and thumbing it open.

"Jonas P. Hollister, captain, United States Army. Born in Tecumseh, Michigan. Graduated from West Point in 1864, assigned to the Seventh Michigan Cavalry under the command of General George Armstrong Custer. Awarded medals for valor at Cold Harbor, Petersburg, and the Winchester Campaign. Received a field commission of lieutenant colonel directly from General Ulysses S. Grant. Court-martialed for assault on a superior officer, found not guilty but reduced in rank to captain in March 1865." Pinkerton paused. "What *exactly* happened there, Captain?"

Hollister was quiet for a moment. He squinted at the man. He still didn't know what this was about. The colonel had returned to staring out the window, giving him no indication as to how he should proceed. All right, then.

"I punched George in the face, sir, because he was responsible for the death of thirty-seven of my men."

"When you say George, you mean General Custer?" Pinkerton asked. Hollister nodded.

"General Custer was your superior officer and you assaulted him . . ." Lieutenant Colonel Whitman said, staring in disbelief. Pinkerton held up his hand and he stopped talking.

"Go on, Captain," Pinkerton prodded.

"*General* Custer, sir, was a glory-seeking jackass," Hollister said, making sure he was speaking directly at Pinkerton. Knowing full well the colonel still held all the cards as far as his future was concerned.

"I see. What is your opinion of Custer's performance at the Little Bighorn?" Pinkerton asked.

"I wasn't there," Jonas said.

"But you must have an idea. Some thought about your former commander. An opinion?" Pinkerton went on.

"From what I heard and read, sir, he divided his command against a far superior enemy with a clear tactical advantage. It's no wonder he got everyone killed. I'm just surprised it didn't happen sooner," Hollister stated. He saw Whitman's shoulders tense.

Pinkerton said nothing, looking down at the ledger again.

"Tell me about Wyoming, Captain," Pinkerton said.

"No, sir," Hollister replied.

"God damn you, inmate, you will answer his questions," the colonel turned from the window and roared at Jonas as he stormed around the desk.

"It's all right, Colonel," Pinkerton said. He had a tone about him that both shut Whitman off and took him down a peg or two. Whitman was about to say something else but decided against it, choking on the words, and spun around, returning to his spot at the window.

"I might be able to help you, Captain," Pinkerton said

"Help me with what, sir?" Hollister asked.

"Get out of here. Permanently, I might add."

"Is that so?"

"Yes. But I need to hear from you what happened."

Hollister smiled. Then laughed. He wasn't sure why he was laughing—and he saw Whitman's face redden, which only made him laugh more. His nerves were jangled, and he felt as though he might burst if he didn't laugh. It was the only thing he could think to do. In Leavenworth, dark humor was one of the few things that could keep you alive, and for Hollister it was all he had right now.

"Is something funny, Captain?" Pinkerton asked.

Hollister calmed himself. "Yes, sir. I'd say it borders right on hilarious. You know what happened in Wyoming. You've read my testimony and my regimental commander's report on the incident. Out of nowhere, the most famous detective in America shows up at Fort Leavenworth Military Prison and asks me what happened on that ridge three years, ten months, and eleven days ago, which, I might add, I never dreamed would happen. So I'm thinking there's only two things that could have happened. One, you've suddenly decided I wasn't lying, which I doubt, since no one else has ever believed me. Or two, it's happened again."

Pinkerton's eyes narrowed and he studied Hollister. Something washed over his face. It was only a flicker, but Jonas saw it, clear as day. Pinkerton had arrived at a decision. Jonas didn't know what it might be, but he clearly had reached some determination of vital importance. Hope stirred in his chest.

"Colonel, I'd like to talk to the captain alone, please," Pinkerton said.

"I'm afraid that's not allowed. It's against regulations for any prisoner to be—"

"Colonel, when I first arrived, you promised me full cooperation, did you not?" Pinkerton asked. "Here's hoping I won't have to send a cable to General Sherman requesting . . ."

Without another word, Whitman threw up his arms and stomped out of his office, slamming the door.

"Pompous jackass," Pinkerton muttered. He strolled casually around the desk to Whitman's chair and sat down. "Please, Captain, sit. Let's talk."

"All the same, I'd prefer to stand, sir," Jonas said. He felt completely in the dark. He had no control over whatever was happening, and so he was determined to hold on to those things he could control. He wasn't going to let this strange man gain any advantage if he could avoid it. At least not until he knew what was going on.

Pinkerton shrugged and turned to another page in the ledger. "Very well. You're correct in your assumption, Captain." He said, looking up at Jonas.

"Which assumption would that be?" Jonas asked.

Pinkerton let out a big sigh. "Captain, I can assure you, I am here as your advocate. However, if you can't at least listen to what I have to say with an open mind, we're not going to get very far."

Jonas said nothing for a moment. "Pinkerton." He paused, thinking. "Weren't you in charge of President Lincoln's security?"

"I was," Pinkerton replied.

"That sure worked out well," he said.

Pinkerton's eyes clouded and Jonas watched as the man's mouth straightened into a thin line. His color changed from pale to bright red and Jonas set his feet, half expecting the detective to launch himself over the desk and pummel him into the floor. Yet the fury subsided as quickly as it had risen, and Pinkerton composed himself, settling in the chair again.

"As I said, Captain, you are correct. We've had another incident, similar in details to what happened to your command in Wyoming. In this case it was a mining camp in Colorado. One man escaped and reported an assault on the camp by what he called 'flesh eaters.' When the creatures attacked, the man jumped across the stream where the sluice box was set up. For some reason they didn't pursue him there. They didn't want to or for some reason weren't able to cross the stream. The rest of his camp was wiped out. Each man was killed and the bodies were then thrown in the back of a wagon and carted away. Does this sound at all familiar, Captain?" Pinkerton looked up over the eyeglasses perched on the end of his nose.

Hollister nodded. He began to sweat, feeling the heat of the rising sun on that Wyoming ridge, watching in horror as the bodies of his troopers were casually tossed into a wagon like sacks of grain.

"The flesh eaters, as the man called them, rode away just before sunrise. This lone survivor finally made it into town and led a posse to the scene. As I'm sure you can guess, there was nothing to see. No bodies, some blood on the ground, a few signs of a struggle, but nothing else to support the man's story."

"Excuse me, Mr. Pinkerton, but why are you here? What

makes somebody with your connections come all the way to Fort Leavenworth to tell me this?" Jonas asked.

"Because, Captain Hollister, things have changed. Your experience in Wyoming is being looked at in a new light."

"Is that so?" Hollister asked quietly.

"Yes. In fact, Captain Hollister, we have a proposal for you. Something we think you are uniquely qualified for," Pinkerton said.

"What might that be?" Jonas asked.

"To find these things. Whatever they are. And kill them."

Chapter Four

Hollister was back in the colonel's office two hours later, bathed, clean shaven, and in a fresh uniform. He tried not to notice the fact that the blue blouse showed captain's bars at the neck, but his fingers went to them and touched them unconsciously. Pinkerton was still there, in Whitman's chair, and he held out a sheaf of papers.

"Just a few formalities and we'll be on our way, Captain. I'll need you to sign a few documents, after that we'll board a train for Denver. My private car is waiting at the station in town," Pinkerton said.

He dipped a pen in the inkwell on the colonel's desk and held it out for Jonas.

Jonas stood, hands clasped behind his back. Not moving and making no effort to take the pen. Pinkerton, head down as he shuffled through the papers on his desk, finally looked up.

"Is there a problem, Captain?" he asked.

Jonas nodded. "I expect there is."

"Would you care to elaborate?"

Jonas stuck out his arm and rubbed the clean, fresh cloth of his new uniform.

"Certainly, Mr. Pinkerton. I'd be happy to. There's too much going on here that I don't understand. First question: you say what happened to my men in Wyoming has happened again in Colorado. I don't see how that affects me. No one believed me then, so why all of a sudden is my story accepted as the truth?"

Pinkerton was about to answer, then thought better of it. He sat back, staring at Hollister, waiting for him to finish.

"Second question: after why me, why you? You are not unknown to me. You are famous and connected. So why are you here?"

"When this is over, I'd like you to consider working for me as a detective. You have a keen mind, Captain." Pinkerton smiled.

"Not according to the United States Army, Mr. Pinkerton."

Pinkerton waved a dismissive hand. "Yes. Well. Admittedly, mistakes were made. We know it now. We'd like make it up to you, but we'd also like your help."

"And if I refuse?" Jonas asked.

Pinkerton frowned. "I'm afraid you'll remain here and finish out your sentence."

"Ah," Jonas replied. "So that's it. You're not really exonerating me. You're asking me to take on a duty that will most likely get me and perhaps others killed. And if I refuse, I stay here digging Whitman's dirt until my sentence is up."

"I wouldn't put it in quite those terms, but yes." He picked up the paper he'd wanted Hollister to sign. "It's all laid out here in writing. If you accept reinstatement you'll be assigned to a special detail of the U.S. Secret Service and report directly to me. You'll be paid, outfitted, and to assure the army's cooperation whenever you need it, you'll be restored to your rank. You'll have authority from General Sherman to use whatever facilities or troops you deem necessary to expose and eradicate this threat."

"Paid, you say. How much?" Hollister asked.

"Two hundred fifty dollars a month, plus board and horses. You'll also be given access to a private, specially outfitted train."

The amount of money stunned Jonas. It was nearly quadruple what his army pay had been before he was sent up the river. However, if he found these "flesh eaters," he'd most likely get himself killed and he'd never spend the money anyway.

Jonas paced. Pinkerton waited patiently.

"Still doesn't answer my second question, sir. Why now? Why does anyone believe me?" Hollister asked.

Pinkerton rested his elbows on the desk. He suddenly looked tired.

"The man who survived this most recent attack is from a family of some consequence. He has made noise. This noise has reached the president."

"Who is this family?"

"Their name is Declan," Pinkerton reluctantly answered.

Jonas recognized the name. James Declan had discovered the second-largest silver lode in the country. He was wealthy and powerful. Jonas understood things a little more clearly.

"I still don't understand. If there were no bodies, no evidence . . ." Jonas's words trailed off.

"You're wondering why attention is being paid to this attack when yours was ignored?" Pinkerton suggested.

Hollister nodded.

"Senator Declan has enormous financial holdings in Colorado. Mining, land, ranching. He started with a small herd of cattle, became a big rancher, then the silver strike happened and he was *rich*," Pinkerton said.

"And since he is now a U.S. senator whose position is compromised, the president dispatched me to Colorado to investigate personally. Based on my observation of the scene, I concluded the story the survivor is telling is true. The senator is claiming it's nothing more than an Indian attack. Utes who are tired of the miners taking more and more land. He is doing this for a variety of reasons; to force the president to send more troops to Colorado, to keep the citizens calm, and Indian attacks are a much easier sell than telling the world what really happened. And then, of course, there are the creatures. People there are in danger, Captain Hollister. Grave danger. The senator doesn't care about them, but if people were to learn the truth and flee the state? What would happen to his finances? It would be a disaster."

"But what if the senator is right?" Hollister said. "Utes know how to fight. I've fought a few of them in my day."

"True, but this was not an Indian attack," Pinkerton said.

"How do you know?"

"Had it been Utes, there would still be bodies left. Scalped and mutilated, but left there to instill terror and inform the local populace that they are back on the 'warpath.' And there was almost no blood, Captain. With that many men, shot or scalped by Indians, there would be blood everywhere. I found hardly any."

"Maybe they were rounded up and killed elsewhere," Hollister suggested, knowing that wasn't the case. He could fill the fear rising in him again: the same feeling he had felt when he spotted the camp through his spyglass. Something wasn't right, and trying to poke holes in the detective's theories was the only way he could quell the rising terror.

Pinkerton reached into his satchel and removed a small glass tube with a cork stopper in one end. It held something white, long, and sharp, and when Pinkerton handed it to him and he looked at it closely, he nearly dropped it in alarm.

"I thought as you did, until I found this," Pinkerton said.

It was a fang. Hollister recognized it immediately. He had seen them on the creatures that'd attacked his men. He handed it back to Pinkerton like it was something hot.

"Might be from a bear or cougar," Hollister muttered, knowing it wasn't but feeling like he needed to say it anyway.

"It's not, Captain. You know it. It must have been

knocked loose in the struggle. My examination of the scene was more . . . thorough. I found it in between the floorboards of the camp saloon."

Hollister was quiet a moment while he absorbed the details of Pinkerton's story. He saw the tall white-haired thing standing in the advancing sunlight, his clothes and skin beginning to smoke. Heard the voice speak to him. He shook his head to drive the memory away.

"Still doesn't answer my second question. Why me? You could send anyone after these things. Why do you believe me now?" Hollister asked.

"There are a few reasons. Aside from young Mr. Declan—"

"Wait," Hollister interrupted. "The survivor of the attack is the senator's son?"

"Yes. I thought I mentioned that."

"No, you didn't. So, the good senator doesn't believe his own son?"

Pinkerton shook his head. "The senator and his son are . . . estranged. And given what he considers to be the young man's 'wild tale,' the president has some concerns. Those concerns must be addressed."

"I've been locked up for four years, Mr. Pinkerton. Explain it to me," Hollister said.

"Senator Declan is trying to convince the local population that this was nothing more than an Indian attack. I . . . we know differently. If word gets out about these 'flesh eaters,' we'll have panic everywhere and the good senator will lose a great deal of money. Whatever these things are, this is the first documented evidence we have that they have killed again. We need someone who has seen what they are capable of to find them. And find a way to kill them. Does that answer your questions, Captain?"

It did. As usual, it was about money. Nobody cared that Jonas was telling the truth. Only that they didn't lose money. He could be bitter about it, but what Pinkerton was offering was a way out. A chance to find the things that killed his men. Vengeance. Redemption. Vindication. All wrapped up in a neat little bow and handed to him with a big fat paycheck. Whatever the reason for Pinkerton's springing him from Leavenworth, this was his chance.

"Major," Hollister said.

"I beg your pardon?" Pinkerton replied.

"If I agree, it will be Major Hollister. It will also be a salary of five hundred a month. Plus all of my back pay at captain's grade since I've been in this hole. The back pay will be wired immediately to John and Nancy Hollister in Tecumseh, Michigan. All of it. I'll want a telegram back from my father confirming he received the money. In the telegram, he's also to reply with the year I broke my arm in the thresher on the farm. That way, I'll know he really received it . . ."

"Captain, this is outrageous! I don't have the autho—"

"It's Major Hollister and I'm not finished," Hollister went on. "I may report directly to you, but I make the decisions as to how, where, and when we take on these things. Eleven of my troopers were killed in a matter of minutes. I've replayed that day a thousand times in my head and I think these things might have *some* weaknesses, but not many. I don't want anyone questioning me, or my methods. Are we clear?"

Pinkerton slumped back in his chair, a man not used to being outmaneuvered.

"And one more thing. There's an inmate in here named Chee. This morning he got thrown in the box for getting the bulge on a tub named McAfee. Whatever he's in for, he's to be granted a full pardon, released immediately, and promoted to sergeant major. He will also receive his back pay, to be distributed at his discretion, and is to be placed under my command."

Pinkerton's shoulders slumped. "Is there anything else, Captain Hollister?"

"Major Hollister. And no, I think that about covers it."

"All right. I'll agree to your terms. But I will need your colonel's clerk to redraw these papers. It will take some time," Pinkerton said.

"Fine. I've got nothing but time," Jonas replied.

"Very well." Pinkerton stuck out his hand. "Do we have a deal?"

Hollister shook his hand, surprised at the strength of the elderly man's grip. He didn't see the pistol until it was right up under his chin and he felt his fingers start to hurt as the grip turned to iron.

"Just two more things, *Major* Hollister. You may think you have the upper hand here, and given the gravity of this situation, you might be right. But never forget who is in charge. And never, ever, mention President Lincoln to me again. Are we clear?"

Hollister's eyes rolled downward, looking at the pistol jammed against his flesh.

"Yes. We're clear," Hollister said.

"Excellent," Pinkerton replied, the pistol vanishing as quickly as it appeared. "Excellent. Now excuse me, *Major*, while I call upon Colonel Whitman's clerk to make a few changes in these documents."

Hollister watched the stooped older man gather up the papers and scurry out of the room.

"Huh . . ." he said to the empty room.

Chapter Five

Chee shuffled along until he cleared the gates of the prison and stopped while one of the guards bent down to undo the irons binding his legs. Pinkerton's papers had made him a free man, something he didn't understand yet, but the colonel had insisted on proper protocol for the release of the prisoner, and that meant leg irons until he left the Leavenworth grounds.

Chee felt a massive weight fall away when the last padlock was undone. The guard said nothing, merely gathered up the chains and returned inside the prison. Chee heard the giant doors shut and the steel bar snap into place, and for the first time in months felt as if he could take a deep breath. He looked down at the sergeant major's stripes on his blue blouse and brushed away a piece of lint on his left arm. One more thing he didn't understand. He'd gone into Leavenworth busted all the way down to private but he'd only been a corporal when he was arrested and court-martialed in the first place. Now he was Sergeant Major Chee. *White people are strange*, he thought.

He walked up the main street of Leavenworth, not bothering to look at the shops or glance in the windows. No one paid any attention to him. He looked like a normal soldier on some errand, not a man who had been locked away in a hole for the last nineteen months. He picked up his pace, hoping to meet up with Major Hollister before Colonel Whitman, the army, or whoever was responsible for his freedom changed their mind and locked him up again.

Chee had been thrown in the box after the fight with McAfee. The temperature inside the all-steel four-foot-square box was well over one hundred degrees and it was just about big enough for Chee to sit in if he didn't stretch out his legs. Chee wasn't afraid of much, but he didn't like cramped spaces. A few hours later Hollister had come with two guards to tell him that they were both being released. He thought it might be a cruel joke Hollister was playing on him. Maybe he was a rat bastard like the rest of the inmates. But it seemed to be true. It was like a miracle, and though he hadn't understood much of what Hollister had said, he agreed right away.

Chee caught a glimpse of black-and-brown fur darting across the far end of an alley off Leavenworth's main street and smiled to himself. It was Dog. He had waited in the countryside surrounding Leavenworth for him to be released. Dog had no doubt been living off the land, hunting the prairie and scrounging for food while Chee was incarcerated. But each night Chee had heard his familiar howl, a signal from Dog that he was still there, and while he might not have understood why Chee was locked up, he would wait there until he got out.

Dog was a variety of unknown breeds. He was big, with a crazy twist of brown-and-black fur. He looked more like a wolf than a dog, and as a result, his presence tended to make folks uncomfortable. He had learned to keep to the shadows, avoiding contact with most humans. He'd been shot at more than a few times, but never hit, and it was enough to make him dislike guns a great deal.

Chee darted down the alleyway, calling out quietly, "Dog! Dog!" and was nearly bowled over when the giant beast burst out from behind a stack of crates lined up near the back door of a general store. He jumped up, putting his paws on Chee's shoulders, and licked his face enthusiastically.

"It's good to see you too, boy," Chee said, rubbing the animal's chest. He cradled the mutt's head in his hands and looked him over. There was a slight tear in his left ear that hadn't been there when Chee had gone to prison, a scar from the hard living Dog had done the last year and a half.

When Chee had joined the army at age nineteen, he'd been stationed at Fort Sill in Oklahoma. While off duty he liked to ride across the surrounding countryside. On one of his rides in the late spring he had found Dog as a young pup, wandering alone, half starved and nearly dying of thirst. Chee gave him water and some jerky from his saddlebags and carried the pup back to Fort Sill with him.

Fort Sill was an open post on the frontier, and Chee was able to keep the pup in a small overturned crate behind his barracks. With regular food and water Dog grew quickly and in a few months weighed well over one hundred pounds. He took to roaming the countryside around the fort but was always outside Chee's barracks in the morning. Chee's sergeant overlooked the fact that soldiers weren't allowed to keep pets, mainly because he was a little scared of both the solitary Chee and the dog.

One night three troopers returned to the barracks too drunk to know better, when one of them pulled his pistol and fired a couple of rounds at Dog. Neither shot hit him, but Chee heard the shots and came bursting out the back door of the barracks to investigate. He arrived in time to see the trooper point his pistol at Dog again, and with great speed and efficiency removed the pistol from the trooper's hand. The man slumped to the ground, unconscious.

It could have ended there. Chee was a corporal, the three troopers were privates. But the other two men took excep-

tion to Chee's intervention and attacked him. The drunks
were hardly a challenge for Chee, given that his father was
half-Chinese and his grandfather had taught him *Shaolin*
kung fu. But one of the men pulled a bowie knife from his
boot, and when Chee threw the man across his hip without
removing the blade from his attacker's hand first, the man
fell on it and bled out before they could get him to the post's
surgeon.

The remaining two men testified against Chee, saying
he went crazy and attacked all three of them. Even though
Chee had an exemplary record, he was a mixed-race loner
and was found guilty of manslaughter and sent to Leavenworth. Chee remembered riding in the prison wagon all the
way to Kansas, watching Dog follow along, mostly keeping
out of sight.

And here he was, nineteen months later. "Come on Dog,"
Chee said. "We got somewhere to be." He took the alley east
and stayed off the main street. As a "mixed mutt" himself,
Chee knew enough about people to realize even his army
uniform wouldn't give him a free pass if some bully decided
to make trouble. Chee could handle himself, but he didn't
want to be late meeting the major.

Not when there were so many questions he needed to ask.

Chapter Six

Torson City Mining Camp, Colorado

The deserted mining camp (Shaniah found it humorous that the humans had called it a city) lay less than half a mile below her. She sat astride Demeter in a stand of quaking aspen trees lining the small canyon rim above the "city." It was nothing more than a few buildings, hastily constructed: a general store, a saloon, three sheds filled with mining equipment, and a few low-slung structures that looked to be barracks or bunkhouses in which the miners slept.

The sun had just set and the western sky had taken on a rust tone, which probably meant rain was coming. Archaics like Shaniah were not comfortable with water. In almost any form it made them weak. When her race was cursed, back in the ancient days, they were technically rendered soulless and therefore burned by the touch of consecrated holy water. Over the centuries her people had learned to tolerate unconsecrated water, but Malachi and his band, now partaking of human blood, would be severely burned by water and even killed by enough holy water.

The Council of Elders had made arrangements with a Russian shipping company to carry her to America, and the voyage had been difficult. They were paid in advance in gold and asked no questions, even though their passenger spent most of her nights in her cabin violently, deathly ill. The prolonged smell of salt water—the very proximity of it— had weakened her and nearly driven her mad. But she had survived. Upon her arrival in Philadelphia she was already several weeks behind Malachi and the others, who had commandeered a ship from the main port of Romania.

Shaniah shuddered to think of what had happened to the crew of the ship as Malachi and his then small band fed on them one by one, leaving only enough crew alive to pilot the ship to the American shore. Shaniah guessed Malachi would have forced the captain to sail the ship up a river until finding a spot to go ashore unnoticed. After landing, he likely killed everyone remaining and burned the ship.

It was only conjecture, but it is how she would have done it if she had gone mad like Malachi, defying centuries of Archaic laws and feeding on humans again.

Weakened and sick from her journey, she left Philadelphia as soon as possible and moved to the countryside. She found an abandoned farmhouse and rested there for several weeks. She stayed hidden, and hunted deer, feral pigs, and even a few wild dogs, until she regained her strength. Demeter had traveled with her aboard the Russian vessel and had survived the trip in fine shape.

She and Malachi had lived for centuries, and every one of her people agreed: one or the other would one day lead the Archaics. There would come a day when Shaniah, like the rest of the Old Ones, would live long enough to become an Eternal. But the process took centuries. Shaniah had become an Archaic during the Middle Ages, but in the human world she passed for a woman in her twenties.

And when the previous leader of her people, Genevieve, had been killed—in an accident, many thought, that Malachi had arranged—the Council of Elders made it clear the choice was between Shaniah and Malachi. There were weeks of private deliberation, dissecting the strengths and weaknesses of each candidate. It was generally agreed among her tribe that where Malachi was aggressive, headstrong and vain, Shaniah was thoughtful and deliberate. He embraced his animal nature. Shaniah knew the survival of her people depended on remaining hidden, separate from humans. It was her steadiness and courage that drew her people to her. Many centuries ago, Archaics had fought against humans and while they possessed greater strength and other attributes that humans did not have, the war between them had been disastrous.

Human beings, the Archaics had learned, were not without their own strengths. Men could be devious and clever, and used technology to their advantage. Their civilization had grown and progressed, while the Archaics' remained stagnant. Soon they were vastly outnumbered and finally retreated deep into the mountains of Eastern Europe, where few humans traveled, and it became their law to avoid contact with humanity at all costs.

There were many in the tribe who disagreed with the decision, and from time to time there had been Archaics who reigned terror on the people nearby. But for the past few centuries her people had lived in peace, hidden high in the mountain passes.

Though many suspected Malachi of culpable actions in the death of Genevieve, there was no proof.

When the Council finished their deliberations, they announced Shaniah as the newest leader of the Archaics. Her word was now the law. Technically, she answered to the Council and could be removed if it was deemed necessary, but that had never happened in the recorded history of her race. For all intents and purposes, her decisions were final.

When she was chosen, Malachi, who long believed he
would rule one day, slowly descended into madness. He was
convinced he deserved the office and fomented rebellion.
His anger at what he considered a betrayal overwhelmed
him. He spoke out, building dissent among the people.
When Shaniah ordered him arrested and brought before a
tribunal, he escaped with a few followers, left their mountain stronghold, and terrorized the towns and villages below.
She and her personally chosen soldiers had not been able to
catch him before he captured a ship and escaped. And it was
up to her alone to bring him back. He must face Archaic
justice. Or he must die.

The sky to the west had gone dark, and a half moon rose
above the mountains to the southwest. Shaniah waited, using
all of her senses to be sure the camp below was deserted.
When she was certain, she spurred Demeter to a slow, careful descent down the canyon.

She rode along the edge of the camp, staying to the far
right of a stream. The sound of the rushing water made her
feel slightly nauseous and she circled away, reining Demeter around behind the buildings. Time, wind, and rain had
removed any sign of the massacre. No doubt Malachi had
dragged the bodies off, and there was no blood visible on
the ground. Malachi had killed here though—she could
smell him.

She dismounted outside the general store and tied Demeter to a hitching post. Inside, the store was full of goods. It
was strange no one had come here to steal the food, guns,
and ammunition still lining the shelves. But she supposed
the stories of what had happened here kept the looters away.

The general store held no clues, and she moved on to
the saloon next door. She found the signs of a struggle and
bloodstains lining the floor. Most of the killing had happened here. She knelt and examined the scene, but it was
harder to single out Malachi's scent because there were too
many smells mixed together. It was there though. Perhaps

if she concentrated, she might be able to lock onto it and follow him to his lair.

He had eluded her repeatedly over the last four years. Being able to travel only at night, her unease in crossing rivers and streams had made her job more difficult. Malachi was feeding on human blood, giving him the ability to more easily tolerate the things that made an Archaic weaker, like rivers and streams. And Malachi was cunning. He knew she would be coming. He did not make it easy, leading her on, doubling back, and sending her down any number of false trails.

Two years earlier, he had staged a massacre of a band of Blackfoot Indians in Montana. But he had left the bodies and his band had refrained from drinking the blood. The massacre had made big news in the territory. The humans made inquiries and decided renegades had killed the Indians. When Shaniah was finally able to examine the site of the killings, she discovered that Malachi had staged the elaborate scene to taunt her. His smell was everywhere, but he was long gone and it was months before she picked up his trail again.

She stood and headed for the doorway, and upon leaving the saloon found three men, all of them dressed in filthy buckskins, standing next to Demeter. The sound of the rushing water in the stream had covered their approach and they had entered the camp downwind, her sense of smell failing to warn her. One of them held her horse by the reins. He was tall, missing his two front teeth and had a long beard, twisted and gnarled below his chin. It was stained and dirty and Shaniah did not want to think about what might have landed in it. The other two men were shorter, and just as ugly and disgusting as the first. One of them, his face lined with scars, wore cavalry pants and a ridiculous-looking top hat. He held a large rifle, which she thought might have been a Sharps carbine, and the other one, his hair greasy and matted to his head, held a lantern, which cast a flickering shadow on the wooden walls of the surrounding buildings.

The man holding Demeter's reins had two Colt pistols with handles out, belted around his waist.

This was trouble.

"Well, lookee here," the tall man said, his tongue pushing through the space of his missing teeth, giving a lisping quality to his words.

Shaniah was dressed completely in black; a long leather duster, riding boots, and woolen pants. She had bound up her shoulder-length blond hair, hiding it beneath her black Stetson, but up this close it was easily apparent that she was a woman. And she carried no weapon except a dagger hidden in her boot.

Shaniah studied the men and for several seconds said nothing. It was quiet as the looters waited to see if she might try to run.

"That happens to be my horse," she said. During her years in America she had practiced her English and her words came out only slightly accented. One of the men standing behind Demeter laughed and shifted his rifle, holding it at port arms.

"Is that so?" The tall man lisped. "Me and Beaver and Jonesy here was just riding along and we seen this fine stallion and thought he might have gotten lost. Where you from, honey?" he asked, as the two men chuckled behind him.

She didn't see their horses anywhere, but they could have left them outside the camp. They were most likely scavengers, here to raid the town of whatever supplies remained.

She ignored his question. "Yes. The horse belongs to me, and I'll be taking him now," she said, stepping forward slowly. She needed to be at just the right distance.

"Well, we'll see about that. You got some proof on you? Somethin' shows you didn't steal him? Awful big horse for a little bitty thing like you. Seems kinda strange, woman like you up here all alone on a fine animal like this."

"He belongs to me, and I would be most grateful if you handed him over. Before this situation worsens."

The scavengers behind the toothless man broke into up-roarious laughter.

Toothless Man reached out and grabbed Shaniah by the wrist.

"Maybe we'll just have us a little party fore'n we decide who the damn horse belongs to."

Shaniah whistled loud and shrilly through her teeth and Demeter instantly kicked out with his back legs. The man holding the lantern screamed as the hooves connected with his midsection. The kick broke the lantern and the coal oil splattered on his clothes and caught fire. He dropped his rifle and batted at the flames consuming him.

Shaniah moved with speed and precision, catching the toothless man completely by surprise. She twisted her arm and broke the man's grip, and turning sideways, drove her elbow into his throat. The man gasped as his larynx was crushed and he clutched at his neck, unable to breathe.

The third man looked at his burning friend, then at Shaniah, and raised his rifle to shoot, but she shielded herself with the toothless man, who was now drawing his last breath. She lifted her leg, pulling the dagger from her boot, and in one fluid motion threw it, watching as it landed squarely in her remaining tormenter's chest.

She released her grip on the toothless man and he slumped to the ground. He couldn't breathe, but with one hand he tried to draw a pistol. Shaniah stepped on his hand and held her boot solidly there until he breathed no more. With him dead, she turned her attention to the last man, who had rolled about in the dust and finally extinguished the flames. He had dropped his weapon when Demeter kicked him and as she started toward him, he cried out trying to crawl away on his hands and knees. For a moment she thought of letting him go. But he would have raped and killed her or watched while one of his companions had. Besides, she couldn't let anyone know she was here. If he lived and talked, word would spread. She was close. He was close. She knew it. Malachi would reveal himself soon. She could not allow anything to interfere with her hunt.

As he desperately scrambled away, she walked up behind him. With a powerful twist she snapped his neck and he died instantly. And for a moment she felt rage, knowing his death had been too merciful.

She looked around. All three men lay dead in the street. It had only taken a matter of seconds. She walked to the second dead man and removed the dagger from his chest. As she did, she smelled the blood and her heart momentarily raced. She brought the dagger close to her face and inhaled the coppery scent. Archaic law forbade drinking the blood of dead humans as well, but she found it an interesting test of her willpower.

After a moment she cleaned the dagger on the shirt of the dead man and restored it to her boot. She carried the bodies to a nearby shed and placed them inside. She caught Demeter's reins, mounted, and rode out of the camp, leaving the bodies behind.

And for a brief instant, the scent of the blood still caressing her memory, she had a better understanding of Malachi and the depth of his desires.

Chapter Seven

Jonas Hollister sat in the main dining room of the Paradise Hotel. He couldn't stop staring at the table linen and thought for a moment it might be the brightest white cloth he'd ever seen. After four years of nothing but the drab gray and dank darkness of Leavenworth, it almost hurt his eyes. But the mug of cold beer sitting before him was another object of rapt attention.

Hollister had never been much of a drinker. He had shared brandy with General Sheridan during the war or when he called his officers together for staff meetings. And he occasionally had imbibed with his commanding officers at various posts on the frontier, so when it came to liquor he could take it or leave it. But the first sip of beer in more than four years felt like someone had tipped back his head and poured liquid ambrosia down his throat.

Hollister fingered the pips on his collar, feeling the major's leaves there, and looked down at the dark blue sleeves of his blouse, something he thought he'd never wear again. He touched his belt and the leather cover of the holster holding the Navy Colt he'd been issued by the prison quartermaster. There was almost too much to take in. He felt slightly disconnected, like he was walking through a parallel world.

The Paradise was the fanciest hotel in Leavenworth. Pinkerton had given Hollister his first month's salary in advance and told him and Sergeant Chee to have dinner, then meet at the railway station, where their train car was being readied.

Hollister sensed motion beside him, looked up and nearly jumped out of his seat, for the newly promoted Sergeant Major Chee was standing next to the table at attention.

"Holy shit, Sergeant! How did you do that?"

"Sir?" Chee asked.

"You snuck up on me," Hollister said.

"No, sir. I'm reporting for duty as ordered, sir."

Hollister studied the man before him. Not quite six feet tall, thin and rangy, his skin was coffee colored, his hair dark and curly. He had gray eyes, a shade Hollister had never seen before, but surmised they were eyes that never missed much.

"At ease, Sergeant, have a seat."

Chee sat in the chair to Hollister's right and Jonas could tell he was uncomfortable.

"Something wrong, Sergeant Chee?" Hollister asked.

"Sir? Uh . . . no, sir," Chee said, shifting in his seat.

Hollister raised his hand and gestured to the waiter, who stood behind the bar across the room, in conversation with the bartender. Hollister watched until the waiter looked at him again. Hollister waved him over but the man stayed rooted to his spot. Another fellow dressed in a black suit walked into the dining room and strolled behind the bar, speaking quietly to the waiter and the bartender. After a moment he approached their table.

"Good evening, sir," the man said to Hollister. He was portly, with a full set of whiskers. His hair was streaked with white, and he had stared hard at Chee as he approached the table.

"Evening," said Hollister.

"Sir . . . Major . . . there is . . . if you would be kind enough to join me in the lobby for a brief discussion?"

Hollister looked at the man and a glimmer of understanding washed over him. "I'm a little pressed for time. Let's discuss it here if you don't mind," he said.

"Sir, really . . ." the man stammered.

"Get to the point," Hollister said.

The man sighed deeply, pinching his nose with his fingers. "Sir, our hotel has a strict policy regarding the . . ."

"Regarding what?" Hollister interrupted.

Chee had been silently watching the exchange, but then understood. He was not welcome in a place like the Paradise Hotel, and he started to rise from his chair.

"At ease, Sergeant," Hollister said. Chee, confused, sat back down.

"Regarding *what*?" Hollister asked the man again.

"Major, you are of course more than welcome to dine with us this evening, but the hotel has a strict policy regarding the service of . . . certain individuals."

"Really? What individuals would that be? It wouldn't be soldiers wearing the uniform of the United States Army, would it?" Hollister asked.

"No sir, of course not . . . it's just that your companion . . . is . . . sir, I'm sure you understand we . . . *the Paradise Hotel* . . . does not allow . . . Negroes to be served on our premises," the man said, choosing his words very carefully.

"Really?" Hollister asked, the incredulity dripping from his voice. He turned and looked at Chee. "Sergeant? Are you a Negro?"

"One quarter, sir," the sergeant answered quietly.

"I'll be damned. Well there you go . . . Mr. . . . I'm sorry . . . I didn't get your name?" Hollister asked.

"It's McLaren, sir, general manager of—"

Hollister interrupted again, "You heard the man. He's only one quarter Negro, so there shouldn't be a problem."

"Sir . . . Major . . . I have no desire to make this uncomfortable for anyone. You, of course, are welcome to dine at
your leisure, and I would be happy to have the kitchen pre-
pare something for the sergeant . . . but I'm afraid he will
have to leave the dining room."

Hollister put his head down for a moment. He thought of
the events earlier in the day, of Chee taking on McAfee in
the yard. He chuckled to himself quietly. He unsnapped the
leather cover of his holster, removed the .44 caliber Navy
Colt, and laid it on the linen tablecloth.

"Sergeant, were you able to test fire your weapon before
you met me here?" Hollister asked.

"No, sir," Chee answered.

"I see. Perhaps we can do it here, starting with the first
row of whiskey bottles behind the bar. My last Colt tended
to pull up and to the right on the recoil. Hollister picked up
the weapon and cocked the hammer, aiming it at the bottles.
The bartender and waiter shouted, ducking quickly beneath
the wooden bar.

"Major!" McLaren shouted waving his hands. "Please.
There is no need . . ."

"You're quite correct, Mr. McLaren, there is no *need*,"
Hollister said. He extended his arm and sighted down the
barrel. "So here is what is going to happen." He paused.
"Look at me, Mr. McLaren, while I tell you how this is
going to play out." McLaren had turned away and buried his
head in his arms, waiting for the sound of shots. He reluctantly uncurled and faced the Major.

"Master Sergeant Chee and I are going to sit here in the
dining room of the Paradise Hotel of Fort Leavenworth,
Kansas, and enjoy two of your finest steak dinners. Then we
are going to pay our bill and leave. Otherwise, I'm going to
work on test firing my Colt right here in your fine establishment. Are we clear?"

Mr. McLaren swallowed hard. "Sir, please, my job . . ."

"Oh, I wouldn't worry about your job, Mr. McLaren. I'd

be more worried about the noise and all the busted glass if we don't get our dinners post haste. Besides you wouldn't want word to get out the Paradise Hotel doesn't welcome patrons from the U.S. Army, would you? Hollister released the hammer on the Colt and put it back on the table.

"We're waiting on our steaks. My companion here would like a beer and I'd like another. And I'll expect them promptly or I may have to reconsider target practice. Am I understood?" Hollister looked up at McLaren.

"Yes, sir, perfectly. Your dinner shall be here momentarily." McLaren turned on his heel and headed back to the bar. Hollister could hear him issuing orders to his employees.

Chee stared in disbelief at Hollister for a long moment.

"Thank you, sir," Chee finally said.

"Don't mention it, Sergeant," Hollister said. "Enjoy your dinner."

Chapter Eight

Pinkerton's car sat on a siding behind the train station. From the outside it looked like a normal Pullman car painted black and silver, and drawing closer in the gathering dusk it was clear the car was brand new. The metal shone and the sunlight glinted off the rounded corners of polished steel. Hollister bounded up the steps at the rear of the car and knocked on the door. A muffled command to enter came from inside.

Hollister entered first, followed by Chee, and both of them stopped for a moment to grasp what their eyes were seeing, for as normal as the train car appeared from the outside, inside it was anything but.

Pinkerton sat at a writing table placed beneath a window at the center of the car. And it was the windows that first drew Hollister's attention. Strange shapes were painted in white all around each window and the far door at the other end of the car. The ceiling had three different trap doors built into it and the paintings circled them as well. A strange aroma filled the car and Hollister thought it was familiar but he couldn't place it.

"*Madre de Dios*," Chee muttered, barely getting the words out.

Pinkerton finished his writing and looked up.

"Ah, Major, so glad you're here. You must be Sergeant Chee?" Pinkerton stood and strode confidently up to the young man. Chee nearly backed up a step and stared at Hollister in amazement as the detective pumped his hand. Hollister shrugged.

"Welcome, Sergeant. Major Hollister has told me all about you," Pinkerton said.

"He has?" Chee answered quietly.

"Yes. Did he tell you he requested you specifically?" Pinkerton asked.

"No, sir. Me and the major haven't had much time to talk yet," Chee said.

"Well, I'm certain he'll give you all the details shortly. But I'm glad you're . . ." Dog, who moved around from behind Chee and advanced toward Pinkerton, his nose working the air, interrupted him. Pinkerton jumped, for he had not noticed the stealthy animal in the low light of the car.

"Jesus Christ! What is that!" he shouted. His hand instinctively went inside his coat toward his shoulder holster.

"I wouldn't do that, sir," Chee said. "This is Dog. He doesn't it like it when people he doesn't know hold guns."

"That is not a dog . . . that is . . . good God I have no idea . . ." He slowly removed his hand from his coat and Dog sat on his haunches, studying Pinkerton.

"Dog," Chee said, pointing to Pinkerton, "friend. Good boy." Dog completely relaxed, reached forward and licked Pinkerton's hand. Then lay down on the floor.

Pinkerton glared at Hollister. "Did you know about this?"

"Nope," Hollister answered.

"I didn't make any agreement for a goddamn . . . half wolf . . . half . . . lion . . ." Pinkerton stammered.

"I think they're a package deal," Hollister said. "And I'm not going to tell him he's not welcome. Are you?"

Pinkerton sighed and his shoulders slumped. He turned with his back to the men and gestured around the interior of the car. He muttered something neither man could hear but had apparently given up on the subject of Dog.

"This will be your home for at least the next few weeks. It's a specially made Pullman car, built to my exact specifications. We've consulted with an expert in these matters—in fact, he will be here to brief you shortly. But in the meantime I suggest you take some time to get acquainted with the car. I have had provisions and extra clothing delivered this afternoon. This car, a kitchen car, another for your horses, and a locomotive will be at your disposal for as long as you need it.

"Mr. Pinkerton, what is that smell?" Hollister asked.

"Garlic," Pinkerton answered, pointing to small cloth bags hanging in the upper corners of each window.

"To what purpose?" Hollister asked.

"It has proven very effective in keeping out certain types of unwanted guests," Pinkerton remarked. He looked at Chee. "Tell me, Sergeant, what have you heard about your new CO?"

"Heard, sir?" Chee replied.

"Yes. You've been in Leavenworth for a year and a half. You must have heard about Major Hollister."

Hollister looked at Chee and saw the wariness creep into his eyes.

"I didn't . . . I don't . . . just rumors mostly, sir," Chee stammered.

"And what rumors did you hear?" Pinkerton pressed on.

Chee looked at Hollister in desperation and Hollister nodded, telling the sergeant it was okay to speak his mind.

"He fought against Deathwalkers, sir, only no one believed him and he was sent to prison instead." Chee had removed his hat when he entered the car and he worked it back and forth nervously in his hands.

"Deathwalkers? I'm not familiar with the term," Pinkerton said, not taking his eyes off Chee.

"My people call them Deathwalkers, sir. They are blood devils: monsters that come awake at night and drink the blood of human beings."

Hollister shifted uncomfortably. He realized, perhaps for the first time, how ridiculous his story had sounded. No wonder his colonel had not believed him. He understood why no one came to his defense. It sounded unbelievable to him, and he had lived it.

"And what do you think of his claim?" Pinkerton asked.

Chee shrugged. "I don't know the major well sir, but I have no reason to doubt him. If he says it happened that way, then it did."

"Really? And what about you, Chee? Tell me, do you believe in these so-called Deathwalkers?" Pinkerton held Chee's stare until the sergeant looked down at the floor.

"Yes, sir. I do," Chee replied quietly.

"Really? Have you ever seen one?"

"No, sir! And I hope I don't. Bad juju. But Deathwalkers are real, all right."

"Is that so? How do you know?" Pinkerton asked.

"My grandmother, Annabel. My people are from New Orleans, sir. My grandmother has told me stories about Deathwalkers," he said.

"I see." Pinkerton nodded. "Hmm. Well, you may hope you're wrong. Did Major Hollister brief you on your mission?"

"No, sir, we . . . had dinner . . . then came here . . . I haven't . . . he hasn't . . . no, sir." Something was very wrong here. This Pinkerton fellow was very odd, and Major Hollister hadn't said two words in his presence. Chee tugged nervously at his collar.

"Well as it turns out, his story may be true. There has been another incident in Colorado. You and the major will go there and investigate. How does that sound to you?"

Chee just shrugged and said nothing.

"No thoughts, Sergeant? You have no problem going after these Deathwalkers?" Pinkerton pressed.

"No. No, I don't, sir," Chee replied.

"And why is that? If Major Hollister has been telling the truth all these years, this could be a very dangerous assignment."

"I expect so, sir. But it beats being in prison," Chee said.

"Yes, Sergeant. From what I know of Leavenworth, I'm sure it does."

Pinkerton chuckled as he walked behind the writing table and sat down.

Hollister took the opportunity to study the interior of the car. The writing desk was to his right and behind it another doorway led to the rear, where Hollister assumed he would find sleeping quarters. On his left between two of the windows a large wooden rack held several rifles and shotguns. There were numerous Winchesters, two Henrys, and a pair of short-barreled Greener ten gauges. Shelves below the gun rack held boxes of ammunition.

"Make yourselves at home, gentlemen," Pinkerton said. "As I said, this car has been specially outfitted and . . ." He was interrupted by a knock at the door. "Ah, it must be our guest. Come in!"

A short, dark-haired man, wearing glasses and carrying a small valise, entered the train car. The better light inside revealed that his hair and the goatee framing his mouth were speckled with gray.

"Major Hollister and Sergeant Chee, it is my pleasure to introduce Dr. Abraham Van Helsing."

Chapter Nine

Van Helsing was an energetic sort. He shook hands, rapidly moving from Chee to Hollister and finally Pinkerton.

"Mr. Pinkerton. So gud to see you! It has been far too long." Pinkerton had mentioned that Van Helsing was visiting the States from Amsterdam, but his words were only lightly accented.

No one spoke as Van Helsing inspected the interior of the car. He traced his fingers over the markings surrounding the nearest window. "Yes. Ah. A devil's trap . . . Babylonian, I presume?"

Pinkerton nodded.

"Gud!" He turned, slowly inspecting every visible part of the car. "Excellent work! You followed my instructions to the letter."

"No expense was spared, I can promise you that," Pinkerton said.

"What is all of this for? What does it do?" Hollister asked.

"In gud time, Major, I assure you. In the meantime, just

know that, hopefully, it will keep you from getting killed," Van Helsing said.

"How will some paint stop one of those creatures?" Hollister pressed. He was curious now. And annoyed.

"We haff learned some things, Major. A great deal, actually. But first some questions."

Van Helsing seated himself at the small writing desk, and Pinkerton made no fuss over the fact he had just lost his seat. He pushed a button on the chair railing beneath the window, a panel in the wall slid open, and a wooden rack holding several folding chairs emerged. In no time, all of them were seated around Van Helsing who was pulling several journals and papers from his valise.

"First things first, Dr. Van Helsing, if you don't mind?" Pinkerton asked. He pulled a small silver coin from his pocket and handed it to the doctor, who handed the detective his own similar piece. Both men held the coins in the palms of their hands for several seconds, then nodded as if satisfied that some unspoken test had been passed.

"What . . ." Hollister asked. Only to be interrupted by Chee.

"Silver?" Chee asked.

Van Helsing smiled. "Ach! Yes, silver! Very gud, Sergeant!" From his pocket he handed each man a silver coin identical to the ones he and Pinkerton held. Hollister inspected his. On one side was an engraved picture of a man with a halo about his head. A saint, he guessed, but which one he didn't know. Hollister had grown up Presbyterian. The small words engraved around the edge read, THE ORDER OF ST. IGNATIUS. On the other side were the words AETERNAM VIGILANTIA. Hollister hefted it in his hand. It was solid silver.

"Mr. Pinkerton and I are part of a . . . society or perhaps association of sorts. We have an interest in the very things you witnessed in Wyoming, Major Hollister. There are many of us, and these coins, forged in solid silver, are one of the ways we can identify ourselves to one another," Van Helsing said.

"I don't understand . . . a society?" Hollister asked. He glanced at Chee, but the sergeant was still inspecting his coin.

"From the time of St. Ignatius. The first to fall. Many years ago we learned of the existence of . . ."

"Deathwalkers?" Chee asked.

"Vampires," Pinkerton said.

"What the hell is a vampire?" Hollister asked, flipping his coin back on the desk, where it rolled around until falling on its side in front of Van Helsing.

"These creatures are called by many names," the doctor said, pushing the coin back toward Hollister. "Your sergeant refers to them as Deathwalkers. As good a description as any, but most of Europe knows them as vampires. The living dead. Beings who were once human but are no longer, and must survive by drinking the blood of the living. As I believe you saw firsthand, Major."

Hollister felt a chill fall over him. The car seemed smaller all at once and his mind's eye flashed on the image of Lemaire dying as the white-haired thing chewed at his throat, its lips and fangs covered in blood. For a while he'd tried to tell himself he had imagined the whole thing. That he and his platoon really had been ambushed by Lakota, and in order to accept the destruction of his command, his mind had concocted an elaborate fantasy to disguise and excuse his shame. But what he'd seen was real.

"I saw . . ." he started to say, but couldn't finish.

"You are familiar with vampires, Sergeant Chee? You knew about silver?" Van Helsing asked.

"I've heard of them, sir. My grandmother was a slave, from Haiti. I mostly thought they were stories told to scare us, but she insisted Deathwalkers were real. According to lore, wood and pure silver can poison them, and I know silver bullets are used for werewolves . . ." the young man said.

It was too much for Hollister. "Werewolves? What the hell are those?"

"Sir . . . they're . . ." Chee stammered. He could sense the major's rising confusion and he had no desire to contribute to it. "A werewolf is a man who has been bitten by another werewolf . . . and when . . . during the full moon . . ." Chee gave up, the stunned expression on Hollister's face making him think he was going to get a dressing-down.

"You're kidding me, right?" Hollister said. "I've been in the army a long time and I've heard all kinds of stories around the campfire at night, but that's all they are: stories. Right?" He turned his attention away from Chee and studied Pinkerton and Van Helsing.

"Much more than stories, I assure you. Nevertheless, the two of you are now the newest members of our society. The Order of Saint Ignatius. You should keep the medallion at all times. We mint them under special instructions with the purest silver available. You will likely come across other members in your travels. We have some of the best minds of our age at work on the study of this . . . phenomenon. The test, holding the pure silver coin in the hand, will tell you if the person is who they say they are. If a comrade has fallen under the thrall of . . . anyone . . . or thing . . . the silver will burn them. It would be an indication for you to immediately . . . kill them," Van Helsing said.

"You can't be serious," Hollister said.

"I assure you we are deadly serious, Major," Pinkerton said. "But there will be time for you to digest this later. Dr. Van Helsing, why don't you begin?"

"Da. Gud. Major Hollister, I have read your report many, many times. I want you to know I believe you. Our order has for years gathered much information on these creatures, not only to verify their existence, which I assure you is beyond doubt. But to discover what their intentions might be, as well as how to defend ourselves against them."

"I think their intentions are pretty clear," Hollister said. "From what I saw, these things didn't have much else on their mind but killing people."

"Yes, but the question is, why? How did these creatures you encountered get here? Where are they from? Have they always been here? If so, why reveal themselves now? Since your incident, Major, we have tracked and chased and followed every lead, no matter how minor, and we have come up with exactly nothing. Those . . . demons responsible for killing your men simply vanished. Not to be seen nor heard of until the Torson City Mining Camp incident one month ago. We believe the same group killed several humans and disappeared without a trace again. It is most odd," Van Helsing said.

"I'll grant you that. But now that you've busted me out of the pokey, how do you expect me to find them, if you've got a whole 'society' trying to track them down and they aren't finding anything?" Hollister asked.

"I'll be frank with you now, Major," Pinkerton said. "Basically, we don't have any other options. Aside from Declan's son, who survived the last attack, you're the only person we know of who has encountered these vampires and lived to tell about it."

"No one believed me," Hollister said matter-of-factly.

"Yes. Unfortunate but true," Pinkerton said. "Now you have a chance at redemption."

"I don't need to redeem myself," Hollister said. "I told the truth. Exactly as it happened. I lived in a hole every day for the last four years, knowing that, and it's the only thing that kept me sane. Save the redemption speech for Sunday school, Mr. Pinkerton."

"Very well. If not redemption, how about vengeance?" Pinkerton asked.

Hollister reached inside the folds of his cavalry blouse and removed a small flask he had purchased that afternoon and filled at the hotel. He took a long swig of bourbon, then capped the flask and returned it to its hiding place. It warmed his gullet as it traveled down to his gut. Maybe General Sheridan had it right. Maybe a good stiff drink wasn't so bad now and then. Especially when you're about to ride off to face eleven kinds of hell. Maybe not a bad idea at all.

"Now you're talking," Hollister said.

The rest of the night was spent around the desk, mostly listening as Van Helsing detailed the history of the vampire as compiled by the Order of Saint Ignatius, with occasional prodding from Pinkerton. At one point, Van Helsing read a passage from his journal.

Their appearance is normal and quite human, until feeding on a human—then their facial structure changes. The chin grows longer, and fangs descend from the roof of the mouth. Their speed and strength is remarkable, but it is possible to kill them. Fire is one way, beheading is another, although given their strength and speed, getting them in a position to remove their head proves extremely difficult.

"I killed one with an arrow," Hollister said.

"Ya. Ve have taken note of this, Major. Yours is the first verifiable recording of killing one by this method. Can you tell me exactly how it happened?"

"There wasn't much to it. It was a woman. She was strong. Unbelievably strong. With one hand she held me up in the air. I couldn't breathe. Her face . . . changed . . . fangs . . . I pulled an arrow out of her thigh and stabbed her through the heart," Hollister related.

"Then what happened?" Pinkerton asked.

"She . . . just . . . disappeared. Her body turned to dust and all that was left was a pile of her clothes and the arrows." Hollister pulled the flask out again and took a little swig.

"Is there anything else? Anything you might have forgot-

ten or something you might have kept to yourself?" Van
Helsing let the words hang in the air, the implication clear.
No matter what shape Hollister had been in at the time, he
had to know how ridiculous his story sounded.

"No, I . . . you said these things could be killed by beheading them?" he asked.

Van Helsing nodded.

"When I pulled my saber, the big one with the white hair
paused. It was only a moment, but he reconsidered. I'd already shot him, twice. I might as well have been throwing
stones. He shrugged it off like a bee sting. But he took notice
of my saber," Hollister said.

"Da. Decapitation is one method of killing them. I would
think a saber would give such a creature pause," Van Helsing said.

"And . . ." Hollister started. He was there again, on the
side of that hill, watching the god-awful mouth descend
toward his neck. And then it was gone. Just as the sun came
over the horizon.

"Major?" Pinkerton said quietly.

"The sunlight," Hollister answered.

"What about it?" Pinkerton asked.

"It was just before dawn when they hit us. I was down.
The big one, I've been referring to him all this time as White
Hair, had clubbed me to the ground. But the sun rose. He
got up right away. They all, the rest of those . . . things . . .
jumped into the back of the wagon, to get out of the sun.
White Hair put on some kind of heavy cloak, covering
himself from head to toe. But just before that, his skin, his
clothes started to smoke. Like they were about to catch fire,"
Hollister said.

"Why is this the first time you mention this?" Pinkerton
asked suspiciously, ever the detective.

"I didn't remember, he'd beaten me pretty good at that
point. I passed out right after that. I just . . . it wasn't there at
the time," Hollister stammered.

"Sir," Chee interrupted. "Begging your pardon, sir. But my grandmother, when she used to tell us stories of Death-walkers, she said they could only come out at night. They slept in the dirt during the day because they would burn up in the sun. They were night creatures."

Van Helsing nodded. "Da. This makes sense. And tells us why they have been so hard to find. We are not looking in the right places. Good. Very good, Major. Thank you, Sergeant." Van Helsing nodded his head vigorously and started to make notes in a journal.

"So where does all of this leave us?" Hollister asked.

"I think we can pick that up in the morning," Pinkerton said. "Let me show you to your quarters and give word to the engineer to get us under way. If you men are hungry, there is food in the galley.

At the mention of food, Dog stood up and stretched, his giant body nearly reaching from side to side of the car. He pushed his nose into Van Helsing's lap, forcing the doctor to stop his writing. Van Helsing laughed and scratched him behind the ears.

"Very sorry, sir," Chee said, stepping forward and nudging Dog away with his hip. "He's not usually so rude."

"Ach. No troubles, sergeant, he is a fine beast. Magnificent animal."

"Thank you, sir. Come on, Dog," he mumbled, following Pinkerton to the rear of the car. Hollister stood and was about to follow Chee, when Van Helsing put up his hand, stopping him momentarily.

"Major, you are sure you are ready for this assignment? It will be quite dangerous, I assure you." Van Helsing studied him.

Hollister considered the man a moment, wondering when he had ever seen such piercing black eyes. It was unsettling. But Hollister had learned to read eyes in the war, on the plains, and in prison. The eyes said everything. Who would fight and who would run, who told the truth and who lied, who was scared and who was without fear. Van Helsing, he decided, was without fear. Whatever these things were, he was determined to kill them.

"No, Doctor, I'm not. I'm not ready at all." He reached out to the gun rack and removed one of the short-barreled Greener ten-gauges. He snapped it open, confirmed it was loaded then flipped the breech shut again.

Hefting the gun, he sighted down the barrel. Then he looked at Van Helsing.

"But I will be," he said. "I will be."

Chapter Ten

Chee sat on the bunk in his sleeping quarters. He had grabbed some beef jerky from the galley, and Dog sat on his haunches, gratefully chewing away at the hard scraps of meat. His cabin on the train held a bed, a small desk along the wall, and a dresser at the opposite end with a washbasin atop it. Hooks on the walls held several changes of uniform and other suits of clothes, each complete with a hat and different set of boots. Chee had never had much beyond his uniform in the way of clothing, so he didn't want to assume the clothes were for him. But the major was a bigger man. Six feet four at least, and none of these looked his size. It was as if everything had been tailored for Chee. How could Pinkerton have gotten so much clothing for him so quickly?

Chee rose and sat at the desk, placed the silver coin Van Helsing had given him on top, and he stared hard at it. Death-walkers. What had he gotten himself into? He had heard the major's story not long after he'd arrived at Leavenworth. Hollister had already been in prison for more than two years by then. The army ran on gossip and even before he'd been sentenced, Chee heard about an officer out in Montana or Wyoming, no one was exactly sure, who claimed that "strange creatures" had wiped out his platoon.

Chee had put no stock in the rumor. Alcoholism was rampant in the army and he assumed it was just another drunk white man who had run into a passel of angry Sioux or Crow and gotten what he deserved for being drunk on duty. And who'd then made up some wild story in order to cover his ass.

Then Chee had met Hollister in prison. He didn't seem like a drunk. As far as Chee knew, Hollister stayed out of the black market, and there had been plenty of opportunities for such activity in a place as rampant with corruption as Leavenworth. After watching him around the yard for a while, Chee realized no one bothered Hollister—not even the bullies like McAfee. Whether it was because of Hollister's nononsense demeanor, or because there was a fear he might be crazy and thus a little dangerous. Then Hollister had intervened on his behalf with McAfee's thugs at the well. There were three of them down in the pit with Hollister when it had started. Yet a single look from the major had kept them all there instead of coming to McAfee's aid. Why? He would need to think about this.

He kept the silver coin in its spot on the desk, like a specimen of something he might be afraid to touch. When Van Helsing had mentioned the Order of Saint Ignatius, Chee had nearly jumped. He had often heard his grandmother speak of the Saint. She claimed he had cursed all Deathwalkers, in the years shortly after Christ died on the cross. Before Ignatius died at the hands of Deathwalkers, he brought down the righteous fury of God upon them. From that point on, the souls of the Deathwalkers were damned and they faded away to the darkness of human history. Chee had thought it was just a story. A fable, meant to scare people and keep little mixed-breed children like him on the straight and narrow.

He reached into his pocket and pulled out a small cloth bag. It held a few things he had kept hidden inside his mat-

tress in his cell, and it was all he'd taken with him when
Major Hollister came to get him from the box. He loosened
the string on the bag and poured the contents out on the
desk: a small French coin with a length of twine running
through it, a pair of tiny bones from the foot of a badger, a
dried garlic clove, and a small plant with a dried, blue flower
on top of it.

Chee removed his boot and sock and tied the coin around
his ankle. A trick his grandmother had taught him. It would
keep evil spirits from sneaking up on him and entering his
body from the ground. He took a new white handkerchief
he'd purchased in town and folded it into a small square
on the desk. He placed the bones, the garlic, and the dried
wolfsbane in the center of the handkerchief, and then folded
the corners up one at a time and placed the small bundle
back in the cloth bag, which he tied around his neck.

He prayed to the north wind in Creek, the language of his
father's mother. The north wind kept evil away. He patted
the medicine bundle over his chest. It felt reassuring. With
Cajun, Chinese, Creek, and Negro grandparents, Chee's
spiritual upbringing had been a crazy quilt of customs, ritu-
als, and beliefs. He took his comfort from whatever branch
of the family tree was most . . . comforting. At the time at
least.

Dog had finished his meal and now sat staring expectantly
at Chee.

"I know, boy," he said quietly. He tried again to wrap
his mind around what he had seen today. Everything had
changed so rapidly. The major getting him sprung from
Leavenworth, the way he'd treated Chee in the restaurant
like an equal. The curious little doctor fellow and, of course
Pinkerton. He had heard of Pinkerton and his men, they
were well known by reputation, even on the plains. But they
mostly went after bank and train robbers. What was Allan
Pinkerton himself doing wrapped up in something like this?

Chee removed his other boot and stretched out on the

bunk. He was unprepared when Dog jumped up on the bed, landing on his chest, the air rushing from his lungs.

"All right, boy," Chee grumbled, sliding over and turning on his side to give Dog more room. The great beast licked his face once and Chee couldn't help but laugh. He thought of Van Helsing, Pinkerton, and Hollister still wandering about the train car, and wondered again why white people were so strange before he drifted off to sleep, Dog already snoring softly.

Chapter Eleven

Hollister felt the train slowly start moving. He lay on his bunk in the darkness, the sensation making him feel as if he needed to put his foot on the floor to keep the world still. After four years of staring at a gray ceiling in his tiny cell, the motion was unsettling.

The flask of whiskey was in his hand, but he hadn't remembered pulling it from his pocket. He fingered it, wondering why he even bothered buying it. He was no drinker. He sat up and put the flask on the small desk. For some reason, given the speed and insanity of the day's events, he'd felt compelled to bring whiskey with him. Like nothing would make sense unless he was drunk.

After digging wells and stumbling through day after day of mind-numbing boredom, he was suddenly a free man, conditionally at least. All he had to do was go find something—man . . . beast . . . he still wasn't sure—that couldn't be killed and find a way to kill it.

Sure. Should be easy. Locate some men-things that weren't men, who hadn't been seen by a living soul for years at a time, and could apparently appear on a whim to wipe out an entire platoon of armed men and disappear without a trace. *What have you gotten yourself into, Jonas?* he thought. *You didn't take the time to think. Just like always.*

Hollister had been posted to the Michigan 7th Cavalry, right out of West Point in 1864. His father, Thomas, was a well-to-do farmer in Michigan, and a prominent member of the state Republican party. It had been no problem for the elder Hollister to secure his son's appointment to the academy. Jonas knew his father had hoped the war would be over before he graduated.

The flaw in his father's plan had turned out to be Jonas himself. When he arrived at the Point, he fell in love with the place. Even the most mundane marching drill and the endless study couldn't dampen his enthusiasm. Jonas felt like he'd found his calling, and he attacked his classes with a vigor he hadn't known he'd possessed. After graduating sixth in his class, he'd taken a commission in the cavalry as a second lieutenant.

And as much as he'd loved West Point, he loved the army more. Jonas Hollister was a born fighter. The way some men are meant for politics or business or medicine, Hollister was made for war. He was a natural tactician and had an easy way with commanding soldiers. When staff meetings were held, maps examined and objectives discussed, Hollister could see the entire field in his mind. He instinctively knew the best ground that must be held or taken, where and how the men should be deployed, when to attack, and when to withdraw.

By the fall of 'sixty-four, the Union was driving the Rebs south out of Northern Virginia. They were winning. The South had lost after Gettysburg, with Grant taking Vicksburg and control of the Mississippi—they just didn't know it yet. After four months in the saddle, riding with Custer, Hollister had been promoted to colonel, given command of a regiment and caught the eye of General Sheridan.

It all had come apart for Hollister near Winchester in March 1965. The men were tired from chasing Lee all over the Shenandoah Valley. No one understood why the rebels just didn't give up.

Near a small Virginia town called Lancy's Gap, Hollister had been ordered by Custer to hold a line south of the town, at the bottom of a long ridge, next to an overgrown apple orchard. It was bad ground.

As always, Hollister saw immediately what would happen. His men would deploy along the fencerow while Custer and his brigade dislodged the rebels from the town. But this is where Custer had it backward. The rebels could retreat at their leisure, cutting through the apple orchard. In those close quarters, with their backs to the fencerow, Hollister's men lost the advantage of being on horseback. Even if Custer succeeded and the Rebs were running, they would still vastly outnumber his troops and cut Hollister's men to pieces. It was a god-awful plan.

Hollister should be flanking the rebels from the east, he told Custer. If both companies attacked on two sides, even with Hollister's smaller force, the remaining rebel force could be caught in the village. A southern retreat would allow Hollister's men to pursue them on horseback and ride them down.

Custer refused. The plan was in place, the order given by General Sheridan himself.

The sun was not quite up yet, but the heat in Custer's tent was already starting to rise.

He knew George was drunk on Sheridan's praise. The previous evening at the staff meeting, Sheridan had told the assembled officers how the dashing Custer had been instrumental in laying the trap here at Lancy's Gap. It was the worst thing he could have said. Custer had an ego the size of his horse and now he was after glory. If he drove the rebels out, he'd make the papers again, probably get promoted. He had fallen in love with the dangerous tactic of dividing his command so he could attack with a smaller force and carry the day with fewer troops. So far he'd been lucky and Sheridan had never called him on it. But his strategy was about to misfire. Most of their engagements the last month had been against smaller forces of Confederates in situations where the rebels were tired, running out of ammo, and desperate. Here, it was different. Jubal Early's men were battle hardened and maybe running low on supplies and ammunition, but these men still knew how to fight. It wasn't going to be as easy as Custer thought.

"Sir," Hollister had said that morning inside Custer's tent, "with all due respect, General . . ."

Custer held up a hand.

"I know what you're going to say, Jonas, and you're wrong. These Rebs have been on the move for weeks with no food and very little ammunition, but their only choice is to fight. Stand your ground and follow your orders. You'll get a few runners, stragglers, maybe a company at most. On horseback they'll be easy pickings." Custer sat at the campaign desk in his tent. He was immaculately dressed; his boots were sparkling. It was a funny thing for Hollister to notice, but he glanced down at his own boots and saw that they were covered in mud and the big toe on his left foot was poking through.

"General . . . George . . . I'm begging you. This is wrong. If you're even halfway successful, they won't stand and fight. They're going to run and I won't be able to stop them. If we ride in from the east . . . hell, sir, I can even have the men dismount along the . . ." Hollister was pointing to the eastern edge of the village where a small stream meandered beneath a covered bridge on the main road.

"That will be all, Colonel," Custer said, dismissing Hollister with a wave.

"Sir, respectfully, I must . . ."

"You have your orders, Colonel Hollister. Now attend to your duty. Dismissed."

By instinct, Hollister came to attention and saluted smartly. He turned on his heel and stormed from the tent. He mounted the bay gelding he had ridden for the last several weeks and rode back to his troopers.

"Orders, sir?" His lieutenant, a rawboned redhead by the name of McAndrews asked him.

"Not good, Mac," Hollister said. "We're to take up a position south of the orchard, along the fencerow. I don't like it, Mac. Not one little bit." Hollister was steamed, but he had very little time to waste.

"Mac, ride to Captain Ferguson. Tell him to take his company east and form a skirmish line along the edge of this orchard. It's going to get hot for us, and when he hears it start, he's to ride through those trees like he owes the devil money. Push hard and keep the Rebs occupied. He needs to thin the herd or we are going to get our asses shot to pieces. Do you understand, Mac?"

"Yes, sir," the young lieutenant said. "I also must respectfully remind the colonel that he was given no such authority to separate his command."

"Noted," said Hollister.

"I must also inform the colonel, in case he should think otherwise, General Custer is full of shit. Sir."

Hollister couldn't help but laugh. "I'll forget you said that. Now get moving. Knowing the general, he'll attack before breakfast. Make sure Ferguson understands."

He watched McAndrews ride off. He was only two years younger than Hollister but for whatever reason, Jonas felt like a father to him. Being in charge of soldiers in wartime makes a young man old. God, he was being morbid.

"Snap out of it, Jonas," he muttered to himself. A corporal mounted on a beautiful black stallion heard him talking to himself and smiled. Hollister just shrugged. Custer had him all jangled up. *Time to get your mind right*, he thought.

He momentarily considered riding for Sheridan's camp, about three miles north of the town. But he'd never make it back in time and that would leave his men without their commanding officer. Something he would never do. Besides, if he went over Custer's head, he'd probably regret it. He had a feeling Custer was gaming the orders. Changing them up so he got the maximum glory, while still technically following Sheridan's command.

He heard a distant bugle sound a call to arms. *Shit*, he thought.

"All right, Corporal. Sound the order. To your mounts, let's ride!" Hollister reined his horse around and broke into a slow trot as he heard the order to mount up work its way down the line of his men. The army had bivouacked in a field northeast of the town the night before, but as always, his regiment was mounted up and ready to go in a matter of seconds. His men had waited for their CO to return from his meeting and give the order. Hollister was popular with his troops. He had uncanny field skills and his troopers had come to understand that when he gave an order, it was always the right move—it would take them through the fight with minimum casualties and maximum success. In return, his men were the most able, polished regiment in Sheridan's whole command.

In less than thirty minutes they reached their objective and Hollister deployed the men along the fencerow. He gave them the order to advance carbines and marveled at how six hundred men drew their rifles from their saddle scabbards almost in unison. What a fine unit. McAndrews returned on his palomino, his face showing some perspiration. He was always a little nervous before the fighting started, but once the first shot sounded, there was not a steadier man.

"Mac, is Ferguson on his way?" Hollister said to the lieutenant. "I think Custer is up to something and I got a feeling a couple thousand rebels are coming through that orchard before long."

"Yes, sir, he said to tell you he'll meet you in the middle. I think he liked your idea," McAndrews said, drawing his carbine from its holster on his saddle. Together, they waited as their horses pawed at the ground and grazed on the grass.

Shortly after sunrise Hollister heard the sounds of the battle start. It was always a puzzle to Jonas how the fighting commenced with the first quiet pops of the long rifles, usually the Enfields the Rebs used. Then the cannon started a few seconds later and it became a cacophony of noise, indistinguishable from either side. Over the sound came the shouts of thousands of men, the Confederates raising their rebel yell while the Union soldiers shouted back. There was never a break in the shouting, as it quickly became a constant roar: the screams as the shooting intensified, the wails of the men as they fell wounded, and the whining cries of dying horses joined in the chorus.

Hollister waited, fidgeting in the saddle. He could not see into the town, as the orchard was densely overgrown. He heard the sound of cavalry approaching from the west. He wondered if it was Custer, and then for a moment worried the Rebs had somehow gathered themselves and sent reinforcements, but it couldn't be. Sheridan and his 15,000 troops were north.

The first Reb came out of the orchard at a dead run and almost collided with Hollister's horse. He was startled to find a line of Union soldiers there, but collapsed when a bullet tore through his chest, skidding to a stop a few feet in front of Jonas.

"Hold . . ." Jonas started to say, but his words trailed off when a bullet whizzed past his left ear. Everything turned to chaos as his men opened fire on an orchard that had come alive with the enemy. He drew his Colt, but saw immediately that his men would be overrun. A wave of gray uniformed soldiers flooded through the trees and the fencerow behind him blocked any hopes to maneuver away.

He had no idea how many times his revolver had clicked on an empty chamber before he realized it was empty.

"Sir, there's a damn lot of rebels!" Mac shouted to him.

And he was right. There were too many. He was going to get
his men killed if he didn't do something quickly.

"Mac, sound the order, about face, retreat! Get the men
through that fencerow and get them out of here, go west and
regroup on the bridge road. Hurry!" He gave the order to his
lieutenant. His pistol was empty and he drew his carbine,
as bullets flew everywhere. The wall of fleeing Rebs had
pushed his troopers up against the fencerow and before they
could move, the ground had become a teeming mass of men
and horses, and still more Confederates poured out of the
orchard.

"Retreat!" Hollister shouted. "Bugler! Sound retreat."
Nothing happened because his bugler had been killed. Hollister saw three Confederate soldiers riding horses back
toward the town, having pulled his troopers from them. It
had all turned to shit. God damn Custer.

Hollister spurred his horse, pushing the nervous animal
through the mass of men. Retreating to the south was out.
"Forward! Move forward!" he shouted. He found some
clear space and rode back and forth, exhorting his men. He
wanted them to follow him into the orchard to fight their
way through the retreating rebels. A few of his men saw him
in the confusion and understood his order. But the chaos
seemed insurmountable and he saw two more of his men
go down.

"Mac! Turn the men! Forward into the orchard! Hurry!"
He shouted at Mac and the lieutenant rose in his saddle
and shouted, "Forward through the orchard! Return fire!
Forw—"

His words died on his lips as a minié ball entered just
below his left eye. Mac catapulted off his horse, his body
falling to the ground, disappearing among the gray uni-
forms.

"MAC!" Hollister shouted "NO!" He was about to spur
his horse toward the fallen lieutenant, but a hand reached out
and grabbed the halter of his mount.

"Sir! No, sir, we've got to get into that orchard sir, come on now. The lieutenant is dead, sir, you need to rally the men." It was a grizzled sergeant named Dawson, from B Company, who had stopped him.

The next hour was lost in Hollister's mind. He vaguely remembered following Dawson into the orchard. His officers had finally understood what he was asking and had rallied the men through the trees until they reached the south end of the village and the advancing Union line. Custer had routed the Confederates out of the town, just as he predicted, but the general's actions had driven the Rebs right into Hollister's regiment, where his men had been chewed up like beef in a meat grinder.

When the buzz of the fight subsided, Hollister returned to the fencerow. It was littered with dead and dying rebels and the medical corpsman had gathered the bodies of his men who had fallen. Thirty-seven bodies were lined in the shade covered by blankets. Hollister sat on his horse staring at the corpses, feeling the anger grow; a small nugget of fire in the center of his chest. No one approached him, asked him for orders, or bothered him. The look on his face was a warning for everyone to stay away. After a while he turned his horse and rode hard for the Union camp.

A half hour later he arrived at General Sheridan's camp. He could hear the sound of celebration coming from the large campaign tent. He handed the reins to a young private guarding the horses and entered the tent. The noise dimmed as the buzzing in his ears became louder. The edges of his vision turned red, and small arcs of light traveled across his eyes like a summer thunderstorm.

Custer sat at the end of a table, his hat off, revealing his long blond hair tangled with the yellow silk scarf about his neck. He was leaning back in his chair with his legs crossed while vanity oozed from his pores.

He heard the clump of Hollister's boots behind him, and turned just in time to see the first blow coming. It staggered him and he slumped to the ground, landing awkwardly on his ass. Hollister kicked the chair out of the way and leapt on the prone man.

"You arrogant son of a bitch," Jonas shouted, and landed another punch on the point of Custer's chin. His arm was cocked for another swing, but it never landed because someone grabbed him, and he felt himself being lifted to his feet. Custer lay on the ground stunned, blood seeping from his mouth and a cut on his chin.

"Fucking bastard . . . you no-good prick!" Hollister shouted.

"Colonel Hollister!" Jonas came out of his rage at the sound of General Sheridan's voice. He didn't recognize the officers holding him by the arms but the general stood between him and Custer, who still lay on the ground.

"Jesus Christ, Hollister," the general said. "Are you going to take a swing at me, Colonel?" Jonas's breath came in ragged gasps but he shook his head.

"Then let him go," the general said. "Good God, man. What the hell have you done?" Sheridan examined the prone body of Custer on the floor of his tent. He nudged him with the toe of his boot. Sheridan was a short man, no taller than five and a half feet, hence his nickname "Little Phil." He was as cocky as a rooster and his voice had always sounded how Hollister thought God's would sound, deep and resonant with just the slightest trace of an Irish brogue. "Sergeant! Get the general to the surgeon. Move it!"

Hollister stood stock still, all the fight gone out of him. He knew he was in trouble, but he didn't care. All he could see was poor Mac, lying on the ground, his face caved in where the bullet had struck him. A sergeant and two privates entered the tent and lifted Custer from the ground. Hollister didn't know it then, but that was the last time he would ever see the man.

Finally he was alone with General Sheridan. Little Phil stood with his back to Jonas, massaging his temples.

"Jesus Christ, Jonas! What the hell was this all about?" Hollister stood silent. Sheridan waited for him to speak, finally spinning on his heel and confronting him. "God damn it, Colonel, you've got one chance here. You better tell me what happened in the next sixty seconds, or so help me God, I'll see you shot!"

Hollister instinctively came to attention. He threw his shoulders back and kept his arms straight at his sides.

"Sir! I was ordered by General Custer to the south of the orchard to attack the rebels from the rear . . . I . . . "

"You what?" Sheridan stared hard at him, then the realization of what Custer had done washed over him. He sagged, and started pacing again. "God damn him, those weren't my orders, I *specifically* told him not to divide his command! The yellow-haired bastard . . ." Sheridan began stalking back and forth. The general was a profane man, and also a bigot and a racist. None of those facts affected his ability as a brilliant cavalry commander.

"What happened?" he asked.

"We were overrun. I only had one regiment and there were at least four thousand rebels on the retreat. I lost thirty-seven of my men, General. Including Lieutenant McAndrews, sir . . ."

"Aw shit, not McAndrews! Kid was going to be something special," Sheridan interrupted. Hollister went on.

"Sir, I pleaded with General Custer not to split the troops, but he assured me you had given the order."

"That vainglorious sonuvabitch. Good Christ, Hollister . . ." General Sheridan's face was a light shade of purple. "You should have come to me," he muttered. Knowing full well Hollister had not had the time, nor would Custer have allowed him any such action. He would have viewed Hollister seeking confirmation of Sheridan's orders as an affront to his command.

"Yes, sir," Hollister said. It was the only answer he could give. This would be made out to be his fault, he was sure.

He saw his mistake in physically attacking Custer. If he'd gone through the right channels, gotten Custer's order on the record, he might have gotten somewhere. Now he was headed for a court-martial at least, a firing squad at worst. And if Sheridan didn't have him thrown in the stockade, he would have to watch his back now for as long as Custer remained in the army. He wouldn't let Hollister get away with this, no matter what the official outcome.

Sheridan didn't say anything else for several minutes. Hollister thought the next words out of his mouth would be an order to surrender himself to custody.

"All right. I'll deal with Custer. The thing is, Colonel Hollister, I can't court-martial him or you. I believe you, Jonas. But this story can't get out, or all of us will be fucked once Sam gets word." Sam was General Grant, commander of the Army of the Potomac. "Sam can't stand Custer and he only barely tolerates me because I win, the drunken bastard."

"I know the skinny, shit-eating little prick wanted to be the one to chase the rebels out of the town and cut them up in the orchard so he could be the hero. And he put your men in the shitter along the way. He's a pompous son of a bitch and we both know it. But he's winning his fights. He's all over the papers, and as much as Sam hates his guts, he likes the good publicity. Grant has the personality of a horse turd and can't stand talking to the press. So he's happy to have someone like that cocksucker Custer woo the reporters. If he's court-martialed the press will crucify us." Sheridan ran his hands through his salt-and-pepper hair in frustration. "Jesus Christ, man."

"So that's it, sir, he gets my men killed and that's it? He gets away with it?" Hollister felt the anger welling inside him again.

"Grow the hell up, Colonel. That's not it, and you goddamned well know it. Are you right? Yes of course, god damn it. But you're going to take it. Go back to your regiment. See to your men and you leave Custer to me. I'm going to bust you but there won't be a court-martial. Consider yourself one lucky bastard. Now get your sorry ass out of my sight. Report here at oh five hundred for staff meeting and orders."

Hollister stood still, seething. He was about to open his mouth.

"Don't you say a goddamn word to me, Colonel! Get out of my sight or swear to fucking God I'll shoot you myself!" Sheridan put his hand on his sidearm for emphasis and dismissed Hollister with a wave, returning to his desk.

As mad as he was, he also realized he was lucky. He knew Sheridan thought highly of him, but he had no indication that the General held him in such regard. He was about to voice his thanks, when Little Phil interrupted him, turning back from his seat.

"So help me God, if you open your mouth you'll be digging latrines until this war is over. Do you understand me? I want you gone, and I mean now."

"Yes, sir," said Hollister saluting smartly as he left the tent. He worked things over in his mind. The word of the dust-up spread through the camp like the clap. Men whispered and pointed at him as he walked back to his horse. He met no one's gaze. Some of the men here were firmly in Custer's corner and wouldn't hesitate to give him a thrashing if he provoked them. Others knew Custer was dangerous. And as far as they were concerned, his beating had come far too late.

The next day Custer was absent from the staff meeting. Word had worked its way back to Hollister that the yellow-haired general had been unconscious for hours with a broken jaw. When the officers convened at Sheridan's tent the next morning, no one mentioned the missing general, and Sheridan was his usual brusque self. Hollister had spent the evening writing letters to the families of the men who had died the day before, but as had happened before and would happen again before the war was over, he found there was little time to grieve. Orders were delivered, the battle plan discussed, and they were dismissed. The fight was forgotten for the time being. There was another battle ahead of them and it required complete focus.

The following week, Hollister was transferred to the 4th U.S. Cavalry. The 4th was regular army and kept him out of Custer's orbit, and a little less than a year later, the war was over.

Custer secured his notoriety for chasing Lee to Appomattox Courthouse from the west. He never spoke to Hollister again. Jonas had narrowly avoided a career-killing mistake.

The army shrank rapidly with the war's end. Hollister re-enlisted and stayed in the 4th. He had no intention of going home. Like most officers who stayed in the regular army after the war, he was reduced in rank to lieutenant and posted first at Fort Laramie. Sheridan was put in charge of the Indian wars and he made sure to keep Hollister away from Custer when it came to assignments. And then came that morning on the plains in Wyoming, where everything went wrong. There were times, as he wrote to everyone he knew during the first year inside Leavenworth, when he was certain his thrashing of Custer had kept some in the army from coming to his defense.

A sharp blast of the train whistle brought Hollister back to the present. He wondered if he would get used to the rickety motion of the car and be able to sleep. The events of the day still tumbled around in his mind like autumn leaves caught in a whirlwind. He had gone from digging holes in Leavenworth to being on his way west on a special assignment in a matter of hours. Then there were Pinkerton and his friend Van Helsing. What odd men they were. And he had dragged Chee along not knowing he came complete with a goddamn giant dog. It was a lot to grasp and he could only think of one thing to say before sleep over took him.

"Huh."

Chapter Twelve

Hollister had slept in his clothes, which only contributed to his disoriented feeling when he opened his eyes the next morning. Waking up in a new place was something he hadn't experienced in four years. There was a broad selection of outfits hanging on his cabin wall, much as Chee had found in his quarters, but he left them there and wandered out to the main car and found Pinkerton and Chee seated at a wooden table that appeared to open up out of the floor. The two of them were eating breakfast and another man Hollister didn't know was spooning eggs out of a skillet onto a plate.

"Ah! Good morning, Major," Pinkerton said. "Did you sleep well?"

"All right, I guess," Hollister muttered.

"Have a seat. Dr. Van Helsing will join us shortly. In the meantime, Monkey Pete here is a fantastic cook. You'll be willing to kill for a cup of his coffee before too long."

Hollister studied the man with the skillet. He was short and skinny, like he hadn't had food in weeks or months. Jonas bet he wouldn't top 130 pounds even if he were holding a ten-pound sack of flour. His shirt was rolled up and his forearms were thick and roped with muscle. A curious expression looked as if it had taken up permanent residence on his face, which was covered with a thick brown beard. Dark eyes peered through a pair of glasses perched on the end of a twisted nose, which looked as if it had been broken repeatedly. He noticeably limped around the table to shake Hollister's hand, presenting one with twisted and broken fingers. Whoever this Monkey Pete was, he'd been through a couple different kinds of hell. His grip was strong though, and Hollister was amazed at the amount of strength on such a thin frame.

Hollister wondered about his broken-up fingers and hands. At West Point, cadets had been drilled in basic hand-to-hand combat, taught by a Master Sergeant Woodson, who had lost a leg in the Mexican War and could still whip every cadet on the campus. He had taught his students three things. First, anyone you meet in any situation is a potential enemy. Second, look at your opponent's eyes. They will advise you of a man's intentions if you learn to read them. And third, look at the hands. If somebody has cut up, scarred, twisted, or broken fingers you are probably in for a tussle. Hands get in that kind of shape from hard living, which usually includes throwing a punch or two. Hollister had never forgotten the lessons. He had studied Pinkerton's eyes and hands, and the detective's words and actions had since convinced Hollister that he was no one to be trifled with. Hollister wondered how this Monkey Pete had come to have his hands in such shape. He was sure there were some stories behind it.

"Pleased to meet you, Major," he said.

"Monkey Pete?" Hollister asked.

"Yes, sir. Served in the artillery during the war. General Hunt gave me the name, after Pickett's Charge at Gettysburg. Said I was crawling back and forth over them Howitzers like a monkey. 'Monkey Pete' he said. It stuck."

"And how'd you find yourself on this train, Monkey Pete,"

Hollister took a swig of the coffee and had to admit it was pretty good.

"Well, fact is, I like to tinker. Got a job with the railroad after the war. Trains get robbed now and then and I've run into Mr. Pinkerton here a few times. First time we met he thought I was the one done the robbin'." Monkey Pete paused and laughed. It was a low-pitched snorting sound and Hollister thought it sounded more like a rutting hog. Mr. Pinkerton just shrugged. "Anyway, I like messin' with engines and mechanical things and whatnot, and Mr. Pinkerton here heard about my ideas during one of our conversations. He liked 'em. Asked me to put 'em on paper and finally one day, come to get me to work for him and get one a my designs built. Once this here engine and cars got built, I figured no one else knew how to run it as good as me, so I stayed on," he said.

Hollister looked at Pinkerton. "What's so special about this train?"

"Finish your breakfast first, then we'll take the full tour. I think you'll find it interesting," Pinkerton said. He said no more and busied himself reading from a sheaf of papers he held in one hand, eating with his other.

Hollister looked at Chee but the young soldier bent to his meal, his expression revealing nothing. Hollister wondered if Chee was ever scared or happy; he doubted the kid's expression even changed when he had been thrown into the box. *Must remember never to play poker with the sergeant,* Hollister thought.

They finished eating, with no sign of Van Helsing. Monkey Pete cleared the dishes and Hollister watched as he first wiped down and then folded and collapsed the table and chairs and slid them neatly into a compartment in the floor.

"Come with me, gentlemen. Monkey Pete, lead the way," Pinkerton said. They followed the engineer outside. The train was stopped on a track siding.

"Last night we stopped in Lawrence to add the rest of the cars," Monkey Pete said. Hollister was surprised he had slept through it. But he had gone to sleep in a real bed for the first time in four years and probably could have slept through the First Battle of Bull Run.

"We picked us up a coal car, a guest car, a car for the horses. The one there with no windows and doors is the armory, don't want no one breaking in and taking all our nice weapons. The one behind the coal car, well, I call it my gadget car. Where I tinker on some o' my designs," he said.

As they walked along the side of the train, they finally reached the engine.

"I've never seen an engine that looks like this," Hollister said studying it from top to bottom.

"I'm certain you'll find the engine to be a great advantage," Pinkerton said. "It's a technical marvel really, and Monkey Pete has even developed a way to transfer ballast on the train so that you can run nearly as fast backwards as forwards. Sometimes there won't be a turntable for locomotives available so it's a very useful feature."

Chee and Hollister had no idea what Pinkerton was talking about, but nodded as if they did.

"I know I've been away awhile, but this engine seems . . . I don't know how to describe it . . ." Hollister mumbled, his eyes locked on the contraption.

"Monkey Pete has made quite a few other improvements to the standard steam engine. First, it's armored. It might not stand up to a continuous assault from a cannon, but rifle or small-arms fire won't hit vital systems and stop it. The engine has been modified—those baffles over the release valves are made of solid steel. They're honeycombed inside so that the pressure is released, but the steam is recaptured and the water vapor is returned to the engine," Pinkerton said with a note of awe in his voice. "You understand what that means, don't you, Major?"

"Of course," Hollister said, nodding. "No. sir. I have no idea what it means. Do you, Sergeant?" He looked at Chee, begging him for help.

"Um . . . I . . . think it . . . must make the train go faster, sir," Chee stammered.

Monkey Pete sighed. "It ain't got nothing to do with speed, Major, it captures the water vapor from the steam so's we don't have to fill the boiler up as often. Improves the range of the train by hundreds of miles!"

Jonas realized he'd never seen a man in love with a train before. The next hour was spent combing over the features of the remarkable machine. Pinkerton was adamant that they know every capability of the vehicle as he had spent a great deal of government money in outfitting it. And, he insisted, it might just save their lives.

Chee visibly perked up when Monkey Pete demonstrated some of the weapons the train had built in. "Major, if you'll step back a few yards so you can see this."

"Follow me, Sergeant," he said. He and Chee went back inside the main car. A second later, Chee's head and torso appeared on the roof above them, the sergeant having popped through a trapdoor inside. Directly in front of him, with a hiss of steam, a large, cylindrical cannon-shaped gun came up out of the roof.

"A portable cannon?" Hollister asked, incredulous.

"A water cannon," Pinkerton said.

"Water? What the hell?"

"You'll learn more from Van Helsing, but his research shows vampires don't like water very much. It won't kill them—well, maybe it will, we don't know yet—but it will keep them away. Water, fire, and sunlight. Remember that and you might stay alive."

Hollister was happier when he saw the next weapon Monkey Pete had altered. Four Gatling guns, modified with a lot of gauges and hoses Hollister didn't understand right away, were mounted on the roof and sides of the car. Whatever the energetic little engineer had done to them, it made them look even more lethal.

Pinkerton pulled back the slide on the magazine of the

closest gun. He removed one of the rounds and handed it to Hollister. Jonas was surprised to find that in every other way it looked like a normal round with a brass casing, except the bullet was made of wood.

"You remember how you killed that thing in Wyoming, Major? We believe wood stabbed into their heart is another way to kill them. They will turn to dust, as you saw. So we've made modifications on the weapons aboard the train. Everything here is new technology developed by some of the best minds in the world, and given a practical application by those men, some of it tested and improved upon by Monkey Pete here, who if you haven't noticed already, is a genius in his own right. He's also a crack shot with pistol or rifle, a munitions expert, a better field medic than most doctors you'll meet, and a hell of a cook. And let's just say he's developed an abiding interest in Dr. Van Helsing's work and is becoming something of an expert on these things. If he weren't so crippled up, I might have been tempted to send him after them instead of you."

Hollister's eyes narrowed, and he studied the detective's face for any sign he might be joking. There was none. He was working up a retort, but swallowed it down. It wasn't the time, and he was sure he'd rather chase the things that killed his men than dig wells all day long. Well, reasonably sure.

Pinkerton met Hollister's stare without flinching.

"All of these things are going to come in handy if you find those creatures, believe you me."

Hollister wasn't quite sure what to say. He'd hoped to have a chance to clear his head a bit this morning, given all of the changes that had taken place yesterday. But that seemed impossible now. He could barely grasp what he was seeing.

"It all looks fancy, Mr. Pinkerton," he said. "But I think I'll rely on my Colt."

Pinkerton looked at Hollister for a moment. "Major, do you remember what happened on that ridge in Wyoming? How effective your sidearm was against those things?"

"Yes . . . I—"

"The answer is not effective at all. If your report was accurate, you shot one of those creatures at least twice at point-blank range. To no effect. Do you really want to pursue these things, who may have grown in numbers to God knows how many by now, with just your Colt?"

Jonas had to admit the detective had a point.

"You make a convincing argument, Mr. Pinkerton. What else should I know?"

When they'd finished, Hollister had a basic understanding of most everything. Chee was like a drunk in a brewery, reveling in the guns and asking Monkey Pete questions about each aspect of every single system. It was clear to Hollister that Chee had been overlooked and ignored by the army because of his race. A capable soldier, certainly, but they had failed to notice his natural curiosity, intelligence, and creativity. He may have served ably for many years, but had Hollister not rescued him, he would have languished in prison and been dishonorably discharged, if he was ever released. The army, especially the post-war army, was not an intelligent or progressive institution. And though the war against slavery had been convincingly won by the North, racism was still alive. Good men like Chee were still going to be chewed up by it.

Hollister hadn't realized Chee's dog had disappeared until it returned, loping around the engine with a rabbit in its mouth. Apparently it was still hungry.

"I'll be damned," Monkey Pete said. "That is some critter. I'll cook us up a nice pot of rabbit stew."

Dog sat on his haunches next to Chee and growled low in his throat when Monkey Pete made to take the rabbit from his jaws.

"Whoa," Monkey Pete said, scrabbling backward.

"Dog . . ." Chee said, snapping his fingers twice. Dog stood and stepped toward the engineer and placed the rabbit at his feet.

"Sorry, Mr. Pete, sir," Chee said. "I forgot to tell him you were a friend. He won't growl at you again."

"How can you be so sure?" Hollister asked.

"He just won't, sir, and he won't growl at Mr. Pinkerton or Dr. Van Helsing either. Once I tell him, that is," the sergeant replied.

"You, 'tell him'?" Hollister asked, incredulous. "How, exactly?"

"I just tell him like I'd tell anyone, sir," Chee replied. "He speaks English. And Creole. And a little Chinese. I didn't have a chance to teach him French before I was . . . I had to go to Leavenworth."

Hollister and Pinkerton stared at each other, then Pinkerton laughed.

"He speaks English, does he?" Hollister asked.

Chee just shrugged as if it were something beyond explaining. It just was.

"Let's get under way, Monkey Pete," Pinkerton said. "And see if Dr. Van Helsing is awake. If I know Abraham, he was up all night scribbling away in his journal."

"Where are we?" Hollister asked, noticing for the first time that the train had pulled off on a siding in the middle of nowhere. Except for the train and the track, which disappeared on the horizon, there was no sign of civilization.

"We are about four hours away from Denver," Pinkerton said.

Hollister was stunned. They had traveled over four hundred miles during the night. How was it possible?

"What . . . that can't be! We just left Leavenworth . . ." Hollister was unable to keep the shock out of his voice.

"It has guns, armor, and an extended range," Pinkerton said. "And there is one other thing you should know about your new train, Major.

"It's fast as hell."

Chapter Thirteen

As the prairie rolled by, Van Helsing and Pinkerton briefed Chee and Hollister with their accumulated knowledge of vampires. The information was sketchy, much of it second- and thirdhand. There was a great deal to digest, and Hollister found Chee's contribution to their discussions both surprising and informative. He'd made a snap judgment about the kid, based on how he'd handled himself with McAfee. Of course he'd seen him around the yard and on other work details, but Chee was quiet and kept to himself. Now he had turned into a different person, and Hollister smiled to himself at the good luck of his choice.

They had worked straight through lunch and gone through Van Helsing's book several times. He handed Hollister a portfolio.

"Da. Very gut! Major, here is a copy of my journal. I've had it transcribed for you. It contains all of the knowledge of the vampire we have accumulated. If and when you track down these vile beasts, I hope you will be villing to share your experiences with us," Van Helsing said.

"Sure, Doctor. I don't mind that at all. 'Course I'll have to survive my encounter first, won't I?" Hollister replied.

Van Helsing threw back his head and laughed. "Ach. So true, Major! So very, very true! You make a very good joke!" Hollister hadn't intended it as a joke and knew Van Helsing wouldn't be laughing either, if he'd been as close to one of those demons as Hollister had.

When they finally pulled into Denver, it was seven o'clock. The train chugged slowly onto a siding at the main station yard. The rails led the train inside a large warehouse. Checking his watch again, Pinkerton stood.

"Dr. Van Helsing, this is the end of the line for you, for now at least. Thank you for your assistance." Van Helsing shook everyone's hand.

"Ach. It is gut to have you with us, Major Hollister and Sergeant Chee. My thoughts and prayers will be with you on your mission," he said.

Gathering up his papers and tucking them into his battered valise, he shrugged into his topcoat. "Adieu, gentlemen!" he said. He took one last look around the train, studying the devil's traps and the markings on the walls; nodding in some internal agreement with himself, he reached the door of the car and paused. "Major, I want you to know something. What happened to you and your men, on that ridge in Wyoming . . . it vas not your fault. You could not have known what you were facing. And I believed you, Major, from the very first time I read the report. I just wanted you to know that. I believed you."

The small man's words were starkly sincere and Hollister could not help but be touched by them. No one had ever mentioned the incident to him in such a manner before. He gave the doctor a small salute. "Thank you, Dr. Van Helsing."

Van Helsing returned the salute and left the car.

"Very good," Pinkerton said. "Gentlemen, if you'll accompany me outside. I think you're going to enjoy meeting your gunsmith."

"We have a gunsmith?" Chee asked. His appreciation of weapons at his disposal was already near euphoria and the idea of a personal gunsmith was close to sending him into hysteria.

"Yes, indeed," Pinkerton said. "You might have heard of him. His name is Oliver Winchester."

Chee and Hollister stared at each other in amazement. Winchester was the most famous gun maker in the country, next to Samuel Colt, who had died years ago. Winchester rifles were famous the world over, and his 1873 repeating .30-caliber model had become the best-selling rifle in history. Practically every home, cowboy, rancher, and cattle thief on the western frontier owned, wanted, or had stolen one. Once again Hollister stopped to consider what he had gotten himself into.

"I'm sorry, Mr. Pinkerton, but a gunsmith? I don't think guns are going to work on these things. As you reminded me, my Colt . . ."

"All true; however, wait and see what Mr. Winchester has created. You'll be going into battle with far more than a Colt, Major."

They stepped off the train. Hollister marveled again that Pinkerton had managed to find a building big enough for the entire train. Almost as if on cue, the door opened at the far end of the warehouse. A slight but determined-looking man with a dark black moustache and beard, and wearing a fine suit with a bowler hat on top of his head approached them. He strode straight to Pinkerton without taking his eyes off him. The two men shook hands.

"Gentlemen, please meet Oliver Winchester, owner and president of the Winchester Repeating Arms Company," Pinkerton waited a moment while the man greeted Hollister and Chee.

"Oliver, do you mind?" Pinkerton said, pulling the silver Saint Ignatius coin from his vest pocket. Winchester closed his hand around the offered coin. The three men waited, and Hollister wondered what would happen if someone, or something, held the coin who was not who they claimed to be. Would lightning strike them or smoke and fire seep out of their hand before they burst into flames?

But nothing happened. Hollister saw Pinkerton relax slightly and when Winchester retrieved his own coin from his coat and offered it to the detective, it felt as if some unspoken challenge had been laid to rest. Yet a small sliver of doubt still crept into Hollister's mind. What if these creatures weren't affected by silver? After all, Van Helsing said the metal "appeared to bother them" but not how, and what happened when it did or even if it really did. Had they tested it? If so, how? He would have to read up in the doctor's journal about all this.

A porter had followed Winchester into the building pushing several large wooden cases on a dolly. The gunsmith thanked the man, who departed without a second glance. Hollister still found it odd, being in a building with a train inside it. Then again, he'd been in prison four years. Maybe things had changed.

Like the weapon that bore his name, Winchester was no nonsense. He got right to the point. He hefted one of the crates onto the table and popped the lid off. Chee inched forward, like an eager puppy, desperate to see what was inside the box. Jonas knew Chee was dangerous enough when he was unarmed. But he also appeared to have an unusual interest in guns. Hollister reckoned this made him doubly lethal.

Winchester removed a rifle from the case. It looked like a normal repeater, one of the big Henry's Jonas had seen in the war.

"Gentlemen, this is an 1866 model Henry rife. It has had some modifications and enhancements made to it. Mainly, changes were made to the barrel that allow various types of ammunition to be used without damage to the mechanism or structural integrity of the barrel. You'll each be issued one of these and there will be another dozen on board the train for your use. Please do not lose them. They are extremely costly and difficult to produce."

"I used a Yellow Boy myself, riding with General Sheridan in the Shenandoah Valley during the War," Hollister said, referring to the nickname given the Henry Rifle. The brass casing on the gun shone nearly yellow when polished and had given rise to the name. "It's a fine weapon."

Winchester beamed with pride.

"Sergeant Chee here was a little too young for the war, but I'm sure you've heard some of your elder brethren in butternut gray talk about the Henry," Winchester said. Chee smiled.

"Yes, sir. Some of my uncles fought with the Eighth Louisiana. They called it 'that damn Yankee rifle you could load on Sunday and fire all week.'"

Winchester laughed. "So I've heard. Well, given these new models and their capabilities, perhaps our enemies will grow to fear them in the same way," he said.

For the next hour, Winchester went over the modifications to the rifles and the contents of the first case. They were given ammo that was modified for their side arms. Some bullets were made of silver and some had been dipped in holy water before they were fitted into the cartridge. Others were wooden as with the Gatling guns on the train, their ends machined into a sharp point. They looked especially deadly, like miniature spears.

When Winchester was finally winding down, Hollister noticed that he hadn't opened or said anything about the second case.

"What's in the other box?" Hollister asked.

Winchester stopped a moment and looked behind him at the case on the ground. He smiled and put one foot on top of it and stuck his hands in his vest pockets, looking for all the world like some carnival huckster.

"This?" he said, feigning disinterest and tapping his foot on top of the crate.

"This gentlemen, is a little something I like to call 'The Ass-Kicker.'"

He then proceeded to show them how it worked.

Chapter Fourteen

It was the damndest thing Hollister had ever seen. It looked like a short-barreled shotgun had mated with a . . . he didn't know what, maybe Monkey Pete's train, and produced a weapon suitable for the devil himself. Winchester held it out and Jonas was almost reluctant to take it from him. There were two large steel baffles along the barrel, gauges and gears everywhere—all shining and polished—and a collapsing stock. It appeared to him the gun might fly apart at any minute.

Winchester flipped a small lever to the side of the trigger guard and the gun broke open exposing four barrels. Winchester held up four rather large shells, nearly the size of small mortar rounds and loaded them into the barrel snapping it shut.

"There's advantages and disadvantages to the Ass-Kicker," Winchester remarked. He took the empty crate and dragged it toward the far wall of the warehouse about sixty paces away.

"It's actually steam powered. There's an attachment here,"

he said pointing to a large brass fitting on the side of the weapon. "Monkey Pete worked with me on this one. With this valve attachment it can be charged from the engine on the train or any sort of standard steam-powered engine fitting. It builds up pressure in the line here, and each time you fire, it sends a pressurized round through the barrel and with these .90 caliber rounds . . . Well, you'll see."

Hollister held the gun, the stock resting on his upper arm, as he prepared to fire from the waist.

"That's it," Winchester said. "You'll want to fire it like you would a shotgun. If you try to get too cute and fire from your shoulder, you'll regret it. Go ahead, Major. I'd be honored if you'd take the first shot."

"The first shot? You're shittin' me right? You mean to tell me you've never test fired this gun before?" Hollister replied, shocked.

"Of course we have." Winchester answered waving his hands in front of him. "In the lab."

"In your lab?" Jonas said.

"Yes, Major, I assure you the Winchester Repeating Arms Company has a first rate research facility. The gun has been tested."

"Then why I am firing the 'first shot?'" Hollister asked growing more and more uncomfortable.

"To be honest . . ." Winchester started, looking at Pinkerton for help, but the detective merely cocked his head and remained silent. "The first models had certain . . . problems. But when Mr. Pinkerton informed me of the severity of it, I put my best men on it around the clock. I'm certain the gun will work as promised, there just hasn't been as much time as I would have liked to test all the . . ."

He didn't get a chance to finish, because Hollister pointed the weapon at the crate and pulled the trigger. The noise alone was enormous and Hollister was unprepared for the recoil as it sent him staggering backward. He tried to keep his balance, but couldn't and landed on the dirt floor on his butt. The gun hissed and clicked as the steam was released and the gears turned then stopped with another click as it readied itself for another shot.

"Oh my God," muttered Chee his face caught between sheer astonishment and an almost childlike expression as if he were about to beg the major for the next shot and would be willing to trade his jackknife and all of his marbles for the chance to shoot the gun just once.

Pinkerton walked to where Hollister lay sprawled in the dirt and helped him to his feet. Winchester cackled with glee as the smoke cleared and the smell of cordite and gunpowder retreated.

"Not going to be a very useful weapon if it knocks you over every time you shoot it," Hollister said in disgust, thrusting the machine back into the hands of the gunsmith.

"Oh. Really?" Winchester said. "Take a look at the crate, Major."

Hollister had nearly forgotten about the target. He had been more concerned with the indignity of landing on his ass in the dust. Now he stared over toward where the crate stood.

It was gone. Only a few splinters remained. Some smaller pieces of wood still fluttered in the air, drifting slowly toward the ground like snowflakes. Hollister looked at Pinkerton and Chee in amazement.

"Huh."

From across the rail yard, a man stood in the gloom of alley between two rail sheds, watching the doors of the large warehouse where the strange train had pulled in a few hours ago. He was six feet two inches tall, whippet thin, dressed in a black leather duster, a black Stetson pulled low on his head. He wore a gun belt holding a nickel-plated Colt, the handle forward for a cross draw. His face was scarred and marked from a battle with small pox he'd barely survived as a young boy. He tried to cover it with a beard but the hair grew thin on his face, not covering the scars completely but succeeding in making him look more dangerous and angry.

His name was Slater and he worked for Senator James Declan. He was many things: ranch foreman, aide-de-camp, and—the role he most preferred—problem solver. Mostly he solved the senator's problems with his Colt, as the gun was second nature to him. But he was happy to use whatever means necessary to make sure the troubles were taken care of. He wasn't above shooting a man with a rifle from three hundred yards, or caving in a skull with an axe handle. Up close or far away, it made no difference to him.

He'd killed his first man at seventeen in Dodge City. He'd drifted into town looking for work, unable to find any, and started pinching from cowpokes outside the saloons when they were all drunked up. One night a cowhand took exception and put up a fight. Slater put a knife in his ribs and watched as he bled out right there in the alley. He thought taking a life might make him feel something: powerful or godlike or remorseful or scared. To Slater it was no different than pulling on his boots, but what he felt was nothing. He took the coin pouch from the dead man and left him there in the dirt.

Slater worked his way west across the plains, partnering here and there with various thieves and rustlers and doing his share of honest labor when he could, even a session as a town deputy marshal in Nebraska, but never any legitimate work for long. Slater was not suited to rules.

Six years ago, he'd arrived at Senator Declan's ranch outside of Denver. He'd heard there might be work. Declan's was one of the largest cattle operations in the state and owned nearly forty thousand acres. Slater signed on and worked for a few months; then a dispute with the foreman rose up. The foreman came at him with a branding iron and Slater took it away from him and beat the man to death.

Slater thought that would be the end. Colorado had just become a state and Declan, now richer than ever with his silver strike, had thrown a lot of money toward the governor to get an appointment as a senator. And he'd succeeded. Declan saw an opportunity.

He was on his way to Washington; with his foreman dead and his ranch in turmoil, he'd need a firm hand to keep things under control. And that's what he saw in Slater, someone who would keep things orderly. Instead of sending Slater off to prison for killing his foreman, Declan promoted him.

James and his wife, Martha, had one son, James Junior, who was a lost cause, in the senator's opinion. Spoiled, weak, vain, and unwilling to *take* what was his, the boy caused nothing but trouble. Now James had caused a whole new kind of trouble. The boy had thought to try his hand at mining, and had been in the Senator's Torson City camp when these . . . whoever or whatever they were had killed everyone but James, who somehow managed to wade into the stream and get away from these things. And no matter how hard Declan and Slater tried, the boy would not be silenced. He insisted he'd seen "monsters," not men.

When James refused to change his story, Declan sent Slater to the camp to investigate. And what Slater saw there had unnerved him. Slater was a killer, without an ounce of remorse for any of the men he'd killed. It wasn't so much what he'd seen as what he hadn't seen. If that many men had died the buildings, the town should be painted in blood. There was very little blood. Almost none, in fact, but everywhere he looked there were signs of struggle. Not just struggle but desperate struggle, the evidence of men fighting for their lives and losing. But not much blood.

There was another thing bothering Slater and it was something he couldn't put into the words. When he had ridden into the camp, seen the general store and the saloon where the men had died, he had felt fear. It had started at the base of his spine and worked its way up till it reached the top of his head. He was frightened for the first time he could ever remember—after years of fights, robberies, beatings, and outright murders, he was never afraid. But being in Torson City, he felt fear. And he'd wanted to leave as soon as he rode in—even his horse was skittish.

He'd never been a gun thug, but he kept track of the men he killed. He didn't put notches in his gun handle or act like the fakers. He just killed and moved on to the next killing. Most of the men he murdered were at the senator's behest, some because they'd just been in the way when a job needed doing. It was not something he felt warranted much careful accounting. But five minutes in Torson City and he knew James wasn't lying. Something evil and dark had been there. It killed efficiently and savagely, then took the bodies and left.

Now at the senator's orders, he'd watched the strange-looking train roll into town and off the siding to its own warehouse. Pinkerton men guarded the outside, and so far neither Slater nor any of his men had been able to get a look inside. He had watched the short man enter with a porter and two shipping crates and a while later heard the muffled sound of weapons fired, followed by an unusually loud explosion, but since then nothing.

He shoved himself upright. It was time for him to report to the senator. Whatever was inside the warehouse had something to do with Torson City. The senator had been sure of that.

Now Slater was too.

Chapter Fifteen

Hollister needed to walk. It was getting close to midnight. Winchester had left a couple of hours ago, after giving them a dizzying array of weapons, and Chee had remained behind at the . . . Hollister couldn't think of anything else to call it but headquarters. It was far more than a warehouse or storage depot. The upper level, reached by a stairway, had rooms for all of them as well as a kitchen, sitting room, and armory.

Jonas was confused. There was obviously money and power behind Pinkerton, Van Helsing, Winchester, and the others. He wondered if the setup was for him specifically or just something set in motion that he happened to be a part of. He was going after some deadly things, these vampires, as Van Helsing had called them. Looking at everything that had gone into preparing him for the task, he still couldn't help but feel a little bit like cannon fodder.

He walked on, fingering his Colts. Winchester had concentrated mostly on long guns during his demonstrations, but his gunsmiths had made some modifications to an array of pistols as well. They had been similarly altered and now could fire a multitude of ammunition. Some of the bullets had small holes drilled into them, the hole filled with holy water and then sealed with wax. One of the most interesting weapons, besides the "Ass-Kicker," of course, had been a large-bore single-barrel shotgun that shot a net weighted down with lead balls attached to its edges. It deployed in the air and could capture a man or a beast "with apparent ease," as Winchester had put it. Hollister snorted at the word *ease*. He didn't think there would be anything easy about catching any of these monsters.

Hollister couldn't help but laugh at that. But he could see the tactical applications of the weapon.

He drew the Colt on his right hip and tested the weight of it in his hands. It felt good to him and he realized again how much he had missed his former life. He missed the army, guns, and sabers, and the trappings of being an officer. Commanding men and fighting and even the rigid structure of the army had been his passion, and he had longed for it.

The Colt slipped back into its slot on the tooled leather holster he'd been given. He had made sure the belt was full of extra rounds, and two speed loaders were strapped securely to each leg. When it came to facing down whatever he'd met on that hillside so many years before, he knew he wanted as much firepower as he could muster.

A light misting of rain started to fall. He felt all jangled up and jumpy and put it off to the fact that until yesterday, he'd been in a jail cell. Walking around like this made him feel out of sorts. Like most cities though, Denver had a rowdy part of town close to the rail yard, and before long he heard noise and pianos and banjos playing from a variety of saloons. He kept going. Denver was a place he'd never visited, and he couldn't see much of it at night, but the freedom of walking, the fresh air, and even the rain felt good.

Before long, he had passed by the saloons and whorehouses and into a quieter place again, lined with shops and businesses long closed at this hour. Jonas wasn't sure when he felt the first prickle of alarm along his neck. Growing up, working on the farm, going to West Point, the constant marching and drilling had kept him fit and he moved quietly and well, even when there was no reason to do so. He had learned on the plains that noise could mean death. And when he reached the next street corner, he left the wooden walkway and stepped out onto the dirt street, his strides much quieter in the rain soaked ground.

He meandered across the street at a long angle, pulling back his duster and resting both hands on his pistols. When he reached the walkway, he paused momentarily, pretending he was unsure which direction to take. In the few seconds of quiet, he heard the clump of a boot on wood and the squeak of leather coming from across the street. Not reacting, he stepped carefully up on the wooden sidewalk and walked on. It was dark, and whoever followed him would have a hard time seeing him fingering his Colts. Unless of course, whoever was watching had excellent night vision—inhuman vision—like one of those things.

"Jesus," he muttered to himself. "Snap out of it, Hollister. No goddamn 'vampire' is going to jump you right in the middle of Denver."

Yet his grip on the Colts remained firm.

He strolled silently down the street, stepping as lightly as he could, pretending to be interested in the shop windows dimly illuminated by the gaslight street lamps. At the next intersection, he turned the corner and put his back against the wall. He drew the Colt from his right holster and waited, counting to ten. Then, removing his hat with his other hand so as not to cast a shadow, he leaned forward and peered around the corner.

Nothing.

Or something.

For a moment, he could have sworn he saw a black-clad figure dart into the alleyway two blocks back the way he had come. The movement was so quick, he wasn't sure he had seen it and he would have discounted it immediately but for the flash of blond hair. Long blond hair, and wearing a black duster. Now he was sure of it. Without moving, and scarcely breathing, he scanned the street but caught sight of nothing else.

Four years of prison had dulled Hollister's sense of smell. He was used to the stink of unwashed men and the other disgusting smells of daily prison life. But men who reeked of cologne were another matter. He spun around, bringing his gun hand up, putting the Colt almost on the nose of a tall, thin man wearing a black Stetson, with a scraggly beard over a pockmarked face. The man didn't flinch, barely moved a muscle in fact, and Hollister found that odd. He moved his hand to his other gun when he saw the dim shadows of three other men behind the first one.

"A very good way to get yourself killed, sneaking up like that," Hollister said.

The man barely shrugged and asked, "Your name Hollister?" Jonas thought he had a voice like a saw on wood, but so far Jonas had moved the Colt an inch closer and the man barely acknowledged it.

"Who wants to know?" he said. And just so each of them understood he was not in the mood for games, he drew back the hammer on the gun. The click sounded like a cannon shot in the quiet street.

"Mister, I'm raising my hands up real slow. And I'd appreciate if you'd drop the hammer on that smoke wagon real gentle-like. You got the jump on me for sure. It ain't right, me coming up on you like this in the dark, and I'm sorry fer it." The man slowly lifted his arms until they were bent at the elbows, his hands floating near his shoulders, the move so nonchalant that Jonas began to worry one of those creatures had found him after all. He kept the gun cocked.

"Mighty generous of you," he said. "Who are you and what do you want?"

"Name is Slater. These fellas here work fer me. And I work fer a man who'd like to talk to you," Slater said.

"The man have a name?"

"You ever hear of a senator named Declan? James Declan?" Slater asked, his preternatural calm beginning to unnerve Jonas somewhat.

"No," he lied.

"Well, I reckon you ain't from around here, then. What matters is he's a-heard o' you and he'd like to talk to you. Right quick-like," Slater said.

"What about?" Hollister asked.

"Don't reckon I know. Just do what I'm told. Just like you, if you are Major Jonas Hollister, United States Army. That is you, ain't it?" Slater asked, his dark eyes darting momentarily as if his knowledge of Jonas's identity had given him some temporary advantage.

"No dice," Hollister said. "I don't take orders from you or any so-called senators. Especially not from ones who send gun hands to request my presence, sneaking up on me like a bunch of Kiowa. You're damn lucky you didn't lose your head. You tell the senator, if he wants to talk, Major Jonas Hollister will meet him at the Oriental Hotel tomorrow morning at nine A.M. sharp. You got that?"

"Listen, Mr. . . . Major Hollister, the senator, he's an impatient man, he wants to talk to you tonight, and if I don't . . ." Slater stopped talking when Hollister pushed the Colt forward till it rested directly on the tip of Slater's nose.

"Tomorrow. Nine A.M. Oriental Hotel," Hollister said. "Is that clear?"

Slater's eyes changed then. Hollister had done a tour at a Fort in Florida right after the war and living there, he'd seen plenty of gators. Right then, Slater's eyes reminded him of an alligator, dark and dangerous and peering out of the water, ready to snap.

Slowly and with great deliberation, Slater took a step back

and then another. He kept his arms up. His voice was even more tense when he said, "Nine A.M. it is then." He backed away a few more paces, then turned and walked up the street, his men following along. Hollister held the Colt ready until they turned the corner and disappeared.

Declan. How did he know Jonas was in Denver? Pinkerton had said no one knew except him, the president, and a few members of the Order. Obviously, that was no longer true. He slipped the Colt back into the holster, but not before peering around the side of the building again and looking for any sign of blond hair and a black leather duster. The street was empty.

He headed back the way he had come, eager to report this news to Chee and Pinkerton, wondering one thing with each step: *What in the hell was going on?*

"Huh," he muttered to himself.

Shaniah watched the altercation of the men in the Denver street from a rooftop. She had returned to Denver having lost Malachi's trail again. She couldn't understand how, but he was growing more and more devious and better able to hide his scent from her. What had he learned in his odyssey from their homeland? Was it the altitude? Unlikely, since they had lived in a high altitude in their homeland. Perhaps the air here was different in some way. Had he uncovered a solution to the natural Archaic fear of water and learned a new way to cross rivers and streams? Or had she lived so long in her high mountain stronghold she had just lost the skills of a hunter?

Then, out of nowhere, she had encountered the man from the Wyoming ridge four years earlier. It was a chance encounter since she had rented a room at a hotel near the tracks. It was not a high-class establishment; it was a place that would not draw attention, run by a Chinese family who asked few questions, but instinctively and respectfully feared her.

She caught his scent as he walked by and there was no doubt it was him: the tall, dark-haired soldier who had survived his encounter with Malachi so many years before. Though she seemed unable to keep Malachi in her sights, her Archaic senses had heightened enough in the months she had been in America, and in a matter of seconds, his walk, his smell, and even the sound of his voice, which she had heard carried on the wind, told her it was him.

Why was this man here? Back then she had traveled near Camp Sturgis and the mining camps at Deadwood a few weeks after Hollister had met his fate, and she'd heard people talking. A captain in the army had lost his platoon—to the Sioux—it was said, and had lied to cover it up. He was going to prison. Shaniah knew this is not what occurred, but understood that the soldier would have had a hard time convincing his human masters what had actually happened. Now the very same man was here in Denver.

Instinct told Shaniah it was not a coincidence. The man may have been released from prison, but with Malachi and his band having slaughtered the miners in the nearby camp, it was unlikely that he was here for another reason. America, she had learned, was too big a place, with too many other places to go. People were talking about what had happened at Torson City; word was leaking out that a survivor of the attack was telling wild tales of monsters and demons on the loose. A local powerful politician—the humans called him a senator—was trying to quell the panic, saying it was only a band of renegade Indians who had attacked the miners. If the soldier had heard these rumors, maybe he had come here seeking revenge. If that was true, the man was foolish.

Shaniah did not believe he was foolish though. She had learned never to make snap judgments. Especially when it came to humans. That day on the Wyoming ridge, the soldier had stood up to Malachi. He had been cautious and even fearful at first, but when Malachi attacked, he'd fought bravely and tried desperately to save his men.

It was odd to see him out at this time of night, so heavily armed and alone. Human men were creatures of the flesh, and at first she thought he might be on his way to find a companion for the night, but when he passed by the brothels without a glance, she became even more intrigued.

After following him a few blocks, she knew he had become aware of the fact that he was being followed. Yet Shaniah was willing to bet that he had no idea he was being stalked by her and four other men. Her curiosity nearly revealed her presence when the soldier stopped and turned suddenly, and were it not for her superior reflexes he might have caught more than a glimpse of her. And a few minutes later, as he encountered the four ruffians in the alley, he likely thought it had been one of those men who had been following him.

She watched the man deal with the men and his behavior intrigued her further. He did not show fear, only the calmness that comes from a healthy dose of self-assurance. By then she was on a rooftop above the confrontation below, two buildings south of them, and could easily hear the entire conversation. It confirmed her suspicions: he was here because of Malachi.

When the man turned away from the intersection and started back the way he had come, Shaniah followed him, this time from the rooftops. As far as she knew, this soldier walking in the streets below her was the only human who had survived an encounter with Malachi. He was following Malachi's trail as well. So she would follow him.

She had nothing to lose.

Chapter Sixteen

James Declan was a rounded oak tree of a man. Medium height and close to three hundred pounds: solid. His hands were the size of frying pans and his face was round and puffy, his bright white hair sitting on his head like a small bush. He had a thick mustache planted in the middle of his face, which always looked as if it were ready to explode in a display of his volcanic temper. He sat at a table near the window in the main dining room of the Oriental Hotel, waiting for Jonas Hollister to arrive and growing angrier with each passing moment.

Declan was self-made in every way. Most of his money had come from cattle. He'd started as a drover on the Goodnight-Loving Trail, bringing beeves up from Texas and into Denver. He wasn't like most cowhands, who collected wages at the end of a drive and blew them all on whores and gambling. He was smart and took his money to the bank. After a few years of drives he had a small stake, and one thing about Declan, he saw the future. Denver was going to grow, no question. Colorado would become a state and once it did and the railroads came, Denver would be the next big boomtown of the many boomtowns on the American move westward.

He started buying land far outside of Denver, where it was still cheap. He found good water and grazing land and then he stopped driving cattle and started buying them. He'd ride out to meet the herds before they got to the city railheads and offer the trail boss a few dollars for a few of the scrawniest, mangiest cows in the herd. Knowing they wouldn't get top dollar for their scrubs in Denver, the bosses usually complied and when Declan led the cattle onto his well-watered grassland, they prospered. Nature took its course, and in a few years, for very little money, he was able to grow his herd to several hundred, then thousand head. He sold off his mature beef, used the money to buy more land and before long he was one of the wealthiest landowners in the territory.

Then had come the silver strike. It had been pure luck. Found on the land of a small rancher he'd run off years ago, it was at the time the second richest strike in history. Combined with his land and cattle, the silver made Declan one of the wealthiest men in America.

Declan though, was dishonest by nature. There wasn't a moment or defining event in his life that turned him that way, it's just how he was. He had come out of the womb a cheat. He pressured smaller ranchers, keeping them from their water rights, even burning them out if necessary. He had brought many a smaller rancher to the brink of ruin, then swooped in with a cash offer of ten percent, or less, of the full value of his land or herd.

When he'd found Slater, he'd managed to remove himself from the dirtier, rougher stuff and clean up his image somewhat. He was loathed in the ranching community, but as the years went by, found his money more than welcome in political circles. When he helped get the governor elected, he was appointed Colorado's first senator when Colorado entered the Union in 1876.

Now he sat cooling his heels, waiting for some goddamn army reject named Hollister to show up at a meeting where Hollister had set the time, place, and agenda. Declan didn't like that, he didn't like it at all. Senator James Declan established the parameters and made the rules, and by God, heads would roll over this when he got back to Washington.

Slater was sequestered in the coat-check room, just to the left of the entrance to the dining room. Just in case this Hollister needed to be taught a lesson, although the senator had to admit he didn't like what he'd heard from Slater; how the man had gotten a clean jump on him in the street the other night. With Slater that never had happened, and the thought that it had was nibbling away at a corner of Declan's thoughts. Just one more thing to make him uneasy.

He had intended for his hired thug to drag the man to his Denver mansion if it was necessary, but Slater said it was like Hollister had eyes in the back of his head. They didn't have a chance to even get close before he skinned his smoke wagon, and from then on, he was in charge. Declan knew Pinkerton by reputation, and when all this trouble started at Torson City, he used his contacts and found out what Pinkerton was up to. There were no secrets in Washington, and he'd found out when the great detective (nothing more than a highly paid thug, in Declan's opinion) had gotten Hollister out of Leavenworth.

The tiny white hairs were standing up in the back of Declan's neck and he didn't know why, though he blamed his goddamn son James Junior and his wild stories. The boy had been nothing but a disappointment to him practically since the day he was born. Then he had come back from his latest venture, running a mining claim in Torson City, with a ridiculous fable about creatures who had killed everyone and drunk their blood. Declan had been angry beyond anything he had ever experienced, and thought for certain he would kill the boy. If it weren't for his wife and Slater's intervention, he might have.

A posse had been sent to the camp immediately after young James had staggered back into Denver, delirious and half mad with thirst. He'd told the local sheriff his story before Declan or Slater could get hold of him and word started to spread. When the posse returned from the camp, they reported some blood and signs of a struggle, but no bodies, and nothing that would corroborate James's story.

It was a wild tale, and Declan had immediately discounted it when he'd first heard about it. He tried shaking young James out of it. It had to be Indians, probably Utes, or else a group of rogue bandits who preyed on mining camps. But when Slater came back and reported to him what he'd seen, Declan began to worry.

Now all the boy did was stay in his room at the mansion. The servants brought him food and emptied his chamber pot and he spent most of his time curled on his bed blathering on and on about blood-drinking savages. James never changed his version of events. The sheriff or one of his deputies had no doubt repeated it, the news spread further, and people began to talk and worry. If Declan didn't get a lid on this fast, it would be a full-fledged panic.

Through it all, Declan had refused to believe any of it. But now this Hollister was in town, brought here by Pinkerton on a fancy train the likes of which no one had ever seen. And Jonas Hollister had told a similar story to what young James had reported and it had gotten him court-martialed and sent to prison four years ago. Things were starting to add up in a way Declan didn't like. And then there were the little hairs on the back of his neck, still standing on end. Why was that? He felt like he was no longer the one in charge of things. Ridiculous. Senator James Declan was always in charge.

Restless and out of sorts, he checked his pocket watch. It was ten minutes past nine and Hollister still wasn't here. He pounded his fist on the table and the china coffee cup jumped in its saucer and splashed a dark stain on the tablecloth. He was about to stand and leave, when Hollister strode into the dining room. Declan had requested a seat near the window and asked the maitre de to keep the tables around them clear so they could talk in private. The room was nearly empty, with only a few tables occupied, as most diners had finished their breakfasts long ago.

Hollister approached the table and sat down in a chair across from the senator, ignoring his outstretched hand. The lack of the handshake further rattled Declan, and he felt an overwhelming urge to throttle Hollister, but he noticed the two nickel-plated, pearl-handled Colts at his waist and the look on his face, which said an attempted thrashing would be a truly bad idea.

"You must be Hollister."

"I am."

"You're late."

Hollister shrugged.

"Are you always late?"

"It depends."

"On what?"

"On whether I happen to be running late or not."

"Is that some kind of joke? You think you're a jokester?"

"No joke, just a fact."

"Hmm. Well you might want to be a little more punctual when a United States senator requests a meeting."

"And you might want to refrain from sending gun hands to *invite* me to talk. First, I don't usually eat breakfast so you're lucky I even agreed to meet, and second, you want to meet with me, you ask me yourself or send a wire. Next time one of your men sneaks up on me in an alley, I'll put 'em down. We understand each other, Senator?"

The senator's face went red, in embarrassment, not anger, and try as he might he could not will it away. He started to speak, but Hollister interrupted.

"One other thing, your gun hand—told me last night his

name is Slater—is waiting in the cloakroom over there. I don't like that. You tell him to come out real slow-like, with his hands clear."

Declan was now nearly crazed with anger, but trying every trick he knew not to show it. How the hell had Hollister figured everything out?

"Slater. You heard the man. Come on out. Slowly, if I were you."

Hollister watched as Slater stepped out of the cloakroom across the dining room. He'd smelled the man's cologne again as he'd passed it by. After last night, he figured Declan, if he were the type to use a man like Slater, wasn't going to leave the horse in the barn. He'd be close by, in case he was needed.

Slater had a better poker face than his boss. He kept the emotion out of it. He came out with his thumbs hooked in his gun belt. Nice and easy so Hollister didn't get jumpy and shoot him, but not out to his sides or up in the air, which is what Hollister had asked for. He took note of this moment and filed it in the back of his mind. Slater now knew he was good. He would still kill him, whenever the senator gave the word. But it wouldn't be as easy as it usually was.

"Now look out the window, Senator," Hollister said.

"What?"

"The window."

Declan looked out the window and saw Chee standing on the sidewalk, leaning slightly against a pillar in front of the hotel. Chee had his eyes on Slater, ignoring the senator altogether.

"Who is that?"

"Master Sergeant Chee. He works for me. He is here to watch Mr. Slater and make sure he doesn't make any sudden moves. If he does, Sergeant Chee will shoot him in the head no less than four times before he hits the ground. Believe me, I've seen him shoot. And if you're thinking about sending your thugs after Chee, maybe to take him out so you can focus on me, you're going to need a lot more men. The sergeant likes to kick people in the face. Hard. He also has a very large dog. I've only just met the dog, but I'm fairly certain it likes to eat people. We left the dog at our offices this morning as it really shouldn't be out during the day where it might scare small children. I say these things not by way of confrontation or hyperbole, merely statements of fact," Hollister said.

"Hyperbole?" Declan snorted.

"What can I say? I went to West Point. Officer and a gentleman and all that. I simply want you to understand me."

There was a silver pot of coffee on the table and Hollister took the handle and filled his own cup, without asking permission. The senator took several deep breaths. Finally getting his color back to normal.

"Are you working for Allan Pinkerton?" Declan demanded, trying to get some measure of control back.

"Why would that matter?"

"Yes or no?"

"Why don't you tell me what happened in the mining camp, Senator? That's what this *meeting* is all about, right?"

"It's nothing really, just some savages raided the camp and killed everyone. My son survived. He's . . . not a strong boy . . . never been well really . . . has a weak constitution, but somehow he managed to get away. But he mis . . . he got things wrong, told some wild tale to cover up his cowardice and now everyone in the territory is spreading rumors and panic."

"I heard though, you were willing to raise an army of volunteers to go after these 'savages.' You were putting pressure on the president to do something."

"Where did you hear that? Pinkerton?"

"I hear things."

"I . . . yes. I suggested to the president the army be sent out to scout and find the Indians responsible for this horrible crime. I would imagine it's Utes. They've been restless lately . . . but I never said anything about any . . . creatures . . . I . . ."

"Wasn't Utes."

"And you know this how, exactly?"

"First, I've fought Utes before. This ain't their style. Second, your boy says he saw what happened?"

"Yes."

"He say anything about a big fella, close to seven feet tall, maybe taller, with white hair, talks with kind of a lisp and an accent, makes him sound sort of like a snake trying to speak?"

Declan thought his heart would stop. Young James had mentioned just such a man, several times in fact. It was real. Dear God. What would happen now? He saw his only son and worse, the Declan name dragged through the mud in what would undoubtedly become a feeding frenzy for the papers once word got out.

He could *not* be associated with this. If Hollister discovered the truth, that there was some type of sinister creatures roaming the mountainsides of Colorado, and the papers got wind of it, Declan would lose everything. The damn Indians were bad enough when they went on the warpath, keeping the settlers away, but this. If word about this got out, not only would new settlers stay away, but people would pack up and flee the state. With no one to deposit money in his bank, buy up his cattle, and lease his farmlands, he faced utter ruin. He had to contain this now. And something else no one knew, not even Slater, was the silver was nearly mined out. He'd lost a lot of the silver money in the financial panic a few years back. He was still wealthy. But not if people started fleeing the territory.

"What are you doing here, Mr. Hollister?" Declan asked.

"Senator, I have been sent to investigate."

"I don't like your damn casual attitude."

"And I don't give a damn what you like. Two days ago I was stuck in Leavenworth Military Prison digging wells, with six more years on my sentence left to go. What happened to your boy also happened to me. But you already knew that. Finding these things and killing them is going to keep me from going back to Leavenworth. And that is what I will do. I will kill them or they will kill me. But I ain't going back to prison. Now. You want to tell me where I can find your son?"

Declan tried hard to stare Hollister down, but it didn't work. He had learned a long time ago, even when he was cheating honest ranchers out of their land, cattle, and money, to leave them with a little something. Men who had nothing to lose couldn't be controlled. Hollister had nothing to lose.

The senator pulled a white calling card from his vest pocket, setting it on the table in front of Hollister.

"My son is resting at our home. This is the address. My butler's name is Silas. He will let you in to see James."

Hollister put the card in his shirt pocket without looking at it. He stood and ignored the senator but gave a small salute to Slater before he stalked out of the dining room.

Both men were quiet for a moment.

"Slater?" the senator said quietly.

"Yes, sir?"

"When this is over, I want him dead."

"Yes, sir," Slater said. Thinking again that killing Hollister would not be easy.

Chapter Seventeen

"What do you think, Chee?" Hollister asked as they made their way through the now bustling city streets back to the train yard.

"About what, sir?"

"Don't call me 'sir.' We covered that," Hollister said.

"Yes, sir."

Colfax was a busy street full of people this time of morning, and they dodged in and out of the crowd, Chee still not saying a word.

"Chee?"

"Yes, sir?"

"What do you think?" Hollister sighed. "And don't say, 'About what?' "

"I think the senator is a very angry man," Chee said.

"No shit. Go on."

"He is also scared. Not for his son or his family. He is scared only for himself, for what he might lose."

They passed by the opera house and Hollister had to

marvel for a moment. Denver was full of theaters and fancy buildings to go along with the gambling dens and whore-houses. Hollister had visited New York City several times as a Cadet at the Point. Denver felt like a miniature New York to him.

"Something wrong, sir?" Chee asked.

"No, Chee, nothing wrong. I was just thinking how civili-zation is spreading everywhere. Here's this big opera house, as fine as any anywhere in the country. And yet we're not on the trail of something civilized, are we, Chee?"

Chee didn't know how to respond to the major. So far, he had found Hollister to be a man who liked to ask questions with no answers. Chee hoped it wasn't a habit. The moment back at Leavenworth, when he had kept McAfee's men from entering that fight with barely more than a look, had told Chee pretty much all he needed to know about his new com-manding officer. He had served under officers good, bad, and average. Hollister had saved him from a life in prison and was giving him an opportunity as an equal he may never have again. But despite all that, he found the major's ques-tions and sudden mood shifts unnerving.

"No, sir, I don't expect we are."

They walked on in silence, the train yard still a few yards away.

"Sir?"

"Yes."

"Are you concerned about Slater?" Chee asked.

"Not really," Hollister said.

Chee said nothing, as if he was chewing on his words, unsure if he should speak.

"Chee, if you got something to say, out with it." Hollister prodded the young man.

"He's dangerous," Chee said.

"So I gathered."

"At some point, he will try to kill you."

"I expect," Hollister said.

"He . . . sir . . . Slater is . . ." Chee struggled to find the right words.

"Like a shark?" Hollister offered.

"No, sir. Not exactly. A shark can't help being a shark. It simply is, like any animal . . . it hunts and kills to survive. Slater hunts and kills because he enjoys it," Chee said.

"I see. Duly noted, Sergeant. You do know he's following us, don't you?" Hollister asked.

"Of course, sir. But there is . . ." Chee hesitated. Not sure how his commanding officer would react to the news.

Hollister noticed the young man's hesitance. "Chee. You and I are about to head into some very dangerous territory. Neither one of us might come out alive. We're going to have a much better chance of surviving if you just feel free to speak your mind. In the army, I learned to trust my sergeants. I already trust you. Implicitly. So out with it."

"Someone *else* is following us," he said.

"One of Slater's men?"

"I don't know for certain, but I don't believe so, sir. He was across the street while you were meeting the senator at the hotel. There was a reflection in the window. He kept staring at the entrance though he pretended to be looking in shop windows. Whoever it was disappeared, then came out of the alley on the same side of the street as the hotel. Now he is behind us, on the south side of the street. Just past the telegraph office."

"How can you be sure it's the same person? There are hundreds of people out and about now."

"It was hard not to notice him," Chee said.

Hollister stared straight ahead, not wanting to turn and look, for fear he might spook their tail.

"Describe him," he said.

"Medium height, slender, dressed in black riding boots and leather duster with a hood. I can't see the face now and . . ." His voice trailed off.

"What is it?"

"I'm not sure . . . I must be mistaken . . ." Chee said.

"Say it," Hollister prodded him.

"The sky is overcast and cloudy, but now and then, the sun comes through the clouds and when it does, he moves to the shadows or the shade. Never stands in the sunlight," he said.

"What? Are you sure?" Hollister asked.

"Yes, sir," Chee said and Jonas thought he detected a mild hint of hurt feelings in Chee's voice, as if the major's doubt had insulted him in some way.

"I'm sorry, Chee. Of course you're sure."

Hollister's mind raced. He remembered that last night, as he'd walked through the streets, he'd felt like someone was following him. And when he'd turned quickly, he'd caught a brief glimpse of a person wearing black cutting down an alleyway. He'd thought it was Slater, believed it could have been one of his thugs trying to surround them.

But now, with Chee finding someone else watching him, he thought it might be something even more sinister. He remembered the hillside in Wyoming, his platoon lying dead, the giant white-haired man advancing on him. He saw the sun come up over the horizon, convinced it had somehow saved his life. And he remembered the man putting on a large black cloak before he climbed into the wagon.

"Sir?" Chee interrupted his thought.

"All right. Let's split up. The next cross street you go left. I'll go right. If this person was watching the hotel, they'll probably follow me. You double back and follow him. Let's try to find out what they're up to."

"Sir, that's not going to work," Chee said, quietly staring straight ahead down the street.

"What? Why not?"

"Whoever it was . . . is gone, sir," Chee answered.

Chapter Eighteen

Shaniah darted down the alley, the black cloak billowing behind her. Her way was hidden by shade and shadow now in the late morning, so she threw back the hood, hoping it would make her less noticeable. Walking quickly, she kept an eye and ear cocked for anyone following her, cursing her laziness and lack of caution.

She had drawn close enough to her quarry to hear that the soldier who had fought Malachi was named Hollister. She did not know if it was his first name or his last, but it was useful. The man Chee was the problem. He had noticed her. He was protecting Hollister and at first she didn't pay attention, but she realized he smelled different from a typical human. The Archaics had lived for many thousands of years, and had outlived species from the earliest times. She knew that there were other races, like her own people, other beings outside the realm of humanity. The wolf people, for example. The Gnazy of the Eastern European lowlands, the ones the humans called gypsies, who could conjure powerful spells, magic that could prevent even an Archaic from killing or destroying them if they were adept enough.

All of these races and beings existed on the fringes of the human world. Humans, though physically weak in comparison to some of these other races, had grown clever and prospered, coming together and forming tribes and societies and civilizations, while the others mostly hunted and fought amongst themselves and with others. Now the humans were far too many. And unlike Malachi, she did not believe they could be destroyed. Terrorized, killed in large volume perhaps, but it was a simple question of numbers. With the weapons they had invented, and their mastery of the elementals, human society was too advanced to conquer. For the Archaics to survive, she had to find Malachi and stop him before he caused the utter destruction of her people.

Discovering the soldier here in Denver last night had raised her hopes. If he was here, knowing the way he had fought for his life and his men those years before, then he was a determined man. And she hoped his determination would lead her to Malachi. But because of this man Chee, he knew of her existence now. He would be watching and it would become more difficult to shadow Hollister.

Finally she reached the corner where she had taken a room at a small hotel on a quiet street far from the center of town. It was near the train station but far enough away that it did not attract a "higher class" of clientele. Her advantage was that near the train station, people were constantly coming and going, leaving and departing every time a train arrived. It made it easier for her to blend in and less likely to be noticed.

Shaniah entered through the side door and hurried up the stairs to her room, closing and latching the door. Chee had unnerved her. It had been hundreds of years since any human had made her feel cautious. Like he might have an advantage over her that she had yet to discover. He had studied her for a long time and she had found when most humans looked at her for too long, they grew restless and ultimately fearful. Instinct kicked in and in some part of their brain, they recognized her as a predator. But Chee had not behaved this way.

She tried to recall his scent, the way he stood in the street outside the hotel, guarding Hollister, silent and unmoving but obviously observing everything around him. Was he Gnazy? Was he a witch? The faintest scent of power had drifted off him.

She went to the window and pulled the curtains back just enough to peek out to the street below. In this part of town, only a few pedestrians passed by, this time of day. Two horses were tied in front of a saloon, three blocks up. When Chee stepped around the corner by the saloon and started walking toward the hotel, she nearly shrieked, dodging back out of sight and letting the curtain fall into place.

Her back against the wall, she peered out again, and saw Chee standing in the street, looking at the buildings on each side, his eyes covering every inch of the sidewalks, windows, doors, even the roofs. He stood there a few seconds more, then disappeared down a side street. She watched for several more minutes but he never reappeared.

She sat on the bed, her mind racing. This man Hollister had found a witch. There was a legend among the Archaics—a story so old most discounted it as a myth. From a time long ago, it was said a small group of humans had known about the Archaics, the wolf people, and the Gnazy. They had learned the secrets of the elementals and passed down this knowledge from generation to generation. Was Chee one of these men? Did he know about the things that could kill or injure one of her kind: silver, wood, and holy water?

Hollister was Shaniah's best hope of finding Malachi before it was too late. Though she avoided taking human lives, this man Chee was a complication. She could not allow complications.

He would have to be dealt with.

Chapter Nineteen

Slater was confused. The senator had left the hotel that morning, after telling him that he wanted this Hollister character killed. Slater knew the senator wanted him to wait, to let Hollister do the work, then step in and silence him. Clean it up like he always did.

Hollister was different though. Hollister was not scared of Slater. He had been in the war, in prison, fought in the Indian wars and he'd seen enough to believe Slater was nothing special. He might not yet know that Slater was a man with no soul. But Hollister would know Slater couldn't be reasoned with, or bought off, or talked out of killing him when the time came. He wouldn't beg or moan or piss his pants like most of the weaklings Slater had ended.

It would come down to who made the first move. Hollister was one of the few men Slater had ever met who would have no qualms about acting first. He would put Slater down if he had the chance.

Killing someone was harder than most people thought. Some men were easier to kill than others. The ranchers—

the piss-poor, dirt-eating farmers he'd shot in the back of the head so Declan could buy up their land in an estate sale, those were easy. They tried to reason, they begged, tried buying him off, or made promises that couldn't be kept, but in the end they got a bullet. Hollister wouldn't go down like that.

And then there was this Sergeant Chee. Not many men unnerved Slater, but Hollister's second did. He stood outside the window and never took his eyes off him, but at the same time, Slater knew Chee was watching everything around him. Leaning against the porch post in front of the hotel, so still Slater wondered if he was even breathing.

He needed to know more, so he left the hotel and followed them, giving Hollister and Chee a good head start. Not because he wanted to know where they were going, he was sure they were either heading back to the train yard or to the senator's house to speak to James, but because he wanted to study them both. They were prey and he was the hunter, and before he moved in for the kill, he needed to learn their habits.

Keeping fifty to sixty yards between himself and them, he followed them as they strolled along the Denver streets like they didn't have a care in the world. After about fifteen minutes the two men split up: Hollister heading right, Chee to the left. But before he disappeared from sight, Chee turned around, his eyes focusing directly on Slater, giving him no time to even make an effort to hide.

He pointed his fingers at Slater like they were a gun and mimed pulling the trigger. Then he touched the forefinger of his right hand to his hat brim, and disappeared around the corner. Slater fumed, angry with himself for being so obvious.

By the time he reached the corner and looked down the street, both Chee and Hollister were gone.

Chapter Twenty

Pinkerton was seated at the foldout desk in the main car when Hollister and Chee returned to the train. There were offices and sleeping rooms available in the warehouse headquarters, but Pinkerton still used the train. His briefcase was open, papers covered the surface, and he furiously scribbled away in a journal.

"Gentlemen," he said, as they walked in. "I trust you enjoyed your meeting with the senator?"

"Enormously entertaining," Hollister said. "Are you always going to be sitting there?"

"Sitting where?" Pinkerton asked, not looking up from his paperwork.

"At the desk, on this train? I just wondered if every time we came back here, we'd find you, is all. Maybe one of Dr. Van Helsing's traps around the windows and doors is holding you here?" Hollister asked.

Pinkerton looked up, studying Hollister to see if he was serious. He couldn't tell.

"What did the senator have to say?" he asked, changing the subject.

"Not much. His son is apparently a weakling, the camp was attacked by Utes, not vampires, and he doesn't like jokesters or people who aren't 'punctual,'" Hollister said. "I'm pretty sure he gave his man Slater the order to have me killed after I left."

"Why would he do that?" Pinkerton asked.

"It's what I would do," Hollister said.

Pinkerton stared off into space a minute, as if considering all the facts.

"I'll have a couple of my operatives dig into this Slater fellow, see what they can turn up. Does the senator believe in what it is we're dealing with here?" he asked.

"I'm not sure," Hollister said. "What do you think, Sergeant?"

Chee hesitated. He was not used to contributing to conversations like this, or being asked for his opinion. Most of his time in the army—his life, actually—he had been overlooked and ignored. He could deal with rowdies like Slater. He was comfortable in that world. But Hollister and Mr. Pinkerton and Dr. Van Helsing and all their educated talk were new territory. Monkey Pete he liked a lot. So far.

"I think at first . . . no . . . he didn't believe it. Assumed it was Indians, like the major says. But he probably sent his man Slater to the camp and Slater knows it wasn't Indians. And now the senator has come to realize he's dealing with something he doesn't know anything about. He's worried of what it might cost him," Chee said.

Pinkerton nodded. "And rest assured, the senator will try to glean any information he can from you. It is incumbent upon you both that it stays with us."

"Going to be hard to keep it under wraps for long if we go traipsing about in this fancy train. It won't be long till somebody from a newspaper knocks on our door to see what we're up to. And if we use any of our fancy gear in public . . ." Hollister let the words hang there.

"Be that as it may, people may wonder about the train,

your weapons, all they wish. But any word leaking out about these creatures can only cause needless panic," he said. Pinkerton reached in his briefcase and pulled out two badges, handing one to Hollister and one to Chee. "I asked the president for one more thing that might help both of you . . . *adjudicate* this matter. He had the attorney general sign the commissions this morning. Congratulations. You're both U.S. Marshals."

Hollister and Chee looked at the badges in their hands and then at each other.

"You have the authority to make arrests, cross state lines in pursuit of criminals, and pretty much anything you might need in the way of legal recourse. You can even go back and arrest the senator as a material witness if you want," Pinkerton said.

"I can?" Hollister asked.

"Don't," Pinkerton said. "I'd keep those in your back pockets, and only use them if necessary." He stood up, gathering his papers. "I'm leaving for Washington within the hour. . . ."

"You aren't taking our train, are you?" Hollister interrupted.

Pinkerton stared at him with knitted brows.

"It's just . . . I've . . . well, I'm very attached to the train," Hollister said.

"Really. After just a few nights?" Pinkerton asked, finally getting the joke.

"I fall easily," Hollister said.

"So it appears. No, Major. As I promised you in Leavenworth, the train is at your disposal. I'll be taking other transportation back to Washington. I *will* expect to be updated regularly. Wires sent by the onboard telegraph will get to me. Monkey Pete is also an accomplished telegrapher."

"Is there anything Monkey Pete can't do?" Hollister asked.

"No," Pinkerton said, snapping his briefcase shut. He shook hands with Hollister and Chee.

"Be careful, gentlemen," Pinkerton said before departing the car. "I'll be back from Washington in a few weeks. Hopefully, you'll have this wrapped up long before then. Try to do it quickly; more people getting killed is not going to be helpful in the long run."

"And don't worry, Mr. Pinkerton, we'll be careful too. Your concern is appreciated," Hollister said.

Pinkerton was again caught off guard by Hollister's specious manner. He made a little growling sound in his throat and left.

"You didn't tell him about whoever was following us," Chee said to Hollister after Pinkerton was gone.

"Knew I was forgetting something," Hollister said. "I had a feeling he might be leaving soon. I wanted to make sure he's gone so we can start on the real work."

"The real work, sir?"

"Yes. We wouldn't be here without Pinkerton, and he's in charge. But I told him in Leavenworth I make the decisions on how we hunt these things. Now that he's out of here we can get started."

"Get started where, sir?"

"James Declan, Junior," Hollister said.

Chapter Twenty-one

Senator Declan's mansion sat on a rise overlooking the city. It was an impressive structure, four stories high, and having just met the man, Hollister had no doubt it was the finest in Denver. The senator did not appear to be the kind of man who would live in the second-best house.

"We should be on horseback," Hollister said.

"Sir?" Chee answered.

"Walking up like this, it's a little . . . diminishing. We should ride up on horses. Big horses. After all we're U.S. Marshals now," Hollister said, fingering the badge in his back pocket.

"Yes, sir," Chee said.

"Chee, we're on a mission here. We aren't in uniform. You're going to have to stop calling me 'sir.' You can call me Jonas. You can call me Hollister. I'll even let you make up a good nickname if you've a mind to. But I think if you keep calling me 'Major' or 'sir,' it's going to be a problem at some point."

"Yes, sir, I understand, sir," Chee said.

"Chee. You just did it again."

"Yes, sir."

"I give up. 'Sir' away, Sergeant."

They had reached the tall wrought-iron gate in front of the mansion. Terraced steps led up in flights of four to a good-sized veranda. The lawn was meticulous, the brick stairs perfectly aligned. The columns were painted bright white and the door, perhaps the largest Hollister had ever seen, was polished oak. Standing in front of it, he rapped the brilliantly polished brass knocker several times. They waited what felt like several minutes, the heat of the day slowly rising, and Hollister was about to knock again when the door creaked open.

An elderly black man answered. He was slightly stooped and his hair was peppered with gray, but his eyes were bright and wide-set in his face. He wore a white waistcoat with trim black trousers and white gloves.

"You must be Silas," Hollister said.

"Yes suh, can I help you?" There was just the slightest hint of a Southern accent in his voice. Hollister knew it well from his time at the Point. His first year, there had still been a few classmates and instructors from the Southern states. But when the war broke out, they all left to fight for the Confederacy.

Hollister handed Silas the senator's card.

"We're here to see young Mr. Declan," he said.

"Yes, suh. I was told to expect you," Silas said. "Please follow me."

They entered the house into a foyer bigger than most counties. It was as if the house grew in size once you were inside. The ceilings had to be at least thirty feet high.

There was a grand staircase on the right, and on the left was a parlor full of fine furnishings, with large couches and upholstered chairs, which Hollister thought looked incredibly uncomfortable. Silas was nearly halfway up the stairs by the time he'd taken it all in.

The stairs were carpeted and led to another high-ceilinged long hallway with a large stained-glass window at the end that gave some light. Silas walked slowly and finally reached the last room on the right. Hollister and Chee stopped gawking and hustled to catch up with the butler, who had already entered.

They found a large, gloomy room that smelled of stale air and unwashed things. Against the far wall was a large four-poster bed, draped in a flimsy canopy. There was a small lump of twisted bedclothes in the middle of it and Hollister thought the pile of sheets and blankets might include a man but he couldn't be sure. A tray of uneaten eggs and coffee sat on a small table nearby.

"Master Declan, suh. I'm very sorry to disturb you, but you have visitors," Silas said.

There was no movement. Hollister glanced at Chee, who stood with his feet spread, his thumbs hooked over his gun belt. He looked uncomfortable and Hollister wanted to ask him why.

"Young James . . . come on now . . . you need to get up and speak to these gentlemen," Silas prodded.

A low murmur came from beneath the bedclothes but Hollister could not make it out.

Silas bent over next to the head of the bed and whispered to the pillows. Finally, a head emerged, covered in shoulder-length black hair that had not been washed in some time. A bearded face turned and one eye opened, squinting to focus on the two men. The familiar fetid aroma of drunken sweat reached Hollister. Declan was trying to deal with what he had seen by living inside a bottle.

"You must be James Junior," Hollister said.

"Don't call me that," the young man groused. "Silas, what are they doing here?" Declan asked with an aching groan in his voice.

Silas had moved to a spot at the foot of the bed, his white-gloved hands crossed in front of him. His stance said he was not listening to the details, but stood ready to intercede on young Declan's behalf, if need be. Hollister thought back to his meeting with the senator and wondered what such a man could have done to inspire this kind of loyalty. But then he had known officers like Custer, who did not deserve the dignity or the honor of the men who served them.

"Master Declan, your father sent them. They just want to talk is all, suh," he said quietly.

"No," James said, burrowing back under the covers.

"I saw them too," Hollister said.

Declan's head reappeared.

"What you saw in the mining camp . . . I saw them before . . . they were in Wyoming then. But I saw them. They killed my men," Hollister said quietly.

Declan stared at Hollister a long time, his eyes wild. Finally, he twisted his way out of the sheets and sat on the side of the bed. He was dressed only in long johns. He was skinny and looked like he hadn't eaten in months, and his chest and arms were streaked with sweat and grime.

"They were fast and strong," Hollister said. "One of them was big, with long white hair . . . he . . ."

"Blood devils!" Declan shrieked, interrupting Hollister.

Hollister flinched. He remembered the young girl, starving and nearly dead from thirst, and how she had cried over and over, mumbling "blood devils . . . blood devils . . ."

"Yes, the blood devils," Hollister said. "I saw them too."

"They killed . . . everyone. Chauncey. Faulkner. Reynolds. Marin. Ole Mack. Red eye. Doyle. Nickerson. Frederick. D'Agostino. Miller. Spencer. Quarles."

Hollister was confused for a moment. After a second he realized what Declan had said and he remembered his own men. "Sergeant Lemaire. Corporal Rogg. Private Whittaker. Private Trammel. Harker, Scully, Runyan, McCord, Franklin, Dexter, Jefferson, and Pope. Those were the men in my unit that those things killed. I can't get them out of my mind."

His words had no effect on the young man, who rolled back into the bed and buried himself in the bedclothes. "Mine," he said quietly. "Mine."

"What's that?" Chee asked.

"Nothing, I don't think. He's just lost. He lost his men. He was in charge. He lost what was his. I know the feeling," Hollister answered.

Young Declan was quiet again. Knowing there was nothing more for them there, Chee and Hollister left.

Chapter Twenty-two

Chee lay on his bunk, his eyes closed but not sleeping. He stood again on the street in front of the hotel as he had that morning. The hooded figure was reflected in the dining-room window. With his breathing slow and deep, he closed out further distractions from his memory, focusing until all else had dropped away and nothing but the mysterious stranger remained.

Slowly he studied the person who had tried and nearly succeeded in staying hidden. His grandfather's stern but melodious voice spoke to him from the mists of his memory. "Concentrate, *sun jai*," he said. "There is only you and the other."

Chee circled the figure in his mind, searching for anything to identify who might have followed them.

There was little to see, as if this person wished to travel as anonymously as possible. The duster was long, below the knees, hooded, and covered in a fine layer of dirt. It had no identifying markings that Chee could see.

"Invisibility is not possible, *sun jai*," he heard his grandfather say. "We cannot see the wind, but we feel it on our faces. You must look deeper."

Chee felt the image floating away, and forced more air into his lungs. He circled the black-clad figure again, starting at the head with the face covered completely by the cloak. His eyes traveled downward slowly, looking for anything, a small rip or tear in the fabric, a stain. But he saw nothing until he reached the boots.

In and of themselves, the boots were nothing. Black leather riding boots scuffed by the hundreds of times they had been placed into and pulled out of the stirrups. But they were small. Very small.

Chee knew then, it was a woman following them. The black duster could hide the size of the body. The hat and hood even added height. But the boots could not be disguised. In truth, a small man could be hidden behind the black outfit, but instinctively, Chee knew this was not the case. It was a woman, he was sure of it.

Dog was on the floor next to the bunk when he sat up and alerted, a low growl sounding in his throat. Chee had heard it also. Someone was walking very quietly along the roof of the train.

His holster hung on a peg next to the door of his berth. He slipped the double rig around his waist, buckling it quickly. Quiet again, he listened. There was no sound, but Dog pawed at the door, his ears still straight up. There was an intruder. Someone had gotten past Pinkerton's guards and into the warehouse where the train was waiting. He opened the door, and Dog charged silently down the hallway, past Hollister's berth and the galley, to the rear door of the car. He waited, body coiled, until Chee reached the door. Drawing his pistol, he lifted the latch, hoping the door opened with little noise.

"Dog . . . hunt," he said.

Dog slipped out the door into the darkness.

Chapter Twenty-three

The man-witch knew she was here. He was awake and moving in the car below. Shaniah stood on the roof of the train and heard the door open and the sound of something moving in the night. She smelled a dog immediately and silently cursed. This man who watched over Hollister had a beast at his disposal. With its superior sense of hearing and smell, it would make her task of killing the man-witch much more difficult.

She stepped over to the very edge of the car, looking down. It was nearly pitch-black inside the warehouse, but Archaics see well in the night.

The dog came around the side of the car, its nose to the ground, body tense and rigid. It paused directly below her and stood on its hind legs, front paws against the side of the train, locking eyes with her. But the great animal did not bark and Shaniah wondered why. It was huge: standing as it did, she guessed it was at least six feet tall.

The door opened wider and the man-witch stepped out onto the small metal porch at the back of the train. Time to leave. With the dog watching, Shaniah bent at the knees and leapt high into the air, grabbing a beam in the roof above and climbing up and out of sight. She had come in through a loose soffit vent in the side of the building, but now she waited high above the train, wondering what the man-witch would do. The dog dropped to all fours and sat on its haunches. She watched Chee come forward, his gun in his hand extended but pointing up, not wanting to shoot someone by accident.

"What is it, boy?" he asked, reaching the animal's side.

The dog whined and barked low in its throat, circling and pawing at the dirt, climbing onto its hind legs again. It looked up into the darkness and though she knew she was invisible to human eyesight in the dark and at this distance, could not help but shrink farther back into the shadows.

The man looked up but could not see beyond a few feet. Shaniah silently cursed the man, for she felt certain he sensed her presence. He had the gift of inhuman stillness. Most humans were impetuous. Not this man. He was careful, thoughtful, and intuitive. But Shaniah had been alive for more than one thousand years and she had learned patience. She would outwait him.

He stood stock-still, as did the dog, which stared up into the darkness like a rattlesnake studying a mouse, waiting for the rodent to twitch so it could strike. Only, in this case, Shaniah was not so certain which of them was the mouse.

More than ten minutes passed, with the man staring silently into the night. Shaniah was about to give up and leave when his voice finally broke the silence.

"I'm watching," he said quietly to the silence above him. "I'm watching over him. And I know you are there."

He returned his gun to the holster and turned toward the door. "Come, Dog," he said. The beast followed dutifully behind its master.

Shaniah waited in amazement until she heard the door click shut, not quite knowing what to think. This man Hol-

lister and his witch Chee were her best chance at finding
Malachi, but the man was a problem. If he got in the way . . .

She could not risk being discovered before Malachi was
found. But Chee knew of her existence and the why and how
of it no longer mattered. Shaniah crept along the beam until
she reached the vent. She knew what she needed to do.

"How do you know it's a woman?" Hollister said. They were
sitting at the table in the galley. It was morning but the sun
coming through the high windows of the warehouse only
dimly lit the interior of the train. Chee would be glad to be
out of the warehouse, on the move, in the open air. Monkey
Pete had made pancakes and bacon. Dog sat on his haunches
next to the table staring at Jonas.

"Does he want something?" he asked, the dog's unrelent-
ing gaze beginning to unnerve him somewhat.

"Probably bacon," Chee said.

Hollister held up a strip of bacon and Dog snapped it out
of his fingers almost faster than he could see.

"Jesus!" Hollister said, wiggling his fingers.

"He likes bacon," Chee said.

"I guess," Hollister said. "So, what makes you think it's
a woman?"

"Small feet. Too small for a man," Chee said.

"I've seen men with some awful tiny feet. General Sheridan had tiny feet. Monkey Pete's feet ain't huge either."

"General Sheridan was a small man, was he not?"

"Exactly my point," Hollister said.

Chee was quiet, the look on his face made it seem to Hollister like he was struggling with something. He'd seen this
look a thousand times on his men before. Usually when
they'd disobeyed an order, or gotten into trouble off the post.

"What is it, Sergeant?" Hollister asked. Try as he might to
make Chee feel comfortable and less formal, the young man
continued to address him as "sir" and "Major," and Hollister

addressed him by his rank to try to get him to relax and speak his mind.

"I believe she was here last night," Chee said.

"What?" Hollister nearly stood up. "Details, Sergeant, starting with why you didn't wake me."

"By the time I determined she was here, she was gone. There seemed no point in waking you."

"And how do you know this is a woman again? You said the person wore a cloak with a hood. Did she take down the hood or something?"

Chee thought for a moment. He did not think Hollister would understand how the identity of the cloaked woman had come to him during his meditation. In the white world such a thing was not evidence. It would be difficult to explain.

"I thought about it, Major. I tried to remember and concentrate on the way she acted in the street. The way she studied the windows, moved through the crowd and last night I tried to pull up details in my recollection and it came to me that her feet were small." He looked away, realizing it was not a reasonable explanation. Luckily, Hollister chose to ignore it.

"And you saw her here last night?" Hollister asked.

"I . . . no . . . Major . . . I didn't see her, but she was here, I'm certain of it."

"How the hell do you know that if you didn't see her?"

"Dog saw her," Chee said.

Hollister studied Dog, who stared back at Hollister impassively.

"Say again?"

"I heard a noise. Someone on the roof of the train. When we went outside, Dog alerted, looking up into the rafters. There was something up there or he wouldn't have acted as he did. She was there, I'm sure of it."

Hollister turned his stare on Chee. The young man sat

there, never flinching under his hardest gaze. He didn't know Chee at all really, not yet anyway. In the army and on the battlefield he'd learned to make snap judgments about men. He trusted his instincts. It's what he'd done in the yard a few days ago when Chee had faced down McAfee. There was something in the kid that Hollister recognized. Will. Strength. Courage. All those things, but something else beyond that, and in truth he wasn't even sure himself exactly what it was. But he'd seldom been wrong about men like Chee before.

"Sergeant, one of these days you're going to explain all this to me," Hollister said.

"Sir?"

"This," Hollister said waving his hands around in the air for emphasis. "All of it. This dog. The crack shooting. The jumping in the air and kicking people in the face."

"Yes, sir," Chee said.

"Until then, if someone of interest shows up, you are under orders to notify me immediately regardless of the time of day, my personal bedtime or any other physical state, understood?"

"Yes, Major," he murmured quietly.

"Eat up. We've got a long day ahead of us," Hollister said.

Chee attacked his breakfast and gave the leftovers to Dog.

"Get your gear, we're headed to the mining camp today. Monkey Pete has us provisioned but I want you to pick out a couple of those special rifles Winchester brought us. I'll be taking the Ass-Kicker."

A short time later, they left the warehouse and the train behind. The day was sunny and Hollister carried the gun down along his leg and hidden in the folds of his black duster. He was dressed all in black: hat, boots, shirt, riding pants, and gloves. Chee carried two of the rifles over his shoulder, apparently unafraid of being noticed. With his two-gun rig riding low on his hips, he looked especially lethal as he walked, with Dog loping along beside him. They were on their way to the livery stable to pick up horses. Monkey Pete had spent the previous day combing Denver for suitable mounts.

"Chee, don't you think you might be scaring folks, with all the ordnance in plain sight?" Hollister said as they walked along the street.

"I hadn't really thought about it, sir . . . I think . . ." His words trailed off.

"What is it? Speak your mind," Hollister said.

"I believe there is going to be trouble ahead, sir, and worse, I think the danger is coming from many places. I would like to be prepared for the trouble and make others aware I am prepared for it as well. My grandfather always said to let your enemy know their aggression will be met in kind. It often stops trouble before it starts," he said.

"Your grandfather really say that, Chee?" Hollister asked.

"Yes, sir," Chee answered.

"Well, I'm glad you're on my side, Sergeant." Hollister laughed.

A few blocks away from the warehouse and they picked up their first tail. Hollister recognized him as one of the men who had been with Slater in the alley the previous night.

"Major?" Chee said.

"I see him. One of Declan's men. Probably under orders to watch us and report back to Slater."

They kept walking, a brisk pace as if they had somewhere to be, avoiding people and not making eye contact with anyone. Before long they reached the livery.

"Any sign of the woman?" Hollister asked.

"No, sir," Chee said.

"She worries me more than Slater and his men for some reason," Hollister said.

"Yes, sir. I believe she is far more dangerous," Chee said.

"Great. Just what we need. A whole passel of blood devils, a bunch of Declan's gun thugs, and now a dangerous woman," Hollister muttered.

"Is there any other kind of woman, sir?" Chee asked.

Hollister laughed. "Well put, Chee!"

Monkey Pete had made arrangements with the livery to have the horses saddled and ready for them. They'd been purchased outright and Hollister made a note to compliment the man on his knowledge of horses the next time he saw him. His mount was a beautiful sorrel mare, strong in the hindquarters and thick through the chest. Hollister thought the horse would do well in the mountains.

He took off his duster and wrapped up the Ass-Kicker, tying it to the back of his saddle. His attention was diverted by Chee, who was muttering quietly to his horse, a fine-looking black mustang with a white star on the forehead and two white socks on its rear legs. Hollister watched in fascination as Chee stroked the horse's forehead and talked softly to it.

"Chee, sorry to interrupt, but what are you doing?" Hollister asked.

"We're talking, sir. I had to ask him his name," Chee said.

"His name? Your horse has a name?"

"Yes, sir, but I needed to ask him if he was willing to reveal it to me," Chee said.

"I see. And did your horse tell you his name?"

"Yes, sir. His name is Smoke."

Hollister was genuinely perplexed. "Chee, I'm sorry, but you give your horse a name, but call your dog just plain old 'Dog'? I'm afraid I don't understand."

"I did not give him the name, sir. It was his all along. Dog is a dog and not a horse. Horses are much more open with people about their true names than dogs, sir," he replied, as if that explained everything.

"Uh-huh. Well, that is right interesting, Sergeant Major. What about my horse? Does she have a name?"

"Yes, sir."

"And what is it?"

Chee suddenly looked uncomfortable. "I . . . they don't . . ."

"What is it?" Hollister asked.

"Horses aren't as particular about their names, sir. But I would still have to ask her permission first."

"By all means, Chee, please do."

Hollister watched in amazement as Chee repeated his exercise with Hollister's mare. A few soft pats on the withers and some quiet murmurs and Chee looked at Hollister.

"Her name is Rose, sir," he said.

"Rose and Smoke. Well, I'll be," Hollister said. The young man who stood before him might be the strangest person he had ever met. But still, Chee's presence made him feel more at ease. He'd seen what these creatures could do, what they were, and it had been proven to him firsthand the world was full of strange things. Whatever you wanted to call it, Chee had a connection to this strangeness, and having him watching his back gave Hollister a measure of relief.

Without further talk, they mounted the horses and in minutes had left the streets of Denver behind and were heading west for the foothills of the Rockies.

Before they had left the train, Hollister had memorized the trails they'd need to follow to reach Torson City. He'd always been good with maps, and two hours out of town, they stopped on a small bluff to study the trail behind them.

"Somebody there?" Hollister asked Chee, who studied the land to their rear. He pulled a small set of binoculars from his saddlebag, scanning the area they'd just ridden through. He saw nothing. The man who had been tailing them had disappeared once they reached the livery stable and Jonas had no doubt he had scurried off to his bosses to report on their movements.

"Yes. Six, maybe eight men, they're staying back, they know where we're going. And someone else . . ." Chee stopped.

"The woman?" Hollister asked.

"Maybe. I'm not sure. I know we're being watched," Chee said, his gaze slowly moving over the surrounding terrain.

"Could be Indians. There's Utes and Arapahoe around here. Neither one of them is too happy with the miners, or whites in general," Hollister said.

"Yes, sir," Chee murmured.

"Dog. Ahead. Hunt!" Chee said. Dog had been lying on the ground resting while they were stopped. At his master's command he leapt up, loping west ahead of them.

"If someone is watching us or waiting, Dog will find them," Chee said.

Hollister nodded. "Excellent. It'll be noon in another three hours. We should be in Torson City by then. I want to get there with plenty of daylight. Let's try to avoid anyone who might get in our way."

He turned his horse and Chee followed, wondering how it was that the major was able to keep his fear in check.

Chapter Twenty-four

"Ain't much of a city," Hollister said. They sat on the hillside above Torson City, studying the small deserted camp below them. There were approximately ten buildings and a few tents, most of them having partially fallen down in the weeks since the attack, the canvas flapping and making a snapping noise in the breeze. Chee sat astride Smoke, not paying attention to the ground below them, instead studying the surrounding woods and mountains.

"They around?" Hollister asked.

"Yes, sir, no more than two miles back," Chee said. "The same group."

"Where's Dog?"

"I don't know, sir," Chee said quietly. "Still hunting I expect."

"I hope whoever is following us didn't catch him or shoot him or something. I'm starting to grow fond of the critter," Hollister said.

Chee shook his head as if such a thing was impossible. Dog would not be caught by Slater and his men or by any

Utes or Arapahoes. Had it been Comanches or Kiowas, Chee might have had a moment of concern. Comanches and Kiowas were crafty and not likely to let a mutt sneak around and spy on them. But he wasn't worried about the others.

"Hmm. Well. Whoever is following us knows where we're headed. No reason for us not to check it out," Hollister spurred his horse and loped down the small rise, entering what would have been the main street if it had been a real town. They rode slowly, Hollister felt jumpy, like something might spring from one of these buildings and grab him. They tied off the horses in front of the general store and walked inside.

There were small patches of dried blood that had soaked the wood floor. The stains had turned a dark brown but Hollister had seen enough of it in his day to recognize it. He didn't know why, but he kept his hands on his pistol. The town was empty, he was sure of it, but instinct told him to be ready for trouble. They moved from the store to the saloon and each of the buildings in turn. There were kicked-over tables and chairs, and supplies and canned goods knocked about, indicating a struggle. But only a few bloodstains—not enough blood for the number of men who had been killed.

"Chee, when these things attacked us in Wyoming . . ." Hollister started to say.

"Yes, sir, you said they drank the blood of your men. It would appear that is what happened here. For a dozen men to be killed, in this small area, there would be more blood. It should be everywhere. Yet it is not," he said.

Chee stepped off the board porch in front of the saloon, studying the ground in front of the general store.

"What is it?" Hollister asked.

"Something. Tracks. A few days, a week old at most. They are mixed in with the hoofprints and footprints of the miners. It must not have rained here in a while. But someone was here, after the first attack by the creatures. Those tracks are too fresh. It was three, maybe four men," he said. He didn't mention the small footprints in the ground. Those, he was sure, belonged to the woman who had been following them. He lowered himself to the ground, peering at the marks, determining that the smaller footprints got heavier and trailed around the side of the building. Whoever had walked this path was carrying something heavy.

He followed the tracks to where they led to a small shed behind the store. Someone had made several trips back and forth from the front of the store to the shed. Maybe for firewood? Could this be where the miners kept their gold dust? He doubted that. It wasn't the most secure place. For a reason he could not yet fathom, someone had returned to the scene and used the shed for something. He knew Declan had sent Slater to check out his son's story, but he did not see Slater's tracks anywhere. In town he had taken notice of the boots Slater wore and he saw no matching tracks. Slater would have been careful not to leave sign behind. He likely rode his horse along the shallow stream until he reached the camp, and then stayed on the wooden walkways, where he would leave no evidence of his having been there. It is how Chee would have done it if he had been asked by Hollister to perform a similar task.

The shed had a broken padlock.

"Major, over here," he said.

Hollister felt compelled to draw his Colt. "What are you looking for, Chee?" he asked.

Chee didn't answer, but threw away the padlock and pulled open the door on the small windowless building. He recognized the stench right away and jumped back a bit as the first body fell forward, landing in the dirt at his feet.

"Holy shit!" Hollister said, startled and taking a step back himself.

Two other bodies lay inside the shed. Chee looked at the major, wondering what he should do.

"Let's get them out here, so we can have a look at them," Hollister said, pulling his bandana over his mouth and nose to block out the smell.

Together they laid the corpses side by side on the ground. They had been dead a few days and were starting to decay, but the shed had saved them from the harshest elements. One of the men was badly burned, another had a large stab wound in the middle of his chest, and the third man had a broken neck.

"You don't think these are miners, do you, sir?" Chee asked.

Hollister shook his head. "If we go by what young Mr. Declan told us, he's the only one who survived that night. And these aren't . . . I don't think they're . . . they don't look like . . ."

"I don't think they're Deathwalkers either, sir," Chee said.

Hollister felt an enormous surge of relief. "The question is, what and who are they?" he said. "And furthermore, how did they end up dead here?"

"And why hide them? If they came to loot the place, or surprised other looters, why would someone go to the trouble to hide their bodies?" Chee asked.

"Good question," Hollister said. And he had no answer. At least not one that made sense.

Hollister stood, straightening his back. He looked up at the mine shaft, which was dug into the side of the hill to the west of the camp, about three hundred yards away.

"Let's see if we can find some torches around here," he said. "We might as well check out the mine."

"Really, sir?" Chee asked. He didn't like closed-in spaces. The thought of venturing into the dark mine gave him an uncomfortable feeling.

"Sure," Hollister said. "Why wouldn't we? We need to be thorough. Then he noticed. "What's wrong, Chee?" he said.

"Nothing . . . sir . . ." Chee said. "It's just I . . . would it be all right if I waited outside while you inspected it?"

Hollister tried hard not to chuckle. "Really, Chee? You'll take on a thug like McAfee. Deathwalkers don't seem to give you pause at all. But you don't like the dark?"

"It's not that . . . I . . . no, sir. I don't like being closed in like that."

"Well, we'll try not to go too far in. But I'm afraid you need to come with me. I might need you to shoot something."

"Yes, sir," Chee said, the reluctance dripping from his voice.

They found two torches in the general store and Hollister retrieved the Ass-Kicker from his saddle. Since Winchester had left it, Monkey Pete had tinkered with it a bit, affixing a sling to the barrel and the stock. It hung at precisely the right position so Hollister could work the action and have one hand free. In truth he would have liked to use his Colt for the other hand, but they needed light. He would have to use his free hand to hold a torch, which they lit once they reached the entrance of the mine. Chee removed the ten-gauge shotgun he had strapped to his back and held his torch in the other hand.

"Are you thinking what I'm thinking?" Hollister asked.

"Unlikely, sir," Chee answered, the sweat appearing on his forehead and dripping down the sides of his face. He held the torch out in front of him, brandishing it like a sword. The thumb on his other hand nervously worked over the trigger on the shotgun, ready to cock it and fire at a moment's notice.

About fifty feet inside they saw the first signs that the killing hadn't been confined to the town below. Here there were more dark brown stains scattered on the walls and in the dirt floor and on some of the timbers holding up the roof of the shaft. It was everywhere. Hollister thought this meant the first killings must have taken place here—which meant the creatures might have hidden in the mine to avoid the sun and waited for the miners to venture inside it before striking.

"Dear God," Hollister whispered.

"Yes, sir," Chee murmured.

"Chee, why do you think there is so much blood here and not in the buildings?" Hollister asked, working his torch over the sides and ceiling of the shaft looking for anything that might provide a clue.

"They were hungry," Chee said.

"Hungry?"

"Yes, sir. Deathwalkers need to feed on blood. They were waiting here for the miners to arrive. And they were consumed with blood lust. They killed the men in here and fed enough to get themselves under control. Then they attacked the town. By then they were more in control, able to kill the men in the camp more quickly and efficiently and with less waste. A hungry man, someone who hasn't eaten in days, is going to eat his first meal much more eagerly. Once his hunger is sated, he'll be less crude at his next meal. A little neater. A little less of a savage. I think that's what happened here."

Hollister nodded his head in admiration for the young man's intuition. "I think you're right, Chee. I think that's exactly what happened."

A loud thump came from somewhere up ahead of them. Hollister raised the Ass-Kicker, thumbing back the hammer, hearing a reassuring hiss as steam filled the firing chamber.

"Sergeant, be ready," he said.

Chee needed no other instruction. Although he wished that Hollister would suspend his examination of the mine and return to the outdoors. What more could they possibly discover here?

Hollister took the lead, the Ass-Kicker resting on his hip, his other hand holding the torch. The thumping noise sounded again, closer this time, and to Chee it very much felt like something was coming toward them. More noises filled the chamber, and try as he might, Chee could not determine what they were. He had grown up mostly in Louisiana, in swamp and bayou country, and hadn't spent a lot of time in mines or caves. The whole environment felt foreign to him.

The individual thumps merged, like a drumbeat, then came a rushing sound, and all Chee could think of was a flock of birds; perhaps some starlings or sparrows had gotten shut up in the mine somehow.

The bats hit them full on. There were hundreds of them.

"Look out!" Hollister tried to shout but the flying creatures hitting his face and chest muffled the rest of his words. He dropped the torch and the Ass-Kicker and fell to the ground, the bats flying over and around him, wanting nothing but to reach the entrance of the mine and fly off into the open air.

To Chee it felt like hundreds of them were striking his face, chest, and arms, and he shouted, waving the torch back and forth trying to keep them off. Hollister was on his hands and knees, his hat lying in the dirt and Winchester's special gun hissing on the ground beside him.

As quickly as the bats were upon them they were gone, rushing past and exiting the mine shaft to their rear, their squeals dying out as they flew away.

Hollister stayed on the ground, breathing hard. He looked at Chee. The young man had restored the usual tranquil look to his face.

"Good Christ," Hollister said, retrieving his hat and using it to fan the embers on the torch and get it burning again. He finally stood up, smacking the grit from his duster and pants. He picked up the Ass-Kicker, which on examination looked none the worse for wear.

"I don't know about you Chee, but I could use a little sunshine right about now," Hollister said.

Chee tried hard to keep the happiness out of his voice. "Yes, sir," he said.

They strode quickly back to the entrance, and were relieved to step out into the fresh air, the sun warm on their faces even in the cool mountain breeze. Both men were quiet for a few minutes, the sun creeping slowly across the sky as they made their way cautiously back down to the shed where the three bodies lay. Each tried to piece together a situation that got more curious by the day. As Hollister was about to inform Chee of his overwhelming desire to be away from the mine before the bats returned, their thoughts were interrupted by a bark as Dog loped into the town, coming from the north. He ran up to Chee and pushed his head into the young man's hand briefly before going to the bodies on the ground and working them over with his nose.

"Good boy," Chee said.

"Not so sure about that," Hollister said, pointing to the mountain ridge to the north and above the town that Dog had just returned from.

A ridge that was now lined with nearly forty Ute warriors. All on horseback and looking mightily pissed off.

"Well, shit," Hollister said. "I suddenly got the feeling we should have stayed on the train."

Chapter Twenty-five

To the east on the mountainside just above the mine shaft and well hidden in the trees, Shaniah sat astride Demeter, watching the scene below and cursing her bad luck. Her plan had been to follow Chee and Hollister and see if they had a plan for finding Malachi. In her mind, she hoped the witch-man Chee would be able to conjure some clue from the scene of the rogue Archaics' last massacre. Any indication that would tell him where they had gone. It was her only hope. The trail had gone cold and Malachi's time was drawing ever near. At the age of fifteen hundred years he would become an Eternal. Virtually unable to die unless killed in battle by another Eternal, and she would need to wait more than a hundred years before she herself became Eternal. By then it would be far too late. His plan to wreak havoc on humankind was foolish and would only succeed in destroying her people.

For now, Archaics lived in the shadows. Hidden high in the mountains. There were nothing but whispers and legends, scary stories told to children to keep them afraid of the night things. Malachi was ruining all of that. If they were revealed, if humans learned of their actual existence, they would use their technology, armies, and superior numbers, and her people would cease to exist, all because of Malachi's vanity. She could not allow this.

She should have hidden the looters' bodies more carefully. Killing the three men had been easy, but she had been careless and in a hurry to find Malachi. In her haste, she had almost forgotten the bodies were still there. And Chee had found them in a matter of minutes. It was becoming clearer to her by the minute that she would need to kill Chee before he discovered who she was and stopped her.

The Indians' arrival gave her pause. She wondered what Hollister would do. Would he try to fight his way out? Or talk? Should she help them if it came to a fight?

The next few minutes would prove interesting, at least.

Slater and his men stayed well back in the trees. The mining camp was in a small valley near the river, and from the rise to the south they could see everything unfolding before them quite clearly. He was certain Hollister and the breed knew they were being followed. And in fact, Slater and his men had made no real effort to conceal themselves other than staying far enough back so as not to be visible to the naked eye. Seven men on horseback weren't easy to hide, and besides, he knew Hollister and Chee were experienced enough to know they would be coming.

He had not counted on running into forty mounted and armed Utes, however.

One of his six men, Baker, a heavyset, slow-witted thug, nudged his horse forward until he was next to Slater.

"What we gonna do, Boss? Should we help 'em out?" he asked.

Slater shook his head. "Not my orders. Mr. Declan wanted them followed, he didn't say anything about fightin' Utes." But he was conflicted. At first, Senator Declan had wanted this whole affair swept under the rug. Let everyone think his son was a coward, a drunk who had run away from an Indian massacre. Eventually all the excitement would die down and things would go back to normal, and the Torson City killings would become just another ghost story.

It might have worked, but Slater had visited the camp and seen signs for himself. This wasn't something that was going away. It hadn't. People were talking, gossip was spreading. A few farmers and ranchers had already picked up and left. Whether they believed what had happened at Torson City had been because of monsters or Indians didn't really matter. People leaving the territory was bad for business and bad for the senator.

And since his own fortunes rose and fell with those of Declan, he needed to make sure this was handled. The only way to do that was to let Hollister and Chee find these creatures and kill them. Then Slater would step in.

Down below, the two men stood rooted to their spots, neither they nor the Utes moving. It was an uncomfortable standoff. Slater had momentarily forgotten his interest in the three bodies they had pulled out of the shed. He was waiting to see what happened next and wishing he could hear what they were saying.

Chapter Twenty-six

"Chee, you got any ideas?" Hollister whispered, his eyes glued to the line of mounted warriors.

"No, sir," Chee whispered back.

Hollister cursed himself. He had been so eager to get here, to find a trail to follow, that he'd acted without any common sense. He had the Ass-Kicker and his Colt, and Chee had his two pistols, all of them loaded with the special ammo Winchester had given them. He wasn't sure how accurate the new guns would be at a distance. And Winchester had said the Ass-Kicker only had four shots before it needed to be recharged by the steam engine, which of course was all the way back in Denver. Crap on a biscuit.

The Ute leader, a tall, regal-looking man, nudged his pony forward as he pulled his rifle from the saddle scabbard. It looked to be a breech-loading Sharps. Hollister cursed again. Favored by snipers and buffalo hunters, it would be accurate at a great distance. The Ute made no other threatening move, but kept his pony striding toward them at a slow walk. After a few paces, the rest of his war party drew their weapons and followed suit.

"Chee, I think we . . ." Hollister started to say, but never finished—for out of the woods to their right and up above the mine shaft, plunged a lone figure on horseback. The horse was a large, black stallion, and the rider was cloaked in a hooded duster, covered in black from head to toe. The horse ran impossibly fast, and whoever guided it was obviously experienced in the saddle.

"What in God's name . . ." Hollister muttered.

"It is the woman," Chee said. "She has followed us here." He had no proof of this, but he was sure of it just the same.

"Get ready, Chee," Hollister said.

Chee said nothing, unsure of what he was supposed to get ready for, but he took a few short steps back, easing his way toward the horses and the cover of the buildings.

She reached the outskirts of the camp, reining the horse around the buildings, barrels, empty wagons, and other obstacles. Surprisingly, she headed straight toward the Ute war party. Dog was up now, his hackles raised and a low growl sounding in his throat as he watched the mysterious rider confront the Indians.

"Dog, hold," Chee said. Dog moved so that he was now in front of Hollister and Chee, his rump pushing into Chee's legs. He quieted but never took his eyes off the rider.

The woman spurred the stallion again and it bounded forward another thirty yards, where she reined to a stop. The Utes looked as surprised and confused as Hollister and Chee did. But after a moment, they regained their senses and started forward again.

The woman threw back the hood of her duster and her long blond hair unfurled.

Chee and Hollister kept backing toward the horses and the general store, taking advantage of the diversion. Dog crept along with them, his muscles tensed and coiled.

A Ute war cry pierced the quiet and the sound of it nearly made Hollister jump. To his surprise, the Utes turned their horses and rode hard back to the north instead of charging. In shock, Hollister and Chee watched until they disappeared from sight.

Their eyes went to the solitary figure on the horse. With the Indians gone, the woman dropped her head, slumping at the shoulders. Hollister wondered if she might be praying, but then she raised back up, stretching back and forth as if she had just woken from a nap. She turned the horse and slowly trotted back toward where the two confused and surprised men stood.

Hollister couldn't be sure, but he could almost swear that smoke was rolling off her face and hair.

Chapter Twenty-seven

Shaniah could not guess what instinct had commanded her to intercede on behalf of Hollister and the man-witch. When she saw the Ute warrior advance toward the two men, it became clear to her the situation was rapidly deteriorating. If Hollister was killed here, she might never find Malachi and his band. Without thinking, she spurred Demeter to action and raced down the rise toward the oncoming Utes.

Her desperate charge had momentarily surprised and stunned the mounted warriors. When she pulled back her cowl, unleashing her long, flowing blond hair, they were further confused. Who was this strange white woman riding to her death toward them? they must have thought. When she skidded to a stop, perhaps thirty yards remained between her and the startled Ute leader. She had only a few seconds. The sun was already heating her skin and she could not be without the cover of the cloak for much longer.

With her back to Hollister and the man-witch, she was able to transform, showing her Archaic face to the Utes. Knowing the superstitious nature of the people confronting her, she was sure they would be frightened away. As her eyes blazed and her face moved, her jaw dropping and her fangs descending, the Indians went wild-eyed with fear. The leader's horse reared and whinnied, nearly tossing him from its back. With all the strength he could muster, he steadied the animal and retreated toward his men, their shouts joining his as they rode off the way they had come, not sparing the quirt to their horses.

When they were gone, she sat still on her horse, feeling her facial features return to normal. Archaics could survive for a limited amount of time in the sunlight. And unlike some other vampire species, it would only burn and weaken them, not kill them. But she could not afford to let it weaken her any further. She raised the cloak back over her head, turning Demeter and spurring him at a trot toward Hollister and Chee. She reined the horse to a stop twenty yards away from the two men.

Chapter Twenty-eight

Chee kept his hands on his pistols as the woman advanced toward them. He knew it was her, without question, could sense it without having ever seen her face. She was the one who had followed them, had come to the warehouse in Denver, for reasons he didn't know. And he was fairly certain she was a Deathwalker. The cloak, hiding her face from the sun and light—all of it pointed to her being one of Van Helsing's vampires.

"What the hell just happened?" Hollister whispered to him.

Chee didn't answer, never took his eyes off the woman, who sat on the great stallion as still as a statue. He was tense, instinct telling him to pull his guns and shoot her down, but he remained calm, waiting to see what the major wanted to do.

"Can I help you?" Hollister said to the woman.

"Sir, I don't think we . . ." Chee started to say, but the major held up his hand, silencing him.

Don't do this, Chee thought. *Don't bring her into your circle, Major. She is death.* He was more certain of this than he'd ever been of anything in his life. The woman on horse-back before them was death.

"I say, can I help you?" Hollister repeated. The woman on the horse said nothing. A few paces behind him he heard the squeak of Chee's holster as the young man gripped his pistols so tightly Hollister thought he might shatter them. The sergeant was tensed and anxious, ready to fight.

"Easy, Chee, let's see what she has to say," he said quietly, "and see if you can steady your friend there." Dog was still on alert, ready to pounce on the woman.

"Major, I don't think this is a good idea," Chee said.

Hollister turned away from the woman to study the young soldier.

"Maybe not. But she just chased off forty Ute warriors without a weapon. I have a feeling if she wanted us dead, we'd be dead already." When he gazed again at the woman, she removed her hood, revealing her face.

With his first clear look at her, Hollister felt her beauty strike him like a punch in the gut. She was beyond gorgeous, her blond hair hanging below her shoulders and green eyes peering out at him from a face carved from alabaster. Her clothing hid most of her figure, but even as she sat in the saddle he could tell she was tall for a woman, her knee-high boots and leather riding pants covering long legs.

Jonas suddenly realized how long it had been since he'd really stopped and looked at a woman. Even after four years locked away in Leavenworth, most of his thoughts had gone only to getting out. And in the past few days, events had moved so quickly, there hadn't been much time to think about anything else. At West Point, and after the war, he had courted women as an eligible bachelor, but he'd never met anyone who really made him think about marriage or a life beyond the army. Now he stood twenty yards away from what he thought might clearly be the most beautiful woman he had ever seen in his life, and for a moment it was difficult to speak.

"Who are you?" he finally asked.

The woman stared at him. Her face was a curious mixture of fear and anxiety. It looked to him like she was wrestling with something: a problem so big the weight of it might crush her. It made Hollister want to help her. Take off his hat and hold it in his hands and ask her, like a Knight Errant might ask his queen how he could be of service.

She stared hard at him for several seconds.

"I am called Shaniah," she said. Her voice was low and Hollister and Chee had to strain to hear her.

"What are you doing here?" Hollister asked.

She did not answer but pulled the cloak back over her head and reined the stallion around, giving him the quirt as she rode hard back the way she had come. Vanishing into the trees almost as mysteriously as she had arrived.

Hollister looked at Chee, who still seemed ready to jump on his horse and ride the woman down.

"Huh," he said.

Chapter Twenty-nine

"Monkey Pete, what does this train have in the way of maps of the territories?" Hollister asked the trainman.

After their encounter with the mysterious woman Shaniah, they had finished their inspection of Torson City, buried the three bodies and returned to Denver just after nightfall. Slater and his men had shadowed them all the way back, but had offered no interference.

"We've got all the maps you might need, Major," Monkey Pete said. From a cabinet in the main car, he pulled several metal tubes and set them on the table in front of Hollister. They had finished their meal, and Jonas wanted to get moving. The encounter with the mystery woman had given him pause at first, but now it felt like he was closer to something, to finding what he was looking for.

Chee sat across the table from the major, quiet and lost in thought. He'd been like that since the woman appeared. Hollister was not surprised that Chee had been right. It had been a woman following them. He was beginning to learn that Chee was right most of the time. At least about Death-walkers and mysterious women.

"Cheer up, Chee. You'll get to shoot somebody soon," Hollister said.

Dog lay on the floor of the car, theoretically asleep but his eyes slitted, always close to Chee.

Monkey Pete was fishing through the maps, finally set-tling on one, pulling the rolled paper from inside the metal tube, and unrolling it on the table in front of them.

"This is a Central and Pacific railroad map, Major. Printed just last month. It's probably the most accurate and up to date of any. What is it you're looking for?" he asked.

"I'm not sure. But something Declan's kid kept saying is sticking in my craw," Hollister said. "He kept saying, 'mine,' over and over. At first I thought he was talking about Torson City, then maybe something personal or a possession he'd lost there when those creatures attacked. Or he was referring to the men he lost. But now I wonder if he meant something else. Chee and I found blood down in the mine. Like maybe they ambushed those men."

Hollister opened his copy of Van Helsing's journal and went to a page he had dog-eared. "Dr. Van Helsing has some notes about 'suspicious' attacks out here. There's a half dozen places where a group of people were murdered in the last six years, and it was put off as Indian massacres. He and Pinkerton weren't sure that was the case."

He thumbed through the diary, marking the locations on the map.

Hollister picked up a charcoal pencil and pored over the map, putting marks on Torson City, the spot in Wyoming where he'd lost his platoon, and where the half dozen at-tacks noted in the journal occurred. When he was finished, he was not surprised to find that three of the eight spots were mining camps. There had to be a connection.

"Van Helsing also thinks these things are mountain creatures by nature. They come from Eastern Europe, where I understand it's very hilly, and the altitude doesn't seem to bother them like it does us. If they were hiding out or had a remote home base, I expect it would be in the mountains somewhere."

Curiously enough, the spots on the map made a rough circle from Torson City on the southern end to the spot in Wyoming just west of Deadwood where he'd been attacked. The circle was a few hundred miles in diameter.

"I don't know, Major, that's a lot of territory," Chee said. "And what if some of those *were* Indian attacks? Makes it even harder to pin down."

"I don't disagree, Chee. I'm just trying to suss it out. One of the two places we know for sure they attacked was a mining camp. I'm wondering if there's a reason for that."

"What kind of reason?" Monkey Pete asked.

"I don't know, but I remember something from when . . . from Wyoming, they don't like moving around in the daylight. Van Helsing said enough sun is fatal to 'em. So they like the dark. What's darker than a mine?"

"But there's got be dozens of mines within that circle you've drawn. Maybe hundreds," Monkey Pete said.

"True. But how many *abandoned* mines? That's where I expect they'd be hiding. They wouldn't be holed up in a working mine. Unless they'd killed or did what Van Helsing called 'turned' everyone working there first."

"Turned?" Chee asked.

"I read it too," Monkey Pete chimed in. "The creatures drink the victims' blood first and then make the victims drink the creatures' blood. Turns 'em into a vampire. I want you boys to promise me something . . . if them things ever gets a'holt of me and starts turnin' Monkey Pete, you promise me you'll shoot me dead."

Hollister looked at the engineer, his face a curious mixture of surprise and some form of admiration for the man's mind. "Sure Monkey Pete. You just promise me you'll do the same to me."

"Oh sure, Major, I'll be happy to shoot you," he said.

"But just to be clear, only if I'm being turned into a vampire. Not for any other reason," Hollister said.

"We'll see," Monkey Pete said and turned his attention to the map again.

Chee shook his head. "It seems kind of thin, sir."

"I don't disagree. But we got nothing else. And these other attacks in mining camps makes it a connection, no matter how thin it might be," Hollister said. "And I've been thinking, maybe when they attacked Declan's group, they were hiding in the mine. The sun went down and out they came. If you can't be in the sunlight, a mine is the perfect spot to spend the daylight hours. There are mines all over the west. Maybe this is how they're moving and gathering a group large enough to make whatever move it is he has planned."

Chee nodded. He had to agree, reluctant as he was. It made sense.

"Let me see that map," Monkey Pete said.

He took it off the table and sat down with it at the desk. Making marks with the pencil, he muttered to himself as he worked. "I've driven trains for Mr. Pinkerton all over this territory. I may not know them all, but I can tell you a lot of the mines that have played out . . ." His words trailed off.

Jonas filled his coffee cup and looked across the table at Chee. The young man sat there looking all jangled up, like the weight of the world was on him.

"Something on your mind, Chee?" he asked.

"No, sir," Chee answered.

"Chee, I told you about calling me 'sir.' Now we had a good first effort in the field today. You did good work out there. When I was in the army I wasn't the type of officer who didn't value input from his men. If you got something to say, I think you need to tell me. I don't want to have to give an order."

"The woman, sir," Chee said.

"What about her?"

"She's the key to this. I think we should try to capture her. If we want to find these things, she's the one who can lead us to them."

Hollister paused while he measured the young man's words.

"Let's say you're right. Suppose this 'Shaniah' is part of this. How do you suggest we go about catching her?"

Chee shrugged.

"And if we do catch her, what if she turns out to be one of the creatures like you figure? I mean, she scattered them Utes in seconds, and God only knows how. She had her back to us, but I'm wondering if she didn't show 'em her real face."

"Her real face, sir?" Chee was curious.

"Yeah. Back in Wyoming, when they attacked my platoon, they came at us, and their faces . . . they change somehow. The eyes turn bright red and their jaws get long and they get these big-ass fangs coming out of their mouths. It's enough to make you shit if you weren't so worried about dying. Out there today, she kept her back to us the entire time she was facing down the Indians. I reckon this Shaniah showed the Utes her real face, and that's what spooked 'em. They probably thought she was some kind of witch."

Chee nodded. There was logic to the major's words. And it did explain what happened when the woman appeared.

"So while I admire your initiative, I'm not so sure I think we're ready to capture and control one of these things yet. Not until we learn a little bit more about them."

Right then, Chee understood even more why Hollister had made such a good commander. He had taken Chee's input, even encouraged it, and given it thorough consideration. And while he hadn't outright rejected it, he had shown Chee the holes in his argument but had done so in a way so as not to discourage him. He had made a command decision. But he had included Chee in the process. Hollister was the kind of officer men fought for.

"Here we go," Monkey Pete said from the desk. He rose and shuffled back to the table where the two men sat, spreading the map out.

"Inside your circle, Major, there're six abandoned mining towns I know of." All of them were on the Front Range of the Rockies, and spread from a point about one hundred and thirty miles north of Torson City all the way up into Wyoming. He pointed to each one.

"How many of them can we reach by train?" Hollister asked.

"These four should still have spurs," the engineer said, pointing out the locations on the map. "The trains don't run there no more, so I don't know what shape the tracks will be in, but we can get close, I expect. But this one, the mine is closed but the town is still there. Train runs in once a week."

Hollister looked at the first spot, a town called Absolution. It was a silver mine, nearly played out but, according to the map, still working. "This might be the place!" Hollister said. "If they want to turn people, wouldn't this be the perfect place to start?"

A small number of people, controllable, and a mine for the daylight hours.

"It's as good a place as any to start," Chee said, nodding his head in agreement.

"Monkey Pete, how long to get there from Denver?" Hollister said.

Monkey Pete put his hand on his chin, calculating the amount of time it would take to be under way. "The horses are loaded up on the stock car. We're ready to go. It's a couple hundred miles to Absolution, and it's about a seven percent grade. Even with our extra speed, it'll take us most of the next day to get there. If we get started right away."

"Well my good man, let's see what this train has got. Get

us going to Absolution and don't spare the whip!" Hollister said.

He scurried off, happy to have his train running again.

Chee reached inside his shirt and fingered his medicine bag. He had a feeling he was going to need it. Something had bothered him ever since he and Hollister had ventured into the Torson City mine earlier. It was the bats. Chee knew that bats were night creatures. They wouldn't normally leave their nests and fly out in the daylight unless they had to. The bats had swarmed out from deep in the mine. Something had scared them recently and when Hollister and Chee had ventured there, they were upset again, frightened enough to ignore instinct and fly out into the daylight sky.

Chee squeezed his medicine bag and wondered what that could be.

Chapter Thirty

Slater watched the train leave the warehouse. It confirmed his suspicions that his adversaries had learned something from the mysterious woman who had ridden to their rescue that day. She must have given them a clue or a direction to go in and now they were on the trail. Depending on where they went, it would be much harder to contain the situation now. Harder, but not impossible.

As the train departed, Slater confirmed the warehouse was still guarded by Pinkertons: two men at each entrance and two others regularly patrolling the perimeter. Whatever was in there, Pinkerton didn't want anyone finding out about it. The train shifted onto a siding and slowly rolled westward. Slater had anticipated they'd be going soon and had stationed his men along the most likely routes, with instructions to report back and to follow the train as far and as long as they were able.

He pulled the collar up on his duster. Even though it was early summer it was unseasonably chilly and rain was coming. Leaving the train yard, he rode through the streets, and was at the senator's mansion in a few minutes. He found Declan inside, sitting in front of the fireplace in his study. The bottle of brandy on the table next to his chair was almost empty. The man was good and drunk. He'd been like this for the last two weeks. Ever since he'd realized his son had been telling the truth. It had unsettled him and he hadn't gotten a handle on how he could fix it. Slater found it mildly disgusting.

"They're gone," Slater said.

"Where?" Declan asked.

"I don't know yet. I've got my men tracking the train. We'll hear soon enough."

"What are we going to do, Slater?" Declan asked, sucking down another big swallow of brandy.

"Whatever we need to," Slater said.

"I don't think that's going to work this time," Declan muttered.

"Meaning?"

"Meaning even if Hollister finds these . . . things and succeeds in killing them, us killing him isn't going to be overlooked. I got a telegraph from Washington today. Nobody knows anything about him."

"So? Isn't that a good thing? No one will miss him when he's gone."

"You don't get it," Declan grunted, rising and leaning against the mantel. "The only things I could get my hands on were his original army records and the fact that his release from Leavenworth was signed by President Hayes himself. That fancy train, the Pinkertons, a mysterious warehouse big enough to hold that gussied-up train—all of it takes massive amounts of money. You don't hide something like that, especially in Washington. If anyone knows anything, they're not saying a word. Which means they either don't know or . . ." He let his words trail off.

"Or?" Slater prodded.

"Or it goes all the way to the top, to the president himself. And that means people are watching Hollister's back. Which means our 'usual methods' won't work."

Slater shrugged. "I wouldn't worry, Senator."

"You sound awful damn confident," Declan said.

"I seen what happened in Torson City with my own eyes. That many men, gone without a trace. If Hollister gets mixed up with . . . in it . . . he ain't likely to survive it. And even if he does, it would be easy to make it look like he didn't," Slater said.

The senator was quiet a moment, turning Slater's words over in his mind. He smiled. "By God, you are an evil sumbitch. I hadn't even considered that," Declan said.

Slater smiled, taking the glass from the senator's hand and draining the rest of the brandy. "It's what you pay me for, ain't it?"

Chapter Thirty-one

The night sky was overcast, but there was enough moonlight behind it to give light to the Front Range, where Shaniah rode Demeter, trailing along with Hollister's train. It was heading north, not into the mountains, and thus her horse had little trouble following it. Of course the stallion would not be able to keep up such a pace forever. But she had captured Hollister's scent and she thought she would have no trouble tracking him.

He intrigued her even more, now that she had faced him in the open. To Archaics, humans were no more than enemies or prey. Viewed the same way a human might view a bear or elk. It had been hundreds of years since she had had close contact with a human in an adversarial way, and she couldn't say why quite yet, but Hollister was different.

She thought most humans, especially males, were ugly. Hollister was not. His face was full of lines and angles, sharply cut, and his eyes were dark. Had she been so inclined, Shaniah would have said they were mysterious, yet that was not exactly right. There were a host of things at play there, not just mystery, but intelligence, integrity, and maybe mischief.

Although she was certain the man-witch with Hollister knew what she was, Hollister had shown no fear of her. Chee had wanted to kill her without hesitation; she could read it on his face. But Hollister had resisted. He had spoken to her. Tried to draw her in.

She remembered him on the plains four years ago. He had fought so desperately to save his men.

Now as she pursued the train, she wondered what Hollister had discovered and what course he was taking. She knew he was going to find Malachi. Of that, she was sure.

Chapter Thirty-two

Hollister stood outside the rear door of the sleeping car, watching the landscape rush by. He was thinking about the woman. There was something in their encounter that had altered things, but damned if he could put words to it. She had upset everything. Chee was jangled up so tight he might gun her down the next time he saw her and that might just be the right thing to do.

What had happened when she looked at him was something he'd never experienced before. It wasn't just that she was beautiful. At the Point, he'd spent a great deal of time in New York City and he'd seen his share of gorgeous women.

Right after the war ended, he'd been invited to a party in Washington. It had been a grand affair at the White House and General Sheridan had gotten him an invitation. He'd been allowed to shake the hand of President Lincoln just three days before the son of a bitch Booth gunned him down in cold blood.

It had been the fanciest affair Hollister had ever attended. After four long years of war, people had been ready to celebrate, and the music, the food, the liquor, and beautiful women had been there in abundance. Some of the prettiest ladies he'd ever seen, in elegant gowns, with their eyes sparkling and their skin so clean and white it was like they'd been dipped in clouds. After months of nothing but the dirt, mud, blood, and gore of battle, the cleanliness of it had made his eyes hurt.

He spent a great deal of time dancing with the daughter of an Ohio senator. She had night-dark hair piled high on her head and ice-blue eyes. He'd even asked her father if he could call on her, but then Lincoln had been shot, and he and his regiment were sent South to finish up with Johnston and he never got back to Washington. Many times, as he'd lain awake on his bunk in Leavenworth, he'd thought of her and of that night and how much he wanted to see her again.

Tonight as the train whistled and picked up speed chugging out of Denver, he could not even remember the girl's name. And as pretty as she had been, she wasn't even in the same county as Shaniah. For the life of him, Hollister could not understand why this mysterious woman had affected him this way.

Part of him wondered if Chee had been right. If she was a Deathwalker, it was certainly possible she could exert some kind of control over him. Mix him up so he wasn't thinking straight. Perhaps this was how these creatures captured their human prey, through some kind of control over their thoughts. He remembered how he'd felt back in Wyoming, with that tall freak advancing on him. He'd felt paralyzed and unable to fight back. Maybe that was what happened.

It made as much sense as anything, for he could not get the woman out of his mind. Closing his eyes and feeling the speed and power of the train move from his feet up through the rest of his body, he tried to clear his head. It was no use. Shaniah's face floated in his consciousness.

"Jesus Christ," he muttered, opening his eyes and watching the night rush past. "What the hell am I doing?"

Chee was right. The woman was trouble.

Clear of the city now, the train whistle sounded again and Hollister heard the steam shoot into the baffles on the engine. He was almost shocked at how fast it accelerated. He smiled. *The woman might be trouble*, he thought.

But my train kicks ass.

Chapter Thirty-three

They ran north through the day, running parallel to the Front
Range. Hollister had no idea how fast they were going, but
after about two hours they switched again and traveled due
west, the elevation starting to rise. Hollister expected they'd
be in Absolution by early evening.

The countryside grew more wooded, with pine and aspen
trees coming nearly down to the tracks. They slowed as they
traveled through a few towns and villages but before long,
most of civilization was left behind. Hollister found Chee in
the armory car, the hatch in the roof open, seated behind the
Gatling. He looked up at the young man.

"Anything to shoot out there, Chee?" he asked.

"No, Major," Chee said.

"Jonas or Hollister, Chee, don't forget," he said.

"Yes, sir," Chee mumbled.

"What are you looking for, Chee?" Hollister asked.

"The woman, sir," he answered.

"The woman? Shaniah?"

"Yes. She's coming."

"Really? How do you figure? That horse she was riding looked fast, but I don't think he could keep up with this train for very long." Hollister pulled one of the Henrys from a rack and started loading it with wooden bullets.

Chee merely shrugged and Monkey Pete, entering the car, interrupted them.

"We're fifteen minutes out of Absolution, Major," he said.

"Monkey Pete, if you're here with us, who exactly is driving the train?" Hollister asked.

"It's got an automatic control system. Steers itself."

"Really? And does it stop itself if there's a missing rail or a cow in the way?"

"Yes," Monkey Pete said, the expression on his face a mix of disgust and irritation as if he'd just been asked the most obvious question in the world. "Fifteen minutes, Major. We'll be stopping at the platform in the town." He left, returning the way he had come.

Hollister looked in surprise at Chee, who just shrugged. "I have no reason to doubt Monkey Pete, it is quite an amazing train," Chee said.

"I'll say," Hollister muttered, returning to loading the modified Winchester. "Chee, I never did ask Winchester this, but I'm wondering about these wooden and silver bullets."

"Sir?"

"Well, suppose we need to shoot something that isn't a Deathwalker. What if we need good old-fashioned lead? Suppose I need to shoot Slater or one of his gun thugs, and these wood bullets don't slow 'em down enough?"

Chee racked a round into the chamber of his Winchester. "Whether it's wood or silver, I suspect it's going to hurt, sir."

A few minutes later, the train slowed, then stopped, as Monkey Pete had promised. It stood next to the platform, which appeared to be on the outskirts of town. The sun was moving behind the mountains to the west.

"Monkey Pete, me and Chee are going out to have a look-see around the town. See if there's a marshal or anyone can give us any information. You stay here. Don't let anyone on the train unless it's us."

Monkey Pete climbed up in the chair Chee had vacated behind the Gatling. He pushed the lever next to the seat forward and the roof hatch hissed open. The chair shot up and out the opening, giving him a commanding view and field of fire.

"No worries, Major. I'll be sure to keep a sharp eye," he said.

"If we run into trouble, we'll fire off two shots from a Henry. You hear 'em, you lock this train up tight and don't let nobody in."

"Don't worry Major," the engineer said. "I know how to keep trouble off my train. What do you want me to do if you don't come back?"

The question caught Hollister a little off guard. He hadn't considered it. This felt more like a reconnaissance mission than an impending conflict. Still, he supposed there could be trouble ahead. It would be good to have a plan in place.

"If we can't make it back to the train, you stay locked down. Send a wire to Pinkerton and have him send the army. And I mean the whole army. If those things are here, we're going to need artillery, cavalry, the whole shebang," Hollister said.

"Chee, I'd like Dog to stay with Monkey Pete. We don't know what we're up against. I figure Dog could discourage just about anyone from taking an unauthorized tour of the train."

Dog had been lying on the floor half asleep, but he sat up and stared at Hollister at the mention of his name. Chee instructed Dog to stay with Monkey Pete. Hollister couldn't be sure, but he thought Dog looked disappointed at the prospect of missing the chance to eat someone. "He'll stay here,

Major, and I've told him to pay attention to Monkey Pete."
Hollister looked at the engineer and shrugged.

"I have no doubt," Hollister said. "Chee, let's go."

Hollister had decided to leave the Ass-Kicker on the train.
It seemed too dangerous to carry it, walking into a town
full of innocent civilians. Instead, he just carried one of
the Henrys, as did Chee, both of them looping two belts of
ammo under their dusters. One of the things Winchester had
done to their Colts and rifles was to modify them so they
were all the same caliber. They could use the same bullets
to load either gun, but he hoped he wouldn't miss the Ass-
Kicker.

There was no station, just a wooden platform next to the
track that allowed them to step down off the train. In the
center of the platform, a set of stairs led down to the dirt. Off
in the distance the main street of the town stood rimmed by
a half dozen two-story structures with one other street crossing it, and that was it. The whole town.

A clicking sound came from behind them and they
turned to see Monkey Pete still in the Gatling seat. He was
working another series of levers. With a hiss of steam, steel
panels appeared out of the sides of the train, covering the
doors and windows. "I'll be damned," Hollister muttered.
He looked at Chee in amazement, but the young man just
shrugged.

"Where to, sir?" Chee asked.

"I'm not sure. Ain't it kind of odd no one comes to meet
the train? Monkey Pete said the Central and Pacific train
comes once a week. I assume this isn't the day the regular train comes, so wouldn't people be curious?" Hollister
asked.

Chee shrugged. Hollister noticed the young man's face
had turned to stone. He was studying the town and the surrounding terrain like he expected trouble.

It took them less than two minutes to reach the outlying

buildings. They marched into the center of the town. A sign-post named the street they stood on as First Street, while the cross street was Second Street.

"Creative," Hollister muttered gesturing at the sign.

There was a hotel on one corner; a hardware store, bank, and assayers office occupied the others. Hollister counted three saloons, a laundry, general store, restaurant, and another building with a sign over the door that just said OFFICE, with no indication of what kind of office might be inside. This comprised the entire business district of Absolution.

Beyond the two-story buildings lining the two streets were a few small houses and what could only be described as huts. There was no one on the streets. With dusk approaching, there were no lights, they could smell no cook fires or wood smoke, there were no horses tied to hitching posts anywhere they could see.

"Where the hell is everyone?" Hollister asked out loud. "It's going to be dark soon. We need to get back to the train. Wait till daylight."

Chee's eyes went everywhere. To the corners, roofs, and every nook and cranny. He saw nothing and no one. Then a noise came from down the street.

Hollister cocked the Henry and carried it at port arms. Chee did the same.

"Saloon," Hollister said.

They separated, Hollister stepping up on the wooden sidewalk, Chee remaining in the street. The saloon was named the Rambling Rose. The swinging doors moved slightly in the breeze. Hollister waited as Chee backed his way up onto the sidewalk, taking a position on the other side of the doors. They quickly cut through the doors, rifles at the ready.

The saloon was empty.

But it looked like the last customers had left in a hurry. On the bar sat a few mugs of half-drunk beer. A bottle of whiskey stood at one end, an empty glass tipped on its side next to it. There was an abandoned piano along one wall and two of the nearby tables still had cards and chips and partially full glasses and ashtrays. To the left of the doorway a set of stairs led to the second level.

Chee advanced slowly on the bar. Holding the Henry in his left hand, he drew his Colt. Hollister stood ready. Instinctively, he felt no one was here, but something was also very wrong in Absolution.

Chapter Thirty-four

As he stepped toward the bar, the major with his rifle up and ready standing at the wall to his right, Chee felt each step was bringing them closer to their ends. The woman, Shaniah, was coming soon. He was sure of it. Since they had left Torson City, every time he looked over his shoulder, he expected her to be there. Chee knew that the Deathwalkers could be killed. But the woman would endanger them somehow. He could not explain the feeling and had quit trying. It was just something that was given.

He raised the Colt, his arm straight and the gun cocked and ready. There was a large mirror over the bar and he kept his eyes locked on it, watching behind them. Moving left toward the stairway, he approached the open end of the bar and swung around, bringing the gun down toward the floor, ready for anyone who might be hiding behind it.

The man had been dead awhile. He wore a white apron with black pants. The front of the apron and his white shirt, was covered in blood. His neck had been torn apart and his face was covered in flies. A small sawed-off shotgun lay on the floor beside the man; four empty shells showed he'd gone down fighting. But not well enough.

"I've got a body here, Major," he said. "He's been dead a couple of days at least. Shotgun, it's been fired." Chee set his Henry on the bar and picked up the sawed-off. He racked it open. It was loaded with two unfired rounds. He slid it into his belt with a feeling he'd be firing it before too long.

Hollister came around the bar at the other end and stooped to examine the body. "Jesus Christ," he mumbled. "All right, let's check the rest—"

Hollister was interrupted by a loud thump coming from the room above them.

"Did you hear that?" Chee asked.

"Yeah," Hollister said, standing and looking up at the ceiling. "I don't like this. We get halfway up the stairs and something comes out of one of those rooms, we're fucked," Hollister said. "I don't want to go up there without more fire-power. Let's go back to the train and get the Ass-Kicker and Dog. He can give us a better idea what's up there. We know what we're dealing with now and we're going to need the—"

From outside a loud scream sounded. It lasted several seconds before fading away. Hollister couldn't be sure, but it sounded like a woman. It was a long, eerie wail, more like anguish than alarm, and Chee and Hollister moved quickly, rushing back out into the street, standing back to back, circling slowly with rifles at the ready. It was quiet again.

"You got any idea where that came from?" Hollister asked.

"No, sir, none," Chee said.

"You don't have some kind of fancy shaman way of figuring it out?"

"I'm not a shaman, sir," Chee said, embarrassment creeping into his voice.

"Sergeant Chee, I meant no offense. But you *do* talk to your horse and your dog. I just figured you had a way of sensing this kind of stuff. All right. We're going to have to do this the hard way. It sounded to me like the scream came from a ways off. We'll start at the end of this side of Second Street. We'll clear the buildings one by one and work our way back. We've got maybe an hour to sundown. Quick and careful. Let's go."

Chee had no other suggestion, so they began their search starting at the end of the street and entering the last building, where the board sidewalk ended. Hollister studied the building itself while Chee kept an eye on the street behind them. It was getting late and the sun was balanced at the top of the mountains to the west.

The first building appeared to be some kind of laundry. It was empty, as was the next and all the buildings on that side of the street. There were no people to be found, not even bodies, but all the signs said the residents of Absolution had left with little warning or preparation. In the back of the laundry a meal had been left to burn on the cookstove, though the fire had long since burned out. Everywhere they went, there was evidence of life interrupted. Dish tubs filled with dirty dishes, pots left on stoves, uneaten meals left on dinner tables.

It took another half hour for them to clear all the buildings on Second Street. Turning their attention to First Street, they headed toward the building with the "office" sign. Upon closer inspection, they discovered the sign had been broken in half, and upon entering, learned they had found the sheriff's office. And it wasn't empty.

Standing there, letting their eyes adjust to dim interior, they heard muffled voices and cries coming from the back. Carefully they made their way to the door and threw it open.

Neither man was prepared for what they saw. Four cells with iron bars lined the back wall of the jail. Inside the cells were several children and women. When they saw Hollister and Chee, they started to cry and scream. The women—there were seven of them divided among the four cells—moved to put the children behind them, out of reach of anyone who might try to grab them through the bars.

Each cell door was wrapped with rope and chain as if some-one had sought to make sure no one could get out.

Or in.

"Get away from us, you devils," one of the women shouted, shaking her fist at the two men. All of them took up the chorus then, shouting and even cursing at Hollister and Chee.

"Quiet!" Hollister shouted. "We're not devils, we're here to help you!"

His words had no effect. They kept shouting and waving their arms. Some of the small children started crying. It was dank and cramped and smelled horrible, and Hollister, for the life of him, couldn't figure out what they were doing here.

"Hold it . . . calm down . . . stop shouting!" he yelled. After a few moments the fire went out of them and the women stood looking exhausted and defeated while a few of the children continued to moan and cry. The smell hit him then, the harsh and gamey odor of human beings forced to live in conditions like this.

"My God," he said. "What happened to you?"

The woman in the first cell who had led the yelling when they first appeared crossed her arms and stared defiantly at Hollister.

"We'll tell you nothing, you demon," she said.

"Ma'am, I don't know yet what's going on here, but I'm no demon. My name is Jonas Hollister, a U.S. marshal, and I'm here to help," he said.

Everyone in the cells was quiet for a moment as if they couldn't understand what he was telling them.

The woman brushed her long red hair out of her eyes and stared back at both men.

"Liar! You're demons! And we'll see you in hell before we open these doors . . ."

The red-haired woman occupied the first cell along with four children. In the next cell, a small older woman spoke to her.

"Rebecca. They don't look like the others. Maybe we should talk to them and—"

"No!" Rebecca shouted back. "There's nothing to say. We can last two more days until the train comes. Then we'll be free of these demons. Help will come. You'll see."

Chee stepped forward, lowering his gun. When he spoke, Hollister almost had to strain to hear him.

"Ma'am . . . ladies . . . I'm Sergeant Chee. The marshal here is telling you the truth. We're here to help you. Why don't you tell me what happened?"

"Demon!" Rebecca shouted and spat at him, but she could not garner much energy for it.

Hollister counted fourteen children in addition to the seven women: three boys and eleven girls. None of the youngsters appeared to be older than nine or ten years old. All of them looked dirty, hungry, and terrified.

"Rebecca, stop that! If they are demons, they can't get to us. Let's hear what the man has to say," the old woman from the second cell said.

"What is your name, ma'am?" Chee asked the older woman.

"Lucinda Hayes. We've been in these cells four days now. We're waiting for the train, like Rebecca said. These demons . . . they come at night. But they ain't been able to get to us. The men . . . my husband . . . the sheriff and a few others . . . they locked us in here after the first night. Said we'd be safer and they'd try to hold them off. The demons cut the telegraph lines and there weren't no way to get help—until the train shows up day after tomorrow."

"Well we're going to try to get you out of here," Hollister said.

"That's all right, mister," Lucinda said. "We got enough water to wait. The children are hungry though . . ." Her words trailed off and she stared at Hollister and Chee with a glassy-eyed and vacant expression.

"I don't understand . . . Chee, see if you can get these

chains off the doors and . . ." He stopped when Lucinda raised a Colt from the folds of her skirt and pointed it at Hollister's chest.

"Mister, I don't wanna shoot you but I will if you come anywhere near them doors," she said. The Colt was huge in her tiny hands but she held it straight and steady. Chee had his rifle up and pointed at her chest.

"Hold on, Chee!" Hollister said. "Ma'am, I think we all need to take a step back here. Don't shoot. We won't touch the doors or these chains until we figure things out." He raised his hands to the sides and stepped back from the cells.

"I am sorry, sir, but if you come any closer, I will shoot you. We know now it doesn't seem to kill you, but apparently it hurts your kind. Quite a bit. And we have plenty of ammunition, in case you were wonderin' . . ." She pulled a box of bullets from the pocket of her dress.

Chee lowered his weapon and stepped back next to the wall opposite the cells.

Hollister paced in the tight hallway. Some of the children took up whimpering again, his presence clearly terrifying them. He was stuck and didn't know what to do. He couldn't leave them here, and his instincts told him they were all in grave danger.

Each of the cells had a barred window on the back wall. The daylight was receding by the minute and the interior of the jail had grown noticeably dimmer, even in the few minutes since he and Chee had entered.

The sunlight.

"Ma'am," he said. "These demons as you call them? Have they been coming after you at all during the day?"

Lucinda lowered the Colt slightly but nowhere near all the way.

"Why . . . no . . . only at night," she said.

"Well we walked in here during the daylight. You must have at least heard our train arriver earlier this afternoon. No one came to greet it. I'm sorry to tell you, but that means either your men are . . . dead . . . or holed up somewhere else in town like you are. But Chee and I, we've been here in the daylight for a while now. Doesn't that show you we're not one of these demons?''

Hollister waited. Lucinda kept the gun on him while Chee kept his rifle pointed at her. A shadow passed over the window, darkening the spot of sunlight on the cell floor. The children screamed.

"They're back!" Rebecca wailed.

"Who's back?" Hollister asked.

"The demons, Marshal," Lucinda said quietly.

A face appeared in the cell window, not human at all, with red eyes and long white teeth. The creature it belonged to made a wild moaning sound, as if it was in pain. Hollister knew the sound: hunger.

Lucinda aimed at the thing, firing the big Colt. She missed but the face disappeared.

"God help us," Rebecca cried again.

Nothing happened for a second, until a chain came through the window. Hands wrapped the chain around the bars and it went taut. At first there was no effect, then the bars made popping sounds and the mortar around them started to crack. One of the bars came free, and the children and women went nearly wild with fright. Rebecca and a few of the other women had fallen to their knees, clasping their hands in prayer.

"Get up, you fools," Lucinda yelled at them. "Children, get behind me. You other women stand up! Protect your children! If you are going to die, you will die fighting!"

In the chaos of the moment, Hollister decided that he liked this Lucinda an awful lot. Even if she had threatened to kill him. The children in her cell did as they were told, as she moved to put herself between them and the window.

"Ma'am," he said. "You've got to trust me and Marshal Chee. We need to get you out of here."

Another bar in the window cracked loose.

"Give me the keys to these padlocks and the cell doors! Please!"

From the folds of her apron, Lucinda handed the keys to one of the boys next to her and he rushed them to Hollister. He started to work at unlocking the fortified cell doors.

"Chee, cut these ropes," he said. Chee pulled the big bowie knife from his belt and slashed through several lengths of rope that had been wrapped around and through the bars.

The entire window in the middle cell exploded out of the frame. Seconds later a man leapt through the window. Chee fired the Henry before Hollister could speak. The retort was deafening. The silver bullet pierced the creature's forehead and tunneled through his brain. The scream was unlike anything he had ever heard before, like the thing's body had been dipped in fire. He was catapulted off his feet, his body slamming into the back wall. He twitched and moaned on the ground, but he wasn't dead. He would heal and come at them again. Hollister had no idea how long it would take, but ended the guess by shooting him in the chest with a wooden bullet from his other Colt. The creature turned to dust after another agonizing scream.

Hollister threw open the cell doors.

"This way. Hurry!" he ordered.

Another creature appeared in the window opening and Chee shot but missed, and it darted away. All the cell doors opened and Hollister drew his pistol.

"Chee, clear the office. Get everyone in there. We'll barricade the cell-block door and figure out our next move."

Chee stepped forward like a cat, slinging the rifle on his back, pulling a Colt and the discarded sawed-off shotgun from his belt. He threw open the solid iron door to the office and vaulted through it.

"Clear!" he shouted.

"Everyone move!" Hollister commanded. The adults and the children scrambled out of the cells and hurried into the office. Hollister kept his gun up, covering the open window in the middle cell.

Lucinda was the last one remaining.

"Come on, ma'am," Hollister said. "Let's get a length of this chain. We can use it on the door from the other side."

Lucinda was just about clear of her cell when a creature leapt through the window, landing lightly on its feet behind her. It had once been a young girl, maybe fifteen or sixteen years old. It grabbed Lucinda roughly by the shoulders and sank its fangs into her neck. Then it bit its own finger and jammed it into Lucinda's mouth. All before Hollister could act. They were here trying to turn more humans.

Lucinda screamed and Hollister remembered the sound his men made as they died on the plains of Wyoming. He shot the girl in the head and the wooden bullet knocked her backward but didn't kill her. She staggered to her feet, ready to launch herself at him, and he shot her in the center of the chest. At first there was no reaction and the creature stared dumbly at her chest wound. An instant later, she looked up at him screaming in pain and disappeared in a cloud of ash and dust.

Lucinda lay bleeding on the floor. He tried to lift her up but she put her hand on his arm to stop him.

"Leave me," she said.

"Nonsense. You're coming with me," he said.

"No. I'm gone now. Give me my gun. You go on and save those children. The bite . . . I've been bitten and I know what comes next. I saw it happen to my husband and a bunch of others. I'm already dead. Let me kill a few more of them first."

"There is no way I'm leaving you here," he said.

She fumbled on the floor, her hands searching, and came up with the gun. She cocked the big Colt and pointed it at him, her other hand trying to staunch the bleeding in her neck.

"Hey . . . easy," he said.

"Let me go, Marshal. You can't help me. Save the others. I'm an old woman. It's all right to let me die. You need to shoot me. Before I come back and hurt one of those children."

"Major!" He heard Chee call from the other room.

"Right there, Chee," He answered.

He was about to argue with Lucinda when, with surprising strength, she dropped her own Colt and grasped his gun hand and pulled it to her chest. Before he could react, she managed to raise her other arm and press his trigger finger.

Her eyes widened as the bullet entered her chest.

"What's your name again?" she asked, gasping.

"Hollister. Jonas Hollister," he said.

"That's a fine name." She died on the cell floor.

Chapter Thirty-five

Hollister backed through the iron door and into the office, slamming it behind him. The door had a small square window in it with bars across its opening. Seconds later a creature appeared in the small window and he fired through it with his pistol but couldn't tell if he'd struck it or not. The door locked with a metal latch that was screwed to the door wall. He wrapped the chain around the handle and the latch. There was nothing to lock it in place but it would slow them down at least.

The office was about twenty feet square and Chee stood at the shuttered window, looking out onto the street through a small shooters' port in the center of it. Hollister momentarily paused to thank whoever had designed and built such a well-secured and fortified jail.

But it wouldn't keep those things out for long. Lucinda had said they cut the telegraph lines the first thing. Then they must have concentrated on feeding, picking off the easy prey around the town. Now they were coming for the hard targets. Maybe the longer they were turned the more they were able to control their urge to feed and could plan and act.

The women and children scattered to the corners as Hollister made his way through them, joining Chee at the window.

The shadows were longer now and it would be completely dark soon. The moon was rising and a hangnail of it just appeared over the mountains to the southwest. In the street perhaps twenty-five or thirty yards from the office door, three creatures stood staring intently at the jail. One wore what used to be a white apron, now covered in blood, and another still had a sheriff's badge pinned to his shirt. The third looked like a bum who may have been the town drunk.

"They been there awhile," Chee said. "Like they're trying to figure out what to do next."

"You still set on ammo?" Hollister asked.

Chee pulled back his duster to reveal three full ammo belts over his shoulders and around his waist.

"Remind me never to make fun of your proclivity for violence ever again, Sergeant."

"My what?"

"Never mind."

Hollister jumped, for Rebecca had approached from behind him and was peering out the port over his shoulder.

"Oh my God! That's Bob! It's my husband!" She tried to shove past Hollister, reaching for the door handle, clawing at the wooden timber that held it shut.

"Whoa!" Hollister said, grabbing and spinning her around in one motion. His back was to the door now. Someone had lit two of the lanterns in the office and he could see the scared faces of everyone in the room.

"We're not going anywhere, at least until daylight. We go outside, those things will be on us before we get ten feet. Good as Chee is, he can't shoot 'em all."

"But my husband! He's the sheriff! He'll know what to do!" Rebecca moaned and twisted her left hand in the folds of her apron.

"Ma'am," Hollister said quietly. "I'm awful sorry for what you been through, but he's not the sheriff or your husband anymore."

She tried once more to go around him to the door and he scooped her up in a bear hug and carried her backward to the center of the room. She kicked and screamed and then stumbled when he let her go, falling to the ground in a heap. She started crying in loud pitiful hiccupping breaths.

"Stay there," Hollister said. He rejoined Chee at the window. "Thanks for your help there."

"Major, it appeared to me you had the situation firmly in hand."

When Hollister looked out the port again, the creatures were gone.

"Wonder where they went," Hollister muttered.

"I expect we'll know soon enough," Chee said.

Hollister studied the group of women and children, many of them now seated on the floor. The children were well beyond terrified and Hollister thought briefly of the little girl who had wandered into Camp Sturgis. How long ago it had been. He wondered where the girl was now and what her life was like.

The women were nearly beaten. They all had empty, vacant stares on their faces. With Lucinda gone, they were losing hope.

"Chee, give me one of your Colts," he said.

Chee handed over the gun with a slight hesitation, like he'd rather pass a kidney stone than release one of his weapons.

"Don't worry, you still have plenty of ordnance." He held up the gun, checking the load.

"Can any of you women shoot?" Hollister asked.

At first no one said anything. Then a hand went up.

"I can, a little," a woman said, her voice small and tiny sounding.

"I'll just bet you can, whore," Rebecca muttered from the floor.

"What's your name, miss?" Hollister asked, ignoring the outburst.

"Sally," she said. She had reddened slightly at Rebecca's comment, but she recovered quickly. Hollister liked her for it.

He held out the Colt.

"You know how to use one of these?"

She nodded, taking the heavy gun from his hand. Pulling back on the hammer, she pointed it at the wall. "You cock it, then pull the trigger."

"Good," he said. "This gun's a little different. It's heavier for one thing, and it's loaded with a . . . unique . . . ammo—"

"Don't you give that whore a gun," Rebecca said, standing up again.

Hollister walked over to her, getting into her space and putting his face very close to hers.

"Rebecca, is it?"

"Yes, my husband is the sheriff here," she said.

"Ma'am . . . Rebecca . . . your husband is dead."

"No . . . no . . . he's outside. He . . ."

"No ma'am, he and all the other men who left you here are either dead . . . or they're not men anymore. Now we need to stay together here, and keep fixed on getting out."

Rebecca threw up her hands and cut her way through the crowd of women and children who were huddled in the corner near the small wood stove. She leaned into the wall and sobbed. One of the other women moved to her shoulder and consoled her, but Hollister thought he saw thinly veiled disgust on the faces of the others, even some of the older children. The sheriff's wife was evidently not a popular woman, which made Hollister wonder about the sheriff.

He turned his attention back to Sally. "As I was saying . . . unique ammo. Aim for the chest and keep pulling the trigger until the gun stops firing . . . if you—"

"Major!" Chee interrupted.

Hollister went to the window again. The moon was over the mountains now and outside there were now five creatures in the street. The same three that had been there before, another man who wore a black top hat and a woman, dressed in a simple housedress. Across the street, hidden in the shadows of the buildings, were more creatures. Hollister stopped counting when he got to a lot.

"Dear God," he muttered.

"I think God has very little to do with it," Chee said quietly.

"What are they doing?" Hollister asked.

"Nothing. Just watching."

As if they had heard him, the man in the ridiculous-looking top hat and the woman took a running start toward the building.

"Here they come," Chee said, raising his rifle and taking aim. Before he could fire, the two things leapt in the air, vaulting off the hitching post in front of the jail, and jumped up onto the roof of the sheriff's office. The noise they made scrambling over the roof caused the women and children to start whimpering and crying.

"Hush now," Sally said quietly, picking up a young girl and balancing the child on her hip while she held the big Colt in her other hand.

"They do that every night. Get up on the roof and stomp around," she said.

"Why?" Hollister asked.

"Don't know. They ain't tried to break through the roof. Lucinda said it was like they enjoyed hearing us get scared."

The stomping on the roof continued, then stopped suddenly. Chee was motionless at the window, his rifle up and ready. Hollister went to the iron door and peered through the window. The cell-block was empty.

"Sally? A word please," he said.

She lowered the child to the floor, patting her on the head and telling her she would be right back.

The young woman approached him at the doorway. The flickering lantern light inside the office made the sudden quiet more menacing somehow. In the dimness he could see the hard years in the lines of Sally's young face. Hollister was willing to bet life had not gone the way Sally had planned.

"Got a question for you," he said to her. "This jail, not that I'm not happy about it right this instant, but for such a small town I got to wonder . . . four cells with iron bars and a reinforced door to the cell block . . . a shooters' port on the front door and window. I mean, it seems like a little bit of overkill. This isn't a cow town, so you don't have cowboys to worry about. I suppose the miners might get a little rowdy on payday, but why all the fuss for a small-town jail?"

Sally glanced over her shoulder at Rebecca.

"The sheriff . . . Rebecca's husband . . . he is . . . well . . . was . . . a hard man. And ambitious. He liked to keep the order. What he said all the time anyway."

"I see," Hollister said. "I guess we owe him some thanks. Why does Mrs. Sheriff have such an intense dislike for you?"

"I'm a whore."

Hollister shrugged. "Seems personal though."

"The sheriff was also my pimp and my best customer, Marshal."

"Ah." He had no further reply.

"How we going to get out of this?" she asked.

"Don't know yet. But I'm working on it."

"We been in here four days, Marshal. I hope you come up with something quick," she said, stepping back to the group and picking up the young girl again. "Your deputy there. He keeps calling you Major. Were you in the army together?"

"Something like that," he answered.

"Major!" Chee said from the window, as if on cue. Hollister rejoined Chee at the window.

"What is it?"

"Our friend is back."

Chapter Thirty-six

Where there had previously stood three vampires in the street, now there were only piles of ash, slowly blowing away in the gathering breeze.

"Where is she now?" Hollister asked.

"I don't know," Chee said. "It happened so fast, I almost missed it. She had a big knife of some kind. She didn't . . . they weren't . . ." Chee looked over his shoulder. He wanted to keep his voice down, fearing news of the woman's appearance would needlessly alarm the women and children. He leaned in close to Hollister.

"What I'm saying is, she didn't cut off their heads or anything. She just stabbed them and they turned to dust. It happened so fast they didn't have time to react. She ran up on the roof. It's quiet up there now. I bet she got the two up there as well."

Hollister thought for a moment, trying to recall anything about stabbing vampires like regular folks that he might have read in Van Helsing's journals. Nothing came to him.

"We'll have to figure it out later. Maybe we can exchange notes if we ever get a chance to ask her—"

He was interrupted by a shout.

"Billy, no!" One of the women screamed. Spinning around, Hollister saw that one of the boys, maybe eight or ten years old, had worked his way close to the door while no one was paying attention. Now he was throwing up the wooden latch and tearing it open.

Hollister was about six feet away and leapt after him, but the kid was small and quick and had the door open. He dashed through it into the darkened street.

"Get back here, kid!" Hollister yelled after him. The boy was fast and he ran across the walkway in front of the jail and down the street. He was about to run after him when from directly above him the man who had jumped on the roof, still wearing his ridiculous top hat, landed on the ground in front of him. Apparently, the mystery woman had missed one of the creatures on the roof. Or she had been killed herself. The thought gave him momentary pause as he tried to scramble backward into the jail, but the creature's hands shot out and grabbed him around the neck.

He couldn't breathe. It felt like his neck had been clapped in irons. His feet started to leave the ground as the creature lifted him up in the air. Hollister was only vaguely aware of the shouts and screams of the women and children in the open doorway behind him. He tried to choke out words, but he could not get any air in his lungs.

Chapter Thirty-seven

Shaniah had slowly worked her way into the town and spent time on the rooftops of the main street across from the Archaics who stood outside the jail and hid in the shadows of the buildings below her. They did not catch her scent, whether it was because of the stillness of the air, or her position downwind of them. More likely it was because they were still initiates, recently turned and not fully familiar with their newfound senses and powers. Her scent blended with the cacophony of smells they were processing at the moment. Experienced Archaics would have known she was there.

Malachi or his minions had been busy. There were dozens of Archaics in the town. The humans sequestered in the jail were going to die. It was only a matter of time, unless someone came for them in daylight. Then they might have a chance. She had eyed Hollister's train on her way into town. It might be their only hope.

It had been smart of the humans to hole up in the jail. She had learned humans were excellent at building jails and prisons, and it was probably the most secure building in the entire town. They could make it through another night. The humans inside did not yet understand the Archaics besieging them. The Archaics were consumed by hunger and were using their strength and viciousness to feed. Being recently turned, planning and plotting eluded them in most cases. Now, watching the jail, she knew there were likely no living humans left in the town. The Archaics were gathering where the food was.

She needed Hollister and the man-witch to find Malachi, but for now, it was time to even the odds. The three Archaics in the street died quickly.

Chapter Thirty-eight

When he turned around, it was Top Hat Man who held his neck. The man's face changed, his eyes went red, and his jaw grew. Hollister watched as the fangs descended from his mouth. Without warning, Jonas was dropped to the ground as there was a loud explosion and the vampire went flying sideways. Chee had shot the man in the head with the Henry and he catapulted off the porch, landing in the street. Of course the bullet didn't kill him, but he screamed in agony, clutching at his head as he rose to his feet, charging at Hollister.

Hollister drew his Colt and started shooting. Hitting a moving target in the heart is not easy. It requires some luck, but the fourth bullet took the creature in the right spot and he moaned in pain again as he staggered backward and collapsed in a heap of dust, the top hat rolling in the dirt.

Jonas staggered back into the office and slammed the door shut. "Jesus Christ!" he said, trying to calm his breath and keep his heart from slamming out of his chest. He reloaded the Colt, nearly dropping the bullets as his hands wouldn't stop shaking.

"Please, mister," he heard a voice behind him, and turned

to find Billy's mother standing there, tears streaming down her face. "You got to help him."

Hollister didn't know what to do. His training and instinct told him he needed to go find the boy, but his encounter with Top Hat had left him shaken.

"What's your name?" he asked her.

"Dowding. Joann Dowding. Please. You got to fetch my Billy," she said.

"Why did he run away?"

"I don't know . . . he . . ." she stammered, unable or unwilling to get the words out.

"Because he's a damn retard," Rebecca interrupted the woman.

"He is not . . . you leave my Billy be!" The woman started crying again and Hollister didn't know what to do to make her stop.

"Your stupid retard is going to get us all killed," Rebecca went on. She was still in her corner, leaning against it. Her eyes were wild and unfocused and Hollister was pretty sure she had lost whatever command of her faculties she might have once possessed. He had seen it happen to soldiers in combat many times. The tense, uncertain atmosphere drove them over the edge.

"If you go after that retard . . . we all . . ." She was cut off by the appearance of Sally, who stepped in front of her, pointing the big Colt at her head.

"Rebecca, you need to shut your hole. You call that boy a name again . . . you open your mouth at all and I'll shoot you myself," Sally said.

"You whore! Don't you point a gun . . ." Rebecca stood up, and while Chee kept his post at the port in the window, Hollister moved to step in. Just as he was about to put himself between them the Colt went off with a loud bang, and the wall next to Rebecca's head exploded, with wood chips flying everywhere. Rebecca and several of the others screamed. Then it was silent a moment as the smoke cleared.

Rebecca stared at Sally and the barrel of the gun, which hadn't moved, a stunned expression on her face. But the sheriff's wife was finally quiet.

"I have had enough of you and your mouth," Sally said. "You're a bitch and a bully. We are through listening to you. This woman is worried for her child and you'll not say another word about it. Is that clear?"

"You filthy whore . . ." Rebecca spat, the shock from the gunshot fading.

"That's right, I'm a whore. I ain't filthy, but I'm a whore. And I think you know your husband was my best customer. I expect every one of us that has been shut up in this jail with you for the last four days can see why. But I ain't like you, so I been too polite to mention it. But you say another word about anything, and I'll go upside your head with this Colt. Do you understand?"

Rebecca had nowhere to go. She was pinned into the corner by Sally. Looking in vain around the room, she tried to find an escape and saw none. Finally she turned and faced the wall, her shoulders slumped, sobbing. Sally lowered the weapon and returned to her spot on the floor, a couple of the younger children scrambling to sit next to her. Hollister decided he liked the fact they had Sally on their side.

He returned to Chee, still at the window, apparently not having noticed the entire episode. Or not caring. Hollister couldn't decide.

"What are we going to do?" Chee asked.

"I'm going after the kid," Hollister said.

"I'll come with you."

Hollister shook his head. "No. You've got to stay here and protect these people. If Billy hadn't run off, I think we probably could have lasted here until sunrise. Either way, you should be able to hole up here. Once the sun comes up, you double-time it to the train."

Hollister checked the loads in his pistol. Chee handed him one of his ammo belts.

"All forty-five caliber, so they'll fit your gun. Those are the bullets loaded with silver and holy water. It will slow them down until you can finish them with wood," Chee said.

"I can see you've given this a lot of thought," Hollister said, wrapping the belt around his shoulder.

"Yes, sir," Chee said.

"All right, you have your orders. Try to keep everyone alive. If I don't come back, send a wire to Pinkerton and have him order the army back here."

"Sir. You really should let me go with you, I . . ."

Hollister held up his hand.

"Don't worry Sergeant," he said. "I think I've got some help out there already."

"You think she can be trusted?" Chee asked. He could not believe the major would be so willing to put his life in the hands of someone he didn't know. Especially one who was . . . supernatural at the very least.

"She helped us with the Utes, she killed at least three of those critters, and maybe more by now. Something tells me she needs or wants something from us. I don't know what it is, but if she wanted us dead she would have killed us in Torson City."

Chee could not argue the point.

Hollister was ready to go, he pulled both of the Colts. He looked at the door a moment, then at Chee.

"One thing, Sergeant. When I come back, if I do come back, you use your coin. First thing. And if I don't have my coin or if I don't want to switch 'em with you . . . and I'm not . . . if I'm no longer me, you shoot me down. No hesitation. Do you understand?"

Chee was staring out the port, keeping his eyes on the street. Finally he glanced at the major.

"Yes, sir," he said. "I understand."

And with that, Hollister disappeared into the night.

Chapter Thirty-nine

Billy was nowhere to be seen. Hollister had debated bringing one of the lanterns with him, but there was no sense
in giving himself away with a light—although he suspected
the vampires already knew he was there. He remembered
Top Hat and his leap to the roof, so once he heard Chee
lock the door behind him, he turned around and backed into
the street with both Colts pointed at the top of the building.
When he cleared the roof over the walkway, he tensed, but
no one appeared there.

He had no idea what to do. These things were so fast he
didn't know where to look first. The moon lighted the street,
but there were shadows everywhere and it took every ounce
of self-control not to start firing at every flickering image he
saw in the corner of his eye.

Where would the kid go? What had possessed him to run
in the first place? Maybe he had a father he thought was still
out here. Once he was out of the jail, he might have wanted
to try and find him. Maybe he wanted to get away from that
bitch Rebecca. Kids do all kinds of reckless things.

He slowly moved south along the street, heading toward the saloon. A door slammed and he nearly jumped out of his boots. It had come from up ahead. Could have been the wind, but he doubted it.

He was certain they were watching him now. No way to tell how many, but certainly more than one. There was an alley between the bank and the saloon and he thought he saw movement at the end of it, but he held his fire, reminding himself not to shoot until he had something to aim at. No sense wasting bullets on shadows. Especially when he didn't know how many of these creatures were out there.

Van Helsing had written that these things turned regular humans into vampires by drinking their victims' blood, then making the victims drink the blood of the vampires. According to his journal, no one had been able to quite figure out how it worked, but something in the human soul was lost in the transformation. Van Helsing didn't necessarily believe they were evil by nature, although they had been cursed, it seemed, but rather they were simply made into predators. They hunted and killed, just like a lion or a wild dog.

Reading through Van Helsing's journal the last few days and having been one of the few humans who had survived an encounter with these creatures, Hollister didn't believe any of it. They were evil. End of story.

Hollister was not a religious man, though he had grown up in a house run by very devout parents. There was nothing beyond chores and church in the Hollister household when he was a boy. They worked the farm six days a week and Sunday was spent at chapel. His mother and father tolerated nothing else. He remembered the countless hours sitting in the pews of the Presbyterian church in Tecumseh, Michigan, pulling at the starched collar of his shirt. Usually wearing one of his brother's hand-me-downs, always so tight around his neck he thought he would suffocate.

He'd spent nearly every hour of his days in the house of God daydreaming. Hoping to leave the farm. He wanted to join the army and fight. So he'd never paid much attention to the sermons or the teachings of the good reverend Forsythe who was so old when Hollister was a boy, he and his brothers had wondered if the man might die on the pulpit right in front of them.

He'd been required to attend services at the Point and he'd done his duty. He'd chuckled to himself a few times then, when he'd caught himself pulling at the collar of the dress grays they were required to wear, mimicking the same thing he'd done as a kid.

The truth of it was, none of the religious teachings had stuck with Hollister much, except for one: the existence of evil in the world.

He had seen enough of it firsthand. Men who were born without souls the way some poor child might be born without a hand. They were nothing more than animals, and during the war, Hollister had put down a few. In Leavenworth he'd found even more: men with a gaping emptiness inside where their soul, the human part of them, should be.

That is what these vampires were. Cursed or not, they were evil. Whatever they represented, they would kill as many human beings as they could. And it was his job to stop them.

He stood in the street, the saloon on his left directly in front of him. Going back in was suicide, he told himself. He didn't know why, but they were in there. At least some of them. And they either had Billy with them or knew where he was. He would keep killing them until Jonas himself was dead, or he found the kid.

Where was the woman? he thought. Wouldn't they be trying to draw her out as well? The guns felt suddenly heavy in his hands and he realized he was very tired. Nothing he could do about it though.

He moved slowly forward, the saloon door coming closer. He held the Colt in his left hand straight out in front of him and his right hand was cocked at an angle at his waist. Holy water and silver to slow them down, Chee had said. Wood to kill them Hollister almost laughed. Chee reduced everything to its simplest terms.

The swinging doors were right in front of him. He couldn't see inside the saloon—it was too dark and not much of the moonlight penetrated the interior. He could sense the vampires inside now, waiting for him. Slowly he reached out with the Colt, pushing on the saloon door. It creaked on its hinges, sounding as loud as a cannon shot in the quiet night.

He was about to step through when, without warning, he was jerked off his feet and pulled backward into the street.

What the hell?

Chapter Forty

As he flew through the air he had enough presence of mind to hit the dusty street in a roll and come up with his pistols raised. Shaniah stood in front of the door to the saloon, a long knife in her hand. It was dripping with blood that was now pooling at her feet.

Hollister kept the Colts leveled at her.

"If you go in there now, you'll die," she said.

"Pleased to make your acquaintance. Again. I'm going to have to ask you to step aside, though. There's a young boy who has gotten separated from our party and I need to collect him," Hollister said.

Shaniah snorted. "You mean the little idiot that ran out of your jail in the middle of the night, with the town full of Archaics?"

"Archaics?"

"I'm not sure what you might call them. Vampires, perhaps, which would be a close description but not entirely accurate. The boy is already dead."

"Oh. Well. That changes everything. Thanks so much for letting me know. I'll just mosey on elsewhere then."

Though she had been chasing Malachi for several years now, she always made an effort to keep her distance from humans. The human language was rich in nuance and subtlety, and she could not be sure if the man named Hollister was serious.

"Good. Now since I have saved your life, it would be easier if you returned to your jail. Wait until morning, when it will be safer for you to venture to your train."

"Sorry, I can't do that. I need to find the kid."

"I told you, he's already dead," she said, puzzled at why he would doubt her.

"So you said," he stood slowly, the pistols maintaining their aim at the center of her chest.

"I don't understand. . . . If he's dead . . ."

"I'm afraid I can't just take your word for it. I'm going to have to find it out for myself. Now, I appreciate what you've done here and in Torson City. You probably saved our hides with those Utes. But I need to find Billy," he said.

"If you go into the saloon you will die," she said.

"Then I guess today is my day for it," he said. "Now, kindly step aside." He took a step toward her, holding the guns steady. In reality he was squeezing the handles so hard he wasn't sure he'd be able to fire them even if he wanted to. She didn't move, and he was sorry for that as he didn't know what his next tactic would be. His only hope was that she wouldn't try to use the big knife on him.

"There are four Archaics inside this saloon. They are waiting for you to come in. You've killed two Archaics tonight. That is far more than any single human has done in centuries. You're too late to save the boy. He has already been fed upon. Walk in this door and you will die. I cannot make it more simple than that." She watched his face expectantly, waiting and wondering what he would do next.

"I'm still going after the kid," he said. "Maybe I can save him."

"He cannot be saved. You can only die," she said.

He was only a few feet away from her now, and even in the soft moonlight he could see the lines of her face. She was stunning. He knew he needed to focus, but his mind was all jangled up, trying to figure out why she was here. Why she had saved him twice and what her endgame was.

There was nothing else to discuss. He moved to his left to go around her and enter the saloon.

If he had to, he would shoot her.

Chapter Forty-one

Shaniah was surprised at Hollister's reaction to being pulled back from the saloon door. Most humans had horrible reflexes, and were she so inclined, he could have been dispatched with little effort on her part. But Hollister had reacted quickly, like a cat, rolling on the ground and rising smoothly, his guns still out, ready to fire. This human confused her. He was sure to die if he entered the saloon, but he seemed determined to do it anyway. All in pursuit of a child who was likely already dead or well on his way to death.

Hollister had been or still was—she wasn't sure—a military man. She wondered if he considered it his duty to find and protect the child. Regardless, for him, entering this saloon would only result in his demise. And if she let him, she would be that much further from finding and stopping Malachi. She had to keep him out of the building.

Her plan almost worked. He circled to her right, his guns still pointed at her, not yet convinced she was here to kill him. She remained rooted to her spot.

"Are you going to move? Or do I have to shoot you?" he asked.

"You won't shoot me," she said.

"What makes you so sure?"

"Because if you kill me, you'll never find Malachi."

"Who's Malachi?"

"The Archaic who nearly killed you in Wyoming four years ago. Tall. Long white hair."

She was not expecting the reaction she got.

Hollister's face turned white, then seconds later red again as the heat rose in him.

"It was you! You were there! Why?" he demanded, his voice low.

As he spoke, his left hand wavered and the Colt dropped slightly, no longer pointing at her chest.

Shaniah made her move.

Her plan worked, at least partly. She grabbed for the Colt, her hands moving like a cobra. She twisted both pistols from his hands, but the major shocked her again. Almost as if he'd been expecting it, he pulled the long knife from his belt and held it at her neck. She dared not move.

"I read somewhere your kind has an aversion to pointy sharp things," he said.

She remained silent.

"Now. Very slowly turn the pistols around, handles first . . ."

"Major . . . you have to trust me. I know you are after Malachi. I can help you."

"Help me what?"

"Find him."

"Why should I trust you?"

"You shouldn't. If I were you, I wouldn't either."

"Well then," he said.

She didn't like the feel of the steel at her neck. She was sure she could disarm, even defeat this man. But something held her back. He knew things about Archaics. The guns she held felt heavier and different in her hands. Unlike other firearms she had handled before. And she'd seen them kill the Archaics. He also understood that decapitation would kill her. What if the blade he held was blessed with an elemental? With even a slight cut, she could be weakened or even killed before she had a chance to counter him.

She sensed a new threat. There were more Archaics stalking them, and those inside the saloon were growing restless, stirring, tired of waiting for Hollister to enter the saloon. She and Hollister were outnumbered. The only advantage they held were that these were new initiates. Freshly turned, they acted like predators, a pack mentality overcoming them, hunting and feeding their only thoughts. Not strategy. Not separating Hollister and Shaniah from each other, making it easier to overwhelm them.

She remembered her turning. It had happened on the steppes of Eastern Europe almost fifteen hundred years ago. Her family were peasant farmers, and Turkish raiders constantly preyed on her village. Her husband, Dimitri, had been killed in a raid two years earlier. She was eighteen years old. They had never had children and she was nearly past the age to marry.

The raiders came during harvest, the villagers were simple people, not fighters, and they had no chance—doubly so, when they discovered that these raiders were not like the others. There was something wrong with them. They didn't just rape and pillage; their faces were strange—and God help her, but they tore at the necks of her parents, her sisters, and their children, and drank their blood. And one of them fell on Shaniah and she felt the fangs sink into her, and a bloody finger was forced into her mouth.

At first nothing happened, then, in a few hours, she began to change. Some of the people of her village could not tolerate the change and died as the raiders drained them of their blood. But she and some of the others became wild with blood lust. They joined the pack and they hunted. And since then, she had been an Archaic. Only, unlike her brethren in her homeland, she kept her human memories. This puzzled the Old Ones. No Archaic had ever remembered their human life. It made them believe she was ideally suited to deal with the oncoming encroachment of humankind. It was one of the reasons she had been chosen leader over Malachi.

Shaniah knew it took time within the change for primal urges to recede and for intellectual capacity to reassert itself. Shaniah remembered her first weeks as an Archaic. She understood that, right now, the newly turned Archaics in the saloon could think of nothing but killing and blood. With time, they would control it; and the longer they survived, the easier it would become.

The major still hadn't moved. His eyes never left hers. Something in his look reminded her of Dimitri, her long-dead husband, a human she should no longer remember. Hollister's eyes were dark, like his had been. He was beginning to show a faint growth of beard on his face, most likely because he found shaving unimportant. His duty came first. At least that is what she imagined. It suited him, giving a clearer definition to his chiseled features.

She snapped back to the moment, silently cursing herself for letting the human distract her.

"Major, please. I beg of you. Trust me," she said.

"Why?" he asked again.

"If you look slowly to your right, just slightly, you will see that there are Archaics standing in the street. We've only got a few seconds."

Hollister pivoted his head, just as she'd said. Sure enough, he saw three Archaics in the street in his peripheral vision. He could hear the rasp of their breath.

He made a snap judgment.

"Can you shoot?" he asked her.

She nodded.

"The gun in your left hand . . . aim for the heart."

The three Archaics leapt at them.

Chapter Forty-two

The sound of the gunfire was impossibly loud in what had been a momentary calm. Jonas had to admit Shaniah knew how to fight. She shot two of the creatures dead center in the heart and they descended with agonizing screams into piles of ash. The third one was going to be trouble.

It landed on the wooden sidewalk in front of Hollister and reached for him. The knife was one of Monkey Pete's inventions . . . a bowie that had silver inlaid in a groove along the blade. It had also been dipped in holy water before he left the train.

As the Archaic advanced, he slashed it across the arm and it howled in pain and drew back. Jonas lunged forward, driving the blade into the creature's chest and twisted it through, leaving the creature in a pile of ash.

The sound of growls and footsteps could be heard coming from inside the saloon.

"Come on," Shaniah said, stuffing one of the guns in her belt. Grabbing him by the arm, she spun him past her so she was between him and the doorway.

Five more Archaics burst through the door. She fired the pistol loaded with silver bullets and hit three of them, sending them spinning to the ground stunned and nearly unconscious.

One jumped at her and she somehow pulled a knife from her boot, pushing it into the chest of the creature. It died instantly. The fifth one stood there, eyes red, fangs snapping, studying the two of them. Shaniah raised the pistol, but before she could shoot, the creature darted back inside the darkened saloon.

Shaniah handed Hollister the pistols and he wasted no time reloading. She took the knife from the dead creature and used it to dispatch the other three, who had yet to recover from their wounds.

"Are they dead?" he asked.

"Yes. This blade is special. The reason why would take too long to explain. Right now it is enough to know it will kill either Archaic or human."

"What do we do now—"

He was interrupted by a strange howl, loud and long, sounding like it came from inside the saloon.

"The one who escaped is calling the others," she said, the worry evident in her voice.

"How many are there?" he asked.

"How many people were there in this town?" she replied.

He shrugged. "Not sure."

"Most were killed," she said. "Fed upon. But many were turned. Part of Malachi's plan. There could be dozens of them."

"Great," he said.

She tensed suddenly, her head up as if she were straining to hear something.

"What is it?" he asked.

"They're coming, Major."

"What do you suggest we do?"

"Run!" she said.

Chapter Forty-three

It was sixty yards down the street, then down the cross street another fifty or sixty yards to the jail, but to Hollister it felt like miles. In the confusion it seemed easier to count the places where there weren't Archaics than where there were.

She was fast. Far faster than he was, and he was not slow by any stretch. He fired as he ran, hitting his targets with the silver bullets, and after the first five or six went down screaming in pain, the others kept their distance. Yet, he and Shaniah were going to lose.

"Hurry!" Shaniah called back to him and slowed, lessening the gap between them. An Archaic came at her and she took off its head with her knife.

"There's too many of them," he said. "Jesus Christ, where did they all come from?"

"Jesus Christ is not a name you should mention to an Archaic," she said.

"Why?" Hollister asked.

"Long story," she said.

Another Archaic charged at them from the shadows. Hollister's gun barked and the creature spun screaming into the dirt of the street. They had another twenty yards to reach the corner, and Shaniah willed him to run faster.

"I've got six shots left, no time to reload," he told her.

"Then you had better make them count," she said.

They reached the intersection and rounded it toward the jail. She skidded to a stop and he nearly collided with her. Thirty yards away, standing in a line across the street, stood more than a dozen Archaics.

"Well, shit," Hollister said. He threw open the cylinder on his empty Colt and pulled a speed loader pre-filled replacement from the belt Chee had given him. He slammed it into place and worked the hammer, ready to fire. "Goddamn Chee, if you were here, I could kiss you right now."

"We're not going to get through them," Shaniah said. She looked behind and the Archaics that had been chasing them from the saloon, another eight in total, were advancing toward them. They were surrounded.

"We should try to make it to your train," she said.

"Can't. If Monkey Pete sees me running toward the train with you, he ain't going to guess, he's going put us both down. The jail is our only shot," he said.

"You have a monkey on your train?" she asked, confused.

"No . . . it's a . . . never mind." He kept his head on a swivel, watching the Archaics at their front and back closing in fast. He fired at one of them and it flew backward, clutching at the wound in its chest. It had the desired effect, slowing the others momentarily as they warily studied the two of them.

"You're only going to make them mad," she said.

"I'm going to make them dead," he replied.

Shaniah tried to think. She was not used to fighting her own kind. It was a simple matter to understand how they thought and reacted, and she had killed Archaics before. Yet it did not come easily to her. She wished Hollister would come up with a plan.

She looked at him and found him studying the rooftops of

the buildings where the jail lay, fifty yards from where they stood. A few feet away, the wooden walkway ended, but it was covered by a roof all the way down to where the buildings ended beyond the jail.

"You're pretty strong," he said.

"Thank you," she said, confused again. This man was unlike any she had ever met. He was about to die—horribly in fact—but he was, apparently, standing in the street daydreaming.

"Not a compliment, a fact," he said. "All right, on the count of three, break for the roof there. You go up first, and then you've got to pull me up. I won't be able to get enough lift to make it on my own. Then we go down the roof to the jail. We've got to be quick," he said.

"Are you joking?" she asked.

"No," he said, and fired at another male Archaic that had ventured too close. The creature managed to dodge the bullet aimed for its head, but they had learned his bullets weren't like ordinary human bullets and they dropped back a bit.

"Because I can't tell. We are not big on the use of sarcasm," she said.

"You got a better idea? I'd love to hear it," he said.

"They'll be on us—"

He interrupted her. "I went to West Point. They may be on us, but we'll have the high ground. It's not much, but it's better than dying here in the street."

"Is Wet Point a place you go to learn how to die?" she asked. He fired again and another Archaic dropped to the ground, but the first two he'd shot had recovered, rejoined the pack, and looked a lot angrier.

"*West* Point. Not Wet Point," he said. "Go!"

His shout spurred her to action, almost against her will. As he had suggested, she sprinted the few feet to the roof and leapt up, landing lightly on her feet. She turned immediately at the sound of Hollister's gun, which he fired three times in rapid succession. She heard Archaic cries of pain, and then saw Hollister leap in the air below her. She grabbed his wrist and lifted him in the air, but an Archaic, a small female, grabbed hold of his legs. The creature threw back her head ready to sink her fangs into him, but with his free hand, he put the Colt's barrel right in her mouth and pulled the trigger.

Even an Archaic could not stand unflinching at such a close-range shot. The silver bullet blew out the back of her head. She didn't make a sound, but let go of his legs and fell into the dirt. Shaniah lifted him the rest of the way onto the roof.

"GO! Move!" he shouted. They ran along the roof, the distraction they'd created only giving them a few seconds. Archaics were running alongside them in the street below and a few were already leaping toward the roof. Shaniah took one down with her knife, and Hollister shot at three more, missing only one.

He raised his Colt and pointed at an Archaic who had reached the roof ten yards in front of him. Shaniah darted into his field of fire and he hesitated. In that instant, something clubbed him from behind and he went down.

He looked up at a face he was sure would haunt his dreams forever: long white fangs, burning red eyes, the mouth and cheeks covered in blood.

This is it, he thought. *This is where I'm going to die.* After surviving the war, fighting Sioux on the plains, and the encounter with Malachi, he was going to be killed here on the roof of a building in a piece-of-shit town in godforsaken who knows where.

"Huh," he said.

Chapter Forty-four

The few minutes Hollister had been gone were some of the longest of Chee's life. He had watched from the shooting portal at the window until Hollister had disappeared in the darkness. The women and children were quiet. He could tell none of them believed the major was coming back, but he was glad for the silence. Even Rebecca was quiet. Billy's mother had apparently cried herself out, perhaps coming to the realization that her boy was most likely dead.

A few minutes later, gunshots sounded and his hopes rallied. Then came a few more shots a short while later and he wondered if Hollister had been overwhelmed. Not long after that, came a faint howling sound he didn't recognize. Not a Coyote or a dog. He had no idea what it meant, but it meant something. He hoped it wasn't an indication that the major was dead.

It would be up to him to keep these people safe, and he wondered if they could survive the night.

The young woman named Sally was suddenly at his elbow, the heavy Colt still in her small hand.

"Do you think he's still alive?" she asked quietly.

"I don't know," he said. Chee was uncomfortable conversing with people. With soldiers and the major, he had no problem, but white people, even whores, generally made him nervous.

"I think he's alive," she said. "He seems like a smart fella."

Chee understood the young woman had gone sweet on Hollister in the few short hours they had been here in the jail.

He kept his eyes on the outside and straightened a little when he noticed several Archaics moving into the street fifty yards down from the jail. They moved slowly toward the intersection and in the moonlight it was difficult to tell what was going on.

But he was sure this meant the major was still alive. Otherwise they would be gathering to attack the jail, not heading in the other direction. A few moments later, he heard more gunshots.

Hollister *was* alive.

He strained to watch the activity in the street, trying to figure out what was happening. Instinct told him something was about to go down. He looked at Sally.

"Miss, I'm going to need your help," he said.

She looked at him, her eyes going wide as if she could read his mind.

"I'm going to go out there and help the major," he said. "You need to take my spot here and keep watch on the street out there. You'll need to bar the door after I leave, and let us in when we come back."

"I can't do that," Sally said, shaking her head.

"Yes, you can," he said quietly. He tried to think of something that would make her believe she could do what he asked. "The major, he believed in you."

Sally swallowed hard.

"But I thought he told you to stay here with us," she said, the fear starting to creep into her voice.

"He did. But he's in trouble. And if we're going to have a chance, we need to help him. He's counting on us. He's counting on you. Can you do it?"

Sally looked down at the floor. Outside there was another gunshot, then another—then the Archaics in the street started running and jumping like a herd of frightened antelope.

"It's now or never, Sally," he said gently.

"All right, I can do it," she said.

Chee went to the door and quickly lifted the beam, looking at the remaining women. "Sally is in charge," he said. "If anyone gives her trouble, I will shoot them."

He stepped through the door, waiting until he heard Sally lower the beam back in place.

Working the action on the big Henry rifle, he ran into the street.

Chapter Forty-five

Hollister didn't die. He opened his eyes, looking up to see the Archaic above him stabbed through the chest by Shaniah and her knife. It fell to the roof beside him and he scrambled to his feet, ready to shoot. The creatures were everywhere. He looked behind him; three more were coming along the roof toward them. They hadn't made it very far; the jail was still a good thirty yards or more beyond.

He fired at the Archaics to his rear, hitting the one in the middle. The other two darted away, the one on his right jumping off the roof of the walkway to the top of a building and disappearing from sight. The one on his left jumped back to the street and he fired at it again, hitting the shoulder and spinning it around, and it darted up onto the walkway underneath him and out of sight.

"This was a bad plan," Shaniah said. She stood holding the knife in both hands, with three Archaics ten yards in front of her, blocking their pathway to the jail. "We're trapped."

Hollister wanted to argue with her but couldn't, deciding she had a point. Maybe he had been mistaken.

Down in the street an Archaic looked at him and growled, its eyes blazing. It leapt in the air and he raised his pistol, tracking it, when he heard a shot and it spun in the air, collapsing on the ground, groaning in agony. The three Archaics confronting Shaniah scattered, moving so fast, he had no idea where they went. Two more still waited in the street below, looking confused as their comrade squirmed in pain on the dusty street. Another shot sounded and one of them disappeared in a cloud of ash and dust. Hollister recognized the bark of the Henry. Chee.

My God.

They had an open path ahead of them now, the roofline temporarily clear of Archaics.

"Go! Go!" Hollister shouted.

Shaniah didn't wait. She took off running faster than Hollister thought he'd ever seen a human being run. Of course she wasn't quite human.

"Chee! It's us. We're on the roof. Don't shoot us!" he hollered, wanting to make sure the trigger-happy sergeant didn't gun them down by accident. Though he knew there was very little the young man ever did by accident.

He took off after her, his boots clomping across the roof. He hoped they hadn't skimped on the lumber, as he would hate to plunge through, after he had managed to elude these vicious critters thus far. The Henry fired again, and another Archaic who had jumped toward them from below was knocked out of the air, tumbling to the street. There was a second of silence as if they had pulled back and slowed somehow. Hollister could only surmise that Chee's sudden appearance and the withering fire he was sending their way had bought them a few precious moments as the creatures sorted through the confusion.

"Move!" Hollister shouted at Shaniah, not knowing why exactly, except that his cavalry training was coming back to him and he was used to shouting orders in combat.

Hollister took a glance backward and discovered two Archaics closing on them. He fired and one of his Colts clicked on an empty chamber.

"Shit!" He holstered the gun and ran faster, hoping Chee would see the two behind him and take care of them.

Ten yards to go until they reached the jail.

Another Archaic jumped in front of them but Shaniah took it out with her knife, this time swinging and connecting at the neck as the creature crumpled to the ground. She ran right through it and Hollister followed. He probably would have been ill at the thought of it if he wasn't likely to die soon anyway.

"Hurry!" Chee called to them from the street below. He was firing his pistol now, having emptied the long gun. "There's more coming . . . Oh My God!"

Shaniah and Hollister reached the roof over the sidewalk in front of the jail and leapt to the ground. Jonas landed hard, feeling the pain shoot from his ankles up to his knees as he spun, rolling on the ground and coming back to his feet.

Shaniah had landed cleanly without a problem and looked at Hollister, her eyes knitted and mouth flattened in a smirk. Hollister stamped his feet, shaking the pain out of his legs.

"Shut up," he said, looking at her and trying to hide his bruised ego.

"Look!" Chee said, gesturing down the street toward the town's intersection.

It was a couple of hours after midnight now, but the moon was almost straight overhead. About one hundred yards away from them were another twenty or more Archaics racing in their direction at a full-on gallop like a pack of rabid coyotes. All of them had obviously been townspeople a few days ago. Not any longer. They were coming to join the fight.

Then Jonas realized that was not the case at all. They were chasing something. His eyes shifted to a moving blur about twenty yards in front of the pack.

Billy.

* * *

"Chee! Reload," he shouted. "Jesus Christ, kid. Run!" He slapped another speed loader into his empty Colt, spinning the chamber, snapping it in place, and twirling the gun back into his holster.

The few Archaics pursuing them along the rooftops had paused momentarily, first wary of Chee and his rifle and now watching the activity in the street below. Three of them turned back and ran toward the oncoming pack, their eyes no doubt set on Billy, angling to cut him off. Predators went after the easiest prey, and right now, Billy, whose little legs were churning up the dirt as he ran, was a much less threatening target than the three of them.

"Chee!" Hollister said, pointing at the three retreating Archaics. The sergeant raised the rifle and fired three times in rapid succession. Hollister couldn't remember ever seeing anyone shoot more effortlessly. Each of the Archaics went down, flopping like fish on the rooftop, the pain of the silver bullets working through them. They wouldn't be down for long, though.

"Chee, cover me," Hollister said. He ran toward Billy, Shaniah's voice sounding behind him.

"Wait! What are you doing?" she cried.

"Going after the kid!"

"Stop! It might be a trap!" she shouted.

Both men could hear the fury in her voice, and it might have given them pause if they'd had time to think about it. Having just fought their way through a swarm of bees only to see Hollister turn around and head back into the hive had put her on edge.

As Hollister ran, he had to give Billy credit. The little bastard was quick. He must have gotten some kind of head start on the Archaics, but they were making up ground fast. *He's going to get me killed*, Hollister thought, *but damn, the kid can run*.

Jonas was fast himself. At the Point he'd often challenge

his classmates to footraces and in four years he'd only lost once, to a plebe from New Hampshire. He couldn't remember the cadet's name now. Simpkins? Simpson? Funny the things you thought of when you were racing toward your doom.

The trouble was, Hollister hadn't run much, if at all, in years. Not since before he was thrown in Leavenworth. There had been no place to run there, and besides, running inmates tended to make the guards trigger happy.

As soon as he started running he knew he wasn't going to reach the kid in time. He hadn't used those muscles in forever, and everything felt stiff and unlimber. He should have sent Chee after him. With all the sergeant's face kicking and leaping around in the air, he would have been a better choice.

He could hear Shaniah calling after him, but her voice was drowned out in the noise of Chee laying down a spray of gunfire and trying to slow the Archaics' advance.

Thirty yards to go, his legs churning, the kid coming at him like a little gray blur. He pushed harder, his boots digging into the dirt.

Something flashed past him on his right, there so suddenly he flinched and almost pulled his pistol to shoot it. It was Shaniah. She was moving even faster than she had on the roof.

She blew past him and Billy a few yards later and skidded to a stop, the Archaics nearly on top of her. Her long knife was in her hand as she threw back her head and shouted in a long, loud cry unlike anything Hollister had ever heard. A strange mixture of animal, human, and something else pierced the night like a blade.

The Archaics stopped in their tracks.

Billy kept running toward the jail.

Chapter Forty-six

The fool! Shaniah cursed as she ran. Chee stayed behind her firing his bewitched rifle and she sprinted down the street in Hollister's wake. He was fast for a human, but not fast enough. It was a surprise to find the human boy still alive. Convincing Hollister to abandon his search had not been easy. She looked foolish now, and had no choice but to attempt to rescue the child.

She rushed past Hollister and put herself between the Archaics and the two humans. This group rushing down the street was made up of initiates, and they might not have known it yet, but she was their queen. It was time for them to learn she would not be disobeyed. The alpha takes the prey first.

The change came over her, eyes burning red, fangs descending, and her jaw pushing forward. Throwing back her head, she gave a great bellowing cry, full of anger, rage, and challenge.

It worked. The Archaics stopped, confused. Crazy and

wild-eyed with hunger, they eyed her warily, unsure what she was, but sensing her power.

Shaniah pitied them. When one is first turned, for days and sometimes weeks, the need for an initiate to feed is nearly all encompassing. The stress and metamorphosis the human body undertakes requires a nearly constant source of food.

But they were also a pack culture and there was an instinct toward hierarchy now imprinted on their newly Archaic brains. Shaniah was about to establish the pecking order.

There were thirteen of them standing. A few more staggered in the streets farther back, still fighting the effects of the man-witch's elemental bullets.

"Hollister," she said, knowing he stood a few yards behind her. "Run."

He couldn't see her face and she was sure he had no idea how she was holding the creatures in check, but for once he did something smart. Billy had already run past him like his tail was on fire, and Hollister spun and ran after him.

A few seconds later, Billy reached the jail and Chee hollered for them to let the boy back in. But he stayed in the street waiting until Hollister skidded to a halt next to him.

Chapter Forty-seven

Stopping next to Chee, Hollister realized the last few minutes had taken a toll on him. His ankles and knees ached from his jump off the roof, he was winded, and his leg muscles were cramping up. He hoped they could get inside the jail and hole up until daylight, when they might have a chance to get out of this mess.

Yet, he had already decided he wasn't leaving Shaniah out here alone. There were too many Archaics here, even for her, and if he was ever going to find the one who'd killed his men, he was going to need her.

"How do you suppose she is doing that?" Chee asked.

"Haven't the foggiest," Hollister said.

"Should I shoot?"

"Not yet," Hollister said, drawing his pistols as he did. "Let's see what happens."

The Archaics from the rooftops had disappeared. One lay in the street about twenty yards away, apparently dead or severely injured and Hollister wondered if the silver or wooden bullets had found a way to kill it—something that was previously unknown to Van Helsing or the other members of the Order of Saint Ignatius who had studied these creatures. But Hollister knew there were more Archaics in this town than the dozen or so Shaniah somehow held in check.

In fact he was sure they were being watched. It was the same feeling he'd had in the army. He could remember riding the plains with the army, chasing Sioux or Cheyenne and knowing they were out there but never seeing them. It was unsettling.

He took his eyes off the drama up the street and studied the buildings, the alleys, the hiding spots, but he saw nothing.

"Chee?" he said.

"Yes, Major, I feel it too. She has done something to capture their attention and though we can't see them, I have a feeling we are surrounded."

"Well, shit, Chee, that ain't comforting at all. How many rounds you got left?"

"Forty-seven," he replied.

"Forty-seven. You're sure. Not fifty-two or forty-three? Forty-seven on the dot?" Hollister asked, unsure if the younger man was pulling his leg.

"I like to keep track of my ammo, sir," he said. "Doesn't everyone?"

Hollister just shook his head, checking the loads in both of his pistols. He made a vow to himself that if he survived this, if he ever faced these creatures again, he would arm himself with far more than two Colts and a knife. Perhaps a pistol in each boot, a rifle and shotgun for his back. A sword. And maybe a cannon, if he could figure out a way to carry it.

"Well, Sergeant, I can tell you I have considerably less than forty-seven rounds, but I don't know exactly. And I thought I left the train with plenty of ammunition. I guess from now on, we need to make every shot count."

"Yes, sir," Chee said.

Their attention went back to the street. Something was happening.

* * *

Shaniah stood her ground. She could not back up, shift her feet, or move in a way that showed any weakness. The Archaics were getting restless. She wasn't sure where the attack would come from, but a big burly man stood out from the rest. He wore a leather apron, what was left of it, torn and covered in blood, and Shaniah guessed he might have been a blacksmith. Where the others had begun to fidget and prance back and forth, wild with hunger but confused and held in place by her appearance, he moved very little, watching her every movement.

She gave another loud howl and swung the blade through the air in a mighty arc. These initiates had not mastered speech yet, their voices stilled by their rapidly changing physiology. Most could not speak in Archaic form for weeks after turning.

"I am Shaniah, your Queen. In time you will come to serve me. Now you obey. You will feed when I allow it. You will follow my commands. This is how it has been and always shall be."

Nothing she said was remotely true. Her position as leader of her people was an elected one. She was not "served" by her people. The Archaics of the high mountains were a small, self-sustaining society and while it was true that she could make decisions for her people, she had been chosen by the Council of Elders because she was the Archaic who was the best hunter, the strongest, the most cunning. She had earned her place through action and example, not by fighting it out as she had heard other groups like the wolf people did.

She needed to exert her will on this group. If they learned to shelter themselves from the sun, they could keep Hollister and the others penned up inside the jail until they starved. There was no time for that.

Her words caused some consternation among the group. It was almost certain they could understand her. Their primitive instincts were just in charge and difficult for them to control. They wanted to kill and eat Hollister and the rest in the jail. For them there was no other course to take.

The blacksmith had slowly worked his way to the front of the group, acting as if he had no interest in anything going on around him. Shaniah set her feet, tightening her grip on the blade. His attack was sudden, and even though she was prepared, his quickness surprised her. He leapt in the air the ten feet or so between them. The blacksmith had been one of the most recent to turn, so he would not disintegrate to ash yet. It was a lucky break for her.

Shaniah did not hesitate. Swinging the blade, she rotated her hips, her arms and shoulders pouring every ounce of strength she had into it. The big knife connected with the man at his neck and his head came off as if she had sliced through a melon. His body collapsed to the ground and with one hand, Shaniah snatched his head out of the air, her fingers twisted in his long dark hair. She held the head up, brandishing it at the Archaics, her eyes burning with rage.

"Do NOT disobey me!" she commanded, tossing the head at the assembled group, who scattered, stumbling over each other to get out of the way.

Now came the dangerous part.

She spun on her heel, walking toward the jail, her back exposed to them, but without haste, as if they were no threat to her at all.

Chapter Forty-eight

Hollister and Chee stood dumbstruck as Shaniah strolled almost casually down the street. The further removed from the Archaics she got, the more restless they became. It didn't seem like their patience would hold much longer and Shaniah quickened her pace a bit, until she finally reached the two of them.

"What the hell did you do?" Hollister asked. Shaniah shrugged.

"I would suggest we get inside the jail, quickly. They have been momentarily cowed. It won't last long," she said.

Hollister wasn't sure bringing Shaniah inside the jail with the women and children was a good idea. Yet she had saved his life a half dozen times in the last ten minutes and he could not see making her fend for herself out here. But he was not taking a fox into the henhouse either.

"Give me your knife," Hollister said.

"What? No!" she said.

Jonas didn't waste time. "Here is how it is. You want my help finding this 'Malachi' as you called him. All right. We can talk about it. But right now, we've got to survive until morning at the least, and I've got women and children inside the jail. I'm not letting you in there with a weapon. So make up your mind."

Shaniah felt like taking Hollister by the throat. But when her flash of anger subsided, she could see his point. And would likely have done the same thing, had she been in his position. She held out the knife, blade down, and he secured it in his gun belt.

Noticing the sullen look on her face, he tried giving her a charming smile. "Don't worry. If the Archaics show up again, I'll be sure you get it back."

"If they come back, you'll likely die," she said.

"Touché," Hollister said. "Sally! We need to come in."

"Hold it, Major," Chee said, raising the rifle. Hollister turned; with one free hand each, they exchanged coins. Both were clear. Shaniah looked puzzled but the two men said nothing.

There came the sound of the wooden timber being lifted from inside, and the door squeaked open. The three of them shot through and Hollister resecured the door. Chee made no acknowledgment of anyone or anything, going right back to the window and peering through the shooting port, rifle at the ready.

Shaniah wasn't sure where to go. The women and children stared at her with a mixture of distrust and fear, several of them cowering and pushing closer together in the office corner. Shaniah herself did not look comfortable standing next to Chee and for a few moments she fidgeted until she took a spot beside the desk and in the opposite corner from where the woman and children had gathered. She studied the door to the cell block, now chained, and pretended to be interested in any mundane thing she could find.

"Who is she?" Sally asked. "I ain't ever seen her before."

"She's new in town," Hollister said, trying to sound at ease.

"How come she's got blood all over her?" Sally continued.

Hollister hadn't really paid attention in all the excitement, but now noticed both he and Shaniah were splattered in blood from their fights with the Archaics.

"We . . . ah . . . ran into a little bit of trouble," Hollister said. "How's Billy?" he asked, trying to change the subject.

Billy sat on his mother's lap. She held him seated on the floor, pulling him tightly to her, sobbing gently and rubbing his hair. Surprisingly, he looked none the worse for wear.

"Appears fine," Sally said, not taking her eyes off Shaniah. "She one o' them?"

"One of whom?" Hollister asked, not wanting to answer and waiting for the trouble he had a pretty good idea was coming.

"You know. A night demon. She don't look right," Sally said.

Hollister couldn't imagine how that could be, because aside from all the blood staining her clothes and the many creatures he'd seen her kill almost bare-handed, she looked like the most all-right woman he had ever seen.

"No. She's not one of them. She's hunting them though. She lost someone who was taken by these things and came to my aid in town. They can be killed and she knows how to do it."

His answer appeared to satisfy Sally for a moment, but she kept a wary eye on Shaniah. The other women were whispering and murmuring among themselves and Hollister had a feeling they were going to figure out Shaniah's true nature before long. Luckily, he didn't have time to worry about it.

"Major," Chee said, his voice barely above a whisper. "We've got company again."

Hollister peered out the port. The Archaics Shaniah had stood off now gathered in front of the jail. They weren't doing anything, just standing, watching. Hollister counted twenty-two now and he wondered how many were left in town. He disliked being pinned down like this, unable to do reconnaissance and find out what he was up against.

The moon was moving lower in the sky. Hollister checked his pocket watch. It was past 3 A.M. Suddenly the Archaics turned to look at something down the street, and from their vantage point neither he nor Chee could see what it was.

A moment later, two more Archaics arrived, each of them carrying torches.

"I thought they didn't like fire," Hollister muttered.

"Where did you hear that?" Shaniah said quietly and he jumped for she was right behind him. He'd had no idea she'd moved from her original spot. "We're quite familiar with fire and its many uses."

"I read it in Van . . . somewhere. From a trustworthy source."

"Well your source is wrong. You are thinking of vampires, not Archaics. Fire will burn us, like a human, but it cannot kill us. From what I have heard, fire does kill vampires. Our accelerated healing makes it an annoyance at worst. A fire will slow us down and only make us angry."

"As if you ain't naturally angry enough already." Hollister snorted.

Shaniah ignored him.

"What are they doing?" Hollister said, changing the subject.

"If I had to guess, I would say they are going to smoke you out," she said.

Their next move surprised all of them.

One of the males holding a torch spoke. "We would speak to the female," he said.

"I think he's asking for you," Hollister said, looking at Shaniah, who never took her eyes off the Archaic in the street. "What does he want?"

"I have no idea," she said. "This is . . . this is . . . not right. Those men should not yet be able to speak . . . unless . . ." she paused thinking, pacing back and forth.

"Unless what?" Hollister demanded.

"Malachi sent them here," she said.

"Malachi . . . just to be clear. He's the really tall guy with the white hair?" Hollister asked again.

"Yes. This means he's getting stronger, he's nearly . . . well, we can discuss it later. Suffice it to say, he's powerful enough now to turn a whole town if he wants to. Those would be his soldiers he sent to start the turning and the killing."

Hollister was caught a little off guard. Tired and sore from his exertions, he was stumbling over what to do next.

"Do you think he's here?" Hollister asked.

She shook her head. "No. I would be able to tell if he was."

"How?"

"Many ways. Smell mostly."

"Nice," Hollister said.

"It is not the only way. Archaics who have lived many years develop a sense of each other—a connection, you might call it. We are always able to tell when another is nearby. I don't sense him here or even anywhere close. But I suspect those two are among his most valued soldiers."

"How do you know that?" Chee asked.

"Because it is what I would do," she said. Hollister wondered if she even noticed how she drew back a little when she spoke to Chee. Something about him made her nervous. He didn't know what it was yet, but he wanted to find out. It might come in handy.

"Sally, can you come here a minute?" he asked the young woman.

She joined them at the window and they made room for her to see out the port. She let out a sharp breath of fear upon seeing all the Archaics.

"It's okay, Sally," he said. "Do you recognize either of the men holding those torches? Are they from around here?"

She studied them and shook her head.

"I don't recognize 'em. I mean there's people comin' and

goin' all the time in a minin' town. But I ain't never seen 'em before." She looked up at him and he thought she might have the brownest eyes he'd ever seen. But there were so many lines on her face for someone so young and he felt a little sad, thinking of the hard life she must have faced. He wanted to get her out of here. Out of this jail and this town. To get her somewhere safe where she might have a chance.

"Thanks, Sally," he said. "Would you mind keeping an extra eye on Billy for me? I don't want him surprising us again and I'm not sure his mother is . . . well, I just need someone I can trust keeping a watch on things."

Sally nodded, and the look on her face told him she knew she was being dismissed, but she had the good grace not to say anything about it. The women were quiet but the children were stirring and he heard one of the little girls whine about being hungry. He realized they had left the food and water in the cells when they escaped. He toyed with the idea of trying to retrieve the supplies but with a glance at the creatures pacing about in the street, he rejected it. They would have to hold out a little longer.

"Just so you know there is something wrong with the one you call Billy," Shaniah said.

"What do you mean wrong?" Hollister asked.

"He doesn't smell right. He may have been turned," she said.

"But you can't be sure?" Hollister said.

"No, it has been so long since I have been near a human child turned Archaic, I can't be sure. But you should kill him, just to be safe," she said.

With that, Chee swung the rifle around so it was inches from her temple. Shaniah did not flinch, but the two of them stared at each other like two bulls sharing a pasture.

"We do not kill children," he said.

Hollister pushed the rifle away from Shaniah and back to its proper place in the shooting port. "Chee, let's try to remain friendly. Shaniah, please avoid talking about child killing as it tends to rile up my sergeant."

Hollister was still struggling with a next step, when one of the torch bearing men spoke again.

"We would speak to the female," it said. The voice was deep, with a raspy, breathless quality and Hollister remembered how Malachi had sounded on the Wyoming plain.

"Like a snake trying to talk," he muttered.

"Sir?" Chee asked, confused.

"Nothing," he answered.

"When they feed on human blood, their voices change. It affects their internal organs. In the old days it was one of the ways an Archaic could be judged for breaking Archaic law by feeding on humans."

The sound of the voice sent the women and children inside the jail into a frenzy.

"Oh God, oh God, oh God," Rebecca moaned from her spot in the corner. This started some of the younger children to crying.

"Hush now," Sally whispered to them. "It's gonna be all right."

"I'm ready for suggestions," Hollister said quietly to Shaniah and Chee.

"Open the door," she said. "Let me talk to them."

"I don't think so," Hollister said. "Let me rephrase that. I'm ready for suggestions that don't involve opening the door. I send you out there and you're overwhelmed. We're going to need you to get out of this."

"I may be able to talk them into giving up," she pointed out.

"They don't look like they're in a giving-up mood. And there's about three times as many as you faced in the street. Plus these two new fellows, they don't look like they'd spook as easy," Hollister said. "Like it our not, next to Chee here, you're my most valuable weapon. I can't afford to lose you."

She was actually worth about ten Chees, but he didn't want to hurt the young man's feelings.

"We would speak to the female now!" the same man hollered again. The other Archaics stood behind the two men, looking nervous and jumpy. Or hungry. Jonas couldn't tell.

A few minutes passed and everyone was silent. Then the next step was taken for them as the two men stepped forward, hurling their torches onto the roof of the jail.

Chapter Forty-nine

The torches spun through the darkness and landed atop the building with a thud. At first, Hollister thought they might be okay, maybe the torches wouldn't catch, but there was a large sound of rushing air and the smell of something burning. The flames lit up the street in front of the jail and Hollister wondered about earlier in the night when the Archaics had jumped on the roof, stomping all around. They must have been preparing it to burn somehow.

The smell of smoke filtered down through the ceiling and now not even Sally's ministrations could calm the children and women.

"You need to do something about your people," Shaniah said to Hollister.

"Like what?" he said, not happy at the distraction.

"You should kill them," she said matter-of-factly.

The words stopped him, although Chee didn't flinch. Not because he would ever consider following her suggestion, but more because he was not surprised by it. Hollister couldn't understand what little dance they were in engaged in, but he would sure as shit find out. When he wasn't so preoccupied with not getting killed.

"You can't be serious," he said.

"They are going to die. Either we all burn to death, or they are killed by the Archaics. No matter the method, they are just as dead. A bullet now is more merciful," she said.

"And you're all about the mercy?" he asked, trying and failing to keep the sarcasm out of his voice.

"The quality is not unknown to me," she said.

"Yeah, well, funny way of showing it. They aren't going to die. Not if I have anything to say about it," Hollister said.

The smoke was now curling down into the room and the air in it would soon no longer be breathable.

"All right. Maybe they don't have the back covered; we go through the cell block, Chee and I exit the window first, the children and the women come next. We might have enough ammo to keep them at bay until we get to the train."

"That's it? Excuse me for saying, but in my country we do not call that a plan," Shaniah scoffed.

"Never been to your country. Don't care what it's called there," he said.

"Major. Sir?" Chee said, interrupting.

"Sergeant?"

"Begging your pardon, sir, but the window won't work, Major. Two of the women yonder are . . . stout . . . they'll never fit through and I don't think it's big enough for one of us to shoot through while the other climbs out of it. One of those things will be on us before we get our feet out the opening," he said. Hollister could tell it bothered Chee to criticize his plan. But he was right.

"In my country we would call this suicide," Shaniah snarled as if wanting to finish her thought.

"It's going to have to be the front door, sir," Chee said. "We're going to have to rush them, guns blazing. Maybe Monkey Pete will come . . ."

"He won't. I gave him orders not to," Hollister said. Everyone jumped as one of the roof timbers cracked and sparks fluttered down from the ceiling.

"Again, you have a monkey?" Shaniah asked.

"NO," he and Chee both answered at the same time.

Hollister tried to think. He had been out of command situations for nearly four years. His decision-making abilities, which had been lightning quick in his army days, had atrophied. He'd not faced anything like this, not in Winchester, Cold Harbor, or anyplace else during the war. The only thing that compared was when he'd lost his men to these things on the plains. He hated the feeling. He wasn't going to lose again. Not if he had to kill every single one of these sons of bitches with his bare hands.

The flames lit up the night, dancing and flickering in the darkness, and by the looks of the reflections in the windows across the street, they were starting to spread to the adjacent buildings. There was another loud crack and more sparks and now smoke rolled into the room and the women and children started to cough. Outside the Archaics had backed away from the fire, and while Shaniah said they had no innate fear of it, he wasn't so sure this was the case. They all studied the flames as if they wanted to keep their distance.

"All right," he said, drawing Shaniah's knife from his belt and handing it to her. "We're going out. Chee, I'll take the point, the women and children next, and you bring up the rear. Shaniah, if you're with us, if you could do what you can to protect our flanks . . ." He drew a Colt from his holster and offered it to her but she shook her head, holding up the knife instead.

"All right . . . we're going to have to make every shot count and we can't assume that's all the Archaics in that group there. Could be more about, so . . ." He stopped as Chee put his hand on his arm.

"Did you hear that, sir?" Chee asked.

"Hear what?"

"It sounded like . . . barking . . ." Chee said, his eyes on the street.

"I didn't hear a th . . ." But then he did. A loud, deep bark.

Down the street came Dog, barking and churning up the ground in great leaps. The Archaics watched in stunned silence as the great beast ran directly to the jail door, where Chee had lifted the timber beam and pulled it open. Dog slipped in, barking, and leapt on Chee, pushing him backward against the door and slamming it shut, his paws on the sergeant's shoulders and licking his face.

Hollister noticed then, the dog was wearing some kind of harness, and held in place by two leather straps was the Ass-Kicker.

"Huh," Hollister said.

Hollister removed the harness from Dog's back. The giant animal appeared not to even know it had been carrying the heavy gun. Hollister hefted the weapon into the crook of his arm and instantly felt about one thousand times better. He checked the gauge, unnecessarily he knew, for Monkey Pete would not have sent it less than fully charged. He drew back the slide and smiled at the slight hiss of steam exiting the valve. *All right, you blood-sucking bastards. Say hello to my Archaic-Ass-Kicking friend.*

Dog had been so happy to see Chee, he had momentarily forgotten about the rest of the people in the room. He ignored Hollister as usual, but he stepped toward the children and women huddled in the corner and huffed, and then stretched so his forepaws were down on the ground like he wanted to play, wagging his tail in joy. The children were scared at first but as they watched Dog clowning it up, their demeanor changed. The cries and whimpering stopped and a few giggles escaped from their tired mouths.

"I bet you wouldn't ignore me if I had a side o' bacon, you big fur ball," Hollister said. Dog looked at Hollister; that was when he noticed Shaniah and his demeanor changed.

He growled low in his throat and took a few cautious steps toward her, his body tense, the hair on his neck standing up. He looked ready to spring at any moment.

"I can easily kill this dog," Shaniah said quietly. Hollister didn't doubt it, but the words did not sit well with his sergeant. Before he had a chance to say anything, Chee spoke up.

"Come near the dog, harm it in any way, and you will walk the *Qui chen* forever," Chee said.

"Chee, what exactly is *Qui chen*?" Hollister asked.

"A river in hell," Chee said.

"Oh," said Hollister. "Easy you two. Let's not walk any rivers anywhere, all right?"

Shaniah stared at him for several seconds as the smoke in the room thickened. There wasn't much time.

"I mean it. No trouble between you two. Sergeant, that's an order. We're on the same side here," Hollister said. "Chee, load up."

"Sally, we're getting out of here. Everyone up and ready," he said.

"No . . . no . . . no . . . no . . . we can't go out there . . . the demons will kill us all. They'll kill . . ." Rebecca had started to moan and wail, but Sally covered the ground between them in a flash and smacked her hard across the face.

"You shut up now, you tired hag. Come with us or stay, but you git ready," she commanded. Rebecca's mind was gone. It just went away to another place, her mind broken like a fine china plate that had fallen to the floor. Hollister didn't think Rebecca was ever coming back from this.

"I'm going out first and I'm going to give those sons-abitches a special hello," he said, holding up the Ass-Kicker. "We all go south on First Street and head for the train siding. We've got help there and we'll be safe. They can't set fire to it and we can outrun them anyway. The three of us will protect you." He was interrupted by a growl from Dog. "Excuse me, the four of us can protect you. We can do this. You have my word." For effect, Hollister worked the handle attached to the main action on his gun, and the sound it made as the steam hissed and the round popped into place was loud in the room, which was reassuring to him at least. It was time.

Chee moved away from the door and returned to the port. He could get off a couple of shots from there if he needed to before they had to exit.

Hollister removed the timber from the door.

"Ready?" he asked. Shaniah and Chee nodded. Dog sat on his haunches next to Chee waiting to see what happened next.

Hollister threw open the door with a bang. The Archaics across the street turned toward the noise as one, reminding Hollister of a herd of antelope spotting a grizzly bear.

"You wanted to talk? Let's talk!" he shouted. He stepped out into the street, no more than twenty yards away from them now. Three of them leapt in the air toward him and he leaned forward, ready for the recoil this time. From the waist he aimed the Ass-Kicker in their direction and pulled the trigger.

There was a quick whoosh of steam, then the weapon fired and jerked in his grip. The noise was deafening. The bullet, which he'd decided was really more like a mortar round, hit the first Archaic and exploded. The percussion wave tore through the creature like shrapnel through butter. His body flew apart in pieces and the other two were knocked backward a good ten yards where they spun into the ground. He didn't think they were dead but they were down. Likely for quite a while.

"Let's go!" he yelled. He started running toward the train and from the corner of his eye he saw Shaniah dart out of the jail, followed by the first of the women and children. Holding the Ass-Kicker in his right hand, he drew his Colt from the left holster. He had a load of silver and holy water bullets and he wanted to use them all before he fired the big gun again.

He aimed for legs. The bullets seemed to cause the creatures great pain and he surmised that if it didn't kill them, perhaps being shot in the legs with ammunition that was clearly poison to them might slow them down even more. His first shot found its mark and a female fell to the ground, her hands clawing at the wound.

His display with the Ass-Kicker had the desired effect. The Archaics shadowed them, still in pursuit but parallel to them and not willing to engage yet. Hollister knew this was temporary, as their need to feed would overcome them before long and they would attack.

He risked a look backward and found Sally and Shaniah leading the group from the jail with Chee behind them. He was running and effortlessly firing the Henry, taking out more targets. The roof of the jail collapsed and he was momentarily relieved to have gotten everyone this far.

They had almost made it to the end of the street when the next wave of Archaics attacked. His Colt was empty, so he holstered it, cocking the action on the Ass-Kicker. The valve hissed and the gear turned, and just like that, it was ready to fire. The rail spur was another hundred yards away. He tried to angle himself toward the Archaics so the gun would cut as wide a swath as possible. It was difficult with them all moving around, running and jumping as they debated whether to come at him again.

"Come on, you sonsabitches!" he yelled.

The women and children were in a tight bunch behind him, with Shaniah and Dog on each flank. Chee brought up the rear, keeping up a steady fire with the Henry. Sally was in the middle of the group toward the front, carrying a small child in one arm waving her Colt around with the other. He wasn't sure if she'd fired it yet or not.

An Archaic charged toward Dog's side of their small column, perhaps thinking it was the weak point. It cost the creature the use of its right arm as Dog leapt, meeting the fiend in the air and taking hold of the limb, twisting them both to the ground. The creature screamed as Dog clamped down, breaking the Archaic's bones and shaking it like a dead cat.

Rounding the intersection, a phalanx of Archaics came directly at them. Hollister skidded to a stop, set his feet, and fired the gun, with devastating effect. It hit the first Archaic in line, blowing through her and the one behind her, and taking off the arm of a third. The rest of the group scattered into the shadows.

"Keep going!" he shouted. He could see the train sitting on the track in the distance. It looked a hundred miles away.

He pulled back the action on the Ass-Kicker and another round ratcheted into the chamber. Two shots left. Hollister had found when testing the gun that each shot lost power until the gun could be recharged. The final shot was about half as powerful as the first, but still did some damage.

Ten yards down Second Street they ran, then twenty. Thirty yards. The Archaics held back but were regrouping. Forty yards down the street, still a long way to the train. *They won't let us reach the end of the street*, he thought.

"Hold on! Here they come!" he shouted.

As if they'd read his mind, the creatures surged into the street. He managed to wound four with the remaining rounds in his Colt, missing two others, but now both pistols were empty. Archaics burst out of the doors of the buildings as if they were running to a fire. Four or five of the creatures stood on the roof of the walkways and beneath them, four more poured out of the general store. They had heard his big gun shoot and were cautious. Hollister aimed the Ass-Kicker at one of the wooden posts holding up the roof over the walkway and his shot obliterated the pillar. The weight of the creatures on the roof collapsed it and crushed those standing below it.

"Bastards!" Hollister screamed. *If I live through this, I will apologize for my language later*, he thought.

"Don't stop!" he shouted. He realized then they had too far to go. They weren't going to make it. He stopped, gestur-

ing for the group to keep moving past him. "Keep going!"
Shaniah and Dog kept the children and women moving
toward the train. Chee pulled up next to him as if to stop,
but Hollister pushed him toward the train. "Get these people
on the train!"

Hollister gave the group a good twenty yards head start
and then spun around, working the action on the steam-
powered gun, his next shot ready. A large group of Archaics,
more than he could count, surged toward him. He fired into
the crowd. There were howls of pain and anger as Archaics
were blown apart and others went down. He spun the gun
around on the sling and used the distraction to slap his final
two speed loaders into his Colts. He ran for the train.

"Monkey Pete! Open up!" he shouted. The train looked
eerily deserted, the iron doors still in place and no sign of
the engineer in the gunner's turret on top of the armory car.
For a god-awful minute he worried that Pete was dead. The
Archaics had managed to somehow breech the train's de-
fenses. Now what? Even if they could get aboard, no way
could he and Chee drive the thing.

A flash of light appeared on top of the armory car and the
ground exploded in small pockets of dirt and sod behind
him. As the sound reached him, he recognized the thumping and crackling of the Gatling gun being fired. One of the
bullets whizzed past his ear.

"Holy shit!" he yelped as the ground around his feet
erupted. He ran faster, trying to put more space between him
and the pursuing Archaics.

The shooting kept up as they covered the last fifty yards,
all of them stopping at the side of the train. The firing had
had a devastating effect on the creatures. There was enough
light now for Hollister to see Monkey Pete in the turret with
a big grin on his face.

"Pete!" Hollister cried. "Let us in! Your fancy shooting
won't stop them for long."

"Yes, sir! Give me a second!" the engineer replied. He

disappeared with a hiss as his seat lowered out of sight. There was no sound from inside for several seconds. Jonas waited for the doors to open, but they didn't.

"Pete! God damn it, haul ass!" he commanded.

He was loading his last four bullets left from his gun belt into his Colt, watching as the Archaics cautiously approached, when the door to the train slid open. Monkey Pete stood there with a hose in his hand. Before Hollister could say anything, he opened the valve and high-pressure water shot out, drenching them all except Shaniah, who with her quick reflexes managed to dive under the train and avoid the watery blast.

"Pete! What the hell!" He spat water.

"Sorry, Major. It's holy water. Ain't letting anybody on my train unless they are who they say they are."

"Well I can vouch for all of us—"

He was interrupted by the sound of someone groaning.

Behind him on the ground lay Billy, twisting in agony as the water burned his skin.

Chapter Fifty

"Demon!" Rebecca shrieked, pointing at the boy writhing in the dirt.

"Get Billy inside," Hollister shouted.

He glanced back at the Archaics. They were regrouping forty yards out, the memory of Monkey Pete's Gatling fresh in their minds. But they were getting ready to charge again. He had learned to recognize their approach.

"No time! For this! Chee! Grab the kid, the rest of you get on the train!" The children and women piled onto the train. Chee grabbed hold of Billy and followed. Shaniah waited.

"What are you waiting for?" he asked her.

"I think I should depart."

"Why?"

"I am not welcome here," she said.

"Maybe not. But I still need your help," he said.

"Yes you do. But you don't listen. You should kill the boy. He is an Archaic now."

"For God's sake I'm not killing a kid, I don't care what he is," Hollister said.

"He is turning. He has made no move yet, because his young mind can't grasp what is happening to his body. But he will become dangerous, and soon."

"Then we'll tie him up or something, we don't have time to argue. Get on the damn train!"

The roar from the Archaics sounded and they bounced forward, leaping in the air and covering great swaths of ground. Shaniah still hesitated.

"I've got questions, and you said you needed my help. Well, I need yours, so what'll it be?" he pleaded, casting a wary eye toward the approaching hordes and hoping like all hell she would say yes. He needed her fighting ability if they were going to live through this.

"All right," she said.

Hollister bounded up the steel steps and through the door. Shaniah tried to follow but was stopped at the threshold. She tried to push through but was stopped.

"What's wrong?" he asked.

"I don't know," she said. The Archaics were thirty yards away.

Hollister remembered the painted markings around the doors and windows. Van Helsing had said they were designed to keep out demons and other creatures.

"Ah crap, the devil's traps . . ." he said.

"What? Invite me in! Hurry!" Twenty yards.

"Invite . . . what the hell? Shaniah, get in here!" he shouted.

The spell broken, she burst through the door and he pulled the lever, watching the iron door slide down into place.

Billy appeared to be recovering but he was huddling in the corner by himself with no one else paying attention to him, not even his mother. Chee had gone to the armory car, and was now in the turret firing away. Hollister could hear the spit of the Gatling.

Something thudded against the side of the car and the train shook momentarily.

"Monkey Pete! Get us going! Back to Denver!"

Far ahead he heard the sounds of the engine starting up, but the train rocked back and forth and he worried it would be derailed before they could get under way.

He handed Shaniah a Colt from his holster and pulled a modified Henry from the rifle rack. Next to each door on either side of the car were small shooters' ports that could be cranked open. It wasn't a large field of fire, but it might drive off some of them.

He pushed the barrel through the port and it was nearly jerked out of his hands. An Archaic tried reaching through the opening, but the space was too small. With his other hand he pulled his Colt and fired point-blank, hitting it in the face and blowing the creature backward off the train.

Slowly, the engine came to life and they rolled back southward, in the direction they had come from. Hollister hoped Pete was secure in the engine room, because they were up shit creek if something happened to the engineer.

More thuds sounded as the Archaics saw their opportunity slipping away. The train gathered speed and huffed slowly away, leaving Absolution behind. After two minutes had passed with no sound from outside, Hollister thought they might have made it.

Two more minutes passed and now the train was going at a good clip. It was hard to imagine, as fast as the creatures were, that they would be able to keep up.

A few minutes later Chee entered the car. "Looks like we made it, Major," he said. "They tried to chase us for a while, but eventually gave up."

"Chee, would you and Sally take these folks up to the galley and get them something to eat? I reckon they're starved. And have Pete telegraph Pinkerton about that town. The army needs to go and clear it out with artillery, nothing less than a battalion. Before somebody innocent wanders across it or that train arrives day after tomorrow. They're going to need to burn it down."

"Yes, sir," he said. He opened the door to the galley and

ushered the women and children into it, leaving Hollister, Shaniah, and Billy alone in the car. Billy now sat in the corner, his knees pulled up, his head down.

"I wondered how he could run so fast," Hollister mumbled under his breath. He looked at Shaniah, who was studying the small boy. "What's going to happen to him? Is he stuck at that age forever now? Like you?"

She shrugged. "Truly, I do not know. It has been centuries since . . . my people . . . we . . . do not normally . . ." She struggled, trying to come up with a way to explain something horrible in a way that wouldn't make Hollister gun her down on the spot.

"Archaics have existed for thousands if not tens of thousands of years. For the last several centuries, we have retreated high into the mountains of my homeland. Humans are too fertile, too clever, and too inventive. We could not keep up. We are hunters. Not inventors or industrialists. Despite our physical superiority, as you have just seen and as you have known from your first encounter with Malachi, we can be killed. Humans have spent many hours and resources coming up with inventive ways to kill us . . ."

"Kill or be killed it seems to me . . ." Hollister interrupted.

"I don't disagree. For many centuries, to Archaics, humans were nothing more than prey. But we could not compete, and since Archaics cannot procreate, no matter how many other Archaics we created, we were losing. Humans found weapons: control of the elementals, ways to thin our numbers, learning that fire and sunlight may not kill us but limits us in ways it does not limit humans. While your kind spread over the globe, we retreated in order to survive. The mountains hide us, and we hunt humans no more. We simply wish to live and be left alone."

"What's this got to do with Billy?"

"My point is, whenever it is, or was, necessary to . . . create . . . a new Archaic, we do not normally choose a child. Our society requires adults to survive. A child would not grow, would not gain the typical strength and instincts of an adult Archaic, so there is no point. I have never seen one, in fact," she said. "I was not able to cross the threshold over your train until you invited me. Since your man Chee carried the boy, perhaps the invitation was implied and therefore did not need to be spoken. Or perhaps your man-witch understood, and put Billy under some kind of spell and . . ."

"Whoa . . . whoa . . . Chee . . . is a . . . you think he's a . . ." Hollister started laughing. He didn't know why, but it was a relief somehow. The idea of Chee casting spells, that was rich. "Shaniah I think the only spell Chee casts comes from the barrel of a gun. But don't change the subject—why Billy, why now?" Hollister asked.

"I have no idea, Hollister. I can only surmise Malachi's intentions," she said.

"Surmise away," he said.

"He wants us to know, as you humans might say, that all bets are off. He wants to show you how cruel he is willing to be," she said.

"But to what end? What does this Malachi want?"

"It's quite simple really," she said. "He wants to destroy you."

Chapter Fifty-one

Slater and his men stayed mounted on horseback, and from the safety of the trees, watched the events at the train take place far below. It had taken some doing, but Slater had found where the train had gone. He managed to gather a dozen men and get there in time to catch the tail end of the "festivities."

Now watching the train puff its way out of Absolution and the creatures give up their pursuit, he had to admit this Hollister impressed him more and more. They had fought well and killed a passel of these creatures—and not only that, but they also managed to save a handful of women and children. It looked like they had hidden some heavy ordnance on their train, and that was duly noted—but fighting their way through those beasts and onto the train had been impressive. No doubt about it.

"Now what, Boss?" one of his thugs, named Nolan, asked.

"Now we get the hell out of here without those things catching sight or wind of us," he said.

"What do you suppose them things are, down there?" Nolan asked. Slater sighed at the man's stupidity.

"I'm sure I don't know," Slater said. "But let's avoid them just the same."

But Slater knew what they were. And he found it even more surprising that Hollister had allowed the woman to come aboard. Letting the fox inside the henhouse was a dangerous and confusing strategy, as Slater saw it.

He rode along, the train ahead of them nearly disappearing from sight. And a flood of emotions rolled through him. Curiosity, confusion, and just like in Torson City, fear.

Pinkerton had a cadre of at least twenty agents waiting at the warehouse when the train arrived. The trip had gone without incident. The children and the women all had blank stares, working through their trauma, trying to achieve some way of dealing with the horror they'd experienced. Billy stayed in Hollister's bunk, the door kept locked, and he and Chee took turns standing guard throughout the day.

Sally and the others mostly kept to themselves. Their world was no longer the one they thought they knew and it would be a struggle for them to find a place in it. Hollister was convinced that Sally would make it because she had the strength. Not to say she wouldn't be haunted by it, but she would find a way to push it down inside and move on.

Now that the Pinkertons were moving the people off the train, the lead man, a big, thick Irish thug named Mullen, came back on the train in the office car and stared hard at Shaniah, then Hollister. Jonas knew what was coming.

Mullen pulled a letter from the inside pocket of his jacket. "Got a letter here from Mr. Pinkerton, says we're supposed to take the woman and the boy with us." He handed it to Hollister, who put it on the desk without reading it.

"Uh-huh. Well, that's a problem. You're welcome to take the lad, but I've got a tactical situation and I am using the woman as an asset. So I'm going to have need of her for a while longer."

Mullen shook his head. A shade under six feet tall, he was a bull of a man, big head atop broad shoulders. For a moment, he put Hollister in mind of Senator Declan, but Mullen wasn't that smart. It was written plain as day on his face, scarred and cut in dozens of places. He wore a bowler cap and his upper lip carried a thick mustache. His nose was wide and flat and had been broken more than once. "I got my orders. Mr. Pinkerton wants any of these captured subjects brought to—"

"She wasn't captured," Hollister interrupted. Chee and Shaniah watched the exchange with quiet but slightly stunned expressions on their faces. "She voluntarily joined us and saved several lives. I'm going after more of these things and I need her."

"That's all well and good, but I have my orders and I answer to Mr. Pinkerton," Mullen said.

"And Mr. Pinkerton has given me full authority to run this operation as I see fit," Hollister added.

Mullen stood up from the chair across the desk from Hollister, making sure as he did so that his suit coat opened so everyone could see the double-rig shoulder holster he wore. The tooled leather held two pearl-handled pistols.

"Be that as it may, Mr. Pinkerton gave me strict instructions, and I intend to follow them." He looked at Shaniah, who had stood idly by. "Ma'am, I'm going to have to ask you to come with me."

Shaniah's gaze drifted between Hollister and Mullen before settling on the Pinkerton man.

"No," she said.

"I . . . excuse me?" Mullen said. He was one of those men whose size and demeanor usually intimidated everyone. Now it wasn't working, and it had thrown him off his game.

"I said, I won't be going with you," she replied.

"Ma'am, there's no need for this. We're just going to take you to a place where you'll be safe." He reached out with his arm as if to take her by the elbow. Hollister knew what was going to happen next, but Mullen had no idea.

With speed that could only fairly be described as inhuman, Shaniah grabbed Mullen by the wrist. She spun him around, his arm behind his back, her other arm wrapped around his throat, lifting him off his feet. Hollister and Chee both winced when they heard the crackling, tearing sound of his shoulder ligaments popping like firecrackers.

"Awww, goddammit, you bitch, turn me loose!" he begged. Shaniah did, pushing him forward as he staggered across the floor of the car, trying to right himself, until he crashed into the wall. He spun back toward them, his arm hanging loosely at his side, his face twisted in pain.

"As I said," Shaniah repeated quietly. "I will not be going anywhere with you."

Mullen looked at her, his eyes darting downward toward the pistol in the shoulder rig on his right side. His left arm was useless and his mind was trying to gauge if he could draw it in time to shoot the woman.

"If you draw your weapon, this time I will break your arm and not merely dislocate it," she said quietly.

Mullen's face took on a curious look. One that Hollister rarely saw in men he had gone up against. He was beaten and he knew it and his expression was neutral; neither angry or full of rage. But his eyes blazed. He needed to reassert himself somehow. Telling Pinkerton he had had his arm torn nearly off by a woman was not something he relished.

"I've got twenty armed men outside, waiting . . ." he said.

This time Hollister said, "Agent Mullen, I've no doubt you're a good man and do your job well. I'd be willing to bet you're one of Pinkerton's best. But I can tell you from personal experience Miss . . . Shaniah here is special . . . and if you had forty men outside it wouldn't matter. I know you're doing what Pinkerton asked of you. And I admire you for following orders. But I work for him too, and he's given me a lot of latitude. I'm telling you I need her."

"I got my orders," Mullen said. His voice was close to breaking, the pain from his dislocated shoulder starting to rage.

"Pinkerton has given me orders too. So let's just call this one a draw. I'll send a letter for you to take to him and explain everything. Will that work?"

Mullen was quiet a moment. Finally he nodded.

Hollister sat down at the desk, and scribbled out a note to Pinkerton. Blowing the ink dry, he folded it inside an envelope and handed it to the detective. "Thanks for this, Detective Mullen. I promise you I won't forget it."

Mullen stepped to the door, turned, and looked at Shaniah, then Hollister. "Neither will I," he said. He lumbered out of the train, slamming the door behind him.

"Do me a favor," Hollister said to Shaniah. "Next time, try not to injure the good guys."

"He put his hands on me. Unnecessarily," she said.

"I know, but the thing is, he's on our side, and if you go around breaking the arms of all the good guys, we're gonna run out of good guys and after what we just saw in Absolution, we're going to need a lot of them."

"Then instruct them to leave me alone," Shaniah said.

Hollister sighed.

"Chee, could you do me a favor and ask Monkey Pete to get the train under way again?"

"Yes, sir. Where to?" the sergeant asked.

"Head west, tell him I'll let him know our final destination shortly. We'll go as far as we can by train, then ride the rest of the way." On their way back to Denver, they had stopped and retrieved Demeter so Shaniah would have a mount if needed.

"Yes, sir."

"But make sure we reload before we depart, ammo, all the stuff Pete used at Absolution, speed loaders, rations, more loads for the Ass-Kicker. Whatever he thinks we need. Oh, and a cannon if he has one. And have him be quick about it. I want to be under way before Mullen and the rest of his Pinkertons out there change their mind."

"Yes, sir, but I don't think Monkey Pete has a cannon, sir," Chee said as he left the main car, leaving Shaniah and Hollister alone.

Shaniah walked along the train car, studying the drawings and paintings around the windows and doors. The weapons and other items stored in the rack.

"These drawings, around the windows, what is their purpose?" she asked.

"Well, I don't reckon if I should tell you or not," he said.

Shaniah looked at him, head cocked. "Really, it is some sort of human secret?"

"Naw, I was just joking with it. I don't think it matters one way or another. According to this fella we met, named Dr. Van Helsing, they are called devil's traps. He said there are creatures called vampires and these markings keep them from coming into someplace you don't want them."

Shaniah straightened up at the mention of Van Helsing. "I have heard of this man, Van Helsing, he has pursued a vampire Vlad Dracul for many years, it is said."

Hollister had questions.

"Do Archaics sleep? Do you have to rest?"

"Only when we have not fed for a very long time. It is one of the differences between us and vampires. Vampires must sleep every night in the soil from their native land. Archaics can go days, weeks without sleep as long as they are feeding."

"How do you know about Van Helsing? I thought you lived way up in the mountains. Don't seem like news would get up that way very easy."

Shaniah shrugged. "We are not without contact with the

human world. Dracul is a vampire, not an Archaic. We are similar but different. But we have heard of Van Helsing's pursuit of him."

Hollister stared at her, plainly not understanding the difference.

"As I have traveled your world, I have seen different species but the same in the animal kingdom. Horses, dogs, cows, all the same, but different, do you understand?"

Hollister nodded.

"Take horses. Certain breeds are faster, stronger, more surefooted. Others are slower of foot but less temperamental. They all have different characteristics. Such it is with . . . my world. We are Archaics. Even vampires know we are the oldest, longest living of our kind. Dracul, who your Dr. Van Helsing bases his studies on, is a vampire and not an Archaic. He can be killed by sunlight, not just burned by it. He must sleep in the dirt of his native soil at night or he weakens considerably. And unlike us, he cannot survive without human blood. Which in a way makes him more dangerous to humans. He is a different species. Does that make sense?

"Or think of it this way," she continued. "You might be able to kill a cheetah with a spear, but you need a gun to kill a lion. That is the difference between Archaics and vampires."

From what Jonas had read in Van Helsing's journals about vampires, and from what he'd seen of Archaics so far, they seemed like the same damn thing to him. But he wasn't going to start an argument.

He sat at the desk, unrolling the map Monkey Pete had marked up with abandoned mining camps. Shaniah continued to study the interior of the train and Chee finally returned from the engine room.

The silence among the three of them was nearly unbearable. Chee was naturally quiet anyway, but finally even he couldn't stand it anymore.

"Where are we heading, Major?" Chee asked.

"Just a hunch, but I've been studying the map here of all

the mining camps." He turned it around on the desk so Shaniah and Chee could see it.

"Something the Declan kid said. It's been bothering me,"
he said.

"What did he say?" Shaniah asked.

"He kept saying 'mine' . . . 'mine' . . . and at first I thought
he was just jabbering away about the mine in Torson City
and so we went to Absolution to see if there was a mining
connection and there is. Or was. But then something Shaniah said . . ." He was drawing circles on the map now, Chee
and Shaniah waiting patiently.

"What did I say?" she asked, growing impatient.

"You said he wants to destroy us, correct?" Hollister said.
Shaniah nodded.

"He does?" Chee asked. "You didn't tell me about this . . ."

"Didn't have a chance, but he's been killin' people right
and left, so it seems obvious he wants us all dead, doesn't
he?" Hollister asked, trying to mollify the sergeant.

"Yes . . . I suppose . . . but . . ." Chee started.

"You're right, Chee, I should have told you. I'm sorry."
Hollister wanted to move on.

"After what we've seen at Torson City, and Absolution,
there seem to be two logical places for him to hide. He
circled two small dots on the map, a town called Clady, in
southern Wyoming, and another called Lamont, in northern
Colorado.

Shaniah looked at the map. "What makes you so sure
Malachi would be in either of these places?"

"Tactics. I studied military tactics at a place called West
Point. It's where the government sends men to train them to
become military officers," Hollister explained.

Shaniah tried not to show surprise or emotion on her face,
but this was another reason she feared her people would
not survive the human incursion. They sent their best men
to places to study tactics and battle. Humans were far too
clever.

"And my study of military tactics tells me two things. Malachi needs a place to hide and gather his initiates, as you called them, and he also needs a place that's easier to defend. Of the two, I'd say Clady is the best choice."

"Why?" Shaniah asked, genuinely curious. She had been following Malachi blindly for years, using luck and intuition. Yet Hollister had come closer to finding him in a few days than she had in all this time. She needed to learn this thing he called tactics.

"Three reasons. One: it's a higher elevation so it's harder for us humans to attack; two: it's an abandoned mine, so it solves the problem with the sun; and three: it's been deserted a long time—no one coming in or out of town they need to worry about. A stranger who might report something," he said. "Also, if he's going to send soldiers out to turn humans, he's going to need a base. It makes the most sense, given where the other attacks have occurred."

Chee studied the map for a second longer then, nodded. No matter what, they needed to find this Malachi. Before he attacked Denver or some other densely populated place. The major's plan was as good as any.

"Chee, would you take the map to Monkey Pete and show him where we are headed?" Chee took the map and left.

"What if you're wrong?" Shaniah asked.

"Then I guess we'll just keep looking," Hollister said. "Until we find him, or he finds us."

Chapter Fifty-two

Monkey Pete had the train resupplied and on its way in a matter of hours. When it came to his train, Pete did not mess around. If Clady was the best choice, it was also the farthest away, and it would take them longer to get there.

While they traveled Chee and Dog made themselves scarce. Chee was clearly uncomfortable around Shaniah and she felt the same about him. He stayed in his bunk most of the time. Hollister had no idea what Monkey Pete did; he appeared with meals and the rest of the trip he remained in the front of the train doing Monkey Pete things.

Hollister and Shaniah spent most of their time in the main car talking, asking each other pointed questions and generally passing time. Each of them knew the other was trying to gather as much intelligence as they could on humans and Archaics, but their conversation was easy. Hollister supposed he should have been more wary, but something about this woman convinced him she was no threat. She would fight, she would kill if necessary, and she wore the mantle of leadership uneasily. And if forced to she would defend her people to the death, but she would not seek out confrontation.

But what he mostly saw in her was someone who wanted to protect her people and be left alone. She told him that until Malachi had gone rogue the Archaics had not fed on humans for centuries. They realized it was a losing proposition and so retreated high into the mountains and fought no more. He had no evidence of this but for some reason he believed her. According to her only a few hundred of her people remained. They were vastly outnumbered and once Malachi was stopped, she repeatedly assured him, they would pose no threat to humankind.

Hollister found her fascinating, and not just because of her beauty, which was immense, and not just because he had not been with a woman in literally years. She had a curious mind and she didn't laugh often, but when he made her laugh, it was like he'd won some sort of prize. As the miles rolled on, he found himself more and more attracted to her. He also knew this attraction was probably not a good idea. And he didn't care.

Nothing would likely have happened had there not been a problem with the train. After they had traveled a couple hundred miles from Denver and they were almost to Wyoming, the train slowed and stopped. Monkey Pete poked his head through the door of the main car.

"Got a problem, Major."

"What?" Hollister asked.

"Don't rightly know yet, something's gone wrong with one of the baffles. Might have sprung a leak and we're low on water, going to have to wait here a spell while I figure it out," he said. He went on with another long explanation, but to Hollister he might as well have been speaking Russian.

"I thought this train was indestructible," Hollister said.

"It purnt near is," Monkey Pete said, his face starting to redden, "but ain't nothin' mechanical that can't break down now and again. So you want to keep insultin' my train or you want me to fix it?"

Hollister held up his hands, "Fix it, by all means, Monkey Pete, I didn't mean anything by it. Do what you need to do."

"Hummph," Pete said, turning on his heel and leaving them behind.

"He makes all of this work?" Shaniah said, waving her hand in the air.

"He does," Hollister said.

"He is a genius?" Shaniah said.

"I guess that's as good a word as any to describe him," Hollister said.

"Where does it all come from?" Shaniah asked.

"What's that?"

"This. All of this," Shaniah said waving her hands again. "Your trains, your weapons, your 'tactics'—where does it come from?"

"I'm not sure I understand," Hollister said.

"We Archaics live in our mountains, away from humanity. We do so purposely, but we do not invent, we do not make advanced weapons or trains," she said. "We hunt. We live simply. It is not in our nature to 'invent.' But the human capacity for invention is . . ." She struggled to find the words.

"Without limits?" he offered.

"Yes. You have an answer for everything. If you don't have an answer, you build something. Or solve it. Or destroy it. How is that possible?"

"I don't know," Hollister said. "Maybe it's just how it is. You mentioned lions earlier. Lions don't invent. They just are. Maybe that's the way it is with Archaics. They just are. They are faster, stronger, more ruthless, so they don't need to invent." Hollister smiled.

"I had a dog when I was a kid. Little black mutt. Named him Apollo, after the Greek God of the sun. That dog loved to chase birds. Chased them every day of his life but never caught one. The birds saw him coming and just flew away. They didn't have to invent anything or shoot back at the dog—they just took to the air. Maybe some things are just like that. Humans like Monkey Pete have to figure things out. You and your people, you don't have a need to."

Shaniah thought about this for a moment. "Perhaps you are right. Except perhaps now it is a skill we need. It is far too late for us to develop this skill, and it is not in my people's will to surrender. So what do we do?"

"I've seen you in action. You don't really appear to need trains or advanced weapons when it comes to fighting," he said.

"Perhaps, but you humans learned not only weapons, but the elementals"—she pointed to the devil's traps—"while we learned nothing but hunting and killing. And now, if Malachi succeeds, we are done."

"Why do you say that?"

"If we do not stop him, you will send armies against us and we will be destroyed," she said.

He said nothing for a moment, because he knew she was right. If word of the Archaics spread, there would be an all-out assault and they would be wiped out.

"If for some reason we don't find him what will you do?" he asked.

"If we don't stop him, if we are discovered, we will die. I will do what I can to prevent that."

"But you just said yourself, you can't win," he said.

"True, Mr. Hollister, but what would you do?"

"I guess I'd do the same, fight, try to survive."

She said nothing else for a while and Hollister tried hard to think of something more positive.

"It'll be dark soon. What would you say if we took the horses for a ride? They could probably use the exercise."

"I would welcome that."

The stock car was at the rear of the train. Hollister had

Rose saddled in a short while, but Demeter was unwilling to let anyone but Shaniah come near him.

"Beautiful animal," Hollister said. "Little temperamental though."

"Demeter is bred for Archaics. Most horses, animals in general, shy away from us. He has been taught since birth not to fear us." She removed her cloak from her saddlebags and shrugged herself into it.

They rode up to the front of the train. Monkey Pete, covered in grease, stuck his head out the window of the engine.

"Pete, we're going for a ride, we won't go too far. When you're ready, give a couple of blasts on the whistle and we'll come back."

"Sure thing, Major. And don't worry. I nearly got this licked."

"I have no doubt, Pete, no doubt at all."

From the back of the train, Chee watched as they spurred their horses and rode away from the train, heading west until they disappeared into the trees.

Chapter Fifty-three

While Shaniah and Hollister had talked on the train, Chee had lain in his bunk, thinking about the woman, Dog taking half the bed as usual. After Absolution, he could not deny that her fighting skills were unparalleled. If what Hollister had told him about this Malachi was true, then she would be a valuable asset. And he had no reason to doubt the major.

Still, there was something off about the woman. There were words she did not speak. Important words. Things Hollister needed to know before he went into battle against this man, and yet she kept secrets. Chee was very good at telling when someone was lying. And what's more, the woman knew Chee was aware she was lying. He made her uncomfortable. Maybe it was his juju, maybe the spells and signs his grandmother had taught him as a boy—the things one could do to protect oneself from the supernatural.

He had tried to tell the major of his concerns, but so far, his suspicions had fallen on deaf ears. And the reason for that, Chee knew, is because the major was smitten with Shaniah. More than smitten. Chee could tell the man had

feelings for her. It was obvious in the way he looked at her.
And Chee understood the major's desire. She was a beautiful woman. No, she was more than beautiful. *Stunning* was
the word. The major had been in prison for many years, and
before that an unmarried officer on the frontier, and had had
little opportunity for female companionship.

But though he could not explain it, this woman brought
trouble with her.

Trouble for all of them.

They rode west over a slight rise through a small stand of
aspen. The land flattened out some into a large valley. The
weather was cooling down, a breeze coming out of the north
and Hollister was sure it would bring rain, probably before
nightfall. The floor of the valley held a large meadow and
they rode along at a gentle pace.

Shaniah tried to watch Hollister without his knowing,
staring at him through the folds of her hood. He rode nearly
effortlessly, moving with the horse almost before the horse
even knew where it was going. No doubt a result of his military training. *What an interesting man*, she thought.

The feelings confused her. Until she left the Archaic homeland to track Malachi, she hadn't interacted with a human in
nearly two centuries. She still had her human memories, and
the Old Ones had reminded her that this made her different. As their leader, she would need to find a way through
the coming clashes with humankind, and her remembrances
were an advantage.

Was this why Hollister intrigued her so? Shaniah did not
believe in destiny as the Old Ones did. Until she met Hollister and her memories of her long-dead husband, Dimitri,
came flooding back.

Archaics did not have children, but they did have sex. In
fact, they had it frequently, often, and athletically. But to her
knowledge, she had never heard of an Archaic having sex
with a human. In fact, she doubted any human could survive

it. But looking at Hollister, with his long legs straining in the stirrups and his broad chest rising and falling with the gallop of the horse—may the Old Ones forgive her, but she wanted to find out if he could.

She wanted to find it out more than anything.

Hollister had left the train not telling Chee where he was going on purpose. Chee was not happy with Hollister's growing closeness to Shaniah. At first, it had been a purely tactical decision. She knew more about Malachi and the Archaics than anyone else; she wanted his help for some reason. It made sense to find out what she knew.

But the part that made Chee uneasy was that it had now gone beyond that. He had heard them talk about things beyond just Malachi and his plans, or the Archaics and their history.

Hollister was attracted to her, and it was here that Chee had a point. Maybe he had crossed a line. She was beautiful, intelligent, and unlike any woman he had ever met. As they rode through the meadow, he tried to watch her without her knowing, but their eyes kept meeting, even through the folds of her hood.

It had been so long since he had even been close to a woman. Were the signals he remembered the same? The furtive looks, the quick smiles? *Forgive me, Sergeant Chee*, he thought. But I need to find out.

Chapter Fifty-four

Hollister reined Rose to a stop, then walked her toward a small stand of aspen and dismounted. Shaniah pulled up next to him, a curious look on her face.

"I thought we might let the horses graze awhile. The grass is good here," he said.

Shaniah slid easily off Demeter's back, stroking his mane and patting him gently on the rump. Unlike most stallions Hollister had seen, he showed little interest in Rose and took immediately to the grass.

Hollister walked to a spot beneath a large aspen and stood looking at the valley. It was about an hour before sundown and the view was gorgeous. The mountains surrounding them were still snow covered at the peaks, the trees were a gorgeous green, and the grass and wildflowers dotted the landscape with brilliant splashes of color.

"Your home," Hollister said. "It's in the mountains, in Europe, you said?"

"Yes," she said.

"What does it look like?"

"Why do you ask?" she said.

"No reason, I just . . . we . . . you and I survived a pretty horrible ordeal in Absolution and I feel like we're friends . . ."

"Friends?" she interrupted.

"Well . . . yes . . . I'd say if you survive a fight to death and you save each other's lives a couple of times, that qualifies as friendship."

"Is that how humans choose their friends these days? It is not how I remember it," she said.

"I just thought . . ." Hollister was thoroughly confused. "I only asked . . . I just wanted to know more about you . . . that's all. . . . I didn't . . ."

Shaniah stepped forward and kissed him. It was a nice kiss, soft at first, and Hollister was instantly aroused. She broke it off and stared at him, her hands on his shoulders.

"So, I guess this means we *are* friends?" he asked.

She laughed and kissed him again, pushing him back against the tree trunk. She removed her cloak and it fell to the ground at her feet.

"What about the sun?" he asked, concern in his voice.

She held a finger to his lips. "It is behind the mountains to the west. Do not worry." The kiss was different this time—more passionate and forceful. Her hands went to his cheeks and she ran them through his hair. She stopped again to look at him.

"Friends don't stop," he said, his breath coming in gasps.

What happened next, happened fast. She kissed him again, and then her hands were everywhere, pulling at his shirt, running over his chest. Her fingers probed the scars on his chest and back, the places where he'd been shot and stabbed during the war, but he was glad she didn't stop to ask him about them then. Time for that later.

The last thing he had any control over was pulling her to him, this time kissing her, his hands running through her long hair, his fingers pulling at the buttons of her blouse.

When he came to or woke up or returned to reality—for

he didn't think he'd been unconscious but he couldn't swear to it—they were lying next to each other on the ground beneath the aspen. The sun had set; he had no idea how much time had passed and didn't care. His entire body ached, but not in a bad way. During the war, after battle he often felt a curious blend of fatigue and exhaustion, his body sometimes so sore it hurt to move. When you were fighting for your life, the aftermath left you completely spent. So tired you believed you'd never be able to stand again, much less fight.

Hollister felt like that now, except he wasn't sore or fatigued. The exhaustion and soreness was there, but he felt unlike he'd ever felt in his life.

Shaniah lay next to him, naked and apparently not caring. Another reason Hollister decided he liked her.

"Can I ask you a question?" he murmured.

"Yes, of course. Anything," she said.

"This . . . what we just did . . ."

"Lovemaking?"

"Yes . . . sure . . . we can call it that . . . lovemaking," he stammered. "Is this the . . . usual way . . . of 'lovemaking' for your people?"

She tried not to laugh. "Yes, I would say it is 'usual.'"

"Dear Lord," he muttered under his breath. "And do you have a . . . over there, or back home, are you married or do you have a custom of . . . I guess what I'm asking is, do you have a husband?" Then he winced; this was probably the absolute wrong time to ask this question. He wanted to kick himself. Except he was too damn tired to kick anything.

If the question bothered Shaniah, she didn't show it. In fact, it didn't appear to affect her at all.

"I did once. No longer. We do marry; we take mates, for life. But in some cases our unions can be dissolved by the Council of Elders."

"I didn't mean to pry, but what just happened"—he turned on his side to face her, trying every way he could not to groan with the effort—"and what we just did was . . . trust me when I say it was indescribable. I just wanted to be sure . . . it was rude of me not to ask before . . . I . . ."

She interrupted him. Shaniah could not help but be charmed by his manners. "You broke none of our rules, Major Hollister, and you are right, it was quite indescribable." As she turned to face him, she pushed him onto his back.

Try as he might, Hollister could not help but let a small groan escape from his lips. Then everything started again, and despite it all, he found himself quite capable of feeling "indescribable" again.

This time, when it was over, Shaniah stood and dressed.

"It was you, wasn't it?"

"Me what?" she said.

"On the ridge in Wyoming. When Malachi attacked me and my men. I was unconscious for a while. But I saw a face. A woman. Beautiful, with long blond hair. It was you."

As she was pulling on her boots, the train whistle sounded.

"It would appear our timing is impeccable," she said. Hollister studied her and knew she wasn't going to answer him. He had just had one of the greatest days of his life. Why press it?

"It would," he said. He made his way to his knees and tried to stand using the trunk of the aspen tree for support, hoping like hell she wouldn't notice that it took him almost five minutes to get his pants on.

"Are you all right, Major?" she asked.

"Right as rain," he said. He somehow managed to get his arms into his shirt and he stepped into his boots. He wanted to throw his gun belt over his shoulder but he knew if he rode up to the train like that, Monkey Pete and Chee would take all of three seconds to know what had happened. Finally, he was ready. Shaniah was dressed and sitting atop Demeter, looking everywhere but at him, trying to be polite so he wouldn't feel self-conscious. He wanted to tell her it was already too late for that.

Before he mounted up, he walked over to her and took her hand. He kissed it gently, and then with his arms holding her, pulled her slowly out of her saddle until she stood in front of him. He kissed her, a soft gentle kiss.

"Whatever you need. Whatever you're looking for. This thing you must do. I'm going to help you see it through. All the way. Do you understand me?" He looked at her, his dark eyes fierce and proud, seeing nothing but her at that moment.

It wasn't possible, it couldn't be. She was an Archaic, not a creature of emotion; but she felt a tear form in her eye.

She nodded and he kissed her again.

"All the way," he said.

Chapter Fifty-five

Slater stood in the parlor, warming himself in front of the fireplace. June in the Rockies could still get cold at night. He had poured himself a large glass of brandy from the senator's decanter. The one Declan usually kept for himself, filled with the good liquor, thinking no one ever noticed he poured his guests the cheap stuff. He never fooled Slater. And he wasn't here yet, so fuck him. He'd drink the best.

Declan finally entered the room. He looked like shit. He had lost weight and his eyes were drawn and weary-looking, like a couple of prunes stuck to his face. When he'd heard Slater's report of what had happened in Absolution, he'd nearly had a nervous breakdown.

"What are we going to do, Slater? What are we going to do?" he'd muttered over and over. "Word gets out. You can't keep this under wraps forever. People start hearing this kind of talk, no one will move into the territory. It's bad enough when the Utes and the Sioux and the rest of the red niggers are on the warpath. This will be worse. Far worse. I'll lose everything," he moaned.

"Word won't get out. Pinkerton will dynamite the mine and seal those things in and burn Absolution to the ground. They'll make up some story, that it was smallpox or something. After a while it will just be a scary story people tell little children at night to scare them. You need to stop worrying."

Slater had assured the senator they were going to be fine. They were going to let Hollister find the leader of these things. The one who'd done all the killing at Torson City, and then they'd take care of everyone. Hollister especially. With no one to back up any of the wild claims, it could all be put off as an Indian uprising that Delcan had been essential in putting down. Hell, he would be a hero in the state again.

"Hollister, the breed and that woman are headed for someplace called Clady, Wyoming," Slater said.

"How do you know?"

"Bribed one of the Pinkertons," Slater said. "They ain't so upright and virtuous once they see a few greenbacks. Told Nolan they loaded up a bunch of ammo and ordnance and left about an hour ago."

Declan nodded. "This is good, this is good. You get the men, take my private train, whatever you need, and follow them."

"I got the men ready, and the train standing by. Don't worry, Senator, we'll clean up the mess."

Declan poured himself three fingers of brandy from his own decanter. He took a large swig and the liquor seemed to calm him. Slater hadn't moved. He stood by the fire staring at the senator.

"What is it?" Declan asked, his voice shaking.

"It's nothing, just . . . we're going to need to make a small change in our arrangements," Slater said.

"What? What in tarnation are you talking about?" Declan asked.

"I'm talking about money and land. I've 'handled' plenty of things for you over the years. We both know what's been done. But this here is a whole different brand of cattle. And a lot more dangerous to boot."

The senator was getting his feet under him now. He knew where this was headed and he didn't like it. "Get to the point," he mumbled.

"After this is over. When I kill Hollister and clean up this mess, things are going to change a little bit. I'm going to want some land, not just money. The two-thousand-acre piece down by the Sweetheart River ought to cover it . . . well, here," he pulled a document from his coat pocket. "I had an attorney in town draw it all up nice and legal so you could sign it before I leave."

Declan snatched the paper from Slater's hand, his eyes scanning it quickly.

"Why . . . you . . . what the hell . . . you can't possibly think I'm going to sign this, you sonuvabitch," Declan said.

"I expect I can, and I expect you will. I don't think you got the time right now to find anyone who does what needs to be done. What I'm willing to do, and let's face it"—he paused to refill his glass, this time pouring from the decanter with the good brandy and making sure Declan saw it—"Hollister and the breed ain't going to be easy to kill, number one, and number two, I been keeping your secrets all these years and you know I'll keep this one. Don't see as how you got much choice, Senator," he said.

Declan glared at Slater. He was trapped. Slater knew everything. Every rule he'd bent, every law he'd broken, everyone he'd had killed and every farmer he'd burned out. He'd known this day was coming. Slater wasn't a church deacon. He was a killer and he was smart. This was the price of doing business. He gulped down the rest of his brandy, and walking to his desk, dipped a fountain pen in the inkwell, signed the paper, and handed it back to Slater.

"Thank you, sir. Now I'll be on my way," he said.

He left Declan standing alone in the parlor, wondering what the hell had happened to his life.

Chapter Fifty-six

Hollister was reasonably sure that Chee and Pete knew he and Shaniah had slept together as soon as they arrived back at the train. The behavior between a man and a woman changes when it happens, no matter how much they try to hide it. The train was ready to go: steam was pouring out of the engine and the ramp to the stock car had been lowered. He and Shaniah rode Rose and Demeter right up into the car and unsaddled the horses, giving them water and straw.

When they stepped off, Monkey Pete pulled a lever and the ramp rose up until the car was secure. Then he locked it into place. He tried hard not to pay attention to Shaniah and the major, while Chee waited outside the main car, wrestling around with Dog. Pete and Chee made every effort they could to not look at each other or at Shaniah and Jonas. Finally, Jonas couldn't take it anymore. Might as well clear the air. But he'd be damned if he'd say anything in front of Shaniah. He was an officer and a gentleman after all.

"You two got something on your mind?" Hollister asked.

"No, sir," Pete said. "Just enjoying the night air."

Chee had some kind of knotted rope that he threw through the air. Dog leapt after it, returning at a sprint to drop it at Chee's feet. This apparently was the greatest game ever invented as far as Dog was concerned.

The quiet hiss of the engine was the only noise disturbing the night. It was almost fully dark now, with a half moon rising in the east.

"Well then, I suggest we get moving," Hollister said.

"Yes, sir," Chee said. "Sounds like a good idea."

"There is one thing I'd like to show you before we leave, Major," Pete said.

"Sure, Pete, what is it?" Hollister said.

He scampered onto the train and disappeared inside. He was so quick and agile crawling around the train, Hollister understood why General Hunt had given him the nickname "Monkey." He returned a few minutes later with another strange contraption strapped to his back. There were two metal cylinders inside what looked like an army rucksack an infantryman might carry. At the top of each cylinder was a gauge and from one of them came a hose attached to a long metal barrel welded to a double-barrel shotgun handle.

"What the hell is that?" Hollister asked. He noticed Chee had perked right up at the prospect that Monkey Pete might have invented another weapon.

"See that pile of scrap wood yonder?" he said.

The two men nodded, fascinated as Pete worked one of the gauges on the contraption he was wearing. He pulled one of the triggers on the shotgun handle and Hollister thought he caught a brief smell of coal oil, then Pete turned another knob and there was a spark near the head of the barrel. Without warning, a flame shot out of the barrel with a mighty whoosh. Pete leveled the barrel at the pile of wood and it burst into flames.

Pete released the trigger and the flame from the barrel died out and disappeared. The wood continued to burn.

"Holy shit!" Hollister exclaimed. "What in the hell have you done, Pete?"

"I got the idea from Winchester's Ass-Kicker," he said, shrugging out of the contraption and setting it on the ground. "I figured out a way to pressurize one of the tanks, just like on the gun, only this tank is a little bigger so it can hold more steam, which means more pressure, and it can push out more of the mixture with extra force and distance. It funnels the mixture out through the barrel, sort of like a beam of fire, and you can aim it how you please and burn up most anything. Think of it like a shotgun that shoots fire instead of slugs or buckshot."

"I'll be damned," Hollister said.

"What's in the mixture that catches fire?" Chee asked.

"My own little concoction of coal oil, kerosene, and corn alcohol," he said. He glanced at Shaniah "and there's some special additives, certain . . . well these things we're after won't like it."

"You can make fire . . . with this machine," Shaniah said, the look on her face a combination of fear and admiration.

"Yes, ma'am," Pete answered.

Shaniah shook her head in amazement.

"Pete, if I'm wearing one of these, can I still carry the Ass-Kicker?" Hollister asked.

"Oh yes, sir. You can store the barrel for the Fire Shooter in the holster, like this." He slipped it into a slot on the canvas straps that fit over the shoulder. "The Ass-Kicker won't get in the way. In fact, you could shoot off your four rounds, leave it on the sling and then draw the Fire Shooter. You'd have hell of a lot more power," he said.

"I'll bet you would," Hollister said.

"How many of these do you have?" Chee asked.

"I made three," Pete said, "but there is one thing. If you're facing someone that's got guns, you don't really want them shooting at you when you your tank is full of mixture."

"Why not?" Chee asked.

"'Cause if a bullet punctures the tank, you'd likely explode and any parts that was left of ya would burn to a crisp." The engineer replied calmly.

"All right. That's a drawback," Hollister said. "But from what we saw in Absolution, the Archaics ain't much for guns. So we should be okay."

Chee nodded in agreement. The young sergeant was a fan of anything that might kill more of his enemies faster and more efficiently.

"All right then," Hollister said. "Let's head for Clady. See what this Malachi fellow has to say for himself."

Chapter Fifty-seven

They spent the rest of the ride in the armory, checking weapons, charging the Ass-Kicker, sharpening bowie knives and generally getting ready to go to war. Hollister didn't like going into a fight like this with so little intelligence. Especially when they were likely to be heavily outnumbered. Chee looked happy as he prepared his weapons. Shaniah's face was impassive. Dog didn't seem to care. He lay on the floor of the car, never far from Chee, chewing on the giant knotted rope the sergeant had made for him. He also never took his eyes off Shaniah.

Hollister tried hard not to stare at Shaniah and he knew she was trying just as hard not to stare back at him. But there were times he couldn't help himself. She was beautiful. He was not a poetic man. The words to say she had eyes like pools of melted emerald, or hair like golden flax—those words weren't in him. For him it was enough to say she was beautiful, the most gorgeous woman he had ever been so close to. He couldn't for the life of him imagine what possessed her to make love to him. He didn't particularly consider himself a catch. Now though, it didn't matter. It had happened. And that was all.

At the Point he'd been required to go to balls and cotillions and had occasionally heard young women speak of him as he passed by, calling him "handsome" or "dreamy" or some other such girly description, but he didn't understand it. And especially after the war, with the way he'd been beat up, scarred, his face pocked by shrapnel, so much so that when he looked in the mirror he saw forty miles of bad road.

But Shaniah had seen something different. She had been the one. While he had lain beaten and battered on the hillside in Wyoming she had come to him. Like a dream. Only not a dream because she was real. And though Hollister didn't believe much in these things, he felt like she was an angel. He knew, intellectually, that she was an Archaic, by all accounts a monster, though she had given up her very nature in order to be more human and though she hadn't specifically been there to help him, that day had led to this moment. At least that is how he saw it. In his mind and in his heart she came from heaven. She had saved him. He didn't know why, he didn't care how he had been deemed worthy of a woman so beautiful, and he was not foolish enough to ask. He would take this blessing and no matter what happened, if he died tonight or tomorrow or next week, he would do so knowing he had found the one.

He couldn't read Shaniah's mind, but he knew she felt something for him. While they worked she studied him and smiled. Her hands lingered over his when she handed him a box of bullets or a weapon, and she watched him as he worked.

"What are you carrying, Chee?" Hollister asked.

"Modified Colts in a double rig. One Henry, two backups on my saddle, and I reckon I'll give Pete's Fire Shooter a try."

"Well, you ought to be able to conquer Canada with that," Hollister said. "Shaniah, what about you?"

"I have the Archaic vengeance blade." She pulled it from

her boot, and it gleamed in the lamplight of the car. She had cleaned and sharpened it since Absolution, and Hollister had to admit it was a formidable weapon.

"That's it?" he asked.

"Yes."

"But you . . ."

"It will be all I need," she said.

"What about one of Pete's Fire . . ." Hollister started to say, though he knew he wasn't likely going to change her mind.

But she held up her hand. "No."

"Why not?" he asked. Chee looked at her curiously as well, wondering why anyone would chose to decline a weapon of such destructive capability.

"The Archaics Malachi has turned are not likely to use weapons. However, there is the possibility. And let's not forget the men following us who do carry guns. And as your Monkey Pete explained, if I am shot at I do not wish to explode into pieces and burn to a cinder."

"Fair enough," Hollister said.

Their inventory complete, their weapons ready, there was nothing left to do but wait.

Chapter Fifty-eight

The opening to main shaft 7 at the Clady mine was crowded with Archaics. Most of them were initiates, although Malachi had sired a few of them when he first landed on American shores. He had kept his band intentionally small then, hiding, feeding either in major cities or remote towns. Places where they could either blend in and find easy food, or out-of-the-way locations where no one would likely notice when they did feed. They moved ever westward until he found what he was looking for. A place much like the Archaic homeland in Europe. Filled with mountains, defensible and secluded, but populated enough so he could begin raising more followers.

The Archaics were waiting for Malachi to ascend from the mine. In three more days he would be fifteen hundred years old and immortal. No human weapon, no elemental, no damnable priest of Saint Ignatius could summon the fires of heaven to consume him. He would live forever. And here he would rule. He would sire more and more humans until his army was too large, too vast to defeat. The centuries of

humiliation, the years of living high in the mountains, feeding on vermin and cowering, hiding from the humans like
frightened dogs would be over. Archaics would rule. As it
had been intended since the dawn of time.

Only one thing could stop him now.

Shaniah. She was nearly an Eternal herself. She *could*
have the power, although he doubted it. Since he'd left the
Archaics in Europe, he had broken the covenant and fed
on humans again. What strength flowed from the *Huma
Sangra*, human blood. He was the most powerful Archaic
alive. He knew this. He also knew Shaniah was a puppet of
the Old Ones. There was little chance she had fed on human
blood while she pursued him, and she would be too weak to
stop him. He smiled at the thought.

But she was coming. He could sense her now. Close by
and not without considerable power. Just not enough. Malachi thought she might have been killed in Absolution, but
instead she and a handful of puny humans had escaped,
and what's more, had killed more than one hundred of his
people. Those who survived the encounter told him of a
great weapon used by one of the humans. It had destroyed
many of them. He had killed the survivors as a lesson to the
others.

Interesting. But he was not afraid. Humans were clever, he
would give them that. Weapons and spells and magics and
elementals they had discovered through the ages had killed
many Archaics. But Malachi knew in his heart they were not
strong enough. If the Old Ones had not given up, if they had
not been cowards and retreated, the Archaics would rule the
planet already.

Now he would make it so.

His army was more than five hundred strong. They had
hidden themselves well here in the Clady mine. The humans
did not know where they were or even for certain what they
were. And they wouldn't realize what hell had descended on
them until it was too late.

But Shaniah was coming and that was . . . interesting. Was she coming alone, or was she bringing help? Had she found some humans who thought their clever weapons could destroy him? Perhaps.

Malachi walked through the crowd, and his followers reached out to touch him, his arms, his hair—stroked his shoulders as he passed by. He stepped up on a cluster of crates that had been pushed together to create a small stage from which to address his people.

"My children," he said. "The time is near." Cheers erupted and he waited for them to subside. He felt invincible. He stood over seven feet tall. His nearly pure white hair now hung to the center of his back. He looked like some ancient warrior, a Viking king, or a knight from the middle ages.

"Our time is nearly here," he said. More cheers.

"But first I must ask from some of you a grave sacrifice," he said. The crowd quieted instantly.

"I've told you of Shaniah, the queen of those left behind. How she has followed me from our homeland. It was she who led the humans at Absolution who killed our brothers and sisters." At this, yells and jeers and yowls erupted and Malachi held out his hands.

"She is coming," he said. "I can sense her, she is close and will try to stop us." There were more shouts and cries of anger and vengeance.

"Do not underestimate her," he said. "She cannot defeat me, I have grown far too powerful, but she is strong and we must not let her delay our plans."

"Shaniah is coming from the south, I would surmise she rides by train to the end of the line near Clawson's Gap. That is where we must meet and defeat her. I ask who among you will meet her challenge?" The shouts were nearly deafening and every one of the assembled Archaics raised their hand.

"I do not ask lightly. Shaniah is cunning. She is brave and strong and fierce—a brilliant warrior. The humans who killed our brethren at Absolution may be with her, and may bring more weapons. Some of you who confront her now will die. But Shaniah must be stopped, or all of us may perish."

He looked to two of his men, Lucas and Jonathan, followers who had been with him since he arrived in America.

"Take one hundred fifty . . . no . . . take two hundred and meet the train at Clawson's Gap. Destroy her," he said quietly.

It took a matter of minutes for his men to gather two hundred angry, vicious Archaics. With howls of rage and anger they ran out of the camp, disappearing into the trees.

On the way to kill Shaniah.

Chapter Fifty-nine

Monkey Pete stuck his head into the armory. The train was starting to slow and the brakes sounded.

"About two miles to the end of the line, Major," he said. A few minutes later the train finally stopped. It still made Hollister nervous, the idea the train was driving itself with no one in the engine room. Pete had tried explaining it to Hollister, but the major had had no idea what the engineer was talking about.

Pete pinned a map up on an open space on the wall. "We're here. The grade was too steep for a rail line to the mine, so they used wagons to haul the ore back and forth from here to the mining camp. There's a road, so it makes for an easy ride on horseback."

Hollister studied the map. "Makes for a good spot for an ambush also."

"Well, there is that," Monkey Pete said.

"We don't have much choice," Hollister said. "Let's do a final weapons check and then we'll ride out at first light . . ."

He was interrupted by Dog, who rose instantly, the hair on

the back of his neck standing up and a growl sounding low in his throat.

"Something's wrong," Chee said.

"He smells them," Shaniah said.

"Smells what?" Hollister asked.

"The Archaics. They're here," she said.

"How do you know?" Hollister asked, looking out the window but seeing nothing in the darkness.

"Because I can smell them too," Shaniah said.

"Well, that changes things," Hollister said.

"How?" Shaniah asked.

"Wasn't planning on a night assault. I figured you could wear your fancy cloak and we would attack them in the daylight, since they don't like the sunlight," he said.

A howl went up from outside the train, and Dog answered with a bark. He clawed at the door, anxious to be outside, ready to attack.

"We'll back up, then return tomorrow in the daylight. Monkey Pete . . ." Hollister turned around looking for the engineer, who had disappeared. Suddenly the outside of the train lit up, the exterior lamps and spotlights coming alive, and through the shooting slots in the armory car, they could see hundreds of Archaics standing in the woods, watching the train.

"Where'd he go?" Hollister asked.

Just then Monkey Pete hustled back into the armory car. "No backing up tonight I'm afraid, Major," Monkey Pete said.

"Why not?"

"Well, Major, them critters"—he looked at Shaniah and tipped his cap—"no offense, ma'am, didn't mean to say *critter*. Those . . . our enemies have pushed about a dozen trees onto the tracks thirty or forty yards behind us. Big trees."

"Pete, this train can practically fly," Hollister said. "Can't you jump over them or push them off the tracks or burn them or something?"

Pete looked crestfallen, as if Hollister had insulted his train somehow.

"No, sir," he said. "Like I said, they're too big to burn and we ain't gonna move 'em, because I'm pretty sure them Archaics outside got other ideas for us. So you better come up with a plan."

Hollister paced back and forth, his hand on his chin, thinking.

"You do have a plan, right, sir?" Chee asked.

Hollister looked up, smiling. "Yes I do. Pete, let's get your fire-shooting contraptions ready to go."

"But, Major, I done told you, we can't burn these trees. They're too big and if—"

"Don't worry, Pete, I got it all figured out. We aren't going to be burning the trees."

"All right," Shaniah said. "The Fire Shooters, then what?"

Hollister grinned.

"Then we open the doors," he said.

Chapter Sixty

"Open the doors—are you insane?" Shaniah said.

Chee said nothing, looking away but actually thinking the same thing.

"Why would we want to do that, Major?" Monkey Pete said. "Sounds crazy to me. Like you're letting them right in."

Hollister smiled. Outside, the Archaics began to howl and scream, and rocks and sticks started thumping against the side of the train.

"Don't forget, we've got the devil's traps and we've got a little surprise for them," he said as he shrugged into one of Pete's Fire Shooters.

Chee picked up his Henry; he was already wearing his double-rig Colts.

"Pete, what about the horses . . . we can't lose them," Hollister said.

"No worries, Major. Them stock doors close up with solid steel, they ventilate out the top and sides. Ain't nothing can get in there except noise. Might spook 'em a little is all."

Hollister nodded. "Pete, you get up on the Gatling and start letting 'em have it. Shaniah, Chee, you come with me."

They left the armory. The sounds of Archaics clamoring over the roof of the train were getting louder. Inside the main cabin, Hollister and Chee each took a door on opposite sides of the car.

Hollister glanced at the paintings and bunches of garlic around the doors and windows. "I hope those work," he said. He worked the gauge on the Fire Shooter.

"Ready, Chee?" he shouted. The howls and squeals of the Archaics were getting louder and louder.

"Ready," Chee shouted. "Dog! Stay!" he commanded. Dog whined and sat on his haunches as if Chee had just asked him to choose a head of lettuce over a side of bacon.

Shaniah, standing at the side of the door nearest Hollister with her blade in hand, threw it open.

Outside, a group of fifteen or twenty Archaics clustered near the train. The open door caught them completely by surprise. But they recovered quickly and launched themselves toward the train. The first one hit the threshold and bounced away, Van Helsing's traps working, at least for now.

Hollister turned the knob on the Fire Shooter and pulled the trigger. Flames shot out through the door and Archaic after Archaic caught fire. Hollister swept the nozzle back and forth like he was watering a garden and the flames erupted, filling up the surrounding woods with light.

The noise surrounding him was nearly indescribable. Dog howled, Chee shouted for the animal to stay. Above him, he heard the sound of the Gatling as Monkey Pete opened fire and cleared the creatures off the roof of the train. Unable to use her blade, Shaniah took up a Henry and fired through the port. Outside, the screams of the Archaics became nearly unbearable; the stink of burning flesh reached Jonas's nostrils and he thought he might retch, but he held on.

Despite the flames, the Archaics kept coming, hurling themselves at the train. Hollister looked at the gauge on his

Fire Shooter. It was more than half empty. Since his field of vision was narrowed to what he could see through his door, he had no idea how many he had killed.

"Chee! How much juice you got left?" he hollered.

"Maybe a quarter tank, Major. There's a lot of them. They keep coming," he shouted over the din.

"When you run out of mixture, you close that door. Van Helsing's charms seem to be working, but let's not take any chances."

"Yes, sir," he shouted, triggering the Fire Shooter again. A new wave of Archaics came through the trees and Hollister bathed them in flames. Some of them began to run away, but he kept the pressure on the trigger.

"They are new! Initiates!" Shaniah shouted over the noise. "Mature Archaics would never stop. They would keep coming until they killed us or we killed them."

Hollister filed this away. It was chaos now, but somehow this was important information. It would come in handy at some point, he was sure. For the time being, he kept pulling the trigger on Pete's Fire Shooter.

A few minutes later, the device sputtered and the flame died. He checked the gauge. Empty. He slammed the door shut and a few seconds later Chee did the same at his end of the car. Monkey Pete was still firing the Gatling from the roof of the armory car.

"Pete! What's going on out there?" Hollister shouted up to the engineer.

"We killed a lot of them, Major. Some of 'em took off and there's maybe fifty of 'em left that I can see . . ." the Gatling fired again. "About forty left now."

"Chee, load up and get Dog ready," Hollister said. "Shaniah, you reload too. We're going out there and kill the rest of them. Before they decide to retreat back to the mine."

"Are you sure that's wise?" Shaniah said. "Even forty Archaics, initiates or not, can be formidable. You do remember Absolution, don't you?"

"I do," Jonas said. "We just killed over a hundred of those things. Maybe more. With what we killed in Absolution we've taken Malachi's numbers down a fair bit. He can't have turned that many. We kill those left out there right now, we weaken him even further. He made a mistake. He didn't know what our tactical capabilities are and he sent too many of his men. Just like Lee at Petersburg. We've got to get them now!"

Monkey Pete's third Fire Shooter was empty, but Hollister grabbed the Ass-Kicker, and Chee and Shaniah picked up their Henrys.

"Pete! We're going out, on the count of three you start singing with that Gatling!"

"YOU'RE WHAT?" Pete hollered back.

"One . . . two . . . three." Hollister threw open the door.

"Dog! Hunt!" Chee shouted. Dog lunged through the door like he'd been shot out of a cannon. He leapt at the first Archaic he met, about ten yards from the train and took it by the throat. It had been a human woman and it was small but Archaic strong, and it tried to push Dog off, but the animal was too enraged. He tore the throat from the Archaic with a howl.

Hollister went out the door firing a Henry. The Archaics regrouped and charged. Chee came next, then Shaniah. The creatures lunged toward the train and Pete's Gatling cut down the first row of them, the wooden bullets stitching them like quilts. A handful of them exploded into dust.

The trio stood with their backs to the train, firing away. When his Henry emptied, Jonas tossed it to the ground, took the Ass-Kicker by the stock, and pulled it to his hip, ready to shoot. He worked the action, the gear clicked into place, he leveled it at the Archaics, and fired.

The percussion wave blasted out of the barrel of the gun and six of the Archaics exploded in a wave of body parts. Three shots left. Maybe twenty creatures to go. He worked the action again, fired, again and again. The final shot took down the last four. It was over. They were all dead. Dog returned from somewhere, and for a moment, Hollister's heart jumped because he had forgotten about the animal and was happy he hadn't accidentally shot it. It loped over to Chee and dropped something at his feet. Hollister thought it might be an Archaic hand but wasn't sure.

The area surrounding the train was a morass of body parts, burned skeletons, and piles of ash. Hollister couldn't believe it. The four of them had beaten off a massive attack.

For the first time since Pinkerton had shown up and gotten him out of prison, he started thinking that maybe, just maybe, this Malachi could be beaten.

One way or the other, they were going to find out.

Chapter Sixty-one

There were a few Archaics wounded but still alive lying outside the train. Chee volunteered to dispatch the remaining creatures. He took Dog and a Henry with wooden bullets and returned to the train about thirty minutes later, the same impassive expression still painted on his face.

Hollister felt nearly euphoric. It was a common condition among soldiers who experienced combat. He and those under his command had survived. Not only that, but they had inflicted heavy casualties on their enemy.

And with Monkey Pete's new device and the Ass-Kicker, he had a plan. It would take a little more of Monkey Pete's genius and it would require a lot of luck. But it just might turn the tide.

It was early morning, and none of them had slept. They sat in the main car at the table, with the littered remains of Monkey Pete's pancakes and coffee. Hollister was busy making sketches on sheets of paper.

The train Pinkerton had outfitted was full of machines, machine parts, and tools and loaded down with weapons. Monkey Pete had attached Gatling guns and hoses that shot holy water, and he'd extended the range and power of the train through his modifications of the engine in ways Jonas would never understand. The train gave them a huge tactical advantage. The problem was, there was no way to get the train to the Clady mine. The grade was too steep. Not to mention the lack of tracks.

Hollister had thought about it for a while and decided that the best thing to do was to send part of the train to the mine.

"Shaniah, can Demeter pull a wagon?" Hollister asked.

"Yes, why?" she answered.

"Pete, you don't happen to have a small wagon on board the train, do you?" Hollister was crossing his fingers here.

"No, sir, I don't reckon . . ." he started to say, and Hollister's heart sank. But then he noticed Pete was getting that dreamy look in his eyes.

Pete smacked the table with his hand. "I ain't got 'wheels' like wagon wheels or anything like that, but I got two extra flywheels in my supply car. Carry 'em as spares in case somethin' goes wrong with the engine. I could rig those into a cart pretty easy."

Hollister wanted to kiss the little guy.

"What is your plan, sir?" Chee asked. He was always so quiet, even when Hollister could tell he had strong opinions about something. When this was over. If they survived, he was going to have to work on getting Chee to loosen up a little bit.

"When the Archaics attacked us last night, and when they stormed the train in Absolution, I think it showed this train is our best tactical asset. They cut down or pushed over a few trees and they've got us boxed in here, but we still fought them off. Almost two hundred of them," he said.

He held up his sketch to show the others. Chee and Shaniah couldn't tell exactly what it was, but Pete got it right away.

"So if we can't get them to the train . . ." Hollister said.

"You're going to take the train to them!" Pete said, unable to keep the excitement out of his voice.

Chapter Sixty-two

Malachi was stunned, though he showed no outward signs of it to his people. Only seven of his followers had staggered back into the camp. They were injured, mostly burned, but healing quickly. The rest had died. How was this possible? How had Shaniah managed to kill nearly two hundred Archaics?

Jonathan and Lucas were both dead, he was told. Before him stood an Archaic who had once been a Blackfoot Indian. He had been turned when Malachi and a few of the others had stumbled across their hunting camp the previous winter. His Blackfoot name had been Walking Cat. He looked as though he had been in a fight.

Most of his chest and face had been burned. Two small wooden stakes stuck out of his right shoulder. Malachi removed one of them to study it. It was made from a hardwood, likely oak, and sharpened to a deadly point. Walking Cat's left arm hung loosely at his side, although it was already beginning to heal. The flesh on his burned face and chest was returning to normal, and a few seconds later the other wooden stake popped loose from his shoulder and fell to the ground.

"Tell me what happened," Malachi said.

"We went for the train, as you instructed. It was stopped at the end of the spur, as you said it would be," he said. Malachi's followers had learned that he loved to be flattered by being told he was or had been right about things.

"We pushed trees onto to the track behind them, big trees, ones humans could not move or lift, so they could not escape. We were lining up, readying ourselves to attack when . . ."

The young Indian stopped. Though he had not been turned long, he should be fearless, Malachi thought. Archaics were afraid of nothing. Yet this man was afraid. As if he was reliving something horrible and could not bear to think of it.

"Go on, tell me," Malachi prodded.

"They opened the doors of the train and . . . they . . ." Walking Cat stammered. Malachi was growing impatient. Wanting to snap the man's neck if he didn't start talking.

"They did what?" Malachi demanded, his voice taking on an angry tone and rising in pitch. The other Archaics were watching now, they were spellbound by Walking Cat's story, but they also grew restless and nervous at the thought of Malachi's anger.

"Fire came from inside the train. Before he died, Jonathan said two of the humans were the same ones from Absolution. They had weapons that shot flame, a great distance. I . . . we caught fire. Another human shot a gun," he stopped and picked up the wooden bullet that lay in the dust at his feet. "The gun, I have seen them before, when I fought the bluecoats. It shoots many bullets, and between this gun and the fire, we . . . many of us died. We kept attacking, but we could not get inside the train for some reason. It was like the doors were blocked somehow. No matter how many times we tried, no matter which direction we attacked from, we could not enter the train." Walking Cat bowed his head and his shoulders slumped when he finished his report.

"Where are the others? Those who came back with Walking Cat? Step forward," Malachi said.

Six Archaics made their way toward him, reluctant looks on their faces. The crowd parted until the seven of them stood in line facing Malachi. Most of them bore similar injuries to Walking Cat, burns and cuts and broken bones, but they were also starting to heal. None of them faced Malachi, they were afraid and disappointed they had let him down, and stood there with their heads hanging low

"Tell me," he said to them. "Is what Walking Cat has told us true?" He spoke loudly so all of the remaining Archaics could hear him.

All of them mumbled yes or nodded their heads, still unwilling to face their leader.

"As Archaics, you were ordered to attack Shaniah, to find her and kill her and you did not. You returned here like whipped dogs with tales of weapons and fire and human tricks, instead of stories of a great victory! Is this not true?"

The seven of them stood motionless. There was nothing to say, they had no defense. Their leader had given them a command and they had failed.

Malachi moved so quickly, the seven Archaics were dead almost before anyone could blink. From somewhere in the folds of his cloak he pulled a long gleaming knife and with the speed of an Olympian god he decapitated all of them in seconds. Where there had been standing, living beings, there were now only bodies and heads, and their screams died before their heads hit the ground, their faces still showing the death grimace of surprise.

The crowd was silent. Malachi looked at the remaining group.

"It will be sunup soon. We will wait until the darkness returns, then we will find Shaniah and the humans who assist her. And we will kill them." He spun on his heel and entered the mine. Leaving the Archaics behind him, the sun just beginning to peek over the eastern horizon.

Chapter Sixty-three

Monkey Pete had shooed everyone away, telling them he could construct the cart on his own, and that they would just be in his way. Hollister had suggested they get some sleep while taking turns standing watch in the gunner's bubble above the armory car. Chee had volunteered to take the first watch. He sat in the seat, his hand on the handles of the Gatling, ready to shoot in an instant if the Archaics reappeared.

Chee was too wired to sleep, so keeping watch had been a good thing for him. But it didn't sit right with him, knowing Shaniah and Hollister were not sleeping. Hollister had made a show of heading for his bunk and Shaniah did the same, leaving the main car and following Monkey Pete, giving every indication she was going to the guest quarters.

Chee was willing to bet one of the two was not in their bunk. She had made her way to Hollister's quarters or he had gone to hers, but they were together somewhere on the train. They were lovers. Chee had seen it almost immediately when they returned from their ride the previous night.

It should not bother him. The major was an adult, his own man, and not to mention Chee's superior officer. He could sleep with whomever he wished. The sergeant just wished it was anyone but Shaniah.

He reached inside the folds of his shirt and fingered his medicine bag, and he could still feel the cord with the coin tied around his ankle. He muttered both a Shaolin prayer and a Creek war chant. Neither made him feel better. He wished his grandmother Annabel were here so he could ask her more questions. How could he protect all of them from this *Brujería*—this witch— in their midst?

Monkey Pete lowered the door on his "lab" car, slowly rolling the cart he'd built down the ramp onto the ground. One of the spare Gatlings was attached to it. Chee continued to marvel at the engineer's ingenuity as he yawned and stretched.

It was almost time to fight again.

Chapter Sixty-four

Shaniah lay next to Hollister in his bunk, with her leg draped over his torso. Hollister questioned his judgment in making love to her again, right before the biggest fight of his life. It was a fight he knew he might not survive.

"What are you thinking?" she asked, her fingers tracing the scar on his shoulder from the bullet he'd taken at Five Forks, right before the end of the war.

"I was wondering if I was still alive," he said.

She laughed. "Oh, you are alive, all right."

"I might not be for much longer," he said. "Is this . . . I mean . . . your people . . . do they always . . . is their lovemaking always this . . . intense?"

"Yes!" she teased him. Enjoying making him uncomfortable.

"You're kidding. It's always this . . . vigorous?"

"Yes, most of the time," she said.

"Dear God," he groaned.

"I'm pleasantly surprised," she said.

"About what?"

"You shouldn't worry, Jonas, your stamina and . . . skill is quite remarkable."

He sighed. "At least there's that."

He had no idea what time it was, but he should probably get up and relieve Chee of the watch and allow him to get some sleep, although he had begun to wonder if Chee ever slept.

He sat up on the bed, feeling weak and dizzy after making love to Shaniah. Was that what it would always be like? The truth of it was, he couldn't remember anyone like her. It was like the women he'd known had all been wiped from his mind and no other woman had existed for him before her. *Strange*, he thought.

"I've got to relieve Chee," he said. "It is almost . . ."

"He knows, Jonas," she said.

"Knows what?"

"About us."

Hollister tried not to react.

"Chee knows a lot of things," he said. "I guess I shouldn't be surprised he figured this out."

"He 'figures things out' because he is a *Vrajitoarea*," she said.

"A what?"

"It is what my people call . . . your word for it would be 'witch.' "

"Chee's a witch?" He looked at her, smiling.

"Yes." And from the look on her face he could tell she wasn't joking.

"Like a 'bubble bubble, toil and trouble' witch?"

She frowned, not understanding his reference.

"It's from Shakespeare . . . a play . . . a story written . . . never mind. I'm pretty sure Chee is not a witch."

"Do not take this lightly, Jonas. You have now come to realize the world is more than what you thought. I am an Archaic, there are many more . . . species outside the human world; Vrajitoareas, the wolf people, vampires, the undead . . ."

"Whoa!" he said, holding up his hand. "I'm having enough trouble dealing with your Archaic pals. I've read Van Helsing . . ."

"You are not listening to me! You have more to worry about than my 'Archaic pals'!" She nearly spat the words at him.

"And you've got a lot to learn about Chee. He's not a Vera . . . whatever . . ."

"Jonas. I am an Archaic. I have been alive for nearly fifteen hundred years. I was a widow, taken in a raid on my village by Archaics. Our society is not structured like yours. We live by rules of strength and guile. Your people, people like Chee, are the ones who found the ways to kill us. To drive us into the mountains and force us to live as we have the past few centuries. Why is that so hard for you to accept?"

"Whoa. Why are you so angry all of a sudden? All I'm sayin' is Chee is just a man, like me . . ."

"No! He is not like you, Jonas," she was angrier now, getting off the bed and putting on her clothes. "Yes, he is a human, but he has a connection to the world that you don't. And if you are smart, if you live through this, you will be wise to remember that there are far more things in this world that can kill you, not just Archaics or humans . . . or grizzly bears!"

"Look," he said, trying to calm her. "I'm trying to understand here . . ."

"No, you are not," she declared, fastening the buttons on her blouse.

"Listen to me, I believe you . . ." He tried to placate her.

"You do not believe me, Jonas Hollister. You have seen plenty of my kind. You have killed them, watched what they can do, and yet you consider me crazy because I tell you of witches and wolf people and vampires and that your man Chee is a witch?"

"Whoa! I didn't mean . . ." He stepped toward her and tried to take her in his arms. He didn't want to fight with her. But she was too quick and dodged away from him. She glared at him and left his bunk, gone so fast it was almost like she'd never been there.

Chapter Sixty-five

Hollister found Chee in the armory. Since it was in between his bunk and the guest quarters, where Shaniah was supposed to be sleeping, he wondered how she had gotten past Chee without his seeing her. He guessed it didn't matter though, because according to Shaniah, he already knew about them.

"Chee, we've only known each other a short time. And its become clear to me you know a lot of things about the world that I don't," Jonas said.

"I'm not sure I understand, sir," Chee said.

"You know things. When Van Helsing was here, not a lot of what he told us surprised you. You knew about Death-walkers, as you called them. And you've got that Chinese fighting style and . . ."

"Kung fu, sir," he said.

"Yes . . . Kung fu. My point is that a lot of what we've learned about these Archaics and the other things we've seen hasn't appeared to surprise you,"

"I suppose not, sir," he said.

"Why is that?"

Chee shrugged. "Maybe it is just how I was raised," he said. "I grew up in New Orleans. I am . . . my grandparents were . . . from many cultures. My grandmother Annabel was a former slave, born in Haiti. Her husband, my grandfather Lu Chi—it was misspelled on the deed of the first property he was allowed to buy—was from China; my mother's father was half Cajun and half Mexican, and my other grandmother was a full-blooded Creek Indian."

"So you're saying . . ." Hollister said.

"I've learned from many cultures. What may seem strange to someone is not so strange to me," he said. "Some believe when we die we are gone. Others say there are ways for the dead to return, as spirits, and through voodoo, which is a type of witchcraft my grandmother Annabel often spoke of. My grandfather Lu Chi believed death was a doorway. It could be opened and closed and walked through both ways. There are many ways of understanding and examining the other worlds we call heaven, hell, the afterlife. Some are different, some are the same, but it all depends on the culture and your point of view. But if the question you are asking me is if I believe in these things, my answer is yes. And hasn't what we've seen given proof to it?"

Hollister smiled. Chee had talked to him about something personal for almost an entire minute. It might have been the longest conversation he had had with his sergeant. He looked at him with a rueful grin.

"Well, did all those grandparents teach you anything about understanding women?" Hollister said.

"No, sir, I don't think any culture has an answer for that question, sir," Chee said.

Hollister thought he might be joking, but the expression on Chee's face was always the same so it was hard for Jonas to tell.

"Shaniah has told me some things, about other creatures,

like these Archaics, witches, and what she called wolf people and—"

"Werewolves," Chee interrupted.

"Yeah, werewolves. Bad enough I've got super-strong, nearly indestructible Archaics on my ass, now I got to go to sleep at night worrying if Monkey Pete or somebody else I know is going to turn into a wolf at the next full moon and come after me like I'm a walking pork chop."

"I don't believe Monkey Pete is a werewolf, sir."

Hollister gave a derisive snort. "How can we be sure of anything?"

"Well for one, Dog would know, sir. And he likes Monkey Pete."

"Dog would . . . of course. Dog would know. Damn dog is probably the smartest one of us on this damn train," Hollister muttered. "Anyway, it's past sunrise, I should have relieved you. I'm sorry about that, Chee."

"No worries, Major. I don't sleep much anyway," Chee said, almost cheerfully. "Besides, I think Monkey Pete is ready to show us something."

Hollister started toward the door of the car, but Chee stopped him.

"Major, since we are on the subject of witches and wolf people and whatnot, I feel there is something I must tell you," Chee said.

"What is it?" Hollister asked, slightly surprised. This was the first time Hollister could remember Chee offering an opinion or a statement without being asked.

"The woman, Shaniah, you are with her now . . ." Chee hesitated. Hollister said nothing, realizing there was no sense in denying it. Shaniah had been right. Chee knew.

"Go on," Hollister said hesitantly.

"She is different. Not just because she is an Archaic, but even among them, she . . . has power," he said.

"What kind of power?" Hollister asked.

"I'm not sure I can explain it, sir. She could kill us easily if she wanted to, but she has not. In fact, she has gone out of her way to help us. At great personal risk. Yet she is holding something back. I do not yet determine what it is. She is dangerous. I wish I could tell you why this is, but I can't. I simply know it. She is not like the Archaics in some important way. It may be the very reason she is here."

"I'm sure she is holding something back, I don't doubt it. But she doesn't seem dangerous to me. I . . . she . . . when . . ." Hollister stumbled over the words.

Chee held up his hand. "Do not worry, and do not try to explain, I understand your confusion. But, Major . . . I will be watching her," Chee said.

"I guess that's probably not a bad idea," he said.

"And, Major, if I see she is . . . if she looks to be ready to betray us, to turn on one of us for any reason or to threaten you in any way, I will kill her."

Hollister looked at his young sergeant, knowing the man had just told him something that had been hard for him to say. Hollister would not belittle him by arguing the point.

"I understand. Now, let's go see what Monkey Pete has to show us."

Chapter Sixty-six

Monkey Pete was proud of what he'd pieced together. As Chee had seen earlier, he had taken two of the spare fly-wheels for the gear assembly on the engine and created an axle out of a spare piece of pipe. The cart was about four feet wide, and he'd apparently stripped some planks of wood from inside the car and made a platform about six feet long.

The metal wheels were thin and weren't likely to travel well in the soil, so Pete wrapped them in several layers of rope to thicken them so they would roll more easily over whatever surface they needed to travel.

He had bolted one of the Gatlings to the cart. The surface of the platform stood about three feet off the ground so the gun could swivel with a 360-degree field of fire.

A Fire Shooter was also strapped to the cart, along with several boxes of ammo, silver, and wooden and holy-water bullets. The cart itself looked lethal just sitting there, and for a second Hollister let himself feel encouraged. They were going in against an enemy more powerful than anything he'd ever faced. But they could be killed, and he might just have the firepower to do it. But then he pushed the thought from his head. No use getting cocky. It would only get them killed.

Jonas checked his pocket watch.

The information he had on the Clady mine was sketchy. Mostly some railroad documents and a one-page report Pinkerton had been able to scrounge up and telegraph to him. It wouldn't be like Absolution. The mine here had been closed for years. There were a few decrepit buildings left and then the mine shaft. The majority of the Archaics would probably be in the mine, until the sun went down. If he were Malachi, he would come at them again, once it was dark. But it would be a different approach. He would try something to draw them away from the train, maybe setting it on fire. Two problems with that approach: first, everything outside of the train was steel or iron and wouldn't burn, and second, he wouldn't know Hollister and his band would be in Clady already waiting for them.

Shaniah stepped out of the train and looked over Monkey Pete's newest contraption. Hollister could tell she was still angry with him, ignoring him completely at first, and instead turning her attention to the cart. After studying his creation for a minute she shook her head in amazement, but smiled. "It pains me to say it, but I think what you have done here, Mr. Pete, is found a way to kill many Archaics."

"Well, ma'am, no offense, but I hope so," Monkey Pete said. "Major, I had these in the armory, and I thought they might come in handy." He pointed to two wooden cases sitting on the cart. Stenciled on the side of each case was the word DYNAMITE.

Hollister smiled. "I think we might find a use for it."

Hollister looked at his watch again. It was now after 10 A.M. According to the map it was just over twelve miles to Clady. It was also mostly uphill. Hollister wanted to be in position well before late afternoon, when the sun went down behind the mountains, in case some Archaics might move about in the hours before the actual sunset.

"All right," Hollister said. "Pete, you stay with the train. We're going to off-load the horses and pull those trees off the track before we leave, in case you need to get out of here. After that, we're leaving for Clady. You stay in the gunner's bubble with that Gatling. If we don't come back or if you see an Archaic, don't fight 'em off. You get the hell out of here. Send a wire to Pinkerton as soon as you can, tell him we failed and he's going to have to try something else to kill these things. Tell him he'll need the biggest goddamn stick of dynamite that's ever been made. Or something."

He looked at each of them. All of them wore solemn expressions on their faces. They were ready.

"All right," Hollister said. "Let's get going."

Chapter Sixty-seven

Malachi sat on a chair in one of the large chambers of the mine. Around him dozens of Archaic initiates slept, hidden from the burning rays of the sun outside. Soon they would be able to go without sleep for weeks as their transformation from human to Archaic was completed. Their mood had changed completely since he had slaughtered the cowards earlier this morning. They had always had a healthy respect for his temper, but now they feared him. Since Shaniah had arrived in Absolution he had found it necessary to discipline his followers for their failures for the first time. If the world was to belong to his people, they would not be the last.

There had been no choice. Archaics could not be afraid. They could never be allowed to retreat, they must attack without hesitation and weakness would not be tolerated.

The mine was clear of bats and rodents, driven out by their preternatural fear of the Archaics, so the only sound was the occasional murmur from the disturbed sleep of his followers. He felt strong. He knew he was more powerful than he had been in centuries, since the Archaics had retreated to the high mountains of the homeland.

He would need his strength now more than ever.

Shaniah was coming. He could feel her presence growing closer. It had been so long since he had seen her. Years. And soon one of them would die.

It would end.

Monkey Pete's cart worked remarkably well and given the terrain and the elevation they were able to make excellent time toward the mine. Demeter had little trouble pulling the cart up the steep incline, and by noon they were more than halfway there.

There was very little talking as they rode. They were alert and a little nervous. Shaniah was cloaked, reminding them that other Archaics could be about and cloaked as she was, and that ambush was always possible. But Hollister didn't think Malachi would risk a daylight attack after losing so many in the night attack on the train. Chee and Hollister rode with Fire Shooters on their backs. The third was bolted to the cart. Each of them carried a Henry across his saddle.

It was four o'clock when they reached the mine. They stayed back in the trees surrounding the clearing where the bulk of the mining camp had once stood. Hollister dismounted and scanned the area with his spyglass but there was no movement or sign of anyone nearby. There were two buildings, both of them nearly falling down, one with the roof already partially caved in, about sixty yards from the mine opening. The other building was to the right of the first, perhaps ten yards closer to the entrance and nothing more than a small shed. He would put Chee with the Gatling and his Fire Shooter there. He would take up a position in the first building with the Fire Shooter, the Ass-Kicker, his Henry, and some of the dynamite, just in case things got really interesting.

"Shaniah, I want Chee in the small building with the Gatling. I don't suppose you'd reconsider using a Fire Shooter, would you?" Hollister asked.

"No," she answered and he decided not to press the issue.

"All right then, if you can cover our flank. And . . ."

"I will be going in to kill Malachi," she said.

"But if we need—" Hollister started to say.

"Malachi has eluded me for years. He may well bring about the end of my people still. I will do what I can to protect and support you in your efforts to destroy his followers. And I will kill all of them who get in my way. But I am here to kill Malachi, even if it means my own death."

"I . . . you . . . Shaniah . . . listen to me . . . please . . ." Hollister pleaded.

"The matter is closed," she said.

Hollister stood there, his mouth open, trying to think of something to say to change her mind, but he had nothing. He could tell she would not be swayed.

"All right then," he said. "Let's get in position."

Chapter Sixty-eight

The horses were secluded in the woods to the south of the camp, the direction they would need to flee in the train if everything turned to shit. They had less than two hours before the sun fell behind the mountains to the west. It wouldn't be sundown completely, but it wouldn't be direct sunlight either, and there was a better than good chance Archaics would exit the mine when the sun set. Hollister wanted to be ready.

Carefully he and Chee pulled the cart toward the building. They went as quietly as possible, and Monkey Pete had thought of everything, even greasing the wheels so they wouldn't squeak as they rolled over the rough terrain. Hollister studied the entrance to the mine shaft with the spyglass again for several minutes. He wasn't sure how far down into the mine the Archaics might go during the day and he hoped like hell they didn't stay close to the opening so any sentries might spot them. But he couldn't tell. The entrance was too dark and shrouded in shadow. He toyed with the idea of just dynamiting the entrance and trapping them all inside.

But such a plan had flaws. It wasn't likely to kill the Archaics and they could dig their way out. And if some were standing guard near the entrance Hollister and Chee would certainly be spotted, then all bets would be off.

"Shaniah," he said. "Can you see anyone inside there? Is there any way for you to tell if there is someone near the entrance who might see us?"

She peered through the telescope for several seconds. Her eyesight, hearing, and sense of smell were superior to his. As near as she could tell, there was no one close to the entrance.

"I don't see or hear anyone," she said.

"All right, we've got to move it anyway," Hollister said. "Let's go, Chee."

With as much stealth as they could muster, they rolled the cart toward the small building. There was no door left in the frame, so they pushed the cart right inside. Part of the wall facing the mine entrance had collapsed, an unbelievably lucky advantage as it gave the Gatling a wide and open field of fire yet a level of concealment. It would do the same for the Fire Shooters. Hollister took one of the cases of dynamite and a pouch full of ammo for the Henry and hefted them over his shoulder.

"This is it, Sergeant," he said. "Make every shot count."

"Yes, sir," Chee said. Hollister scratched Dog on the ears. This time the giant beast didn't growl or pull away.

"Well, look at that," Hollister said. "I'm probably going to die in ten minutes and now he decides he likes me."

"He's very particular," Chee said. "I think you've grown on him."

Again, Hollister couldn't tell if Chee was joking or not. And it was getting damned annoying.

"Sergeant, if we survive this, I swear to God, I'm going to figure you out. And your damn Dog too," Hollister said.

"I doubt it, sir," Chee said.

And then he smiled.

Chapter Sixty-nine

Shaniah was waiting for him in the other building. He set the dynamite near the window and pried off the lid. He checked the load on his Henry and leaned it against the wall next to the window. The Ass-Kicker was charged, the gauges on the Fire Shooter showed full. He was ready.

"I'm sorry," she said.

Hollister drew his Colt and rolled the cylinder along the sleeve of his duster. Each chamber held a round.

"For what?"

"What I said earlier."

He holstered the Colt. Jonas was jumpy as a cat, wishing the goddamn Archaics would pour out of the mine right now so he could start gunning them down.

She came to him and took his hands. "For hundreds of years we have avoided humans because we considered them enemies, and most of my people believed one day that our civilizations would meet and clash. With so few Archaics and so many humans, my people believed we would die. All of us. The Old Ones chose me to be the leader of my people, to be the one to see us through this. They believe I possess the skills to convince humans that we only wish to be left in peace—that we would continue to live as we have for centuries, without killing or feeding on humans. As long as we can stay in our homeland, left alone, we would remain peaceful. The killing we were responsible for centuries ago would be over. It *is* over."

She stopped, unsure of herself. As if she had lost her train of thought. Finally she figured out what she wished to say.

"Malachi may be the death of my people. He is vain, and he is cunning, but most of all he is evil. And if I do not kill him first, I promise you this. He will not murder hundreds but *thousands* of humans before he is stopped. If he survives and continues on this path, there will be no hope for peace between our peoples." She let go of his hands and paced back and forth in the shed a few times.

"Have you heard of dinosaurs, Jonas?" she asked.

"Yes, I read about them at the Point. Giant reptiles, lived millions of years ago, they figure."

"Exactly, they lived for millions of years and then they all died. Extinction, they call it. Many species of creatures gone, as if they had never existed. This is what will happen to us. It is what will happen to me, if I do not stop him," she said.

"I understand," Hollister said.

"Do you? I do not mean to be curt, but I do not think you do. There is greatness in you, Jonas Hollister. I sensed it when I first saw you face Malachi on the plains. Malachi saw it too. He drew back from you. Physically, he is your superior in almost every way, but you are brave and you are fearless, and you frightened him, if only for an instant. But what is most important about you, what sets you apart is, you have a sense of compassion that other men lack. Your strength is not just your courage or your abillity to shoot a gun, or the 'tactics' you study at this place you've called the 'Point.' You know what is right and what is not, when to fight and when to stand down. You make instant judgments about men. And you are never wrong. Take Chee as an example. You told me you hardly knew him in prison, but then you saw him fight these men and you judged him. You were right about him. Now he follows you and will continue to follow you without question, forever. You have shown him these same qualities in you that I just spoke of and he will now ride with you through the gates of hell. He trusts you with his life.

"In Absolution you were bold and daring. So much so, that you could have gotten everyone killed, but he followed your orders without hesitation because he trusts you. And from the moment you took him from the prison he will never not trust you."

Hollister didn't know what to say. He'd heard his commanders at the Point and generals he'd served under in the war say he was a natural born leader, but he didn't believe there was any such thing. Apparently, Shaniah thought otherwise.

He had to make her understand something. They were running out of time. "The reason I said what I said, about you covering our flank . . . it's only because . . . I . . . I don't want you to die, Shaniah. You've taken something from me, and I don't know what it is . . . but there is a piece of me that belongs to you now and . . . I don't want . . ." He couldn't get the words out. "I'm no good with words. I know it sounds impossible, foolish even, but it's how I feel and it makes no sense . . . but . . . isn't that what love is?"

"I love you too, Jonas," she said. "And you are much better with words than you think."

She kissed him then. It was a kiss that comes only a few times in your life. When you know you have found the one. Time stops. The world becomes clean and bright. It was that type of kiss. It bonded them forever from that moment. If Jonas believed in God he would have said, "God help me, but I love her so." But he didn't believe in God anymore: he just knew that whatever had happened between them over these past few days—he knew he loved her. How could he love her? How could they be together? She wasn't even a human, not in any way that made sense. It would be like a pirate loving a mermaid. And he didn't believe in mermaids but he damn sure believed in her.

"I . . . no one has ever said that to me before," he said. "And what I told you yesterday, in the valley. I'm with you all the way, I will kill Malachi with my bare hands if it means saving you, because I . . ."

But before he could finish the first of the Archaics emerged from the mine.

It was on.

Chapter Seventy

One came out first. Then three more, then they straggled out in groups. Surprisingly to Jonas, they looked almost like humans waking from a deep sleep. Rubbing their eyes and stretching, as more and more of them emerged.

"They look like they've been sleeping. You said that's good, right?" he asked.

"Yes. Malachi has chosen this place because it is very similar to our homeland. Mountainous. Largely deserted. But he has gone through the surrounding territory, found enough humans, and started raising his army.

"As a result there are few if any humans left nearby to feed on. And what humans they have found have been given to Malachi. Feeding on *Huma Sangra* makes an Archaic much stronger."

The Archaics continued to pour out of the mine, more than a hundred so far.

"He's been feeding," Hollister said. "But his army hasn't. At least not as much. So that makes them weaker."

"Yes, but do not be fooled or careless. Even without *Huma*

Sangra, they are much stronger, faster, more vicious than humans. They likely have been feeding on animals from the woods and plains nearby. Just as I have. They will still be formidable. And Malachi . . ."

"What? What about him?" Hollister said.

"He will be the strongest of all of them. You must leave him to me," she said.

"But you haven't had human blood either, have you?"

"No, it is forbidden by the Old Ones, and I have kept my vow. But they have also prepared me. Do not worry, Jonas. Malachi is strong. But so am I." She smiled.

He tried not to worry, but it didn't work. All he could see was Malachi as he had seen him on the plains so many years ago, the bullets bouncing off him like pebbles. Being thrown on the ground like a rag doll. Sitting on Hollister's chest, Malachi's fists pounding on his face like anvils dropped on his head. Only he saw Shaniah being beaten this time and the thought terrified him.

"What are you going to do?" he asked. It was all he could think of to say.

"I need you to open fire when Malachi appears. The wind is with us. They will not smell us yet. Pray the wind does not shift. Concentrate on the Archaics. You are unlikely to hit him anyway. He will be too quick for most of your weapons. I will focus on him," she said.

"What if you don't find him?" Hollister said.

"Then he will find me," Shaniah said. "You see, Jonas, he has been waiting for this moment ever since he escaped our homeland. He will not let it pass."

"I don't like this," Hollister said.

"I know," Shaniah replied. "But you made a promise to me. Do you intend to keep it?"

He looked at her, memorizing her face because he knew he might not see her alive again.

"All the way," he said.

* * *

More and more Archaics flooded out of the mine. Through the collapsed wall of the building, he could see Chee in the shed, hands on the Gatling gun, ready to wreak havoc. He couldn't see Dog, but he imagined him next to Chee, coiled and ready to attack anything that moved when given the command.

At the Point he'd been trained to determine enemy strength by counting a group of ten, getting a read on the size of those ten then roughly counting the number of groups that size in the force arrayed against you. Using the technique, Hollister guessed there were about three hundred Archaics. He'd expected more, so he was somewhat relieved; but killing them wasn't easy, so he'd count his blessings. He readied the Fire Shooter.

Something was happening at the mine. The crowd was parting. Malachi emerged. Even after all this time, Hollister had no trouble recognizing him. It was the same man who had killed his men. His hair was longer and even from this distance he seemed taller. But there was no doubt in Hollister's mind it was him. He stepped up on some crates that had been pushed together like a small stage, as if he were about to give a sermon at a revival

"There he is." Hollister turned to tell Shaniah.

But she was gone.

Malachi looked out at the crowd of his Archaics, their faces eager for him to lead them. They were hungry and desperate to feed. He would send them to destroy the train and then . . .

He was about to speak when images of Shaniah flooded his brain. She was here, and very close by. He knew she had been coming but this surprised him. He studied the woods and the nearby mountainsides. To the south he smelled horses. But she was not there. Even after all this time, he would know her scent anywhere. The woods surrounding the mine clearing were also devoid of her presence. Where was she?

His eyes settled on the buildings. They were less than one hundred yards away from where he stood. She was not there either, or was she? Strange smells came from the structures. Had she masked her scent somehow? Someone was there, and from the buildings came another odor he faintly recognized. Whoever it was would need to be dealt with. Quickly.

"Listen!" he said loudly and the Archaics surrounding him quieted instantly. "We have been discovered. Shaniah is here. And she is not alone. We must find her. Those buildings hide those who seek to destroy us. Kill them."

The Archaics turned in concert, readying themselves to charge.

The buildings were just far enough away that neither Hollister nor Chee could hear what Malachi was saying. When the entire group of Archaics looked at the buildings, they knew they been discovered.

Hollister wanted to wait until they got within forty yards before using the Fire Shooter to make sure they were within range. First, he started picking them off with the Henry. It was extremely accurate at this distance and he'd chosen the load of wooden bullets dipped in holy water. Whenever he could hit one directly in the heart it made for an agonizing death.

Once Hollister had fired off a few shots, the group targeted his building. Hundreds of them running and leaping across the ground. To Jonas it felt like they would be upon him in seconds. Until Chee opened up with the Gatling.

It cut them down like a scythe in a wheat field. Archaics might be stronger and faster than humans, but they were not immune to pain, and the sound of their screams echoed off the surrounding mountains as they went down in waves, twisting and writhing on the ground.

Yet, some still made it through and while Chee kept the big gun chattering away, Hollister opened up with the Fire Shooter. It caused mass confusion at first, then more cries of agony as body after body burst into flames. In the course of two minutes, they had greatly reduced the numbers heading toward them.

Hollister still saw no sign of Shaniah, but he could see Malachi standing on the crates, watching the devastation take place before him. Hollister kept the trigger down on his Fire Shooter because there were still Archaics charging forward. But he looked at his Henry rifle leaning against the wall and for a moment toyed with the idea of picking it up and taking a shot at Malachi. From this distance, if he could hit him in the heart, he could end this whole thing. But he couldn't risk it. There were still too many of them coming and they could be on him before he could get the shot off.

He looked at the gauge on the Fire Shooter. It was already down by half. This was going to get interesting in a hurry.

Chapter Seventy-one

Malachi could not believe what was happening. His followers, the army he had sired, gunned down and burned to near death before his eyes. How? This was not Shaniah's doing. He knew that. It was humans who had created weapons that killed and maimed his people. Impossible.

He remembered centuries before, when the Old Ones had decided that mankind had grown beyond the ability of the Archaics to treat them simply as prey. He had argued against it then and he had opposed it again when the Council chose Shaniah to be their leader. *We are Archaics!* He had reasoned. *Humans should tremble before us!* But the Council had been too weak. They had always been too timid. Afraid of tiny beings no better than insects.

When the decision to avoid human contact was made, the Archaics fractured. Most went along to the high mountains of Eastern Romania. But a few scattered, never to be heard from again. There were times he wondered about those who had chosen freedom; had they survived? Had they lived and prospered in the human world? Did they still feast on the *Huma Sangra*?

Malachi had decided to wait. He went along with the others to the high mountains. But one day he would become an Eternal. *Then* he would take control of his people. And he would show them that humans were not to be feared. Humans were nothing more than food.

Once he left, after Shaniah's ascension to leadership, he had quickly learned on his journey to this place about the advances of humankind and their remarkable ingenuity. He had seen human weapons up close. Had felt them cut his skin and pierce his flesh. And he had found them to be no match for a true Archaic. A mosquito bite. Even those humans who had learned control of the elementals did not instill fear in him. He was unbeatable.

To Malachi, humans were nothing more than walking meals. He remembered that, a few years ago, he had been on the plains of Wyoming and his band had killed a group of soldiers. One of the soldiers had shot him several times. He felt the bullets stinging his skin but hardly slowing him down. The soldier had no idea how close he was to death. How Malachi would feast on his blood. But the sun came up and he did not have time to kill and drain the man.

Archaics owned the night. Another reason they could decimate the human race when he raised his army. Humans feared the night. Darkness was a great disadvantage to them. They could not see, did not feel or hear the presence of an Archaic stalking them until the fangs sank into their necks. And they died, as they should.

He had come to America to get away from the very Archaics like Shaniah and the Old Ones who could have stopped him if he had stayed in the old country. Every step of the way he had planned carefully, turning followers when they were needed, but carefully planning and growing.

He was close to unleashing his full fury on the human

race, but now he saw before him these puny creatures that stood toe to toe with his Archaics unafraid, with weapons he could not imagine. The cries and screams of agony of his people brought him back to the present.

He was angry and confused, and for a moment not sure of what he should do. Should he retreat? Let his soldiers die here and start afresh somewhere else? All he needed to do was live three more days and he would be an Eternal. Nothing, no weapon, no spell, no elemental could kill him after that.

"I tried to tell you this would happen."

The voice from behind him actually startled him, but he showed now sign of it as he turned to face her.

"Hello, Shaniah," he said. "It is good to see you again."

Chapter Seventy-two

Hollister emptied the Fire Shooter and then shrugged the other one onto his back, twisted the knob, and pulled the trigger. Fire shot out of the barrel and more Archaics screamed and died. In Absolution, Shaniah had said that fire would not kill an Archaic. He had to consider the possibility that she was lying or withholding something in case she needed some tactical advantage later. Because to Hollister it looked like the Fire Shooter took the flesh right off their bones. He wondered if they were able to regrow skin. Maybe they could come back to life as skeletons or something. Or maybe Monkey Pete had put something in his "mixture" to give it a little extra kick. Holy water, maybe? Whatever it was, the Archaics sure looked dead.

The ground between the two buildings and the mine shaft was littered with bodies. By Hollister's count there were maybe only sixty Archaics left alive. It was almost over. If they killed the rest of them, he could go after Malachi. He checked the gauge on the Fire Shooter and it now was about a quarter of a tank full.

He was swinging the barrel back and forth, the fire knocking down Archaics like bowling pins. Up near the mine entrance he saw Malachi still standing on the crates. It was like he was glued to the spot, forced by someone to watch his army crumble before his eyes. Suddenly Malachi broke for the mine shaft, and Hollister thought for sure he saw someone in a dark coat and flash of blond hair following him. Shaniah. Going into the mine after Malachi. A bad idea. Really bad idea. He couldn't let her do it alone. She had taken a part of him. His heart, his soul. He just knew he couldn't let her face Malachi alone.

He glanced across at Chee in the shed, still working the Gatling.

"CHEE!" he hollered, hoping he could be heard over the sound of the gun. The sergeant looked in his direction.

"I'm going after Malachi. You clean up the rest!"

"Major! I don't think—"

"Shaniah is in there with him!"

"Sir! Please don't, she will be able to . . ."

But Hollister was no longer paying attention. He slung the Ass-Kicker over his shoulder. For good measure, he put a couple of bundles of dynamite in the pockets of his duster. He grabbed the Henry with one hand and kept the barrel of the almost empty Fire Shooter in his other. He glanced out the open wall. He had a clear path most of the way to the mine. Chee was still working the Gatling and Hollister reminded himself to thank Monkey Pete for packing so much additional ammo.

Hollister broke through the door frame and cut to his left around the building. There weren't any Archaics closer than thirty yards away, so he sprinted toward the mine. Five or six noticed he was out in the open and came his way. He pulled the trigger on the Fire Shooter. And as often happens in dangerous or combat situations, a strange and silly thought entered his mind. He really didn't like the name

"Fire Shooter" for Pete's weapon. He made a mental note to work on a new name for it.

The fire shot out of the barrel and drove the advancing Archaics back, giving him time to run toward the mine shaft. And he would have made it just fine if he hadn't tripped and fallen face-first into the dirt. He wasn't hurt—mostly embarrassed, and afraid he was going to die like a fool, letting six Archaics jump on him and tear him apart. When he got to his knees though, he saw how close he was to serious trouble and his embarrassment disappeared. An Archaic had seen him tumble and lunged in his direction. Hollister swore they could cover twenty yards in a single bound. It would be on him in an instant. He dropped the Fire Shooter and tried to bring his Henry up so he could shoot, but the slings and belts were all tangled up from the fall. Only ten yards left, he pulled his Colt and was raising it to fire when Dog knocked the Archaic flat on its ass.

The creature had once been a young boy, and though he possessed newfound strength and agility with his new Archaic abilities, he was no match for the massive, enraged animal. There was no question Dog had developed a passionate hatred for Archaics. He wasted no time, grabbing the throat and shaking the creature as easily as he might shake a rabbit. Hollister staggered to his feet, raised the Henry, and shot the Archaic in the heart. It exploded into a cloud of dust. If it was possible for a canine to look disappointed, Dog did.

"Sorry to ruin your fun, boy. I appreciate you saving me and all, but I'm in a rush," he said.

He checked the Henry and both pistols. The dynamite remained in the pockets of his duster. But the barrel of Fire Shooter was now clogged with dirt. He knocked it on his boot trying to clear it, and some of it came loose but it was still plugged, deep in the barrel. He shrugged out of the apparatus and left it there. He didn't have time to try to fix it and it was almost out of fuel. The Ass-Kicker was probably a better choice anyway. He slung the Henry on his back and pulled the Ass-Kicker around to his waist. He worked the action, heard the small hiss of steam as the round chambered and locked in place. He was ready to go. All of his preparations had taken place while Chee continued firing the Gatling, keeping the remaining Archaics at bay.

"Thanks again, Dog," Hollister said. "I'll see you on the other side."

He ran toward the mine shaft, surprised to find Dog loping along beside him.

The Archaics had been whittled down to a few clusters scattered between the shed and the mine shaft. Hollister ran as fast as he could while shooting with some level of accuracy. Dog worked like an anti-sheepdog; when an Archaic approached, he chased it away, never getting too far away from Hollister.

Finally he reached the entrance. It was dark inside, and he wished he'd thought to bring a torch. He glanced quickly around, but there was nothing serviceable nearby. Luckily he had Dog.

"All right boy, let's find Shaniah," he said. He tried to think of how Chee addressed the animal, compelling it to do what the sergeant commanded. He remembered something Chee always said to the giant animal.

"Dog! Hunt!" he said.

Chapter Seventy-three

As Malachi ran deeper into the mine, he could hear Shaniah following behind him. The Old Ones had sent her to kill him. He assumed they would just let him go, figuring that a human with a new weapon or an elemental would eventually kill him. Yet, here she was. Impressive. The Council had decided he was too dangerous. If he succeeded with any part of his plan, he would bring human wrath down on the Archaics. From tonight's events it looked as if he had miscalculated and the Council of Elders had been right to be concerned about the advancement of the human race.

The mine was played out long ago and no more gold remained, but the structure of it and its darkness made it ideal for Archaics to use. And he and his followers had made some modifications. Up ahead they had dug a wider, more open space. A chamber most often used when they brought captured humans here for feeding. It was perhaps forty feet by forty feet and well lit by torches.

Shaniah was getting closer. The blade was at his belt. Where the shaft widened into the larger, open space he stopped and stood to the side of the entrance. It was an old trick, but she had been tracking him for years, and hopefully, her exuberance would make her foolhardy. When she ran through the entrance he would kill her. Poor Shaniah. The Council had sent her, but she had accepted her assignment and her fate was her responsibility. He gripped the blade.

He waited. The sound of her running had stopped. She was being cautious. He could smell her, but . . .

Shaniah exploded into the room. She came in low, rolling through the door, and his mighty swing of the blade hit nothing but air until it caught in the wood beam that supported the doorway. He worked to pull it loose, but as quick as a cat, she was on her feet and staggered him with a kick to his midsection. He regained his footing and she crouched as they faced each other, circling slowly like two rams about to charge.

"I didn't think you'd come," he said.

"Yes, you did," Shaniah replied.

He lunged at her, swinging his blade, but she dodged easily away, pulling her blade from her boot.

"We don't need to fight," he said. "We both want the same thing."

"No we don't, Malachi. We never have. I want our people to survive. What you want leads only to their destruction."

"You couldn't be more—" He slightly lowered his weapon as he spoke, giving her the opening she had been waiting for and she swung her blade with all of her might. But he ducked it easily.

"As I was saying," he said, backing farther away from her. "You couldn't be more wrong. The Council is full of weak and ancient fools. They ask us to live like cattle."

"What they ask is that we survive." They continued to circle each other.

"Survive." He spat out the word as if it tasted bitter. "We are Archaics, a race far older and stronger than humans. We conquer. We do not succumb."

"No, Malachi, you are wrong. We are dinosaurs."

"Dinosaurs? I'm afraid I'm not familiar with the term," he said. Shaniah lunged at him, swinging her blade, but he blocked it again easily, pushing her violently into the wall of the chamber. His strength was incredible. It was the *Huma Sangra*. It had restored him. She scrambled to her hands and knees, trying to stand, but she had hit the wall solidly and it had stunned her. Before she could move again or react, he was behind her, his hand grabbing her hair and pulling her head back exposing her throat. He held the blade close to her, wanting her to be afraid as the steel kissed her skin.

"Do you feel it, Shaniah?" He yanked her by the hair, pulled her head back so far she felt the muscles of her neck strain to the point where she was afraid they were going to snap.

"It is the power of the *Huma Sangra*, Shaniah." He tightened the grip on her hair and with the hand holding the blade he held his wrist close to her nose. "The *Huma Sangra* flows through my veins. You can smell it, Shaniah . . . taste it . . . go ahead. You can feel it."

And the truth of it was, she *could* feel it. And part of her wanted it. She knew it was wrong, she had resisted it for centuries, but now . . . so close . . . so near Malachi and his power. It was overwhelming her.

"No . . . I . . . will . . . not," she said. Her free hand went to his wrist holding her hair in a twisted mass. She tried hard to break his grip but it was like iron. She twisted and struggled and clawed at his hand, but found she was loosing her strength.

There was a loud explosion. Suddenly Malachi's grip was broken and he flew through the air, hitting the far wall with a hard thump.

Hollister and the Ass-Kicker had arrived.

Chapter Seventy-four

Chee had watched as Hollister and Dog disappeared inside the mine. The major was following Malachi and Shaniah. Unless Chee acted, and soon, Jonas Hollister was going to die. He pulled back the slide on the Gatling and loaded a new belt of wooden bullets. Hollister had found an opening in the Archaic line and made it to the entrance. But there were another twenty or thirty Archaics still standing, and they needed to be dealt with first.

He pulled the trigger, but nothing happened. This was not good. He pulled the slide open and immediately saw the problem. One of the wooden bullets had fractured into several pieces and jammed the action on the gun. He tried clearing the splinters but there were too many. The gun was momentarily useless.

The Archaics realized the shooting had stopped and slowly they ventured closer to the shed. Chee tried desperately to free the action of the gun. No time. With the butt of the Henry, he knocked open the crate of dynamite left on the cart. He removed two sticks of dynamite and lit them. There were howls and shouts coming from outside as the Archaics grew bolder. The fuses on the dynamite hissed as he stepped back to the window and was shocked to see how close they had gotten. He tossed the dynamite through the window.

The Archaics were hit full-on from twenty yards by the concussion wave of the explosion. A few of them tried to turn and run when they saw the sticks spinning through the air, but they had ventured too close to the shed and they were blown down like dead stalks of wheat. Chee poured it on, keeping the flame working over them until there was nothing left but piles of charred flesh.

Looking out through the opening in the shed wall, he could not see an Archaic standing anywhere. He picked up one of the Henry rifles and hung it on his shoulder. Monkey Pete had designed the Gatling to be released from the cart by untwisting a large screw. He took the sling from the spare Henry and fastened it to the Gatling gun so it hung at his waist. Looping a belt of ammunition around his shoulders, he left the building. He worked his way through the mass of destruction and dead bodies that lined the ground between the buildings and the mine.

At the entrance he looked behind him, making sure there were no signs of life among the bodies on the ground. Archaics could heal quickly, and he wanted to make sure no one was left alive to attack from the rear. The Archaics in the field lay still. Their weapons had reaped mass destruction on these creatures. He and Major Hollister had brought killing machines to this fight. And they had won. At least this battle.

He heard noise up ahead, coming from deep inside the mine shaft. It sounded like a fight.

Chapter Seventy-five

Hollister was never happier in his life than when he saw Shaniah still alive. If he could rush to her right at this moment and hold her in his arms he would. But that would get them both killed.

Malachi should be dead. Or at least unconscious. But after receiving a direct hit from the Ass-Kicker, Malachi was climbing to his feet. Shaniah was crawling around on the ground looking for the blade she carried.

"Holy shit," Hollister muttered as he watched Malachi, now standing.

Malachi had changed. His jaw was elongated, the fangs had descended, and his eyes had turned red. He charged at Hollister, who barely had time to work the action and shoot before Malachi was upon him.

Dog came to his rescue again and charged at Malachi. Malachi laughed at the thought of the hound attempting to stop him, and when Dog leapt for his throat, he backhanded him across the head. Dog spun through the air, hitting the chamber wall with a loud yelp and fell silently to the ground.

Hollister fired the Ass-Kicker a second time and Malachi tumbled backward, the shell catching him square in the chest and knocking him down. He had to be dead now, the shot should have felled a bull elephant. Malachi lay on his back, not moving.

Shaniah rose, the blade now in her hand.

"I think that did it," Hollister said.

"No, it is not finished. Not yet," she said. Holding the blade in both hands, she walked toward Malachi. Hollister remembered what Van Helsing had said. Decapitation was the surest way to kill an Archaic.

Standing over him, she raised the blade over her head and brought it down in a vicious whistling arc.

An inch before the blade reached his neck, Malachi caught it with both hands. He leapt to his feet, twisting the blade from her grasp.

"How the hell do you kill this bastard?" Hollister shouted.

Malachi laughed.

"I remember you now. You're the bug I nearly squashed on the plains of Wyoming almost—when was it now, four years ago?"

"Yeah, but I'm still here, aren't I, you piece of shit," he said. "And this bug bites back."

Hollister worked the action on the Ass-Kicker but he couldn't shoot because Shaniah was in the way. He dropped it on the ground. It only had two shots left and it wasn't having any effect anyway. He drew one of his Colts, knowing those shots wouldn't kill him but they might distract him like a bee sting. Long enough to get Shaniah away.

"Shaniah, watch out . . ." he cried. But he was too late. Malachi threw Shaniah against the rock wall of the chamber and Hollister knew she was hurt now. But he had a clearer shot and he fired the Colt, hitting Malachi in the shoulder. There was no reaction. He shot again, this time hitting him in the side. Still no response. He fired a third time.

Malachi turned toward him.

"Ow. Stop," he said, his voice dripping with sarcasm.

He leapt across the chamber to where Shaniah lay in a crumpled heap and grabbed her by the throat, raising her up and slamming her into the chamber wall. Jonas fired again, hitting him in the arm. The bullet had barely entered his flesh before it popped out again. Whatever had happened to him since their first encounter in Wyoming, he was much stronger now.

"You are only wasting bullets," Malachi said. "If you are smart you will put one of those bullets in your head. Do it now and I promise to kill Shaniah quickly."

Shaniah was conscious now and clawing at Malachi's hand at her throat.

"Fuck you. I've got plenty of bullets," Hollister said. He raised both Colts, firing at Malachi until both guns clicked on empty chambers.

"I almost killed you too, you fucking bastard, but you were too afraid of the sun to keep going," Hollister said as he slapped two new speed loaders into the Colts.

Malachi laughed. "You almost killed me? You are humorous, human. What is your name? I wish to know it before I drain you of your blood." He casually threw Shaniah aside like she was someone's doll. "I will kill you first," he said. "You are suddenly more interesting to me than Shaniah. I can always find another wife."

The words hit Hollister like a punch in the gut. A wife? Malachi was her husband? Well, this was news. He tried hard not to let his face show anything, but failed. And Malachi noticed.

"You . . . are you . . . ? Incredible. She has taken a human as a lover? You? A puny, pitiful man? And she never told you?" He threw back his head and laughed. "We have been lovers for centuries. Longer than you can ever imagine, and now you think . . ."

Hollister had heard enough. His first Colt empty, he raised the Colts again and fired, point-blank, trying to hit Malachi's heart, but the bullets could not penetrate far enough. Hollister emptied the gun, making a nearly perfect circle of bullet holes in the Archaic's chest. Malachi looked down at his chest, then up at Hollister.

"I give you humans points for ingenuity." A bullet was working its way out of his skin and he removed it, holding it up to examine it.

"Silver on the tip, projectile made of wood, and judging by how much they burn, I'm guessing you dipped them in holy water?"

"Go to hell," Hollister muttered. Malachi was less than an arm's length away.

"Oh, we will all go to hell," Malachi said. "That is no question. Except for me of course, as I am about to become immortal."

His hand was closing around Hollister's neck when there was a loud explosion and Malachi flew sideways, hitting the wall. Chee stood in center of the chamber holding the Ass-Kicker. Malachi shook his head, rolled on his back, then got to his hands and knees and looked at Chee.

"We *may* all go to hell, but I think we'll send you first," Chee said.

Chapter Seventy-six

They were dead now and Hollister knew it. Nothing worked. The Ass-Kicker had one shot left and it would be the least powerful. Chee was wearing the Gatling somehow slung over his shoulder, but who knew if that would even stop Malachi? It appeared that nothing short of a mountain dropped on him would work. And maybe not even that.

Chee raised his Henry and shot Malachi in the face. The bullet collapsed Malachi's left cheek just below the eye and the force of the shot staggered him backward. But almost instantly, his wound started healing. *For the love of God*, Hollister thought. *How much blood has this asshole drunk?* The way it was going, he must have drained the entire city of Chicago.

"Sir!" Chee shouted. He tossed Jonas the Henry and with both hands free, turned the Gatling toward Malachi.

"The Gatling, Chee! Now!" Hollister shouted.

Jonas had one speed loader for his Colt left and that was it. He loaded it up. They needed to get the hell out of here.

Hollister shot Malachi again, to distract him, but the Archaic paid him no attention; he jumped across the chamber toward Chee and tried wrestling the Gatling from his grip. Chee saw his chance and opened up with the Gatling at point-blank range.

The wooden bullets had effect this time. They drove Malachi back. As he staggered toward the opposite chamber wall, Chee advanced, and as the belt of bullets writhed through the action of the gun, Malachi actually cried out. The stone wall finally stopped him, and Chee, from no more than five feet away, fired and fired, until the gun was completely empty.

Malachi staggered toward Chee, and Hollister took careful aim and shot him in the eye. He dropped to the floor of the chamber. Hollister shot again trying for the heart, and again and again, and then he pulled the trigger and his heart sank as he felt the hammer land on an empty chamber. He pulled the trigger again and again. It was no use: the gun was empty.

Malachi looked up at them from the stone floor.

"You've done well, humans. I will grant you that small satisfaction. You've killed far too many of my people and no one has damaged me to such a degree in centuries. But you cannot kill me. I will leave here and heal, and raise more followers; then I will kill all of your kind. Every last one of you. Remember . . . in a few short days I shall have lived for fifteen centuries. Nothing will stop me then," he said.

With a degree of strength Jonas could not fathom, he climbed to his feet. He backhanded Chee, who tumbled backward onto the ground and was still. He was upon Hollister in an instant, pressing him against the wall of the chamber. His hand closed around Jonas's throat. Somehow, through it all, he had maintained his grip on his blade; he thrust it into Hollister's gut and Jonas remembered thinking that he should have told Pinkerton to go fuck himself when he'd come to Leavenworth that day. Digging wells was far better than having your guts strung out by this pompous asshole. Malachi pulled the blade out. Hollister clutched his gut, blood seeping out of his stomach, as he slowly slid down the wall toward the floor.

"You will all die," Malachi said "Remember that . . ."

But Malachi died first, as Shaniah rose behind him, swinging her blade with all of her might, connecting at the spot where his neck met his shoulders, and his head came cleanly off his body.

His face had one last instant of surprise and shock as it rolled onto the chamber floor.

"You know what, Malachi? Go fuck yourself," Hollister said as the head rolled to a stop a few feet away from him, the empty eyes taking on a curious look of amazement.

Chapter Seventy-seven

Shaniah stood over Malachi's dead body, holding her Archaic blade. Jonas pressed at his wound, but the blood still seeped through his fingers. He'd seen enough wounds like this in the war to know he wasn't going to make it.

She secreted the blade in her boot and rushed to his side. Dog came to then, standing on unsteady feet and shaking his head. He went to Chee and licked his face, but Chee didn't seem to respond much.

Shaniah held Hollister's face in her hands. He was gravely wounded, but she knew a way to save him. The blade Malachi had stabbed him with lay on the ground a few inches away. She picked it up, and drawing it across her palm, she opened a cut.

"I thought you told me your blade was all you needed," he said.

"I lied," she said.

"Hmm. Lied about a couple of other things too, apparently?" he said. "You forgot to mention the whole married to the evil mastermind thing."

"Would it have mattered?" she asked him, putting her hand on his cheek.

He tried to focus on her face but it was hard. It seemed like someone was taking great pleasure in making the world spin. He finally found her, with one eye closed. She was still beautiful.

"No, it wouldn't have made an ounce of difference," he said.

She held her hand, the cut seeping blood up to Hollister's face.

"You need to drink this," she said.

Without warning there was a gun against the side of her head. Chee stood there, his Colt pressed against her temple. Dog was next to him, growling. How she hated that goddamned dog. Chee pulled back the hammer on the pistol.

"What are you doing?" Shaniah said.

"Don't move," Chee said.

"He's going to die," she said.

"He might not," Chee answered back.

Hollister was losing blood and getting the giddy, nearly drunken feeling one can only experience with too much blood loss.

"What are you two doing? You need to stop arguing and start getting along. And stop calling each other witches. I mean it," he said. Then he giggled, slightly delirious.

"Archaic blood can heal him. He only needs a little," she said.

"Better he dies than turns into one of you," Chee said.

"He won't. He can't become . . . he won't turn. He has to be bitten first, then he has to drink the blood of the one who bit him, the sire. That's the only way it works. But this will keep him alive, it has healing powers."

"I don't believe you, *Brujana*," he said.

"Chee," Hollister said. His voice was weak. "It's all right. Let her do it. It might work, it might not, but I'm done otherwise."

Chee stared at Shaniah hard. Dog still looked like he wanted to see if he could fit her entire head in his mouth.

Finally, he lowered the gun. "Dog, off," he said. Dog stopped growling instantly and sat on his haunches.

Shaniah pushed her bleeding hand to Hollister's mouth. She pulled open his lips and squeezed blood into his mouth. She kept at it until his face was covered with it. He slipped into unconsciousness.

"What now?" Chee asked.

"We wait," Shaniah said. They waited several minutes. Chee checked Hollister's pulse.

"Shit," Hollister said, his eyes open again. He had slumped over onto the floor when he had gone unconscious, and now he came to, staring face to face with Malachi's dismembered head. Staring at the head locked in a death grimace, he said, "Remind me never to make you angry."

"You're alive," she said, falling to the ground beside him and taking his head in her hands.

"Either that, or we're all dead. Can dead people talk to each other? Chee, you know a lot about dead people."

Chee shook his head. "I don't know, Major." But he smiled. Glad that Hollister was alive.

The color slowly returned to Hollister's face. "All right. I think we've killed everyone we were supposed to, so let's get out of here. Help me up."

Chee and Shaniah lifted him slowly to his feet.

"Getting stabbed sure does hurt," he said. "Got stabbed a couple times in the war and it always hurt more than getting shot. Which always surprises me." Hollister realized he was babbling, but he was so happy to be among the living he didn't care.

Shaniah laughed. They slowly left the chamber behind, Dog in the lead, Chee and Shaniah on either side of Hollister, holding him up.

"Wait, I forgot something." He reached into the pocket of his duster and pulled out the two bundles of dynamite. There were six sticks in each bundle and the fuses were wrapped around the bundles.

"What do you say we make sure old Malachi stays put?" Hollister said.

"Keep going, I'll back up and set the charges," Chee said.

Every step brought Hollister searing pain, but he could also tell he wasn't going to die anymore. Shaniah's blood was bringing him some relief. They were a few feet away from the entrance when Chee came sprinting back.

"Probably best if we hurry," he said. He took Hollister's other arm and they picked up the pace, wanting to be outside before the dynamite went off. Twenty yards or so ahead of them, Dog starting barking and growling, sniffing the air ahead of him, the hair on his neck standing up.

Chee racked a round into the chamber of his Henry. Shaniah took hold of her blade with her free hand. "You think some Archaics survived out there?" Hollister asked.

"Don't know," said Chee. "That's not his Archaic bark."

Even though it hurt, Hollister had to laugh. "He has different barks?"

"Yes, sir," Chee said. "That is his 'bad man' bark."

They finally cleared the entrance and found why Dog was barking. It wasn't Archaics. Standing just outside the mine was Slater, holding the Fire Shooter Hollister had abandoned before he entered the mine.

"Howdy," Slater said. "Good to see you survived."

Chapter Seventy-eight

Slater was standing in front of six mounted horsemen, deployed in a semicircle behind him. Some of them held torches, painting the area in a flickering orange-blue light. Slater was pointing the barrel of the Fire Shooter at the ground but in their general direction. All six of his men had their guns pointed at the three of them.

"Mr. Slater," Hollister said, trying not to grimace as he spoke. "It's awfully nice of the senator to send you here as our backup. But as you can see we managed to put these things down and everything's fine, so your service is no longer required in this campaign."

Slater lifted the barrel of the Fire Shooter, studying it, running his free hand over the barrel if he were inspecting a horse he wanted to buy. He smiled an ugly smile and looked at Hollister.

"I think you know he didn't send me here for no backup," Slater said. "You don't look so good, by the way."

Hollister could only imagine what he did look like, his

shirt and face covered in blood and his body battered from being tossed around by Malachi inside a room made entirely of rock.

"Never better, actually," Hollister said. "We got a lot of paperwork needs doing after all the shooting and exploding we did here. And Pinkerton and his men are on the way. So we're going to get to it, if you'll excuse us."

Slater snorted. "I don't think you got any backup coming. And even if what you're saying is true, it'll take Pinkerton a while to get here. And you'll be dead and we'll be long gone before he arrives."

"Chee, why the hell hasn't the dynamite gone off yet?" Hollister muttered quietly.

"What's that? Didn't quite catch it," Slater said.

Chee had his Henry held at port arms and would never be able to get a shot off before one of Slater's gun thugs shot him down.

"I was just telling Sergeant Chee here to shoot you first, once the shooting starts," Hollister lied, trying to buy time until he could think of a way to stall Slater and his men. He tried to stand up straighter, but his wound sent another wave of pain through him and he bent forward again. The dynamite must have been duds, because there was no explosion.

"You know Shaniah here, she's impervious to fire, plus she's fast. Faster than Chee."

"Well, Major Hollister, I never went to West Point, so I don't reckon I know what 'imperialist' means . . ." Slater started to say.

"Impervious, not imperialist, you moron," Hollister interrupted. "Means fire can't kill her." *Where is the damn dynamite?* he thought. "Chee," he muttered out of the side of his mouth. "You still got ammo?"

"Yes, sir," Chee replied. "Six shots."

"Crap on a Cracker," Hollister said. "I'm out."

"As soon as you two finish your little conversation there,

please let me know. I'd like to get to the part where I kill the three of you," Slater said.

"Kill these men," Shaniah said. "Burn me with your contraption there, empty all of your guns into me. I will not die. And when I heal, which will only take a matter of days, I will find you, Mr. Slater. I have your scent. I will hunt you down and I will kill you. Without any hesitation."

Hollister was growing impatient. Standoffs like this were not his forte. In the war, on the plains, he attacked or retreated to find a better tactical position. Waiting for the fighting to start was annoying as hell. It also led to stupid mistakes, he reminded himself. He wanted his explosion, he wanted his stomach to stop hurting like a bitch, and he wouldn't mind putting a bullet in Slater's head just to top off his day. He was out of ideas though.

Slater stared at Shaniah, his reptilian eyes slitted nearly closed, as he considered her words.

"You know, I've done a lot of killing over the years," Slater said, looking at the barrel of the Fire Shooter again. "Shot people, strangled a few, stabbed a fellow once in Wichita . . ."

"Was that you?" Hollister said. "Because I've heard Wichita doesn't usually get a lot of stabbings, but this one year . . ."

"Shut your mouth!" Slater shouted. "Like I was saying, hung folks, pushed a rustler off a cliff, pretty much killed every way you can. 'Cept I ain't ever burned anybody to death before."

He lowered the Fire Shooter and pointed it at Chee. "While we was watching you fight these . . ." He looked around at the piles of dead bodies. " . . . whatever the hell these things are, I got real interested in your little flamethrowers here."

"Hey. Flamethrower, that's a pretty good name. We were calling them Fire Shooters, but I didn't much care for that. I like flamethrower a lot better, don't you, Chee?" Hollister said.

"Yes, sir," Chee said, never taking his eyes off Slater. Next to him he could sense Shaniah growing tense, waiting to spring. Chee held Dog in check some way Hollister wasn't sure of. Probably by using his mind, for all Hollister knew.

"But wait," Hollister said. "Did you say you were watching us fight these things? And you didn't help us? Well, excuse me, but that's just rude." The dynamite was a goddamned dud; that was the only explanation. Hollister was angry he wouldn't live long enough to tell Monkey Pete they had survived fighting a billion Archaics but were thwarted by faulty dynamite. If the three of them survived, Monkey Pete was going to get an earful. Hollister gave a sideways glance at Chee and rolled his eyes toward the mine, but Chee only shrugged.

"Shut up, Hollister. You ain't funny. I ain't the one sat in prison all them years like an idiot. I get to kill people and get paid for it and ain't never got caught once. And now I'm gonna burn ya'll, starting with the breed." He looked at Chee "What do you think, Breed?"

"I think you better not miss," Chee said.

Slater laughed, he turned the knob on the handle of the flamethrower and pulled the trigger. At that instant the dynamite inside the mine went off with a mighty blast. What Slater didn't know was that the weapon Hollister had left behind had a barrel jammed with dirt and mud. The pressure mounted inside it, exploding in a burst of flames and engulfing Slater. Screaming in agony, he dropped to his knees as Monkey Pete's fuel mixture burned the flesh from his bones.

The explosions threw the horses into a frenzy, their riders trying desperately to regain control of their mounts. The dynamite's pressure wave knocked Shaniah and Hollister to their knees. Yet somehow Chee remained standing, and he fired the Henry shot after shot, killing five men. The rifle was empty. The last man tried to keep his horse under control and draw his pistol at the same time, until he was knocked backward out of the saddle by Chee's bowie knife landing in the middle of his chest.

Then it was quiet. Dust filled the air. The torches had fallen to the ground and there was a little light left. Dog walked over to Slater's remains and sniffed at him. Then he lifted his leg and peed.

"Good boy," said Hollister. Even Chee laughed.

Chapter Seventy-nine

By the time they arrived back in Denver, Hollister was almost completely healed. Even the scar where the blade had entered his stomach was slowly disappearing. Chee developed an uneasy truce with Shaniah when he saw Hollister's improvement. She remained on Dog's bad list though.

Monkey Pete was happy to hear his contraptions had worked, but less so when he found out his equipment had been left behind.

"Sorry, Monkey Pete," Hollister said. "In all the excitement we forget to grab the Ass-Kicker also, so it's gone too, and I expect Winchester ain't going to be too happy about that either. Besides, your damn dynamite nearly got us killed, so stop whining." Pete groused and muttered a few curses but eventually came around.

The train chugged into Denver, and Hollister was happy to see the warehouse again. He'd come to think of it as home. Which was strange because there was nothing homelike about it.

On the way Shaniah and Hollister made no attempts to

hide their relationship. But to Jonas it felt as if a veil of melancholy had descended over her and he couldn't tell why. And no matter how hard he tried, he couldn't jolly her out of it.

They arrived about three o'clock in the afternoon. The warehouse became a hub of activity as the train was resupplied and restocked. Shaniah and Hollister stayed in his cabin until it grew dark.

"There's something I've got to go do," he said. "When I get back, let's take a walk. Sound good?"

She stood and took him in her arms. She kissed him, a long lingering kiss.

"What's that for?" he asked.

"For what you did for me. For my people. For keeping your promise."

"Huh," he said.

Chapter Eighty

Declan hadn't heard from Slater or any of his men and he was starting to get nervous. He entered his mansion at dusk and went to the study.

He was pouring the bourbon from his decanter when he realized a man was sitting at his desk. "Jesus Christ!" he shouted, spilling bourbon all over himself and the floor.

"Good evening, Senator," Hollister said.

"Is that you, Hollister? What the hell are you doing here, trespassing in my house? By God, I'll have you arrested!" His heart sank. If Hollister was here, then it meant Slater was probably dead. This was not good. Not good at all.

"I don't think you'll have me arrested. I don't think you'll do much of anything. In fact, in another forty-eight hours I don't even think you'll be a senator anymore."

"What? Are you out of your mind? Get out of my house," he said.

Hollister pulled a letter out of his vest pocket.

"I found this letter in Slater's saddlebag. He's dead, by

the way. Pretty interesting, you transferring all this land and money to him, right before he comes trying to kill me."

"That letter doesn't prove anything," the senator said. "I was simply rewarding an employee for years of loyal service."

Hollister stood up and walked toward the senator, who instinctively backed up.

Hollister kept moving forward, the senator backpedaling until he was nearly standing in the fireplace.

"I think whether it proves anything or not isn't up to you or me. I think I'll send a copy of it to the governor and the president. Just for the hell of it, see what they think about it."

"You—you—wouldn't do that . . ." Declan stammered.

Hollister folded the letter back up and put it back in his pocket. "Your reaction tells me everything I need to know. Here's what's going to happen."

Hollister stepped over to the table holding the decanters and poured himself a large glass of bourbon.

"First, you are going to get your son some help. Get him out of that bedroom, find an asylum or some doctors somewhere who will help him. Then you're going to resign from the senate and you're never going to run for any kind of office again. Ever. And third, you're going to give back all the land you stole from the farmers and ranchers. Every acre. Give it back to the state, land grants, I don't care. It goes back to the original owners if they still want it."

"You're insane," Declan said.

"I am. If you'd seen what I saw, you'd be insane too," Hollister said.

"I'm not doing any of these things." Declan snorted.

"You will. You have two days." Hollister put down the glass and walked back to where Declan stood. He drew his Colt, thumbing back the hammer. He put the barrel under Declan's chin. The senator closed his eyes, tears escaping and running down his cheeks.

"You will do it, in two days. Or I'll come back and kill

you. Your choice," Hollister said. "And don't try sending anyone after me. Slater was as good as there was. Just not good enough."

He left the mansion, the senator's eyes still closed and tears cascading down his cheeks, long after Hollister was gone.

Chapter Eighty-one

•

Shaniah went to the stock car and led Demeter down the ramp. He was saddled and ready to go. It was best this way. She was an Archaic who needed to return to her people. Hollister was a human being who needed to get on with his life and though she should not have these feelings for him, she did. It would be a clean break.

She mounted Demeter and was startled to find Chee standing on the other side of her horse, the ever-present Dog at his side.

"You're leaving," he said.

"Yes. It's best this way," she said.

He studied her a moment. "I agree," he said.

"You don't like me," Shaniah said.

"No. Not really," Chee answered.

"Why?"

"You think you love the major and he loves you. He does. But it cannot be," he said.

"And so you hate me because he fell in love with me?" she asked.

"No. I hate you because you are an Archaic. And we are enemies, like the lion and the lamb," he said.

"We leave humans alone," she said. "We have for centuries."

"For now. But it will not always be that way," he said.

"Then hate me. If as you say, that is how it must be," she said.

He nodded.

"Will you tell him I said good-bye?" she asked.

"I will not," Chee answered.

"Why not?"

"It will only make it harder for him," he said.

"I do not understand you, witch-man," she said.

He shrugged.

She reined Demeter around and started on her journey home. Before she reached the warehouse door, she heard Chee call out to her and she stopped, wheeling Demeter around to face him.

"Did you tell him?" Chee said.

"Tell him what?" Shaniah asked, her voice cracking. He couldn't know. It was far too soon. How could he tell? She was more convinced than ever he was a witch.

"To leave without telling him you are carrying his child is cowardly. He has a right to know," Chee said.

"He can't know . . . I'm not . . . it isn't possible," she stammered.

"But nevertheless it has happened. And you must tell him. It is only right," Chee said.

She spurred Demeter close to Chee.

"You will not tell him. If you do, so help me, I will kill you, witch-man," she said.

"First, I will not tell him because it is not my place. That responsibility belongs to you. Second, you may try to kill me at your convenience," Chee said.

She looked at him for a long time. Then she turned Demeter toward the warehouse exit. He called out to her.

"Shaniah," he said. "I will be watching."

She rode away, his warning echoing in the empty warehouse.

Chapter Eighty-two

Two weeks later

"Is that where he spends most of his time?" Pinkerton asked.

"Yes, or at the Golden Star," Chee said.

"God damn, I feel sorry for the man," Pinkerton said.

Chee did not answer.

"Let's go," Pinkerton said.

"Before we do . . ." Chee pulled the Order of Saint Ignatius medallion from his pocket and flipped it in the air. Pinkerton caught it and held it out in his palm so Chee could plainly see it.

"Well done, Sergeant," Pinkerton said, giving Chee his own coin. Chee repeated Pinkerton's action, and satisfied, they left.

They walked through the streets of Denver until they reached the saloon. As he usually was, Hollister sat at the corner table farthest from the bar. A single glass and a bottle of whiskey sat in front of him, and his head was down as if he were trying to stare a hole through the table.

"Major Hollister," Pinkerton said as he approached.

Hollister recognized the voice and glanced up. He looked briefly at Pinkerton and said nothing and returned to staring at his whiskey glass.

"I have something for you," Pinkerton said, pulling a folded paper from his suit coat pocket.

He unfolded it and handed it to Hollister. Jonas looked at it, then tossed it onto the table. Across the top of the paper in large type it read, PRESIDENTIAL PARDON.

"Just as we agreed," Pinkerton said.

"Thanks," Hollister muttered.

"I have something else," Pinkerton said.

"What? Because if you don't mind, I really like to drink alone." Hollister looked at Pinkerton. The detective could tell he wasn't much of a drinker. His eyes weren't bloodshot and the bottle was mostly full. He came here and sat and sipped his whiskey because that's what a man with a broken heart does.

Pinkerton removed a leather wallet from his suit pocket.

Hollister was a little drunk. "You keep pulling shit out of your pockets, Pinkerton. You haven't got a monkey in there, have you?"

Pinkerton handed him the wallet. Hollister opened it. On one side was a badge. On the other was a small picture of Hollister from his army days, printed on a card that said, DEPUTY INSPECTOR, U.S. DEPT. OF THE INTERIOR, OFFICE OF PARANORMAL AFFAIRS.

"What's this?" Hollister said.

"It's a new job, now that you've completed your original assignment. Sergeant Chee here has already said yes. You'll travel around the west, and investigate . . . things. Like you just did with the Archaics. Incidents that are strange, curious, and don't add up. You'll keep the train and Monkey Pete. You'll get a raise in pay. You'll save lives. In fact we've already got a case for you down near the Mexican border.

Might be Apaches. Might be something else. I'd like you and Chee to find out."

Hollister snapped the wallet shut and handed it back to Pinkerton. "Can I let you know? Think on it for a few days?"

Pinkerton stroked his beard with his gnarled fingers. "All right, fine," he said. "But don't take too long, Jonas. People are dying."

Jonas picked up the glass and stared at the detective through the amber liquid.

"Mr. Pinkerton," he said. "Someone, somewhere, is always dying."

Chee and Pinkerton turned and left the saloon, leaving Hollister alone with his whisky bottle and his thoughts.

Chapter Eighty-three

Four months later

The ship tossed and rolled in the storm. The smell of the salt water made Shaniah so nauseous she thought she might pass out. Never had she felt this ill.

It had taken her three and a half months to reach Boston from Denver. She took a combination of riverboats and trains, and some days she rode Demeter, afraid that Hollister might try to find her and bring her back. She could not go back.

At Boston Harbor, she had found a ship with a captain who would be willing to take her back to the Black Sea. The gold she offered kept him from asking questions. She had known she could not travel such a great distance alone in her condition.

In the name of the Old Ones, what had she done? Hollister, she saw his face every time she closed her eyes. She had left part of herself behind in Denver. She did not know what the Old Ones would say when she returned. When they saw her. Would they cast her out?

She had been forced to break her vow regarding *Huma Sangra*. There was no other way. She traveled to a section of Boston filled with Gnazy from Eastern Europe, what the Americans called gypsies. The Gnazy knew what she was and were spooked immediately. As she walked the streets they disappeared until she passed; crucifixes and cloves of garlic went up in storefronts and the smell of garlic was everywhere. Businesses closed at sundown, no one walked the streets.

But she finally had found what she was looking for: an elderly woman, a midwife, who lived alone. She could not enter the woman's home without an invitation, so she caught her on the street one night on her way to see a patient that could not wait until morning. The woman could not fight her off. She sank her fangs into the gypsy's neck. After so many centuries without it, her blood should have tasted like ambrosia, but instead it made her ill, like she wanted to vomit. Still she kept her composure long enough for her to bite her own arm and force the woman to drink her blood. She turned. It was done.

Now they were on the ship in the middle of the Atlantic, and Shaniah thought she might die. Her face was bathed in sweat. Archaics never sweat. She felt pain in her joints like she never had before.

The woman, who would remember her midwifery for a while until her human memories faded, gave Shaniah a drink of some god-awful concoction. Shaniah threw it up immediately.

"What is happening to me?" she asked the woman. She made the woman watch over her constantly, letting her feed off of animals she had bought and loaded aboard the ship. Only enough to keep the woman from going mad and attacking the crew.

"It is time," the woman said.

"Time! Time for what? It is impossible," Shaniah screamed, as another wave of pain rolled over her body.

"Perhaps it is not. Perhaps the legends are not true?" the woman asked.

"No!"

"Was there an Archaic?" the woman asked.

"God, no! You miserable hag!" Shaniah shouted at her.

The old woman shrugged. "Then it is a miracle. She lifted Shaniah's blouse and put her hands on her round and swollen belly, the movement of the baby easily visible beneath her skin.

"AAAAAH!" Shaniah screamed.

"It is time," the woman said. "This baby will be born tonight."

MARCUS PELEGRIMAS's

SKINNERS

HUMANKIND'S LAST DEFENSE AGAINST THE DARKNESS

BLOOD BLADE
978-0-06-146305-1

There is a world inhabited by supernatural creatures of the darkness—all manner of savage, impossible beasts that live for terror and slaughter and blood. They are all around us but you cannot see them, and for centuries a special breed of hunter called Skinners has kept the monsters at bay, preventing them from breaking through the increasingly fragile barriers protecting our mortal realm.

But beware…for there are very few of them left.

HOWLING LEGION
978-0-06-146306-8

TEETH OF BEASTS
978-0-06-146307-5

VAMPIRE UPRISING
978-0-06-198633-8

THE BREAKING
978-0-06-198634-5

EXTINCTION AGENDA
978-0-06-198638-3

HARPER VOYAGER
TRADE PAPERBACKS

THE INHERITANCE
and Other Stories
by Robin Hobb
978-0-06-156164-1

THE WATERS RISING
by Sheri S. Tepper
978-0-06-195885-4

GHOSTS BY GASLIGHT
Stories of Steampunk and Supernatural Suspense
Edited by Jack Dann and Nick Gevers
978-0-06-199971-0

BY THE BLOOD OF HEROES
The Great Undead War: Book I
By Joseph Nassise
978-0-06-204875-2

THE TAKEN
Celestial Blues: Book One
by Vicki Pettersson
978-0-06-206464-6

THE THACKERY T. LAMBSHEAD
CABINET OF CURIOSITIES
Edited by Ann VanderMeer and Jeff VanderMeer
978-0-06-211683-3